A SNAKE
FALLS
TO EARTH

A SNAKE FALLS TO EARTH

DARCIE LITTLE BADGER

LQ
LEVINE QUERIDO
MONTCLAIR · AMSTERDAM · HOBOKEN

This is an Arthur A. Levine book

Published by Levine Querido

LQ

LEVINE QUERIDO

www.levinequerido.com • info@levinequerido.com

Levine Querido is distributed by Chronicle Books, LLC

Library of Congress Control Number: 2021931960

ISBN 978-1-64614-092-3

Printed and bound in China

Published October 2021

First printing

With love, I dedicate these stories

to my mother, protector of knowledge

to T, healer of animals great and small

and to the families we find in unexpected places.

NINA, AGE 9

On the hospital bed, her delicate body cradled between thin white pillows, Rosita dreamed. Pictures in metal, plastic, and wooden frames surrounded her, displaying images of friends and family, giving the appearance of an audience. However, the only visitor in the room was Nina, who sat on a tin chair beside the hat rack-shaped IV pole.

Nina couldn't stop looking at the sepia-toned photograph in an oak frame. Propped on the window ledge, it featured a portrait of Great-Great-Grandmother Rosita as a young woman. The picture came from an era long before digital cameras. In those days, people posed in front of a boxy camera and had to wait days to learn whether they'd blinked. In her portrait, young Rosita wore a hundred strings of pale seed beads around her neck, against her buckskin-clothed chest. Some had glinted, each glass bead a mirror for the sun. Young Rosita's fine black hair had symmetrically framed either side of her face. With dark, intense eyes, she'd stared directly at the camera lens, as if challenging the photographer to blink first. In most old-timey photos, the subjects didn't smile, but young Rosita's lips quirked in the suggestion of stifled laughter, as if she'd remembered a joke, one she could barely wait to share.

In the hospital room, Rosita's hair fanned across her pillow in thin white wisps. Her eyes, now opening slowly and wearily, were sunken; advanced age had sculpted her face against the contours of her skull, revealing sharp ridges that had once been hidden by plump cheeks. Without her dentures, Rosita's thin lips curled inward. Rosita looked toward Nina. Did she need something? Water? More medicine? In anticipation, Nina opened the speech-to-text translation app on her phone.

"Don't worry," she said. "Dad's coming back soon, and after lunch, Grandma will visit." Nina's father was speaking with doctors beyond the closed door. "Are you okay for now? A . . . abuelita?" Great-Great-Grandmother didn't speak much English. Unfortunately, Nina knew even less Spanish, but her attempt to communicate worked, because at the word *Abuelita,* Rosita's lips quirked, creating the same anticipatory, gentle smile that shone from the old photograph.

"Quieres escuchar una historia?" she asked, her voice raspy but strong. The translator on Nina's phone automatically typed out the question: **Do you want to hear a story?**

Nodding, Nina scooched her chair closer, flinching at the nails-on-chalkboard *screeeeech* of metal legs scraping against the smooth white floor. Rosita patted her cradle of pillows, finding a gray remote control between them. One press of an arrow-shaped button caused the back of her bed to lift with a soft mechanical whir, gently raising her into a sitting position.

"Esto es importante."
This is important.
"Recuerda nuestra historia."
Remember our history.

Again, Nina nodded, hiding her confusion. The first time Rosita said *historia*, the phone app had translated the word as "story." Now, it translated the word as "history." Which version did her great-great-grandma mean?

As Rosita began to speak, it occurred to Nina that the app was an imperfect interpreter, despite its 4.8-star rating and how it had worked for her in the past. Most of the story Rosita was telling now was being classified as an "unknown language." How was that possible? The app had advanced linguistic AI and could understand thousands of global dialects. Occasionally, Rosita used a Spanish phrase, but they were so sporadic, Nina couldn't piece together the story—history?—using the Spanish translations alone.

However, Nina didn't dare interrupt her great-great-grandmother. In her nine years on earth, she had never heard the elder speak like this before, as if each word was connected, one flowing into the next. At last, her voice raspy with overuse, Rosita said two last words: el pesadillo. In the silence that followed, she turned away, closed her eyes, and snuggled back into her pillows.

According to the translator, el pesadillo meant "the nightmare."

"Did you have a bad dream?" Nina asked. Gingerly, she touched Rosita's vein-threaded hand; finding it to be cold, Nina entwined their fingers together. "Abuelita?"

This time, there was no smile. Just deep, steady breaths.

"Abuelita? Are you okay?" How could she ask that in Spanish? The word *bien* meant "good," right? "Are you . . . bien??" Nina started panicking. "Dad! Dad, help!"

In an instant, her father and a nurse in pink scrubs jumped into the room—they must have been standing right beyond the door. Nina's father wore his best pair of tattered blue jeans and a black felt cowboy hat, the fancy one embellished by yellow and red beadwork around the rim. "What's happening?" he asked.

"She stopped talking and fell asleep, Dad."

The tension seeped from the nurse's stance. "Oh, honey," she soothed, pressing a button on the bed that made it flatten out, "your great-great-grandmother gets very tired, but that's okay. She needs lots of rest to recover."

"Dad, just now, Abuelita told me a story," Nina explained. "I . . . think."

"That's great! She's feeling like herself again." Rosita was an entertainer, the keeper of ten thousand stories, each stranger than the last. Now and then, she'd share one with Nina, and though she was sure much of the nuance was lost in translation, the app had usually been able to capture the essence of her words.

"Do you know what this means, Dad?" Nina held up her phone, sharing the jumble of nontranslated words and translated Spanish.

"Hm." Her father stepped near the window, waving Nina close. After studying the screen, his brow split by a vertical wrinkle of concentration, he guessed: "It may be an Apache dialect.

Rosita's parents spoke Lipan, 'round when our people had to go culturally incognito for survival."

"Wait, what?"

"Shh," her father hushed, glancing across the room, where the nurse in pink was taking Rosita's blood pressure. "Don't wake her up."

"Sorry," Nina whispered. "I just didn't realize Rosita understood it, too." Years ago, Nina's parents taught her that Lipan needed to be "revitalized"—people knew phrases, simple sentences, and words, but nobody spoke it fluently. Not even Rosita. Plus, that timing didn't make sense. If baby Rosita had survived the U.S. government's attempts to slaughter Texas Natives, she'd been alive during the 1800s, which would make her over 150 years old.

Sure, Nina's family tree had a lot of centenarians, but humans didn't get much older than 100, right? Was Nina in the presence of a record-breaking elder?

Possibly. Stranger things had happened.

"I didn't, either," Nina's dad said, and kept reading the story transcript. "The spelling's messed up, but that's Lipan for 'home' . . ." He scrolled through the wall of text, pausing near the end. "That phrase probably means 'animal person.' Gawd, what a treasure. Save her words, okay? We may never understand, but . . ." Now, he turned to regard the sepia portrait in the oak frame. ". . . it'd be a shame to lose them."

After that morning, Great-Great-Grandma Rosita spent a week longer in the hospital, surrounded by her photographs and family. When awake, she told fanciful, ancient stories about the days when humans and spirits lived together. Stories with titles like "Coyote Person Traps the World's Sweetest Ballad in a Locket" or "Clever Sisters Escape from Kidnappers and Spend the Winter with a Groundhog Family."

On the last day, when Rosita was at her strongest, Nina prompted: "Abuelita, um, what about el pesadillo? Que es . . . la historia . . . del pesadillo?"

The smile again. Slight, knowing. And gone just as quickly, as if carried away by a flood of sorrow. When Rosita spoke, she tilted her head toward Nina's phone, which translated:

> That was the last story my mother told me. Remember, she said. Creator, I was so young when my parents died. Now, I carry sounds without the meaning. Isn't that sad?

"¿Cuántos años tienes?" Nina whispered, scooting to the edge of her seat. In response, Great-Great-Grandmother only shrugged.

"It's okay," Nina continued, leaning over the bed to kiss Great-Great-Grandmother's forehead.

Later that year, Rosita died in her home. It happened peacefully, everyone said. As if she had simply decided, "Tonight's the night," shut her eyes, and strolled into the underworld during a gentle dream. Born among family in the tumbleweed-spawning desert, Rosita had no official documents listing her birth date. But when Nina's father removed her portrait from its frame to scan the image for her wake, he found a single date written on the back: 1894.

COTTONMOUTH IS CAST FROM HOME

I can't remember when I learned about the path to anywhere-you-please. It's one of those stories everybody seems to know, like a persistent thread of gossip. But I'll never forget the day it found me, completely by chance, in the terror of Robin-Kept Forest. Thing is, I didn't realize the path was special until I'd already walked it. Where would I be now if I'd known?

Momma was overprotective; she didn't chase me from home till I was fifteen years old. It happened during a calm midsummer morning. I was napping on the riverbank, dreaming about the sunlight. Real sunlight, the kind that's so bright and warm, it almost burns. You can still bask in the dimly radiant light that slips into the Reflecting World, my home of spirits and monsters. The pseudosun, we call it. But it's no perfect substitute. Without so much as a greeting, Momma plopped a rucksack full of supplies onto my chest, and hissed, "Wake up, Oli. You're ready."

I clutched the bag in a death grip against my skinny chest, hoping I was just having a nightmare. "Really? Today?"

"Yes, today. Of course today. When else is there, little snake?" She dropped a tightly folded blanket on top of the rucksack, and the weight of densely woven sheep wool caused me to hiss with discomfort and sit up, shifting the parcels' combined weight to my lap.

"Can I live down the river?" I asked, fumbling for my spectacles. The world sharpened when I slipped them over my eyes.

"If you do, it better be so far downstream that I never see your scaly tail again, kid." At my dismayed gasp, Momma's expression softened, and she added, "If I let all my children stay here, we'd run out of food, space, and patience."

"You could make one exception?" I ventured. "For me?"

"Absolutely not. That'd be unfair." Momma pointed south with her nose. "Leave now, and you'll reach the dammed town before nightfall. The beavers usually have room for a lodger."

"And if they don't?" I muttered.

"Pfft. You're a cottonmouth," she snickered. "Sleep under a bush."

As if to demonstrate, Momma switched from her false form to her true form. She slithered out of her dress and bared curved, venom-filled teeth in my direction, warning me to skedaddle.

"Okay, okay." With a final, wistful look at my favorite sunning rock and the family cottage, a squat dome of moss-covered stones, I heaved the rucksack over my shoulder and scooped up the blanket. Its fabric, which smelled of sage and smoke, felt dense under my fingers.

"Goodbye, Momma," I said.

She remained silent until I'd turned my back on home and

started trudging down the riverside. "Goodbye, Oli. You'll be all right."

I should have been prepared for my ousting, should have already scoped out the territory for my new home. It wasn't as if Momma had failed to give me forewarning. That winter, she'd borrowed a massive loom from the sparrow woman who lives across the valley. Then, she'd haggled for brown and green wool at the market. "I'm making you a good blanket," she warned me, "and it'll be my last gift to you." But Momma spends most of the day in her snake form. Her fingers—in her own words—feel like alien appendages. They'd moved hesitantly over the spun yarn, warp strings, and batten. I thought I had another year. Guess she had been determined to finish by summer.

That haste was for the best. If she'd sent me away during a cold season, I probably would have frozen solid outside the cottage. Even in our false form, cottonmouths do poorly in low temperatures. I suppose that's one reason why Momma's last gift was a thick blanket.

I walked in a glum daze until my stomach tickled with hunger. Momma had probably packed rations in my rucksack: chewy smoked fish and dense, honey-soaked cornbread. But I didn't want to break into the emergency food so soon. There'd be fresh meals at the dammed town. Rich stew, baked yucca, and fire-seared corn with juicy kernels. I may even have a mug of thick chocolate if a trader from the south had visited recently. The thought of a warm feast urged me forward. I even tried jogging, only falling back into a brisk walk because the rucksack kept thumping against my back. I'd changed into a tunic, but the fabric did little to cushion my bony spine and shoulders.

It'd been several years since my last trip to the dammed town during a family outing by boat, but if I recalled correctly, I didn't need to run to reach the dams before the pseudosun set. Everything will be fine, I told myself. And it was.

Until I reached the split in the river, a wishbone-shaped division of my path. I hesitated, trying to remember whether I should follow the right or left branch of the bifurcation.

That's when I realized that I couldn't remember ever seeing the split before, much less which direction would take me to town. It was too easy to nap on the warm deck of a riverboat. I'd never been awake for this part of the journey.

For a couple minutes, I searched my surroundings for anyone who could help. Although there were crickets in the grass and silvery minnows glinting under the ripples of the river, they weren't animal people like me. Believe it or not, there are a lot more animals than animal people in the Reflecting World. If I had to rank us by numbers: plants, fungi, and animals—in that order—are most abundant. Then animal people. Then monsters. Then others.

So I had a choice to make: right or left. At the time, fifty-fifty odds seemed pretty good. If I made the correct choice, I'd have a warm meal and soft cot before nightfall. The wrong choice meant I'd just have to dig into my rations, camp overnight, and retrace my steps the next morning. For a worst-case scenario, that didn't seem bad.

I had no idea how terrifying a real worst-case scenario could be. If I had known? Well, I probably wouldn't have made such a risky gamble. In fact, I might have scampered back home to venomous Momma at the prospect of spending a night in Robin-Kept Forest.

Instead, I picked the branch going right. It meandered deep into the forest, past elms, oaks, and sap-glistening pines. There was no dearth of wood for the dammed town, particularly since the beavers replaced every tree they gnawed down. Aware of their activities, I quickly became uncomfortable. Even after an hour of walking, there were no signs of logging. No tree stumps bearing the marks of teeth or metal tools. No saplings growing in orderly rows. I should have trusted my instincts. Instead, I committed to my choice. Maybe there'd be evidence of logging by the next mile. Or the next. I could have underestimated the distance to town. My gamble could still pay off.

It didn't.

When the river glistened orange under the setting pseudo-sun, I had to accept that there'd be no stew and drinking chocolate for supper. My feet sore and my stomach empty, I searched the riverbank for a good place to camp. I wanted to sleep near the water; in my true form, I could escape most threats by swimming. Not many land animals are able to outswim a cottonmouth. Plus, when I was little, Momma often warned me that it was unbelievably easy to become lost in the forest. Even trees could get confused. For the longest time, I thought that was an exaggeration. Didn't seem possible for a tree to get lost—even in their false forms, plant people must remain rooted, their legs or torsos sprouting directly from the ground. Then, Momma explained that she once met an elm person who was a thousand years old, with bark tougher than the plates on an armadillo's back. Everyone called her the screaming elm, because she wailed "Where am I?" all day long.

As I searched for a friendly-looking patch of land to spend the night, I felt a deep pang of sympathy for the homesick elm person. Then, I came upon a clearing, a semicircle of flat, dry, inviting land tucked against the bright river. It was perfect. I could envision building a cozy, one-snake cottage in the center of the clearing. There'd be a fishing dock crafted from beaver-cut logs. Weeklong trips to town and naps on the warm riverbank. I dropped my blanket and rucksack in the center of the clearing and sprawled on the cool grass. Already, from the shadows of the forest, the night bugs and toads were singing. The voice of a lovesick frog person wove between the cacophony of screeches and chirps.

"Where have you been?" the frog person sang, his voice mellow with longing and hope. "Where will you be? Will you be with me?" The song faded, as if carried by the wind. He must have been singing as he walked through the forest. I wondered how anyone found each other in a place where it was so easy to become lost.

Before bed, I devoured half the smoked fish in my rucksack and drank deeply from the river. I'd spend the night in my true form; to protect my supplies from thieves, I hid my bag under a layer of dry leaves. Then, I folded my clothes, transformed, and curled up beside my blanket. In my dreams, I tried to sing, but my voice was drowned by the screams of trees. "Why are you shouting?" I asked the forest. "It's okay. You're home."

"Then why are you here?" the trees asked. "If this is our home, who are you?"

A sharp pain in my tail shocked me awake; my bones felt on the verge of snapping. Driven by pain, confusion, and lightning-fast instinct, I sank my teeth through skin and muscle.

"AIIIE!" somebody screeched.

Next thing I knew, I was soaring through the air, flipping head over tail until gravity slapped me into the brush. I thrashed around on my back. The violent motion finally snapped me right side up, with my belly to the ground. The unknown culprit who'd stepped on my tail and then kicked me into the forest was making a big fuss nearby, shouting "Snaking snake!" and stomping all over the clearing, pulverizing leaves and sticks under her heavy feet. That could've been me.

In the dark, my round eyes couldn't see a thing, but I pieced together details from the taste of the air, its chemical signature. The stomper was an alligator person. A mature one. If she found my hiding spot, I was dead. I couldn't even bite her again; I'd used all my venom, and that defense mechanism was doing a shoddy job dampening her strength. I could transform and make a run for it, counting on her swollen foot to slow her down. But she might have ranged weapons.

Instead, I wrapped myself around the base of a shrub and waited. Before long, the commotion of her furious tantrum petered out. Then, I heard her flop onto the ground, grumble a few mean-spirited curses, and sink into persistent silence. I didn't dare leave hiding while my attacker was still awake. But how could I tell the difference between sullen silence and unconscious silence? Impossible. I'd be stuck there all night!

My worries multiplied as the sky brightened from black to deep, nearly-dawn blue. Would she notice my leaf-covered rucksack? What about my blanket? My special blanket! I shifted, peeking between sharp, sparsely leafed branches. My tongue flicked through the air, tasting anger, blood, and the sourness of venom-damaged tissue. I made out a blocky shape hunched in the center of the clearing, fussing over a large item. It was too large to be my bag. Even aided by the faint light that trickled through the canopy, my eyes were useless for details. They sensed motion, shapes, and the hint of color. In my false form, I was nearsighted and had to wear a pair of silver-framed spectacles with round glass lenses. I probably needed spectacles in my snake form too.

That said, it didn't take perfect vision to puzzle out the alligator's next move. She started hammering poles into the ground, occasionally grunting with pain, and then folded a tarp over the pyramid-shaped frame.

She was setting up a tent just feet away from everything I needed to survive.

I threw back my head and opened my mouth in a silent scream. How did everything go so wrong? I hadn't lasted a day! Maybe I should slither back to Momma's house and beg for mercy. Just one more year in her cottage. One more blanket.

I'd be better off taking my chances with the foulmouthed alligator.

In retrospect, I should have suspected that the clearing would be a prime campsite for other fish eaters. The alligator could camp there for days. It was only a matter of time before she noticed my rucksack, and imagining a stranger rifling through my possessions, then stomping on my spectacles with spite, made me throw back my head a second time in a dismayed silent scream.

I resolved to wait until the alligator was distracted and then sneakily grab my stuff and escape. She'd probably rest soon; alligators were supposed to be big fans of day napping. Sure enough, that midmorning, a long snore rumbled from the tent. The rhythmic thunder of her breath encouraged me to stiffly unwind from the shrub stem and slither around the perimeter of the clearing. When I reached the little mound of leaves blanketing my rucksack, I transformed. The ground crunched under my bigger, heavier body. I froze, wide-eyed, waiting. When the snores continued, I exhaled with relief and squatted beside the hidden bag to gingerly, leaf by leaf, remove the layer of camouflage. Then, I lifted my rucksack from the ground at a snail's pace, flinching at every minute rustling sound it made and relaxing only when it hung from my shoulder. The strap dug into my bare skin, reminding me how delicate my false body was without clothes. I needed my moccasins and pants; where were they? Oh, right. I'd folded them on top of my blanket, which was tucked behind a tree on the other side of the clearing.

Fantastic. I had to sneak past the tent on legs. Couldn't slither in this body but I sure couldn't carry all my supplies as a silent little snake. I just had to be clever about it. Sync up my footfalls with the snores. With every rumble she made, I took a step.

Snore/step.

Wait.

Snore/step.

Wait.

It was working! I now stood a couple feet behind the tent; the air seemed to tremble with every snore. Or maybe I was shaking. Just a few more steps, I reassured myself.

A robin dropped onto a nearby branch and puffed his red chest feathers. "What are you doing?" he chirped. "Creeping around Miss Bruhn's camp. Troublemaker!"

"No, no, no," I hissed. "It's not like—"

"Wake up, Bruhn!" the robin screeched. "A naked thief is stealing your gear!"

"It's my gear!" I cried. "I was here first!"

The snoring stopped. I tried to sprint to my blanket and clothes before it was too late, but the robin dove at my face and pecked at my eyes as he chirped, "Liar! Liar!"

"What is happening out there?" Miss Bruhn hollered. Before anyone could respond, the tent flew into the air, thrown aside by the volcanic fury of its occupant. In front of me, surrounded by tentpoles and dressed in a long white nightgown, loomed a six-foot-tall alligator woman. Like mine, her skin was sprinkled by patches of scales. But my scales are smooth and shiny, sleeves of black ones down my outer arms and brown ones in the place of eyebrows. Hers were spiny, covering her neck, shoulders, and—most alarmingly—knuckles, like armor. She showed her sharp teeth in a snarl and pointed at me rudely with her finger. "You're the little worm who bit me!"

"You stepped on my tail!"

"Your tail had no business in my fishing spot." She lowered her finger quickly, pointing to her right foot. It was red and puffy, with a pair of purple tooth punctures above the big toe. "If any of my toes fall off, I'll eat you for breakfast."

"They won't! It'll be fine in a couple days, I think . . ."

"Get lost!" She grabbed a wooden tentpole from the ground

and swung it at my head, but I ducked in the nick of time. The wood swished over my ear.

"Can I just grab my blanket and—"

"No!" she roared. The second swing grazed my shoulder, leaving a couple splinters. With a startled shout, I ran. I could hear Bruhn's heavy footfalls: *thump THUMP thump THUMP.* They were uneven, as if she had to use the strength in only one leg to propel herself forward. The robin flapped around my head, cheeping, "Don't come back! You better not come back! I'll catch you again, punk!" He followed me, flying from branch to branch and shouting accusations from above. Troublemaker, foot biter, creep!

When it became difficult to breathe, I slowed to a jog and glanced over my shoulder. Thankfully, Bruhn was nowhere to be seen. She must've given up the chase. Finally able to take a break, I dropped my rucksack and untied the bow keeping it sealed. My spare leggings, pants, and shirt were packed between a set of dishes and my brush collection: hairbrush, toothbrush, and paintbrush. There was also a rough scrubbing brush for heavy-duty cleaning tasks and skin removal. Sometimes, after shedding, patches of dry, dead scales cling stubbornly to my body. It's not a good look to carry around dead skin. As I slipped into my pants and shirt, I shouted to the robin, "See? This bag is filled with my stuff. Stop harassing me."

"And what about the bite? You tried to murder my friend!"

"First, she's going to be fine."

"You *think*." Emphasis on *think*.

"I'm ninety-nine percent certain. Plus, I didn't mean to bite her. It was instinct."

"Oh? Oh? You can't control yourself? That makes you even more dangerous."

I tied my rucksack shut with a frustrated hiss and slipped my spectacles over my eyes. "I'm leaving now. Happy?"

"Tsk. Hurry up. And remember that birds can see everything in this forest. Don't come back."

"I . . . I won't. I don't even want to be here." But that wasn't completely true. My blanket and good moccasins were still at the clearing, hostages to the alligator's wrath. I could replace the footwear, but when I thought about losing the blanket? That hurt. It was my mother's last gift to me, her attempt to keep me warm long after I'd left her hearth. I was almost willing to risk another physical altercation just to get it back. Almost. I shoved my dirty feet into a pair of casual slippers. Around me, the tree branches swayed and bounced, even though there was no wind.

An army of birds—robins, swallows, sparrows, mockingbirds, warblers, jays, and too many others to list—landed one by one in the canopy. Their little round eyes flashed, and their sharp beaks clicked in annoyance. I wouldn't make it halfway to Bruhn's clearing before the feather faces swarmed me.

So, I marched deeper into the forest, watched by the robin and his many friends. Eventually, I couldn't taste the river in the wind anymore. The absence of its flavor—silt, freshwater, and sweet grasses—terrified me. I could always discern the chemical composition of the air, even in my false form. I'd never lost track of the river before, never been so far from my element.

After I'd wandered far enough to lose most of the birds to boredom, I took a meal break. Unfortunately, Momma had only packed enough fish and bread for a daylong journey, no doubt assuming I'd reach the dammed town before my rations ran out. If I hadn't taken the wrong branch in the river, my morning would have consisted of boiled eggs and pleasant conversation. I'd have been surrounded by friendly, generous hosts.

Could I find another way to the town, perhaps by looping back through the forest? The loop would have to be wide, which meant another day or more of hiking.

What other option did I have?

My inner bad-mouther warned that I'd get lost. It hissed: *Oli, if you can't follow a billion tons of running water, how will you navigate through a strange forest?* Luckily, unlike earlier, my surroundings were now teeming with life. So, I decided to wave down the first kind stranger I met and ask for help. Maybe somebody would even accompany me to my destination, shielding me from additional misunderstandings with the locals.

Unfortunately, after being chased by a thousand birds, I was being avoided by everyone else. That's how it seemed, anyway. The farther I walked, the darker and denser my surroundings became, but nobody revealed themselves to me. There were others out there, somewhere. I sensed them. Suggestions of squirrels, possums, voles, and even other snakes lingered in the air. There was movement in my peripheral vision, rustling leaves and crunching shrubs somewhere nearby.

"Can anyone point me to the river?" I shouted. "Anyone? Please?"

You know the old saying: if a tree falls in the forest, but nobody's there to hear it, does it make a sound? Well, I started to wonder: If an Oli asks for help in the forest, but nobody makes a sound, does anybody hear him?

Even the angry birds had left me.

Judging by my sleepiness, it was midafternoon, well past nap time. But as much as I wanted to find a sunny spot and rest, I had to reach the river before nightfall. Before the deep forest monsters came out to hunt.

But here's the thing about monsters.

Sometimes, they prefer to hunt in the light.

NINA, AGE 13

So much for an easy A.

Surrounded by markers and pieces of construction paper, thirteen year-old Nina sat cross-legged on the living room floor, staring at a scanned copy of Rosita's portrait. She had to make an ancestral chart for class; it was a social studies project worth 10 percent of the class grade. Due to her tribe's enrollment requirements, Nina already knew the recent branches on her family tree, so the project should have involved minimal research. And initially, yeah, it had been easy. First, Nina Arroyo had written her name, date of birth, and birth town on the bottom of a bright green piece of poster paper. Two branches extended upward: Richie N. Arroyo (father, bookstore owner) and Alicia T. Arroyo (mother, translator). Next, her parents grew four grandparents (one living, three deceased), who grew eight great-grandparents (three living, five deceased), who grew sixteen great-great-grandparents (all deceased). And that's when things got tricky, since Nina's teacher would never accept that

Great-Great-Grandma Rosita was born in the 1870s (give or take) and died over 150 years later. But everything Nina knew about her ancestor supported this impossible truth.

Plus, there were the others.

All three of Rosita's children, including Nina's great-grandfather (who'd retired to an assisted living home in South Carolina after marrying his fourth wife), were still alive. None were younger than one hundred. "It's lucky genes," her father had once claimed, whatever that meant.

"Do you have lucky genes, too?" she'd asked. "Do I?"

"Only time will tell," he'd say.

Nina often wondered if she'd like the Earth one hundred years from now. The future could be a wondrous place of androids, cloned dinosaurs, and VR glasses. That's what Nina wanted to believe. However, when the anxious hum of the evening news slipped into her bedroom, carrying prophesies of disease and pain, it seemed more likely that the future would be a place of nightmares.

In her father's words: only time would tell.

Now, Nina's thoughts returned to Rosita's final story. The mystery of what she had said nagged at her in the years since, rarely straying far from her mind. Sometimes, it felt like Nina's great-great grandmother had bequeathed her a locked treasure chest. Who could be satisfied until the chest was opened? Not Nina. There was a reason why videos with titles like "I Found A Weird Sealed Door Behind the Wallpaper" or "Unboxing Mystery Time Capsule" went viral online. Plus, Rosita—practically lying in her deathbed—had tasked Nina to remember their historia. And she wanted to! Really!

If only riddles could be opened with a lockpicking kit or a sledgehammer.

After Rosita's death there'd been a family-wide effort to make sense of her words. Unfortunately, the translation app recording had mangled most of the Lipan phrases beyond recovery. Even Nina's mother, a genuine polyglot, ultimately gave up. "There just isn't enough information." She'd thrown up a helpless shrug. "A voice recording would have been more useful. If we had that, I could compare the words to a related language. Jicarilla or Navajo. But the app made a mess of everything. It's not equipped for Athabaskan languages."

That's why, all this time later, Rosita's story was still largely incomprehensible, except for a few phrases:

> "Homeland/home"
> "She was in pain"
> "The healer"
> "The nightmare"
> "Animal people"

Animal people.

Everyone knew they had left Earth thousands of years ago after the joined era, but considering their prodigious lifespans, Nina had to ask the question.

"Dad!" she shouted. "Daaaad!"

His response, also shouted, came from the kitchen: "Whaaat?"

"If I fail this project, it's your fault!"

"Why? I bought you green poster paper!"

"Your side of the family has the life span of parrots! It all begins with Rosita. Is she actually a bird person? Are we descended from spirits? Is that the big mystery of her story?"

A series of audible footsteps indicated that her father had gotten tired of their loud back-and-forth—he'd probably had a busy day at work, considering his fondness for amiable hollering—and was crossing the hallway, which always creaked like the floorboards in a haunted house. He dropped onto the overstuffed recliner near the window and looked down at Nina's homework. "We're not one-sixteenth parrot people, no," he said. "That's thankfully impossible."

"What should I do? I can't write 'lucky genes' under Rosita's name."

He shrugged. "Just leave her birth date off the poster. If your teacher asks, explain that Rosita doesn't got reliable records. It happens."

"It's not the truth, though. We know our family history, and that's more reliable than a birth certificate."

"Play with the wording. There's no need for lies if you're clever. How about this: Rosita doesn't got reliable paper records."

"Yeah . . ." Nina chewed the end of her marker before drawing a big question mark in the space under Great-Great-Grandma's name. "You know, she oughtta be in a world record book, Dad. There has to be evidence to prove her age. What about more pictures?"

In response, he rolled his fingers against the recliner armrests, drumming a soft beat into the fabric. With a start, Nina realized that her father did the same thing on airplanes—and flying made him nervous.

"What's wrong?" she asked.

He shook his head, smiling now. "Rosita would've hated that. Remember when we tried to make her a Picture Place account?"

"Heheh. Yeah. That was a disaster. She never did trust the Internet."

"Oh, the Internet was all right." He stood and ruffled Nina's hair as he strolled back toward the kitchen. "She streamed all her old telenovelas online. It's the attention Rosita hated. Social media. Targeted ads. Some people don't want to be known by the unknown, believe it or not."

"Her Picture Place account was going to be private."

"It's my fault," he admitted, the volume of his voice increasing as the distance between them grew. "I might've told her about hackers."

Nina called after him, "What should I put as her career?" In her long life, Rosita must have done a dozen or more odd jobs to earn money and survive, but she'd always described herself as a storyteller. To Nina's knowledge, though, she'd never earned a wage for stories.

"Entertainer," her father responded, now back in the doorway. He glanced at his wrist, checking the time on his smart watch. Although its square-inch screen was too small for his fingers, it obeyed voice commands. The watch's AI could even tell jokes and pretend to hold conversations; sometimes, Nina got low-key jealous of the watch's company. "Don't forget to call your mother," he reminded. "It's a halfway decent hour in the middle of the ocean."

Nina hoped there'd be a strong connection; the last time she tried to contact the ship, the onboard Wi-Fi went down. Of course, Nina spent hours in a state of panic, convinced that the research vessel and all eighty souls onboard were at the bottom of the North Pacific. Thankfully, her mother sent a comforting message as soon as the Wi-Fi returned:

All's well, my darling.

There'd been a one-minute gap. Then:

By that, I mean "As well as can be on a 4-month cruise with strong-willed scientists from 15 different nations." I wish I could describe the arguments I've translated. Needless to say, the situation became very tense after the galley ran out of sweet biscuits. I can't wait to return home. Love you—Mom

She'd be back soon, and for one season, they'd be a family together again. Then, Nina's mother would return to the Pacific. It was all for the money, she claimed. No translation job in Texas could pay even half the salary of the ocean gig. The family certainly needed it. But sometimes, Nina wondered if her mother really enjoyed the adventure too.

Honestly, who could blame her?

Finished with her work for the night, Nina shoved her school supplies under the coffee table—it was messy, but at least nobody would trip on a marker—and moved to her bedroom. There, she dug through a pile of old journals in her closet, looking for a bright green spiral notebook, her third-grade diary. She found it near the bottom of the pile, the cover decorated by dinosaur stickers and loops of glitter glue. If Nina recalled correctly, she'd written several entries about Rosita then. Maybe, the wisdom of hindsight could extract secrets from that year. If nothing else, she wanted to refresh her memory about the events leading up to the story. Something had sparked Rosita's memory of those Lipan words. Nina's parents believed the spark had been medicine. Maybe that was true. People said strange things when they were in the dream-like fog of IV-delivered morphine. But Nina suspected that something else had first reminded Rosita of la historia.

The fish, for example. The talking fish.

Nina opened the diary. She'd survived a hard-core gel pen phase in third grade, exclusively writing in absurdly colorful ink, as if completing math and spelling worksheets in neon shades of pink made the schoolwork more exciting. If nothing else, the habit taught her to think carefully before she wrote, since gel pen marks could not be erased. Still, as Nina flipped through rainbowy entries, she noticed several scratched-out sentences. A whole page from October 1 was obscured by a whirlwind of frustrated blue scribbles. Nina paused, trying to remember that day. It must have been a bad one. She held the page directly under her bedroom lamp and concentrated on the order among the chaos. With effort, she could still read the original entry:

Philipa is really gone. Now, all my friends have moved away. Kevin and Julio kicked ants at me during resess. I'm easy prey. Alone. I went to the swingset and flew back and forth until I felt like throwing up. The movement is bad for my stomic but at least nobody can hurt me when I'm in the air. In stories from the joined era, people could fly. I miss that freedom almost as much as I miss Philipa. Is it possible to miss something you never really experienced though?

Nina keenly remembered when her best friend moved to Iowa. Philipa's plea: "Don't forget about me." Her tearful response, a promise: "I won't."

As if fleeing the memory, Nina rapidly flipped through her diary, passing the new year and the ides of March. On April 7, Rosita was hospitalized. That day, using deep maroon ink, Nina had written:

After Grandpa died, Grandma moved into Rosita's house. Its weird how a tragidy can save a life. Rosita still gets drinking water from a old well on the ~~ege~~ edge of her massive yard. She says it tastes better than anything from a sink. To me the well water has a flavor like seltzer without bubbles. Some people like that. Anyway, this morning, Grandma woke up and could not find Rosita in the house. She got worried because snakes like the footpath to the well. Its sunny and warm, which makes reptiles happy. Usually Rosita takes a walking stick and taps the ground so copperheads, rattlesnakes, and cottonmouths know shes coming but its possible to get bitten anyway.

Grandma went outside. She shouted "Rosita! Where are you?" She probably shouted that a hundred times because her voice is ~~horse~~ hoarse now, like she gargled sand. Grandma looked behind the oak tree and in the long grasses. Then she found Rosita's flask near the well, and the water bucket was still lowered. So Grandma leaned over to look into the black water. Do you know what she saw? A HEAD OF WHITE HAIR! Grandma says she thought poor Rosita must be drowned.

But Rosita looked up and said "I can't climb out. Throw down a life vest." (In Spanish because she does not speak very much English). Right away, Grandma got a pool floatie and called 9-1-1. Then she called Dad. Guess who arrived first? Dad. He was 20 minutes away but he drove so fast, he got there in 15 minutes. Right away Dad looked into the water and shouted, "Rosita what are you doing in a well?" She was too weak for talking so Dad climbed down using a rope and made sure. Grandma was safe. He says The water was warm up top but biting cold at his feet. Its a good thing not all of the well was that cold Dad says or hed be in the hospital now, too, with hipothermia.

"I saw a little girl down here," Rosita whispered. "She had such frightened eyes. But when I tried to rescue her, the girl became a fish and swam away."

"How?" my dad asked. "Theres nowhere to swim."

"Down. I think shes still there. Under our feet."

After the EMTs and fire service came, everyone—including Rosita—decided that the fish girl had been a hallucination. A figment of dementia or mental stress. Then they got to focusing on getting Rosita better. But Nina was starting to put faith in a stranger possibility.

Nina flipped past the last day of third grade. Next came entries detailing her vacation and sweltering days spent indoors, holed up in air-conditioned sanctuaries like her bedroom or between the fiction shelves of her father's bookstore. All summer, she'd waited for messages from Philipa. Messages that never came.

On August 19, Rosita passed away. The entry for that day was written in black:

My great-great-grandmother is ~~no longer with us~~ dead.

Following the single-sentence entry, Nina had filled three journal pages with a copy of Rosita's story, replete with the jumbled-up nonwords from the app. Looking at them, Nina felt like she'd been handed ten pieces of a hundred-piece jigsaw puzzle and tasked with describing the full image.

She'd have a better chance with a reference. Similar stories, perhaps, or a more thorough understanding of Rosita's early life. Maybe Grandma could help with that. After living with Rosita for decades, she probably knew the woman's history better than anyone else in Texas.

Nina pulled a blank journal from her closet. Across its red cover, she wrote one word: *Evidence.*

COTTONMOUTH IS HUNTED
BY A MONSTER

*I*t started with a beat. *Clack, clack, clack.* Like two drumsticks tapping against each other before the beginning of a rock song. However, the song never began. Just *clack, clack, clack.* I couldn't pinpoint where the sound originated from. It seemed to echo off the trees, bombarding me from every direction. Confused, I stopped walking.

The sound stopped, too.

When had the forest become so quiet? Even the white noise of bird chirps was gone. Earlier, I'd felt avoided. Now, I felt alone.

Well. Almost alone. The drumstick tapper clearly sensed me, because the moment I resumed walking, the clacking started again. What irony. Only minutes earlier, I'd been desperate for company, but now I was so afraid to meet the beat maker, I started to run. Look, there are sounds that warn of danger. For example: thunder or a rattlesnake's tail. The clacking was scarier than all of those sounds combined. It accelerated. In the air, I tasted something profoundly wrong, as if it came from a different world. The chemicals did not resemble anything I'd sensed before. That's the only way I can explain it. They didn't belong to a mammal or a reptile or an insect or a bird or a plant. Still, my brain classified the chemicals as organic. Something living. What else were there?

Monsters.

Shoot.

I didn't even know where to run. It could be approaching from any direction. So, I went very still.

Again, the clacking stopped. I wondered if that meant the monster had stopped too. Maybe. The sound certainly resembled wooden shoes tapping on a hard, flat floor. Thing is, the forest ground was soft and spongy. There, footsteps weren't sharp. I doubted that the monster was actually running around and tapping a pair of drumsticks over his head. Perhaps, it was carrying a bag that clacked with every stride, the same way my rucksack thumped as it bounced against my back when I ran.

If that was the case, the monster moved when I moved. Stopped when I stopped. Which implied the creepy thing had to be tracking me by vibration, either through sound or by feeling my footsteps.

To test my theory, I stomped the ground once.

Clack, clack, clack.

At that moment, I would have easily traded my whole rucksack for a pair of wings. I'd fly away and go so high above the canopy that I could see both horizons, as well as the blue thread of the river. In the sky, a day's journey by foot can be made in a couple hours. No wonder winged animals rarely transform into their false forms. The ability to fly is a gift.

Heck, as a bird, I could've made friends with the nasty robin and joined his team of forest protectors. Instead, I was trying to will my empty stomach not to rumble in case the sound attracted my hunter.

Birds almost always had an escape route: up.

Wait.

Technically, so did I. Cottonmouths aren't little boa constrictors; that is to say, we don't like to chill on branches. But in a pinch? Sure. We can climb a tree.

Nearby was a towering, ancient white ash tree. Slowly, I removed my rucksack and looped its strap over a low branch. Then, I eyeballed the distance between me and the trunk: one long jump. There weren't any convenient handholds or footholds for my false form. That was fine. I climbed better without hands and feet, anyway.

When I transformed, my clothes, shoes, and spectacles plopped onto the ground, and the monster made another inquisitive pair of clacks. I disentangled myself from my white linen tunic and grabbed my spectacles by one ear hook, carrying them in my mouth as I slithered with my head held high toward the tree. The monster made another hesitant clack, and I worried that it was very near. How else could it hear my movement? I practically threw myself at the trunk, gripping it tight with my muscular body, and zigzagged upward. A couple feet up, I heard a shrill, repetitive braying. If the monster was trying to scare me, mission accomplished. But I wouldn't be startled into a rash decision. Wouldn't try to flee on the ground. Tightening my grip on the trunk of the tree, I continued the grueling but steady journey upward. Soon, I passed the lowest branch. It was sturdy; my heavy bag still hung from one of its ends. I didn't stop there, though. The higher, the safer.

The monster didn't wail again, but when I was ten feet above ground level, I heard it clack-clacking in little bursts, as if it were scurrying back and forth, searching for a lost trail. I climbed faster, slithering in loops around the narrowing trunk. There were loads of branches at this height, and I could've made any one of them my perch, but I'd chosen a whopper of a tree. It must've been hundreds of years old. Maybe thousands. If I could reach the highest branch, then nothing on the forest floor would be able to sense me. And even if the monster realized that I'd escaped up that tree, how could it follow me? The high branches would snap under its weight unless it was the size of a squirrel.

I passed a bird nest full of little white eggs. Late bloomers, like me. They'd hatch in the late summer, if at all. I wondered how many of my siblings had survived their first day of independence. How could all of them thrive in a world that was so vicious and uncaring?

I was a nontuplet, born in a clutch of eight others. The most daring sibling, my sister Sona, hopped onto a passing ferry at the age of ten and never came back. She didn't even wait for Momma to make her a gift. The others left home between the ages of eleven and fourteen, their departures staggered, such that everybody left alone. My sibling Bleak was gifted a pistol and a holster; Pilot, Al, and Fourier got kayaks; my brother Elvin really, really, really wanted a flashy outfit, so Momma sent him to the tailor in the dammed town, and he marched into the sunset wearing a vibrant silk shirt, blue jeans, a silver and turquoise bolo tie, and a twelve-gallon hat. Everyone else got handwoven blankets. I guess all those gifts were supposed to improve our chances at survival. Even a flashy outfit, on the right person, can open doors to safety and good fortune. However, if my first day and a half were any indication of reality, Momma couldn't give us enough gifts to even the playing field against the world.

I reached an elevation above most of the other trees, but there was still plenty of ash to go, so I continued climbing. Sixty feet above the ground, the vertical body of the tree was so thin, I could wrap around it at least twice. At last, eighty feet high, I lifted my head and peeked above the shell of delicate green leaves at the top of the ash tree.

From my vantage point, I could see previously hidden details of the forest: the mushroom-shaped, domed heads of deciduous trees mixed among conical conifers. Gray clouds huddled along the western horizon. It was raining in a not-too-distant part of the world. I searched for signs of community, such as cooking smoke or road-shaped gaps in the canopy, but did not find anything promising. No river, either. Of course, the world was a bit fuzzy. I tightened my bite on the spectacles, considering my options. If I transformed, my extra weight would snap the tip of the ash off, and in the unlikely event that I survived the fall, I'd probably land in the open mouth of the monster. Instead, I squinted and tilted my head, trying to force sharpness into my vision. There was a south-to-north gap in the green patchwork of leaves, a narrow line of emptiness that resembled a seam in the very fabric of the forest. It was difficult to be certain, but it might have been a sign of a trail. Something narrow, perhaps worn by the same set of feet over a period of many years. Wherever the path led, it led somewhere, which was a lot better than my track record of going nowhere. Once the monster had lost interest in me, I would head toward that path.

Slowly, I drew my head back and squeezed the tree, waiting. Listening. The clacks started again, bursts of distance-muted sound that fired off like the rapid explosions of a machine gun. That went on for ten minutes, give or take. The whole time, I kept my eyes shut, afraid of what I might see far below. In my imagination, the monster had scythe-blade-sharp mandibles that snapped together as it shuffled over the forest floor on one hundred legs. Or, it carried a clattering bag of bones, souvenirs from its many victims.

Finally, there was silence. I opened my eyes but did not uncoil from the tree. It was still too quiet. Where was the birdsong? With my mouth clamped tight on my spectacles, I was unable to taste the air for the otherworldly sting of danger. The one sharp as smoke. I had to trust the birds. As the annoying robin said, his kind were observant.

The air cooled, and the sky darkened from bright blue to deep blue. If I wanted to reach the path before nightfall, I had to start descending now. It would take a while to slither down the tree. Plus, I was exhausted, sluggish with the chill. But while I didn't want to spend the night on a branch, the silence was still broken only by the wind.

Was I being overly cautious? My inner bad-mouther chided: *Timid little snake. Last of your siblings to leave home. You never had enough guts to survive. You'd run back to Momma if you weren't lost. Stop trembling in a tree, waiting for the world to be as safe as her cottage. That'll never happen.*

My inner bad-mouther made a compelling argument, but I

was so scared. Was the monster waiting? I might feel pathetic coiled around the ash tree like a tight spring, but I'd feel a million times worse if the monster ripped out my skeleton and used it as a necklace because of my self-loathing and impatience. So, my cautious side and my inner bad-mouther came to a compromise. I moved to a sturdy branch halfway down the tree and spread out to prepare for a long stay. After hanging my spectacles on a twig, I even managed to snap up a couple of flies for supper. That's one perk of the cottonmouth form: it doesn't take much to satisfy your hunger. Well, that's not exactly true when you're older. Snakes don't stop growing. Every year, we get a bit longer and wider. Slower, heavier. Our appetites grow, as well. That's why elders rarely transform into their true bodies.

I once met an elder cottonmouth in the dammed town. He was eating lunch at a food cart counter, hunched over a bowl of stew. He noisily slurped the rich broth from a wooden spoon. At the time, my siblings and I were so young, we still had green-tipped tails. We had never seen a cottonmouth person with such magnificent wrinkles. Momma just had a spattering of creases around her eyes and one vertical crease down the middle of her forehead.

"How old do you think he is?" Pilot wondered in a secretive hiss. "Is he an originator?"

"No way," Sona said. "They wouldn't be caught in a nowhere place like this."

"It's not that bad here," I muttered.

"He's at least two hundred," Elvin guessed. "His scales have gone all black."

In his false form, the elder had scales down the back of his neck and upper arms. They were as dark and sleek as obsidian chips.

"I'm just going to ask him," Sona declared, marching right up to the elder. He put down his spoon and watched her with amusement as she climbed onto the empty stool beside him. Me and the other siblings huddled nearby, always less bold than Sona. "Grandfather, how old are you?" she asked.

"I don't know," he said.

"You don't know? Really?"

"Do you know how many breaths you've taken?" he asked her.

Sona hummed, like she was actually trying to calculate the answer, but she soon gave up with a reluctant, "No."

"Why not?" he wondered.

"Because it doesn't matter," she said.

The elder swiveled in his seat and looked directly at me; my other siblings shyly ducked behind my back. "What about you?" he asked. "Do you keep track of your breaths?"

"One and a half million," I guessed.

In response, he shook his head, hissed with amusement, and swiveled back to his soup.

"Well, how big are you?" Sona persisted.

"How big do I look?"

"No, I mean as a snake!"

"Big enough to swallow a cow, kid." He clapped his hands, mimicking a jaw snapping shut. "But too big to catch one unless it skips into my mouth."

To be honest, I still don't know whether to believe the elder. Cows aren't remotely bite-sized. Sure, we keep growing end-lessly, but the rate of growth decreases over time. A snake my age can gain half a foot in one year. A snake Momma's age might grow a few centimeters. With elders, we're probably talking millimeters. So he was either telling a fib, or he was very, very, very old.

Originator old. One of the first cottonmouth people.

I wished I could swallow a cow. Then, I could've yawned wide and invited the monster to be my dinner. Skip on up, jerk.

At dusk, a fluctuating wind batted my branch side to side like a bobcat pawing at a fieldmouse. I remembered the distant rain clouds and wondered if they were not so distant anymore. It was already uncomfortably chilly. What would nightfall bring? A deeper chill? Stronger winds? Freaking lightning? My tree was the tallest in sight. It would make an excellent lightning lure. I couldn't stay here if it stormed. I'd fry. Could that be the reason why the birds were silent? Were they sensitive to the approaching nasty weather? Maybe they were all just tired. Most birds don't chirp at night.

You could have been at that trail by now, my inner bad-mouther informed me. I tasted the air. There was no monster. However, I had not tasted anything but the trees since I left the ground. I grabbed my spectacles and descended to a slightly lower branch. It was still at a safe height, but if the rain started, I'd have less distance to travel in order to find shelter. The thicker branch was sturdier and less prone to swaying in the wind, and I was able to relax my grip. Night fell rapidly; there was no lingering sunset, and unlike Earth, the sky was devoid of other stars. There was no moon, either. So imagine my surprise when I was able to clearly see the leaves in front of my face. They were lit from below by a dim red glow. Curious, I peeked over my branch and looked down. Two pinpoints of light the color of hot embers were swaying in the tree a couple branches below me.

The lights flickered when the monster blinked.

Clack.

I huddled against my branch and prayed to both the Creator and my momma that the monster was too heavy to go any higher.

In the morning, the birds sang again. There were deep, sap-dripping scratches up the trunk of the tree, evidence that something with claws sharp enough to slice through bone had pawed against the wood. The fresh scratches stopped at a branch about five meters below mine. My rucksack and clothes below were thankfully undisturbed. They clearly had not been the monster's target.

Exhausted after a sleepless night, I transformed into my false form, dressed quickly, and started hiking toward the path I'd observed from the tree. I only paused to drink from the puddle of dew shimmering in a concave leaf. I did not bother to look for friendly strangers. That would be a waste of effort. There did not seem to be any kindness in the world beyond my childhood, and I could never return to the past.

The path, although modest, was well worn; down its center, all but a comb-over of wimpy grass had been stamped away. I chose a direction and started strolling. My neck and shoulders ached under the rucksack weight. I idly wished for the convenience of a wheelbarrow; the path would've been perfect for wheels. It was absolutely straight, as if planned by a mathematician. The gentle sun, which caressed me in patches of warmth squished between leaf-shaped shadows, felt so nice against my face. I almost forgot about my anxieties.

They say the path to anywhere-you-please is not concerned with the rules of space or time. It slithers snakelike through forests—mostly in the world of spirits and monsters, but occasionally on Earth—fleeing from the people who want to catch it. That's why no map leads to the path, just like no map can lead to a roaming pack of wolves. Guess that's also why most people who walk the path do so unwittingly.

Of course, there are stories of determined individuals who managed to successfully track the wiggly thing. Like the human father. Have you heard that one? Centuries ago, he lost his son in a flood. A river overflowed and swept the little kid away. Everyone assumed the man's son had drowned, but a body was never found, and that ambiguity sharpened the father's grief. He'd stay awake all night, moaning, "Where did you go? Where did you go?" If his son was still alive somewhere across the land, the father wanted to bring him home. And if he was dead? Well, the father wanted to bury him. Do it properly. Get closure, too, you know?

Like I said, the path to anywhere-you-please is one of those stories everybody, including the father, seems to know. He also knew that it hated being chased. So he got an idea.

Once a year, on the anniversary of his son's disappearance, the father camped in the center of his forest. Meanwhile, his friends searched for the path, trying to herd it toward the grieving man.

It took fifteen years. Fifteen years of patience. Fifteen years of disappointment. Fifteen years of hope. At last, the father walked down the path to anywhere-you-please, saying, "I want to be with my son." He vanished in the mist and was never seen again. Many people believe that the path gave the father exactly what he desired, reuniting him with his child in the underworld.

But we'll never actually know, huh?

Thankfully, I didn't think anything dangerous when I ignorantly trudged down the legendary path. Instead, with my face angled upward to catch the sun, I dreamed of a happy little home. Somewhere safe where I could bask on a comfy rock, catch plenty of fish, and say "Good morning!" to my neighbors. My pleasant, nonhomicidal neighbors.

Suddenly, my ears popped, as if the pressure had changed rapidly. I stepped onto the bank of a calm, blue lake. Creator bless me, the water stretched farther than the horizon. How did a lake that size appear in front of me? Baffled, I spun three-sixty degrees to take stock of my surroundings.

Behind me, the path was gone.

And before me was a flat granite stone half-buried in the ground, its surface warm and inviting. Silver-bright minnows swam in the shallows, and there were plenty of good materials to start a house, a dock, a raft! Everything I needed to thrive.

Don't get too excited. The last time you found a perfect home, it already belonged to a jerk. Bet a whole family of vicious reptilian tail-stompers lives just beyond those reeds.

"Does anybody claim this rock?" I hollered. Crickets chirped, and cicadas hummed, but nobody chased me away. With a pleased sigh, I lay on the toasty granite bed, spreading my arms to soak up the heat. "It's mine, then," I said, closing my eyes.

It seemed like, apart from the chatty insects, I didn't have any neighbors. However, that turned out not to be the case. Before I slipped into a proper nap, I felt a gentle pat against my cheek. It didn't sting like a mosquito bite, so instead of smacking my face, I opened my eyes. A little toad sat an inch away. He was an unusual species, delicately built and spattered with spots of brown and mesa red. He waved a four-toed hand.

"Is this your spot?" I asked. "Sorry . . ."

The toad shook his head: no.

"Oh. Okay. What is it, then?"

Again, he waved at me.

"You just wanted to say hi?" I realized.

A nod.

I rolled over onto my stomach and propped my chin atop my folded hands. From that angle, I had a clearer view of the little amphibian. "My name's Oli," I said. "Three days ago, Momma kicked me outta her cottage, and it's been a complete nightmare since then. How does anyone live long enough to get black scales?"

He patted my finger reassuringly with a hand that was no wider than the pad of my thumb.

"Do you talk?" I wondered.

A head shake.

"Not even in your false form?"

Another shake of the head. We stared at each other a moment. It was an oddly companionable silence. Then, a blackfly landed on my wrist, but before it could bite my soft, unscaled skin, the toad's tongue snapped out. Crunch.

"Hey, thanks," I said. "Or maybe you should thank me for attracting lunch . . . Ami."

I just had to look at him for the name to pop into my head. It was like reading text on a page. See, all animal people have a knack for communication. We don't all speak the same language, but we're adept at understanding all languages, get it? And I have a particular knack for the skill.

The toad half-opened his mouth in an expression closely resembling a smile. For the first time since my independence, I smiled, too.

Maybe now you can appreciate why I recruited a group of daring spirits for a mission to Earth. Some things are worth protecting with your life.

Before I get into that part of the story, though, I should introduce the adventurers.

NINA, AGE 13

*N*ina sat cross-legged in front of a coffee table, her back steadied against a stack of toy-filled cardboard boxes. Grandma, always questing for presents to give to her grandchildren, often scoured the local garage sales and flea markets for toys. She seemed to forget that, every year, another grandchild aged out of dollies or relocated north of the peril zone. Nina was among the last remaining family in Texas, and at thirteen, she hardly needed a button-eyed teddy bear (her bed was already overflowing with plushies). But that didn't stop her from accepting Grandma's gift with a grin, and an enthusiastic "Aw, thanks!"

Somewhere, thunder rumbled, and the overhead lights flickered. With the bear sitting on her lap, Nina shifted anxiously; her cotton shirt, flattened between cardboard and skin, was sticky with sweat. Even under the shade of storm clouds, South Texas was dangerously hot. A busted air-conditioning unit could mean death, especially for elders like Grandma, who could not or would not move. Not for heat. Not for drought. Not even for hurricanes and their entourage of tornadoes, floods, and blackouts.

The land under and around the three-bedroom house had been their family's homeland for generations. Before Texas became a state, Nina's ancestors had lived there, and they didn't ever leave. Not really. When Federal Indian Removal became the law of the land, and bounties were put on Apache heads, her people resisted. In many ways, they still did.

Officially, Rosita had bought fifteen acres of South Texas land in the early 1900s. She'd allowed most of her property to grow unimpeded; beyond a well-trimmed backyard and a fenced-in patch of longhorn grazing land, the earth sprouted thick tangles of brush, mesquite trees, and allthorn plants with leaves shaped like green porcupine spines. Every morning, the chachalacas cheered. Every night, the screech owls cooed. And as the nearby suburbs spread in the century that followed, covering the land with identical yellow houses, pink condominiums, and gated neighborhoods named Paradise and Sunny Vale, the fifteen acres became an island.

The situation got sticky in the late 1900s. Rosita's property had grown too wild, too ugly: that's what the city charged. Fix it or lose it, they said. So she'd surrounded the whole thing with a stone wall, her younger family members laying each rock over the course of a skin-searing summer. If the people of Paradise and Sunny Vale thought her land was ugly, they didn't have to look at it.

These days, sections of the wall were missing, crumbling around the trunks of ever-growing mesquite trees. Other rocks, especially at the far end of the property, where the family seldom ventured, were bright with graffiti. That didn't matter. Nina's grandmother, who'd taken over the house when Rosita died, seldom worried about fussy neighbors, 'cause there weren't many left. Paradise and Sunny Vale had closed after a terrible case of foundation subsidence, flooding, and a class-action lawsuit. That meant the nearest neighbors were two introverted, off-the-grid married women who shared a highly modded RV. They were friendly enough and mostly kept to themselves: in other words, perfect. However, Nina worried, maybe the neighborhood dynamics would be changing again soon. She'd noticed a fresh Sold sign down the street from Grandma's place. Somebody had purchased the ruins of Paradise. Why would anyone do that? Did they plan to renovate and reopen the graffiti-painted adobe houses? Or tear it all down to build something new? Only time would tell, and the family was powerless to do anything but wait.

That was true of so many things these days.

Nina glanced at the television screen, which was playing ominous maps from the Weather Channel. Last she checked, most projections showed the hurricane veering east. The worst would miss them. Maybe. As her father always said, when it came to weather, a lot could change quickly. It was risky to trust predictions until the final day.

"Want a hint?" Grandma asked, noticing Nina's reluctance to continue losing their game of checkers. Her voice was dulled by the metallic, quickening *plop-plop-plop* of raindrops on the roof. The first half of summer had been thirsty, but just when the fruit trees and crops got too weak and withered for a decent harvest, the storms started. First, a category 2 hurricane collided with Puerto Rico, its winds rippling west. Then, a week of thunderstorms spun tornadoes throughout Arkansas. Now, more rainfall preceded a category 4 hurricane that was arcing through the Atlantic, veering straight toward Florida.

There was one slender, faintly shimmering silver lining around the roiling clouds of hurricane season: every time the Weather Channel predicted a big storm, Nina and her dad visited Grandma's house to check on things. They'd top up the pantry with canned food, prep the generator, and check the batteries in all the flashlights. At the moment, her father was buying sodas, canned soup, and bread at the nearest grocery store. Once he returned, they'd head straight home. It was a two-hour drive, and the risk of bad-weather driving increased after sunfall, since even a mist of rain could transform into a glowing, disorienting curtain in the truck's bright headlights.

"Can't you come with us today, Grandma?" Nina asked. "I know the hurricane won't go through Texas, but . . ." Nina could recall a time—she must have been four, five, six years old—when Grandma ventured away from the homeland and Rosita to visit the bookshop every month. They'd read together and bake oatmeal cookies in the narrow apartment kitchen. What had changed? These days, Grandma rarely left her property, much less traveled beyond county limits. ". . . it could be fun. You oughtta see the renovations we made to the nonfiction section. I painted historical quotes on the wall."

"That sounds perfect. Do you have photos?"

"Pictures aren't the same as being there."

"Nina, I wish I could." Grandma rubbed her forehead, as if massaging away a headache. "Lately, travel doesn't sit well with me. I guess it's part of aging. Some people cry when they're homesick. I get terrible migraines and indigestion. It's rough to enjoy anything when you feel like death warmed over, honey."

"Have you visited a doctor about that?"

"Of course," she said. "And if I ever meet one who can help me, you'll be the first grandchild I visit."

"I better be." Nina used her fingertip to scoot a checker piece diagonally. She only had a few left, with no queens among the lot. "Thank you."

"You're welcome."

In other words, conversation over. In the pause that followed, Nina considered asking a follow-up question anyway. In the end, her respect for Grandma's wishes won out.

"On a different note," Nina said, "I have a question about stories—"

"Which ones?" Grandma sounded grateful for the change in subject.

"The old ones from the joined era, when there were still animal people on Earth."

A smile now. "Rosita's favorites."

"Yeah! I guess . . . I don't really know what they look like. Do animal people resemble furries? Or are they like humans with animal features?" There were a million different theories online, but since cameras didn't get invented 'til way after the joined era, the best visuals people had were cave art, sculptures, temple paintings, and pictographs, which seemed to vary based on artistic license. Nina didn't trust the online videos promising "real footage of animal people on earth!!!" It was too easy to fake that stuff for views.

A pause. "Furries?" Grandma finally asked. "Some had fur. The mammals."

"No. Sorry. That's not what I meant. Furries are anthropomorphic . . . actually, let me show you. Visuals will make this description a million times easier to get. Where's the computer?"

Grandma pointed to a metal desk piled with letters, notebooks, and magazine-filled reusable grocery bags. Nina pushed aside a twine-bound tower of birthday cards to reveal an early 2000s monitor. Its black square screen was streaked with oily fingermarks. "Did somebody mistake this for touch-sensitive?" she asked, laughing at the absurdity of her question. The machine was vintage.

"Little Jon visited last week," Grandma explained. "He kept pawing at the computer."

"Did he eventually try using the mouse?"

"Of course. He's very clever."

Nina knelt and found the power button of the obelisk-shaped computer. "I'm surprised Aunt Peele let Jon mess with this. She says he can't even know the Internet exists till he's past kindergarten."

"It doesn't get Internet," Grandma explained.

"Seriously?" Nina sat up so fast, she nearly bumped her head on the edge of the desk. How could she explain the phenomenon known as furries without access to their natural habitat?

"Yep."

"Hold on. There's another way." Nina grabbed her smartphone off the coffee table and checked its power. It was clinging to 10 percent charge. In her defense, when she'd arrived at Grandma's place that morning, Nina hadn't expected to stay more than two hours. And she certainly hadn't anticipated that a house that resembled the world's most cluttered thrift shop would not contain a charger compatible with her phone. Oh, Grandma possessed miles of electrical cables and cords, with loops of insulated wires in every drawer. Earlier that afternoon, Nina had rummaged through chargers for devices ranging from digital cameras to defunct game consoles. Nothing could connect to her phone.

A quick image search wouldn't zap too much power, though. Nina typed "furry" into the browser search bar on her smartphone. Then, she clicked on a G-rated illustration of an anthropomorphic fox guy with bright pink fur. He wore a flight attendant's uniform, complete with a tray of sodas and pretzels.

"Do animal people look like this?" Nina asked.

Grandma shook her head adamantly. "Doubtful."

"Then how did a coyote person trap the world's sweetest song in a locket? I dunno that a coyote could close a locket with paws."

"I always assumed that they have two forms. An animal body and a false body, one that resembles humans."

"They must really like opposable thumbs. I'd choose tentacles instead."

A snicker, and then Grandma hunched farther into the cocoon of light blankets wrapped around her shoulders. In the raindrop-interspersed silence, Nina pushed one of her checkers pieces forward and counted the stains on the coffee table. Grandma owned plenty of coasters, cork or cardboard freebies from various restaurants. But her grandchildren, with their heaping cups of juice and sweet iced tea, never used 'em, and Grandma never attempted to enforce a coaster rule.

Maybe she liked the rings their glasses stamped on every flat surface of her kitchen and living room. Did they keep her company when she was alone?

"I've considered that choice," Grandma said. "There are different possibilities, but the one that rings true"—she tapped her chest, indicating her heart—"is that at the edge of memory, when humans became the most dangerous species on Earth, the false forms adapted. Like butterfly spots resemble owl eyes, to mimic a dangerous hunter."

"That's an iffy solution, considering how often we hurt each other."

Grandma looked Nina directly in the eyes. "I know." Then, Grandma stole two white checker pieces in a single move: hop, hop. "Queen me."

"I resent that you're so good at this game."

"Practice."

As Grandma returned the game pieces to their starting positions, Nina said: "If you're right about the two-body thing, it means a spirit could temporarily look like a scared little girl and then transform into a fish."

A knowing smile. "Like Rosita's hallucination?"

Conspiratorily, Nina leaned over the coffee table and whispered: "Was it, though?"

"Why would a fish girl be in our well, centuries after the joined era?"

"That's what I'd like to know. Have you ever noticed other

weirdness out there?" Nina pointed to the window, which overlooked an expanse of wind-tousled wilds. The well was there, somewhere, at the end of an overgrown trail. Deprived of Rosita's daily walks, the trail would soon vanish completely.

To Nina's surprise, her grandmother did not respond immediately. Instead, she considered the question, distractedly tapping a black game piece against the tabletop. *Tck. Tck. Tck.* Then, "The Odd Jobs Man. He was very strange."

"Who?"

"I can't recall his real name. Maybe he never provided one. Some details are vague, since we met so long ago. It's been almost fifteen years."

"That's okay, Grandma. His name can be Odd Jobs Man. But what made him so strange?"

"Well, back then, Rosita raised a few chickens for their eggs. They lived in a coop outside the house. I did my best to help. There's the water, the feed, and the constant repairs. Out here, coyotes and foxes will chew through metal to steal a chicken. Vigilance is important. Cleverness, too. Believe it or not, the moment you underestimate a coyote's ingenuity, they win. That chicken coop needed constant upkeep, endless adaptations. Don't ask me how, but a coyote once turned a childproof latch on the outer gate. Luckily, there was a second door—a padlocked door—between the chickens and death.

"Anyway, Rosita and I were cleaning the coop when we saw a man wandering around the distant mesquite. He wore a long wool coat and a fishing hat. Carried a hiking backpack. Sometimes, people mistake our fifteen acres for campground; they don't know anyone lives here. Rosita didn't mind, 'long as the campers were respectful and treated the land right. No fires when there's drought, no littering, you know. So we waved, and he waved back.

"This man approached, and I'll never forget his face. He had a five o'clock shadow from his neck to his cheeks, white stubble. But he must've gone gray early, because his face hadn't had the chance to wrinkle, except for laugh lines around the eyes.

"He first complimented the chickens, 'Pretty birds you got. I've never seen healthier hens.' Then, Rosita asked him, 'What are you doing out here, wearing wool in late spring?' Turns out, he was only passing through. 'I carry all my belongings,' the Odd Jobs Man explained. 'It does get hot, but I'm used to wearing a coat.'

"I was reluctant to entertain strangers. Sometimes, there's venom behind a friendly smile. 'Don't let us keep you,' I said. 'The nearest town is miles away.'

"But then he asked, 'Before I leave, do you need any work done? For a modest fee, I can mow lawns, trim trees, and patch up houses. I'll even remove beehives.'

"That touched Rosita's heart. I guess she'd experienced so much hardship, she could empathize with nearly any pitiful traveler. 'I'll give you twenty dollars to feed our hens,' she said, handing him a bag of pellets. 'And breakfast, if you're hungry. We're having coffee, beans, and toast this morning.'

"He blessed her generosity, and before long, we were sitting around the bench on the open-air patio, and the Odd Jobs Man took his coffee black, just like us, even though Rosita offered him cream. Even I dropped my guard. We chatted like three old friends. Sometime, during breakfast, the conversation turned to your father's bookshop. I mentioned that our economy was punishing for small businesses. 'He's got commitment, determination, and dreams,' I confessed, 'but with a baby on the way, I doubt that'll be enough. My boy's preparing to sell.'"

At that, Nina thought about her mother and the ocean between them. About the tense discussions she overheard at least once a year. Dad offering to sell the store to bring Mom home. Mom asking him where they'd find better jobs in "this economy." Had so little changed in her lifetime?

"Odd Jobs Man said, 'Missy, you helped me. Now I'll help you. I know folks who are hankering for books. They'll pay good money in exchange for discretion.'

"That request worried me. I asked, 'What kind of books do they need? We're a . . . family-friendly establishment, if you catch my drift.'

"He looked me straight in the eyes and rattled off, "Textbooks, pulp mysteries, romances, fantasies, nonfiction and fiction. Old books. New books. Any books and all books. I hope that answers your question, because I—and my nerdy friends—won't answer any others. Like I said: discretion. It's a matter of life and death. So, are you interested?'

"Took only a second to answer, 'Yes.' What was the harm? It's not like customers owe us their life story.

"A couple weeks later came a knock on the door so early in the morning, neither the rooster nor the chachalacas had arisen to scream their songs. Three people in trench coats stood on the porch. They asked for directions to the bookstore, and then promptly left by foot."

"Trench coats? Seriously?"

"Sunglasses, too."

"In the dark? That's a choice." Why would an animal person wear sunglasses, of all accessories? Had they studied human behavior by bingeing spy movies? Were movies even a thing in the world of spirits and monsters?

"Nina, I doubt Rosita saw a fish girl in her well," Grandma continued, "but it's closed-minded to discount the possibility that there was something otherworldly about Odd Jobs Man and his bookish friends. Many claim that no animal people remain on Earth. That's the price those spirits paid to survive us. But there must be exceptions to the rule. It's not like they all went extinct after the joined era. So . . . perhaps brave ones still visit us now and then. In secret. I'd be reluctant to pester them. As the Odd Jobs Man said, discretion can be a matter of life and death."

Silence, broken only by raindrops and faraway thunder.

Then, Nina looked up sharply.

"Grandma, I think those trench-coat guys still visit the bookstore."

COTTONMOUTH MEETS
THE COYOTE SISTERS

*R*isk and Reign are twins, which is rare for their kind; coyotes usually come in litters of three or more. I wonder if their pack spoils them 'cause of that. As a nontuplet, I struggle to relate.

I met the twins after two months of independence. Thinking back, the day seems like a lifetime ago, and maybe it is. You know the way it feels to shed your skin and emerge bright and new? That's the way I felt after meeting Risk and Reign.

I was napping on my granite basking rock. Although I entertained half-baked plans to build a stone cottage, I still lived in a tent in a secluded nook along the banks of the bottomless lake. My home territory was a grassy crescent of land between the water and forest. I could hide my raft in a patch of reeds within the shallows, and I never lacked fish or insects for dinner. Plus, the lake itself was a good avenue to escape danger, considering its depth. Which—for the record—is extremely, ridiculously deep, but definitely not infinite. The name *bottomless* is misleading; I guess the lake doesn't technically have a bottom, but it doesn't go down forever, either. It's a horseshoe-shaped tunnel in the ground created by something ridiculously giant in ancient times. If you dove and kept swimming—assuming you could swim for days and survive the frigid, crushing, monster-infested depths—you'd go down, swoop, and then go up, eventually emerging in a different pool of water on the other side of the world.

Some even claimed that the water connected us with Earth. At the time, I assumed that only the strongest, bravest swimmers could confirm the truth.

Midnap, I heard a crunch of multiple feet behind me. It took less than a second to leap off the rock and into the water. Like I said, my first instinct is usually "run and hide;" as my encounter with Miss Bruhn showed, the venom in my bite might not deter an attacker (especially if they're big and angry) and takes forever to come back. I switched from my false form with arms and legs (which are so unwieldy in the water; how does anything with limbs manage to swim?) to my true form and was a long leap away from the shore when a high-pitched voice called, "Hey, wait! It's okay, viper! We didn't mean to scare you!"

I poked my head above the surface and flicked my tongue, scenting the two young coyotes on the bank. They weren't pursuing me, so I switched back to my false form to get a better look. The coyotes were about my age and could have been mirror images in different sets of clothing. In their false forms, both had brown-gray hair—the kind that's so thick and straight, it bristles in the wind—wide-set yellow eyes, and long noses. The sister to the right wore an oversized red sweater; its sleeves were rucked up to the elbows but probably would've dangled below her fingertips otherwise. The sister to the left wore a patchwork of pastel, multi-textured cloth that had been stitched into what I can only loosely describe as clothing. She resembled an upside-down rose flower bursting with differently colored petals.

"You startled me," I hissed, brushing my soggy bangs out of my eyes. "Don't sneak up on people when they're napping."

The sweater sister grinned slyly; one of her pointy canines jutted over her lower lip. "You heard our footsteps, didn't you?" she asked.

"Well, yes . . ."

"Then we weren't sneaking. Listen." She danced in a circle; I didn't hear a thing. "That's real sneaking."

"Point taken. What do you want?"

"Is that your boat?" the colorful sister asked, pointing to my raft. I'd fastened several logs together, making a sturdy but unremarkable platform that floated well on calm waters. It was large enough to hold five people, but I'd never had company. I used it for fishing. If I ever needed to leave in a hurry, it could also carry my tent and other belongings across the lake.

"It's mine," I confirmed.

"Can we borrow it?" she asked.

I swam closer to shore and stood where the water was waist deep. "When you say 'borrow,' do you mean forever or . . . ?"

They laughed at me, a high-pitched frenzy of yips. "You're a suspicious fella, huh?" the sweater-wearing coyote asked. Then, she held up a burlap sack. It clattered and clinked, as if full of solid objects. "For one afternoon of boating, we'll give you all these phones. They won't go bad for another ten days, at least! Some of them have games. Want a look?"

Honestly, yeah, I did. Earth stuff ages fast in our world, eroded by something in the air. I learned that disappointing lesson as a child, after I found a little toy horse jutting from the muddy ground. It was made from a smooth, colorful, decidedly human-concocted material. Plastic. I couldn't believe my luck. Sometimes, relics fall from the sky. More often, they're smuggled here by scavengers who travel between worlds. I carried the toy home and tucked it in a basket beside my sleeping bag. It was safe there, I figured, but within a few days all that remained of the toy was a pile of white and pink grains. They resembled sand but softer. Less permanent. A couple days later, even the grains were gone.

Still, I was reluctant to part with my raft for a nonemergency purpose. It wasn't that the sisters were coyotes; I'm not the kind of small-minded fellow to buy into stereotypes like "all coyotes are tricksters." But they were strangers, and since my precious blanket was still missing, the raft was the most important thing I had. It wasn't irreplaceable, per se, but the replacement process would take a season of hard labor, since I'd have to do everything alone. It had taken me forever to cut down five trees with a little hatchet, drag them to the water's edge, lash them together, and waterproof them with resin. The ordeal left my hands raw with splinters, my back aching with strain. My dear friend Ami had been a lovely source of moral support, but the most his tiny hands could carry were scraps of twine.

"Sorry," I said, "but I can't risk my boat unless it's a life or death situation."

They stared at me, inscrutable.

"A vole woman named Feint—she lives a mile that way—has a couple kayaks," I added, hoping the information would speed their departure so I could get back to my nap. "Try asking her instead."

The twins exchanged a long glance, communicating with their eyes in one of the few languages I did not understand. Then, the colorful sister eased to the ground, sat on her knees, and beckoned me to listen with a smile and a twitch of her clawed fingers. She had heart-shaped patches of fur on the back of her hands, with the rounded part under her knuckles. "I'm Reign. That's my sister Risk. To be honest with you, we need to row to the center of the lake, where it's deepest, but the pack raft is in use, and nobody else trusts us with their boats today."

Risk remained standing, but she leaned over slightly to look down at me. "Guess why."

"Guess why nobody trusts you?"

"Heh." She snorted. "Nah. That would be insulting. Guess why we need the boat."

"You need to dispose of something embarrassing?" I ventured. Lots of naïve land-based peoples rowed to the center of the lake to chuck their bags of incriminating junk overboard. They didn't realize there were low-down aquatic scavengers who made a living off blackmail.

"No," she said. "Anyway, I don't get embarrassed."

"She doesn't," Reign confirmed. "It's a marvel!"

I yawned, flashing my milk-white inner mouth to the sisters. "Sorry. That wasn't intentional. Warm days make me sleepy. Cold days make me sleepy, too. Come to think of it, sleepiness is my body's response to any extreme in temperature."

"It's fine," Risk assured me. "I'll cut to the chase. You know the ancient water monsters who live deeper than the deepest catfish? Way below the light?"

I nodded. Anyone who lived near the bottomless lake knew about the abyssal monsters, who had bodies longer than mountains and mouths wide enough to swallow whales. Specifically, we knew to avoid them.

"Our aunt . . ." Risk looked both ways, as if reluctant to be overheard, and then knelt beside her sister. Her voice dropped to a murmur; I had to tilt my head to listen. "Our aunt," she continued, "knows how to communicate with them, and she taught us the method."

"Is there a reason you want to bother a monster?" I asked. "A good reason?"

Risk responded with a slight smile, one that hinted at secrets. It was almost a smirk.

"Because of the benefits," Reign explained. "The knowledge. The gifts. Imagine being older than the creation of Earth. Spending all that time in the darkness, in thought, guarding the secrets of generations. Alone and surrounded by sunken treasures. You have so many answers but so few opportunities to share. Then, one day, you receive a greeting from the surface: 'Hello! How are you?' It's been so long since anyone has spoken to you. Maybe this is the beginning of a conversation? A friendship?"

I shrugged. "That's possible."

"Plus, they never leave the deep lake," Risk added. One of her sleeves slipped down her forearm; she distractedly shoved it back over her elbow. "That means if the monsters hate our messages, the worst they can do is snub us."

"That'd hurt my feelings," Reign admitted.

"At least you'd live to get over it," her sister said, laughing sharply. The sound resembled a bark. "So, naked guy. Can we borrow your boat, or nah?"

Naked. Right. I'd initially been wearing a pair of shorts and boots, but all my clothes fell straight into the lake during the transformation from legs to no legs. Luckily, they weren't beyond recovery, and I'd safely removed my spectacles before the nap. "My name's Oli," I said. "I'll escort you to the middle of the lake. It's safer that way—"

"Aw," Reign squeaked. "That's sweet."

"—for my boat." Plus, access to a wealth of knowledge was somewhat more exciting than another nap, even on a warm day.

My slice of the lake was relatively safe. Aside from the rare thief, there were few threats willing to target animal peoples. As long as we traveled straight to the deep end—no detours around the fringe islands or through catfish territories—we'd be fine.

After fishing my clothes out of the muddy shallows, I slipped into the shorts and arranged my leather boots on the sunning rock to dry.

"We'll leave in a minute," I said. "Gonna ask my neighbor to watch the tent."

"Neighbor?" Risk wondered. "We didn't notice anyone." Based on her grimace, the possibility that they'd overlooked somebody was personally offensive.

"Hah. Were you two casing my place or something?" I asked.

Risk chuckled drily, and Reign shook her head.

"I'm joking," I reassured Reign. "Follow me."

We walked into the edge of the forest, where an old pine was surrounded by a ring of its own needles, which were as thick and bright as a woven rug. The tangled roots at the base of the pine formed a natural cubby, the perfect home for a field mouse, or—in this case—a toad. I crouched and tapped the roof of the root home.

"Hey, Ami, are you there?"

In response, a serious little face peeked outside.

"Do you mind watching my place this morning?" I asked.

He puffed out his blue throat.

"Thank you," I said. "While I'm out, do you need anything from the middle of the lake?"

After a thoughtful pause, he shook his head. No.

"Hey, is it a good idea to communicate with the deep lake monsters?"

My toad friend made a shrugging gesture with his tiny arms. I'd never seen Ami in his false form. Sometimes, I wondered if he could even transform.

"Yeah, I don't know either. See you later. Hopefully."

My friend lifted his foreleg, raising one unwebbed foot. I booped it with the pad of my index finger in a tiny high-five. Well. He had four long fingers in his toad form, but you get the picture.

"He's cute," Reign observed as we returned to the lake.

"Yeah," I said, smiling. "I'm lucky he's my neighbor."

"We're kinda your neighbors, too," she noted. "Our pack lives in the valley. It's less than an hour away if you cut through the forest. You should visit someday! There's lots to do. Birthday feasts happen every weekend in the spring, and there's plenty of community parties, especially when traders visit. How good is your aim, by the way?"

"Aim with what?"

"Gun, bow, sling—"

"All terrible." I tapped my spectacles. "Even with these."

"Aw, that's okay. There are other types of competitions. Can you sing?"

"My pitch is worse than my aim. But you had me at 'feast.' It's been two months since my last good meal. I'm still learning how to cook."

I wrangled my raft out of the reeds. It was equipped with two long paddles. Normally, I saved one for backup, but I'd never had an extra set of hands before. "Here," I said, offering the second paddle to Risk. "You two can take turns. Row to the right. I'll handle the left."

She nodded, accepting the paddle and gracefully hopping onto the raft. It wobbled slightly, but she calmed the motion by shifting her weight closer to the center of the platform. Next, Reign threw the burlap sack over one shoulder and climbed aboard with help from her sister. Once they were settled, I grabbed my travel bag, which was filled with survival essentials and rations of smoked fish, and joined them. With my paddle, I pushed against the mud of the lake bottom to maneuver us into deeper waters. Then, Risk and I stood on opposite sides of the raft to row, while Reign sat between us, her legs buried under a waterfall of fabric strips.

The sisters didn't speak again until we were well into the lake, probably afraid to press their luck. "What changed your mind about helping us?" Reign asked.

She sounded hopeful. At the time, I didn't understand the motivation for her question. But now, I suspect that Reign wanted me to admit, "I decided that I like you." As if I'd chosen to lend them the boat for their sake, not for mine. I wish that had been the case.

"It just happened," I lied. Truthfully, I'd never seen anyone communicate with the deep-lake monsters before, and it seemed like a useful trick.

"Before we go much farther," I said, "can you explain how to contact something that lives under miles of water?"

"Yeah, sure," Reign said. "Like this." She loosened the twine that cinched the burlap sack shut and began unpacking, spreading its contents in front of her knees. Among the objects were a book of short stories, several shiny, paper-thin phones, a glass bottle, and a spool of tightly wound thread. It was fine and white, like braided spider silk.

"Careful," Risk warned, grinning. "You might drop them in the lake before we're ready."

Reign stuck out just the tip of her tongue, making an expression I usually associated with disgust, although on her face, it was softened to mild distaste. Then, she pointedly turned away from her sister. "See this, Oli?" Reign asked.

I nodded, able to paddle with my motor memory while concentrating on her demonstration. Reign put the lip of the bottle against her mouth and whispered into it. Then, she pressed the palm of her hand over the opening, as if trapping a firefly in a jar, and stood. I braced for the raft to wobble, but it didn't budge. Step by well-balanced step, she moved to my side. After lifting the Coke bottle to my ear, Reign swept her hand away to free its contents.

"This is the trickiest part," the bottle whispered, sounding as diffuse and hollow as a distant echo. "It's not easy to trap your voice in glass."

"Took us months of practice," Risk drawled from across the raft.

That meant the technique might take me years to learn, if I was diligent. It was a world-shaper, an act that momentarily tweaked the natural laws through willpower alone. On Earth, some humans call it "magic." They're afraid of it or fascinated by it or—most commonly—don't believe in it. All those responses make sense, I guess, since nothing completely originating from Earth can do world-shaping. It's supposedly a lot more difficult to influence Earth's natural laws, too, but I'd never tried.

Frankly, Momma discouraged the whole practice. Once, after a salmon escaped her fishing line, I asked, "Why don't you pull on the river and fling that fish onto land?"

At that, she propped her hands on her hips and grimaced at me, like I'd suggested something distasteful. "How can I pull on water, Oli? It's a liquid."

"Using world-shaping? Sona says we're semiaquatic snakes, which means we're good at influencing the water."

Momma hissed in laughter. "That girl. Has she been talking to the owls again?"

"I . . . don't know? But she's right. Look what I can do!" Concentrating, I wove my willpower into a thimble-sized basket and mentally lifted a drop of water into the air. It bobbed around Momma's face.

"Stop that, Oli." Momma flicked the water away and unholstered her slingshot, a sturdy Y of wood with a dark rubber band and leather ammo pouch. "See this?" she asked, holding the slingshot in front of my face. Its band dangled loose, like a swing with no rider. I nodded, and Momma continued. "I'm about to get metaphorical. Pretend this slingshot is the world. The floppy rubber band represents our natural laws in their resting state. Do you follow?"

"Yes."

She stooped over, plucked a pebble off the ground, and placed it in the sling. Then, Momma aimed at the water and pulled back the sling a couple millimeters. The rubber band barely stretched. "This is me doing a tiny bit of world-shaping," she said. "After I'm done, the laws will go right back to their original state." She released her slingshot, but there hadn't been enough tension to send the pebble sailing. Instead, it plunked in the mud at her feet.

"Now," Momma continued, "what you asked me to do? That's not a small feat. Rivers are mighty forces, kid." She retrieved the pebble, reloaded her weapon, and pulled back the sling so far, the rubber band was thread-thin with tension. "This is me redirecting a river's current in order to fling dinner onto land. And this is the world bouncing back to its resting state."

With a snap, the pebble shot into the distant river, landing with a sharp *splsh*.

"Thing is," Momma finished, "with both world-shaping and

slingshot firing, aiming is the important part. You don't want to be on the wrong end."

As if emphasizing her point, a glittering gray body bobbed belly-up to the surface of the river. As the current gently carried the dead fish downstream, it leaked a red trail of bright, warm blood. I could taste iron in the air. My mother's mouth dropped open, but she snapped it shut quick. "Stay put, Oli. I gotta fetch our dinner!"

With that, she shifted to her true form and slipped into the water.

In any case, trapping a question in a bottle seemed to be a minor feat of world-shaping. The kind that, if it backfired, would cause less damage than a pebble plopping in the mud.

"Can you use a different type of canister?" I asked the coyote sisters. "Would that trick work in a clay jar or stone vase?"

"Anything solid," Reign said. "We just chose the Earth-crafted bottle because it'll disappear in a few days."

"Like Auntie says," Risk added, "guests shouldn't leave a mess behind. Hey. Is that another boat?" She swept up her paddle and used its rounded end to point at a boxy shape on the horizon. I recognized the silhouette and recoiled with a hiss. If I hadn't been distracted by the voice trick, I might have noticed it earlier. Maybe even early enough to escape undetected. But it was too late for that; the boat was coming straight at us. I spun around, identifying the nearest land.

"Backtrack," I said. "Go, go, go!"

"Why?" Risk asked. "Who is it?"

"Catfish cultists," I said. "Pretty sure, based on the look of that boat."

"Hold up. Fish on a boat?" Reign snorted.

"Yeah," I said. "Better hope they stay on it, 'cause things get really dangerous when they're in the water."

Remember when I claimed that my slice of the lake was relatively safe? The catfish cultists were the exception to the rule, the main reason I anticipated the need to move camp someday. They lived in a squadron of houseboats, drifting from bank to bank in a terrible, unpredictable cycle.

And, to put it lightly, they were volatile.

Under different circumstances, I would have switched to my animal form, slithered overboard, and swum away to hide. However, I didn't know how far the sisters could swim and refused to abandon them. Well, certainly not as a first resort.

"Are they thieves?" Reign asked, repacking the bottle and spool of thread. "We can throw the phones into the water. Maybe they'll get distracted."

"Worse," I said. "Much worse." My arms burned with the strain of paddling. To her credit, Risk easily matched my pace. Her sleeves slipped, hiding her hands and pooling against the paddle pole, but she didn't pause to right them.

"How so?" Reign wondered. "Murderers, then?"

"Are they your enemies, Oli?" Risk asked. "Is this attack personal?"

"No! I don't pick fights with anybody. Except once, accidentally. An alligator stepped on my tail, and—you know what? Never mind. Just trust me: I've lived here less than a season, but that's all it takes to appreciate that the catfish cultists are bad news. Listen. Whatever you do, don't admit that you eat fish, okay?"

"Oooooh," Reign said. "I think I've heard stories about them. Isn't their official title 'guardians of the finned and whiskered?'"

"Yep."

For every species on Earth, there are animal people. A couple truths are known. First, we're strong and plentiful when our species do well. Second, we suffer when our species suffer. Bison people used to be among the most common folk in the land. They even built a city. When my great-grandmother was a child, still living hand in hand with her twelve siblings, she visited their homeland: loops of long, hoof-hardened paths winding through well-kept prairie gardens and blocks of earthen buildings. There, farmers tended fields of maize: the bright, jewellike kernels brought living rainbows to the land every harvest season. Adobe towers overlooked the meandering trails, and clear bathing pools glinted under the pseudosun. It was the most prosperous city in the central continent, a hub of agricultural trade and art. Then, with no warning, all the bison people fell ill. Even the originators, who'd lived for centuries. They were too fatigued to farm, too exhausted to transform. They no longer strolled down the mazelike garden paths or tended their crops. No more bison babies were born, and deaths washed across the city like a flood.

When my great-grandmother described the fall of the city, her voice was a frightened hiss. "Even the great healers could not stop the plague. They tried. For years, they tried. At best, they could only ease the pain of a lingering death."

"But why?" I'd asked. "Why couldn't they do more?"

"The healers feared that the worst had happened."

"What is that?"

"An illness with no cure in this world. Scouts were dispatched to Earth, and after making the dangerous journey through the pseudosun, they confirmed the healers' fear: the bison species was going extinct."

"So quickly?" I asked; I knew that species ebbed and flowed through time. That nothing lasted forever. But the process was usually slow, spanning countless generations—time measured by the erosion of mountains, not weeks or years.

"They were slaughtered," she said. "A human breed known as colonizer killed millions."

"Their appetite must have been enormous!"

"Hah. They didn't hunt the bison for food. The colonizers desired to annihilate another group of humans. Indigenous peoples. They knew that the Indigenous ones relied on bison. So the bison had to go. Thankfully, the species did not go completely extinct. With time, the number of Earth bison has grown. But where there were once tens of millions, there are now only thousands. The city remains in ruins. Never forget how quickly our end can come, Oli. Never take your life for granted."

However, much is still unknown about the creation of animal peoples and the meaning of our existence (if there even is meaning). The catfish cultists—the guardians of the finned and whiskered—were one of many groups who believe that we are guardians of our species. Gods, even. Unfortunately, instead of protecting their wards on Earth, they seemed preoccupied by harassing other animal peoples in the Reflecting World.

Land was a vague line of green delineating the horizon, separating the water from the sky. We were still too far! I looked over my shoulder to estimate the speed of the houseboat. It was close enough that I could clearly see the pilot catfish standing at the wheel. He was in the amorphous "midadult" age category, ranging from thirty to three hundred years. In his false form, the catfish man was six feet tall and built like a pro wrestler. His wide mouth curved into a grin, revealing white gums and sharp little teeth. He had a thick mustache of whiskers and spiny fins down his arms.

"Howdy!" the pilot shouted. "Fine day, isn't it?"

"Double time!" I urged, speeding my paddle strokes. "Don't engage!"

"Hrgh," Risk groaned. "My hands are two massive blisters."

"Trade spots," Reign volunteered. "Three, two, go."

I was going to beg them to stay where they were, 'cause we didn't have time for tradesies, but in one fluid routine, Risk tossed the paddle in the air and rolled to the center of the raft, while Reign took a long stride and caught the paddle before it could land in the lake. The whole exchange happened in a heartbeat.

"You weren't exaggerating," Reign said, huffing with the strain. "This is difficult. How's the houseboat moving so fast?"

"Steam power," I said.

"They have a steam-powered boat? We can't outpaddle that!"

"I know. But when they inevitably catch up, the closer we are to land, the better."

"Hm." Risk crawled to the back of the raft. She lifted her hand; in my peripheral vision, the gesture resembled a wave. I turned to get a better look, relieved to find she was only using her hand like the brim of a hat to block the sun, as she stared at the approaching boat.

"We won't let them hurt you," Reign promised.

"You have good moves," I said, "but acrobatics won't win a physical fight with adult catfish. They're massive."

"Fight?" Risk asked, bemused.

"We oughtta reason with them first," Reign clarified. "Like Auntie always tells us, deescalate."

"Plus, I think he's alone," Risk said. "If it does come to blows, three against one strikes me as encouraging odds."

"That might make sense on land, but this"—I pointed at the water—"is solidly fish territory—"

"Hey," Reign interrupted. "I think the time for paddling is over."

The catfish pilot, now close enough that I could clearly see the gray of his eyes, was jumping up and down and waving his hands in the air, clearly pleased to have our attention. "Howdy!" He shouted. "Pleasant day to go fishing, huh?"

"It's a trick," I hissed. "Don't answer." Although we weren't trying to escape anymore, my grip on my paddle tightened with fear. I vividly recalled snippets from true horror stories, conversations I'd overheard on dark nights. Warnings like "Never talk to those catfish. They'll punish you for anything. Wrong answers to confusing questions, breaking laws you've never learned. They'll suck you into a cavernous mouth, grind off your skin with tiny teeth, and leave you bleeding in the water."

"We aren't fishing," Risk said.

"What are you three up to, then?" He crossed his arms on the houseboat railing, leaning over, smiling ever wider.

"Meeting a friend."

"Anyone I know?"

The sisters exchanged a look. Then, Reign said, "I doubt it. Nice meeting you, but we're in a hurry. Let's paddle, Oli."

"Just one minute. One measly minute. It's not like your tail's on fire." He slapped his leg and chortled, as if the mental image of a coyote with a burning tail was the funniest thought he'd had in a long while. "I waved you over for a reason."

I clenched my jaw to stop myself from doing anything embarrassing; when you're a cottonmouth, one instinctual response to fear is a wide-mouthed hiss. That's fine in your snake form, when you have a nice pair of venom-full fangs, but it looks a bit silly in your fake form.

"One minute," Risk agreed. "It's yours." She tilted her head, prompting the houseboat captain to speak.

"The open waters are no place for coyotes," he said. "Your viper friend's leading you astray. I urge you to paddle back to land. Live in a manner befitting your kind. Would the coyotes of Earth swim into the ocean? I suspect they rarely swim at all. At an instinctual level—an honest level—they are repelled by the depths. Because your kind is made to drown." The catfish stepped back, still smiling. The expression seemed genuine to me, as if he'd enjoyed our meeting. "Thanks for the minute of your time. I hope you'll consider my warning."

I didn't unclench my jaw until the houseboat started puttering away; the waves from its wake rocked my raft. "Was that a threat?" Risk asked. "Or was he just creepily trying to be helpful?"

I shrugged. "Both? Sorry, but I'm not taking you farther today. If you want to come back another time, then—"

"Okay," Risk said. "That's cool."

I didn't gasp, but my surprise must have been obvious anyway, because she and Reign giggled. "What?" she asked. "Did you think we'd force you to paddle us onward? That's awful!"

"No, but I did expect an argument. And honestly? I wouldn't blame you. That stuff he said about coyotes and land peoples staying in their place? Um. Excuse the language, but it's bullshit. And I'm sorry I didn't say that to his face."

Reign patted my head. It struck me as a very canid form of affection. "Don't stress, Oli. We understand. He could've torn your raft apart. Or drowned us just to prove his stupid point."

"Gotta pick your battles carefully," Risk added. "Weigh the risk against the reward. That's what Auntie always says."

I smiled. "Another bit of good advice from your aunt. She must be very wise."

"Oh. We have a hundred aunties. I don't know if I'd call any individual auntie wise. But all together? Yeah. They are a deep well of wisdom."

"Do they all live in the valley?" I wondered.

"Most, yeah. Our pack's massive. There's other families in the valley, too. Even some wolves! Hey, the day's early. Want to visit after we're on land?"

I imagined feasts and lively conversations. Friendly competitions. Inside jokes and ongoing arguments. A sense of longing tightened around my heart. "Sure," I said. Then, a slight sigh. "I still wish I could've seen that bottle trick in action."

"Wait! What if we demonstrate here?" Reign grabbed the bottle and held it high; pseudosunlight glinted off the clear glass. "The message could still reach a monster. And if it doesn't, at least you'll still learn the basic technique. What do you want to ask? I'll whisper your question into the bottle."

"Um!" The questions I'd accumulated over two months of independence seemed to evaporate under the heat of Reign's undivided attention. She waited, smiling and staring at me with bright yellow eyes. In the distance, the houseboat had stopped retreating, too. It was as if the world had decided to pause, so it could judge the next few words that came out of my mouth.

Given the chance to speak with an ancient being, what question would a wise person ask?

I didn't know. I wasn't wise. I was Oli.

I blurted out, "Are my siblings okay?"

"Heh," Risk snickered. "How would a lake monster know that?"

"They know a lot more than we do," Reign snapped. Then, she brought the bottle to her lips and whispered my question into its glass belly. Next, she poured a few translucent pink crystals into the bottle, explaining, "They have dual functions as both weights and beautiful gifts. We harvested these from the quartz fields." At last, the bottle was sealed with a cork.

"Normally," Reign concluded, "we'd tie the string around the bottle and lower it slowly. If the monsters feel chatty, they can send a message back. But for now, I guess we can improvise."

She chucked the bottle overboard, aiming towards the deep zone of the lake. After arcing through the sky, it landed with a soft plop and immediately sank.

"Uh-oh," Risk said.

"What?" I asked, my head whipping away from the ring of

diminishing ripples, the only remaining sign of my question in a bottle. Both of the coyotes were staring at the distant houseboat.

Only, it wasn't so distant anymore.

"Does he need another minute of our time?" Reign groaned.

"I don't want to find out," Risk growled, and then she and her sister simultaneously lunged for the paddles. With quick, powerful strokes, they urged the raft toward shore.

The boat must have been approaching at maximum speed, because it gained distance quickly, spewing a thick cloud of steam from a vertical copper pipe. The chug, chug rhythm of its two paddle wheels, which churned the water on either side of the boat, was loud enough to scare a nearby group of geese into the sky. I wished I could have sprouted a pair of wings and flown away with them.

Then, the wheels stopped turning. For a naïvely hopeful moment, I thought the catfish had stopped chasing us. Maybe, the whole pursuit had been a warning. The pilot catfish's way of saying, "Quit dawdling, and return to land."

That's when I noticed him step away from the wheel of his boat and climb over the outer rail. With a wave, he unceremoniously plopped feetfirst into the lake.

"Oh, no. Oh, no!" I stood. "He's coming! Don't let him swallow you!"

In a synchronized motion, Risk and Reign both dropped the paddles and plucked hunting knives from their boots. The blades might help, if they aimed right and got lucky. But old catfish had thick hides. Ancient ones could deflect an arrow off their back.

I peered at the water. The pilot had become a dark shape under the clear blue surface, a long shadow approaching the raft.

From nose to tail tip, he was over sixteen feet long, bigger than most of his people. His back fin jutted above the water, cutting V-shaped ripples.

"Here we go," I said, grabbing one of the paddles. It was no spear, but I might be able to poke him in the eye with the handle. The sisters stood side by side; Risk wore the burlap sack over one shoulder, as if protective of its contents.

"What's up?" she shouted. "Let's talk."

The catfish halted his approach. Then, in a fluid arc of motion, he dove.

"Everyone to the center of the raft," I said. "I don't know where he'll pop up!"

We stood shoulder to shoulder in a triangular huddle, facing the lake. "Go away!" Reign cried. "If you hurt us, our aunties will skin you!"

"Don't tell Mom, though," Risk growled. "She'd skin our hides first."

I closed my eyes and tried to ignore the vibrations of their high-pitched voices, instead focusing on slower rhythms, subtle variations in the pressure around me. There: a crescendo signaling his approach.

He was under our feet.

I narrowly managed to grab the sisters by their sleeves and yank them into the lake before the catfish flipped the raft in an explosion of freshwater spray.

Catfish are like cottonmouths: they don't stop growing. Sure, the rate of growth slows with time. But animal people, if we're lucky, have as much time as we need. Judging by the power and length of our attacker, he was far heavier than any flathead on

Earth. In the murk of the bubble-thick water, I saw a yawning space, a white pit that could have been the basin of a pond within the lake. With horror, I recognized it as the catfish's mouth. He could swallow a coyote whole.

The first time I bit somebody, it was an accident, an instinctual reaction to pain in my tail. That's why I'd wasted my venom on the sturdy meat of Miss Bruhn's foot. This time was different. My bite would be a conscious decision. So I aimed for the gray-ringed globe of the catfish's eye. If I got it just right, I could send him scampering to a healer.

Problem was, if I aimed wrong, I'd shoot straight into his mouth.

When I transformed, my clothes ballooned around me like a fabric tunnel; I flicked my tail, propelling through the open water, and then shot forward in an undulating motion, my body a physical manifestation of a propagating wave. Compared to the bulk of the catfish's head, his eye was a minuscule target. Thankfully, when I was submerged, I felt like grace itself. Sometimes, I wished cottonmouths would evolve gills or become proper aquatic snakes like the banded sea krait. Were we in a transitional state, gradually transforming from an animal of the land to an animal of the water? Or would we always live with our tails in one home and our heads in the other?

Time seemed to slow as I neared the catfish. I tried to adjust for every micromotion of his body, aware that I'd probably have only one chance. A near miss would accomplish nothing. But it might get me swallowed whole. At the last half-second, his eye rolled toward me; that's when I opened my mouth wide. The moment my teeth collided with a solid surface, they clamped down, sinking into something with the consistency of a ripe grape. I held off on the venom; he might be tough, but hemotoxins were especially dangerous in the head. I didn't want to kill him, even if he was an unneighborly bully.

"AAAAAAOOOWWW!" Sound travels more quickly in the water than in the air, so I wouldn't be surprised if the deepest monsters in the bottomless lake heard the catfish's enraged holler. He thrashed and dove, trying to knock me loose, but my teeth were hooked deep into his eyeball, and he couldn't break my grip. Finally, in desperation, the catfish swam toward his boat. Once in the shadow of the houseboat, he transformed into his false form. I let go as quick as I could and zipped away. He tried to grab me with his muscly fingers, but they were too slow.

"You lowdown, slithering son of a whip!" he shrieked after me. "I can't see a thing outta my right eye!"

"What did you expect?" I shouted back. "Go to a healer! The venom will spread fast, and your head is a bad place for it." With that, I rapidly swam toward the raft. Risk and Reign had climbed aboard during my tussle with the fish and were now kneeling near the edge, beckoning to me urgently. As I approached, they scooped me out of the water and dropped me in the middle of the flat surface. I squinted warily at the smudge of a houseboat. Splash, splash, splash went its paddle wheels.

"Is he coming or going?" I asked, hoping that he'd fallen for my lie about the venom.

"Going!" Reign cheered.

"We should, too," her sister added. "Where's the other paddle?"

"Got it," Reign said.

Still in my true form—I wasn't about to transform until there was land firmly under my belly—I coiled up and tried to enjoy the short ride home. It had been a long time since I'd been a passenger on a boat.

"Saved the bag of electronics," Risk commented, interrupting my memories of the river, of siblings, and of naps in the sun. "They may not work anymore, though. You still want one, Oli? I could also fetch a new batch of phones. You deserve them."

"What about the book?" I asked. "Is it ruined?"

She shrugged. "It's soggy, but they dry in the sun."

"If you don't mind," I said, "I choose the book as my gift."

"Can you read quickly? It'll disappear in two days."

"Yes," I told her. "I've got a knack for reading. Momma always praised my language skills. She said I oughtta lean into my gift, 'cause it might save me. There aren't many chances to practice, though. Where did the book come from?"

"The wolf pack," Reign said. "They live just beyond the valley. Most Earth stuff in the region comes from the pack's smugglers."

"Our uncle is friends with the alphas," Risk continued. "They supply books to a group of local scribes. We could talk to them. Redirect a few paperbacks your way."

"Oh, thank you! That would be wonderful. I'll lend you my boat every week—"

Paddling one-handed, Reign reached out and patted my head. "That won't be necessary," she promised. "Friends do nice things for friends."

"Like bite a catfish in the eye," Risk added. "I hope you didn't make a dangerous enemy today."

"Me, too. I think I'll be all right, though. He probably couldn't tell me apart from the next snake."

Supposedly, catfish cultists were motivated by two goals: be guardians of the finned and whiskered, and ensure that the natural order was maintained. Payback for a minor personal slight did not further either goal—or so I told myself. Nevertheless, that particular cultist seemed mean enough to seek bloody retribution for my act of self-defense. That night, I pulled my tent into the high grasses and drowned my campfire so thoroughly, no glint of embers remained. At bedtime, I left the tent flap partially untied so I could escape at a moment's notice. Then, I lay on my side, my face toward the lake. From my position, I could only see a sliver of the sky and the tips of the wispy yellow grasses. That was fine. I expected my sense of hearing to warn me of the houseboat's approach. Even if the catfish swam to land and tiptoed through the grass, I'd hear the water fall from his body, pattering against the ground like drops of rain.

Instead, it was the smell of mud woke me. It wasn't the silty brown sludge at the cusp of the lake—the mundane, inoffensive mud I often tracked around the campsite. This mud smelled as ripe as oil, like it had been stewing in the water for aeons. I tasted the air, confused.

Among the mud was another flavor. Something sharper, more ancient.

I shouldn't have trusted Risk and Reign to know the limitations of monsters.

The grass rustled, scraping against my tent with gentle swishes of sound. I closed my eyes and pressed my ear against my woven mat, trying to discern the vibration of footsteps. But there were none.

And yet, when I opened my eyes again, a darkness blocked the narrow opening of my tent, as if something large loomed over me, a wave suspended before crashing. I froze, my false body tensing in suspense.

From outside, a voice gurgled softly, "To answer your question . . . yes." A pause, almost thoughtful. "For now."

Then, the darkness slipped away like mist.

NINA, AGE 14

Nina had been to the well several times before her fourteenth birthday, but now, she came prepared to demystify its greatest mystery. Namely: how deep did the water go? She was visiting Grandma outside hurricane season, her birthday wish.

"Wouldn't you rather invite friends to our house?" Nina's father asked. "I can convert the bookshop into party central."

"I'd need friends for that." Nina tried to lighten the statement with a smile. She was just being realistic, pragmatic. Nobody would come to her birthday party, but that didn't bother her or anything. "I don't feel like celebrating until Mom gets home, anyway." Nina wouldn't have to wait long. In the meantime, she wanted to investigate the fish girl story. Some species of fish lived in water-filled caves, flooded mine shafts, and deep-sea caverns. If the well went deep enough, it could be home to a hidden community of animals or—fingers crossed—a sanctuary for animal people.

Although Nina's birthday fell on a Tuesday, her father

approved time off from school, since she was making good grades and had requested makeup work in advance. During the two-hour drive, instead of music, Nina listened to St0ryte11er videos on her phone. She knew they were getting close to Grandma's place when a pinwheel-shaped "buffering" icon started spinning over the frozen face of YourPal David, a young man with bright bleached hair. He'd been midway through a story about a grease fire in his kitchen, and now Nina would have to wait until high-speed Internet access returned on the drive back to learn whether his apartment had burned down. She stared out the window, briefly entertained by a line of ten windmills, their blades dark against the empty sky. Then, Nina opened her messages, rereading her mother's most recent communication:

TUESDAY 4:35 A.M. (MOM)
> Happy birthday, Sweetest! Call me when you wake up. We're finally on the move again, docking in Greenland. Do you want a souvenir? Anything that fits on a plane is fair game. Let me know—enjoy your cake, and don't forget to make a wish. Love you.

She scrolled up, finding an earlier message.

SATURDAY 9:15 P.M. (MOM)
> Our ship is fine. We've survived choppier waters. Unfortunately, the damage to the harbor is considerable.

SATURDAY 9:16 P.M. (NINA)

Does that mean you can't come home on time?
SATURDAY 9:20 P.M. (MOM)
   There will be a delay. Captain's seeking a different
   location to dock. Greenland looks promising. Any
   day now!
SATURDAY 9:21 P.M. (NINA)
   You missed my birthday last year, too.
SATURDAY 9:21 P.M. (MOM)
   I'm sorry.
SATURDAY 10:13 P.M. (NINA)
   Is it worth it?
SATURDAY 10:41 P.M. (MOM)
   I hope so.

She scrolled more quickly, skimming hundreds of messages, weeks of conversation.

WEDNESDAY 8:24 P.M. (NINA)
   Dad got depressed. He's afraid we'll be forced to
   move someday.
WEDNESDAY 8:24 P.M. (MOM)
   I'll talk to him.
WEDNESDAY 8:24 P.M. (NINA)
   Is it true, though?
WEDNESDAY 8:24 P.M. (MOM)
   That's what we're trying to learn out here. I wish I
   could be more certain about things. You know how
   difficult it is to predict the path of a hurricane just
   one week in advance? Imagine trying to predict the

whole tangled fate of global climate years, decades in advance. Under conditions nobody has witnessed before.

WEDNESDAY 8:24 P.M. (NINA)

My teacher says it'll get worse.

WEDNESDAY 8:24 P.M. (MOM)

What will?

WEDNESDAY 8:24 P.M. (NINA)

The droughts, heat, and storms. The vortex freezes. All that.

WEDNESDAY 8:24 P.M. (MOM)

Yes, but we'll survive together. I promise.

Too far. She scrolled down.

FRIDAY 11:10 P.M. (NINA)

How do your scientist friends measure water depth?

SATURDAY 3:14 A.M. (MOM)

They lower machines into the ocean and track pressure changes. Do you know why pressure increases with depth?

She must have realized that Nina wouldn't answer that question, considering the time in Texas, because she continued with an explanation.

Saturday 3:20 A.M. (MOM)

All that water presses down, accumulating. One

meter below the surface, it's like carrying a bucket of water on your head. With every meter you sink, the number of buckets increases. Is this for class?

SATURDAY 10:01 A.M. (NINA)

No. I'm studying Grandma's well. Is there an easier method?

SATURDAY 9:13 P.M. (MOM)

A long rope with a small weight on one end! Mark every meter, and count the distance as you lower it. Don't forget to wear gardening gloves. You don't want blisters.

Lowering her phone, Nina again looked through her car window, but instead of staring upward, her eyes dropped to the land. Emaciated orange trees, their branches bare and dry, grew along the road. They were the fruitless stragglers of a long-abandoned orchard. The familiarity of its ruin comforted Nina. She'd never seen the orchard flourish, though it must have once, if only for a few sweet years. To her, the emptiness and silence were home. This wasn't a ghost town. Not when the heart of her family still beat within the land.

As they approached Grandma's house, Nina noticed the first sign of change: parked near the ruins of Paradise, a tin camper sparkled like a prehistoric beetle. The small domicile was surrounded by a chain-link fence: ten feet high and topped with a tangle of barbed wire. The new neighbor had moved in. It had to be just one person. There wasn't enough room for two people to happily coexist in the camper, unless they completely disregarded personal space.

"Who is that guy trying to keep out?" her father wondered aloud.

"Bears," Nina joked.

At Grandma's house, they ate finger sandwiches and a fruit tray for lunch, and then Nina opened her birthday presents. The yard-sale toys were wrapped in salvaged silver wrapping paper, which was precreased by the shape of another child's present. "Thank you!" Nina said, cradling an antique game of chess, surrounded by an audience of plastic dolls. "I love everything."

"Do you want to play a match?" her grandmother asked. "I haven't won a game of chess lately."

"Defeat Dad first," Nina suggested. "I need to measure the well." She gathered her supplies and, rising, brushed bread crumbs off her jeans.

"Why?" Grandma wondered, her tone wary. "You aren't fishing, too, are you?" The implications were clear: Nina better not meddle too much.

"Of course not."

"Be careful," her father added.

"Don't worry, Dad. I'm just lowering a rope."

"Well," he conceded, "I guess that's safer than basejumping."

"Huh? What's basejumping?"

He ducked his head. "An extremely boring hobby. Go have fun with your science experiments."

"And don't be too long," Grandma warned. "Cake is waiting."

"I'll be back before you win that game," Nina promised, exiting the room with a wave goodbye.

The trail to the well was now completely overgrown, only

distinguishable because Nina knew where to look. She followed the thin, snakelike line of new grasses, tapping the ground with Rosita's wooden walking stick.

Tap, tap.

Tan grasshoppers scattered as she walked, their wings humming in shrill bursts of flight. An eighty-foot length of rope was loosely wrapped around Nina's free arm, its coils dangling in loops from her bent elbow. Last night, she'd marked every foot with a brand of cherry-scented nontoxic marker. Although nobody used the well anymore, the thought of contaminating a potential source of drinking water made Nina feel icky. She wouldn't take chances. Plus, fish people—children!—could be using that well as a tube-shaped inn when they visited Earth.

"Who are you?" The deep, unfamiliar voice was so abrupt and startling, Nina raised her walking staff defensively. She'd thought she was alone, aside from the grasshoppers, but a man stood off to the side of the path, not too far from the stream. No wonder she'd overlooked him: he wore khaki pants and a brown shirt, colors of the desert. A metal disk glinted in his hand. Under different circumstances, he might have been an innocuously average-looking man. He stood about five feet, nine inches tall. Had a thin build, and was clean-shaven, with vertical laugh lines down his cheeks. His hair was dark brown and neatly trimmed. But his eyes? They regarded Nina with intense, guarded scrutiny. Like a stray dog glaring at somebody from the pound. If she didn't know better, Nina would have suspected the man was afraid of her.

"This is my grandma's place," she said. "Everyone's visiting." She didn't clarify that "everyone" just meant her and her dad. It seemed wise to let him assume a family of twenty was partying in the house.

In a snap, the wariness and tension drained from his stance. "You mean this wild-ness actually belongs to somebody? I thought it was buffer between your house and mine."

"All the land inside the old stone walls is my grandma's yard."

"Even the stream?" he asked.

"Um. Yeah. Most of it."

Shaking his head in disbelief, the man tried to approach. But when Nina stepped backward to maintain distance between them, he stopped and raised his hands in a exaggerated show of harmlessness. Now, Nina could see that the metal disk was a compass. Its needle spun round and round, as flighty as a broken clock. When her eyes flicked to the navigation tool, the man snorted in laughter. "It always goes useless around here. Do you know if there's an old mine on the land? Iron ore can make a magnetic compass fail. I wish gold did, too . . ."

"I don't know."

"Fair enough."

For a moment, they simply looked at each other. What did he want? An invitation to her birthday party? Finally, once the silence had stretched uncomfortably long, the man said, "Guess I'll vacate your property. Be careful out here. My wildlife cam spotted a coyote this morning. I'm trying to find the old thing. It looked half-rabid and hungry."

"There's a bunch of wildlife here. I won't let any bite me."

"Right." He turned and started trekking in the direction of Paradise, his steps long and decisive. However, as Nina's guard fell, the man paused, turned around, and shouted out: "So all this land belongs to your granny?"

She simply nodded.

"That's a lot of upkeep for one lady. No wonder it's a mess. I'll introduce myself properly someday. The name's Paul, by the way."

Nina cringed. He had a lot of nerve to call Grandma's land "messy" considering the state of Paradise. Instead of protesting—she didn't want to fight with the man—Nina just stared.

"Well, good to meet you too, Nameless," he huffed, as if she'd been the one to insult him. "Don't dump anything in that stream. It may bubble out of your land, but it empties into mine."

"I won't," she said.

"Good. Don't." With that, he turned back around and resumed walking. Vigilantly, Nina watched him shrink with distance. By the time Paul reached his beetle-bright camper, he seemed tinier than a plastic army man, hardly threatening at all. Just a huffy little man who had to get the last word with a 14-year-old girl.

But there was still something unnerving about him. The interaction didn't make sense. Maybe it was the compass; how far had he planned to hike? She didn't believe for one second that he'd wander miles to track a coyote. What was he doing, then? Looking for iron and gold? Even if there were metals in the land, Grandma would never hollow out her home.

It seemed to her like he'd been following the stream. Granted, the land was easiest to navigate near the water, where the foliage thinned out. She didn't like his focus on the water, though. Grandma still drank out of the well now and then.

Whatever the case, Nina planned to keep one eye on the camper in case Paul tried to come back. She checked her phone, made note of the time, and continued to the well.

At the end of the trail, a waist-high ring of stone peeked over the yellow brush. Its bucket and pulley system were gone, likely removed after Rosita died. Nina shone a flashlight into the well, noting that the water was as transparent as glass. Still, the well floor was hidden below darkness. Steadily, Nina unwrapped the rope looped around her arm. She'd knotted a large steel washer to one end, and the bright metal ring seemed to radiate glinting ripples when it plopped into the water. Whispering, Nina counted the distance markers as they passed her hands.

. . . ten, eleven, twelve . . .

She was surprised that the well hadn't dried up yet. It must be connected to a big aquifer, a pool of water in the Earth. There were other signs of a hidden water source: based on old photos, the plants on Grandma's land hadn't changed much over fifty years, which meant they weren't being hurt too bad by the increasing droughts. Plus, there was the narrow stream near the well. Chatty grackles enjoyed huddling in the mesquite trees along its banks.

. . . thirty, thirty-one, thirty-two . . .

A bird with the impressive wingspan of an average-sized kite glided over Nina's head. Turkey vulture, she thought. The bare-headed scavenger flew past the well, circled twice, and then landed between two spiky bushes.

. . . sixty-eight, sixty-nine . . .

Nina was reaching the end of her rope. She'd have to return with a longer one. At least she'd confirmed one thing: the water was deep enough to hide plenty of secrets. Steadily again, she pulled the washer up, fighting the press of water. As the washer swung out of the well, there was a crunch nearby. Turning, Nina saw the turkey vulture hop back quickly, its wings spread, as if startled.

Moments later, a plaintive, high-pitched cry erupted from behind the bush. A single, pained meow. Nina dropped the rope in a messy pile and sprinted through the brush. As she approached, the turkey vulture fled to the air, abandoning the lanky black kitten, which was sprawled across a brick-red patch of dirt.

The dirt had originally been brown.

"No!" Nina cried, kneeling beside it. "Little cat, what are you doing here?" Gingerly, she touched the kitten's head, looking for injuries. His eyes were closed, and he breathed in quick gasps, as if the single meow had exhausted him. There were tacky patches of fur on his stomach, indicating bleeding from several punctures. He must have been attacked by a coyote, narrowly escaping before collapsing here and bleeding into the ground. That meant Paul had been telling the truth! She experienced a surge of embarrassment for assuming the worst about a neighbor—maybe, he wasn't so bad. But that emotion was quickly buried under Nina's concern for the kitten. He had no collar, and there were fleas caught in his drying blood; perhaps he was from a wild-born litter. Or he might have gotten separated from a human family.

Nina lifted the kitten carefully, cradling his head in one hand and his body in the other. After a moment of consideration, she flipped up the bottom of her T-shirt and used it as a makeshift cradle. There had to be a veterinarian near town; they could stitch the little guy up, save his life. If she had to return all her presents to pay for the treatment, so be it. Leaving the rope and staff at the well, Nina speed-walked toward Grandma's house. Looking down, she observed the kitten's condition deteriorate over the span of minutes. Now, his breathing was irregular: shallow gasps separated by seconds of nothing. Instinctually, she knew that he was dying.

"I'm taking you to a doctor," she promised. "Stay alive."

Upon reaching the back porch, Nina kicked open the swinging screen door, shouting, "Dad! Dad! It's an emergency!" She stood half in the kitchen, half outside. "Dad, come here! Hurry!"

"*What?* Did you get bit by a snake?" Two pairs of footsteps—one pair heavy, the other pair light—sped down the creaky hall to the kitchen. It occurred to Nina that her father and grandmother both went extremely wide-eyed when they worried. Now, they gaped at her from the doorway. "Is that a raccoon you got?" her dad wondered, looking at the black tail hanging over the hem of Nina's shirt sling.

"It's a cat. He was attacked. We need to get medical help fast, Dad! Hurry, grab the car keys!"

Grandma snagged a clean kitchen towel from a hook on the wall. "Give it," she ordered. "Let me have a look."

As instructed, Nina passed the unconscious kitten into her arms. "This is dire," Grandma agreed, wrapping the kitten in the towel.

"Please, can we help him? Please!"

"We can try," Grandma said.

The nearest animal hospital, a twenty-four-hour critical care center, was thirty-one minutes away by car. Nina's father drove, while Grandma sat in the passenger seat with the kitten bundled in her lap. He was still unconscious, but his breathing had become more regular. That gave Nina hope as they handed him to the critical care team.

"If they can help," her father said, settling onto a black waiting room chair, "he may need to stay the night. Shoot, I hope surgery isn't in the cards."

"If money's an issue, I'll cover it," Grandma said.

"How are you going to cover a five-thousand-dollar bill, Mom?"

"Yard sale."

"Let me get this straight: you'll throw a yard sale to get rich off stuff you bought at other yard sales?"

As the adults discussed the wisdom of that plan, Nina walked to the drink dispenser on the other side of the waiting room. She put a paper cup under the nozzle and pressed the hot chocolate button. The machine whirred for thirty seconds before spitting out 0.5 oz of pale brown liquid. It smelled like chocolate but tasted like hot dishwater. Cringing, Nina wistfully thought about the uneaten cake at Grandma's house. The unmade wish. Given the chance, she'd ask for the kitten's life.

One hour later, a red-haired vet tech leaned into the waiting area and waved Nina's family into an exam room. There, supervised by a smiling veterinarian, the black kitten sat on a metal table. Although his stomach had been shaved, there were no signs of puncture wounds. "He bounced back," the veterinarian, an elderly white woman in scrubs, explained. "We couldn't find any sign of injuries. How long ago was the attack?"

"I . . . don't really know," Nina told her. "But he was covered in fresh bites. I saw them."

"Perhaps you mistook old blood for new bites," she said. "I'm not even sure the blood is his. There are no scabs, no scars. It just took food and water to bring him around."

Nina was too relieved to argue. Her voice high-pitched with affection, she asked the kitten, "Was that it? You were hungry?"

He padded toward the edge of the table, meowing twice. The vet tech—with a single hand on his chest—gently slid him back.

"Does anyone own him?" Nina's father asked. "Or is he up for grabs?"

"We didn't find any microchips," the veterinarian explained. "Plus, he's about five months old, but hasn't been fixed, and there's no local reports of missing black cats. All those point to no. Of course, we need to follow protocol. But I suspect that, when all is said and done, he'll be available for adoption."

"Well, Nina? If that's the case, do you want a birthday cat?"

"Thank you! That would be the best present." She rubbed the kitten's head; he leaned into her hand, his yellow eyes closing with appreciation. "I've already thought of a name. Tightrope!"

"I was partial to Phoenix," Grandma said, "but Tightrope is very cute."

Much later, before Nina collected the rope and walking staff, she visited the spot where she'd rescued Tightrope. The ground was still spotted with red. A lot of blood for a kitten to lose, and there was no sign of dead mice or something else that bled. But the alternative—the possibility that Tightrope had healed miraculously within one hour—was too far-fetched. So what was the truth?

That morning, Nina had intended to solve a mystery. Instead, she gained another one.

And a cat.

COTTONMOUTH MEETS COOPER'S HAWK AND A SINISTER STRANGER

*A*fter many disappointingly tasteless, charred, or displeasing meals, I finally learned how to cook fish like Momma. Trust me: the result was worth every aggravation of practice. My new life was composed of a few simple but cherished pleasures: warm naps, books about the absurd dramas of Earth, conversations with Ami, and—finally—satisfying meals. With the introduction of well-seasoned dishes into my schedule, it felt like I'd finally transitioned from simply surviving to living.

Anyway, a couple months after achieving culinary perfection, I was about to dig into a plate of sage-rubbed, slow-roasted fillets when an eager-sounding voice called out, "Hey! Hi! You there!" A Cooper's hawk flopped onto the ground and bird-walked to my picnic blanket, which was spread across my favorite basking rock. In their true form, the hawk had a pair of deep brown wings, intense yellow eyes, and a soft belly of white and brown feathers. That meant they were my age, give or take. The

adults have slate blue wings and red eyes; quite a striking transformation. I was slightly jealous.

"Oh. Hi." I lowered my dinner plate, a hand-carved maple
board. "Can I help you?"

"I'm looking for my good friend. Have you seen a toad? He
has a bright blue throat and is about this tall." The hawk lifted a
taloned foot slightly above the ground, their wings spreading for
balance.

"Oh, Ami! I think he's catching flies right now. How did you
meet?" Honestly, I was surprised that Ami had other "good"
friends. Don't get the wrong idea: he was as sweet and lovable
as honey cake. Anyone would be lucky to know Ami. But he also
mostly kept to himself, rarely venturing from the land immediately around my basking rock. He always turned down invita-
tions to visit the valley with Risk and Reign, instead preferring
to hear about the outings at night. That was our routine. Every
night, when I built a fire to brew a pot of yaupon, Ami climbed
onto a nearby log and listened to me talk, occasionally interject-
ing with signed commentary. I'd always ask, "How was your
day?" and he'd respond with a lopsided shrug, indicating "Same
as always." That meant fly catching and thinking. That's all I saw
him doing, anyway. If Ami ever left home or visited other neighbors, he did so secretly.

"We met when I was as prickly as a porcupine," the hawk
said. "That age when you're too young to fly, but too big to share
a nest without annoying your siblings. You know what I mean?"

"Not about nests," I admitted, "but I've definitely annoyed
my siblings before."

"Yeah. It's unavoidable sometimes. See, I always do this when

I yawn—" They squeezed their eyes shut, threw back their head, opened their beaked mouth in a deep inhale, and stretched. I had to stifle my own sympathetic yawn. "—and that day, during a big yawn, I smacked my sister in the face. Mom and Pop were hunting, so she kicked me out of the tree. I bounced off a couple branches on the way down. Made me dizzy. Must have knocked the common sense outta my head, too, 'cause I decided that I should track down my parents to tattle on her. Everyone knows— straight from the egg—it's safer to wait if you tumble from the nest. Just hunker down and shriek."

"That wasn't right of your sister, though. None of my siblings ever tried to murder me."

They squawked in laughter. "She just misjudged a kick. It wasn't attempted hawkicide. I think."

"Hope so. How did you meet Ami, then?"

"Oh, I transformed and ran through the forest, shouting, 'Mom! Pop!' My false form was a tiny thing, barely able to move on hind legs without toppling. That's why they call 'em toddlers. Because they toddle. I still somehow ended up all the way here, at the lake. I'd never seen so much water. It looked scary. Like a giant bird nest filled with water. That's when I flopped onto my back in the mud and screamed." They demonstrated by blasting a full-on hawk screech into the air. *SCREEEIIII!* "Suddenly, a toadlet jumped on my face. Tiny guy. The size of a cicada. Obviously, he's grown since then, but not by much. Anyway, he patted my nose until I stopped wailing and proceeded to keep me company all morning. When Pop found me, the toadlet left, and since then, we've been friends."

"That sounds like Ami," I agreed. "He basically did the same thing when I came to the lake. Except I was a grown snake, not a lost baby."

"Ami—" The hawk pinned me with an intense stare. To be fair, I doubt any hawk can manage a chill-looking stare. They just have a high-intensity resting face. "You keep using that name. I didn't realize he had one."

"Uh-huh."

"I've known . . . Ami . . . all my life, and he's never shared his name. You two must be tighter than a boa constrictor's hug."

"We are, but"—I blushed, uncomfortable—"I learned his name the first day we met. See, I'm really good at communication. When I look at a page of written characters, the words make sense almost instantly. It's the same with signed and spoken languages. Ami has a very unique way of telling people things."

"Wow! Is that so? Welcome to the neighborhood, smart stuff. What's your name?"

"Oli," I shared. "Yours?"

"Mine's Brightest. Mom and Pop always said I had the brightest, keenest eyes. I hatched with them wide open. You know how rare that is?" They fluttered their upper eyelids at me. "What do you think?"

"Very nice."

"Thank you, Oli! Where'd your name come from?"

"Momma just liked the sound, I think."

They shuffled closer. "You know what? Ami may be busy catching grubs, but that's fine. Because fate brought me to you."

"Fate? What's going on?"

"I found a natural wonder. It's great. Wanna see?"

I stared longingly at my dinner, which was cooling by the minute. "What is it?"

"Part of the joy is the surprise. Trust me."

I'd been living on my own for almost a year at that point. From experience, when a stranger's introduction included the words "trust me," under no circumstances should they be trusted. On the other side, the hawk seemed to know Ami well, and I couldn't imagine that Ami would be friends with a scoundrel. Still, I had to cover my bases. "Is this a plot to steal my raft?"

"Wha! No!"

"My fishing pole?"

"I prefer nets, but that's not relevant 'cause nobody is stealing nothing. Look, I simply found an extremely interesting thing in the forest and was moved to share the experience. So, are you in?"

"Mmmaybe. I was about to eat supper . . ."

"Luckily, it's nearby."

"Nearby for somebody who can fly, or nearby for everyone?"

"Thirty-eight point seven meters that way." With one wing, Brightest pointed into the forest. I weighed my curiosity against my hunger, and for a moment, the hunger was winning. Then, with a crunch of leaves, Ami shuffled out of the brush and waved his arms excitedly.

"You're back!" Brightest cheered. "My buddy, wanna go on an adventure?"

An enthusiastic nod in agreement.

"Awyeah! Let's hustle!"

What followed was the slowest hustle I'd ever witnessed.

Brightest bird-jogged across the ground, their wings spread for balance, and Ami followed hop by hop.

"Hold up," I said. "Need a lift?"

Ami clapped and climbed onto my offered hand. Gently, I transferred him to my shoulder, and followed Brightest into the forest. They flew from tree to tree, shuffling on the boughs with anticipation in between flights. At one point, I lost sight of them, but after a dizzying five minutes, they dove over my head and urged, "This way!" Finally, at the end of a journey that was definitely more than a mere thirty-eight point seven meters but didn't drag out too long, the hawk landed on the ground and spread their wings toward a majestic oak tree. Its lower branches were so large, they drooped under their own weight, nearly touching the ground. I'd passed the tree before, and although it was older and more picturesque than the average oak, there was nothing especially thought-provoking about it.

"Behold!" Brightest cheered. "Do you see?"

"No. What?"

"No? Don't feel bad," they continued. "As you know, I've lived in these parts since the egg, but have never noticed the chain before. There." They jabbed at the trunk with one long, sharp talon.

I leaned forward until my face was just a foot from the tree. Sure enough, a rust-speckled chain link, the size of the loop my forefinger and thumb make when I sign "okay," protruded from a knot of gnarled bark. "Huh. You're right. That's odd."

"There's more," Brightest said. "One, two, three. One hundred little bumps of metal half-swallowed by the tree."

Now that I knew what to look for, it was easy to spot the

exposed links around the trunk: they resembled a necklace, one fused with the neck.

"What do you make of it?" Brightest prompted.

"I guess somebody looped a chain around this oak," I ventured, "and as the years passed, the tree grew and engulfed it."

Ami clapped his hands; they didn't make a sound, but I understood the meaning: *nice one; I agree.*

"But why?" Brightest wondered. "That's the question that keeps me up at night."

"It does?"

"What was the chain for? Good, solid metal: why would anybody abandon it to rust? And is it part of the oak now? Does that mean the tree and the chain are the same entity? When you eat a slow-roasted tilapia, Oli, at what point does it cease to be fish and become you?"

I shrugged slowly, careful not to jostle Ami. "When it goes into my stomach, I assume."

"Not in your mouth? It has to be the stomach? What if it's not dead? What if it's still swimming? Thrashing and struggling to escape."

"Hey." I planted my hands on my hips. "It's dangerous to let something with pointy fins flail around inside your innards. I'd never swallow a live fish."

"Forget about food, then. Picture this scenario: you're a jewel thief."

"Okay." I tried to envision their hypothetical. There weren't many jewels I'd be tempted to steal. Maybe a hunk of turquoise with rich veins of brown, a stone reminiscent of scales. I'd take it to an artisan to commission a cuff for my wrist. In my false form, I adorned myself in stones and textiles that resembled my natural skin. That day, I wore leather pants and a sleeveless shirt I'd dyed brown with leaves from the forest.

"You steal a pendant," they said.

"I'm imagining it. Go on."

"But you're cornered by an angry mob. They lust for justice. To hide the evidence, you swallow the pendant. When it plops into your stomach, does that mean it's yours? Or you?"

"Huh," I said. "That's a good question. I revise my earlier answer. No more stomachs. If something isn't part of me at a cellular level, it's not me. What about that?"

"Are your thoughts you?" they badgered. Ami tilted his head in deep thought.

"What in the worlds does that have to do with a chain in a tree?" I demanded.

Brightest ruffled their chest feathers, seemingly pleased. "The connection is part of the fun, pal," they said, and I know beaks can't technically form a smile, but I swear they grinned at me. "Thought provoking, am I right?"

"Yeah," I conceded. "It's interesting." I might have been more enthusiastic about the philosophical back-and-forth, but my stomach was pinched with hunger. Why hadn't Brightest visited at a more convenient hour?

Suddenly, the hawk looked up, their body tensing. Then they said, "You need to get back to dinner. That fish sure smelled delicious." It wasn't a question. It was a command. "I won't keep you two any longer."

Ami squinted, as if uncertain about something.

"Uh, yeah," I said. "Maybe we can talk later. You still live in these parts?"

"Yep. Around this lake, the strangest trees are my favorite cribs. Chain tree will make a nice vacation perch, I think."

"Hope to see you around, then." I waved. "Bye, Brightest. Nice to meet you."

"Heh. Oh, yeah. See you around." There was something vaguely strange about the promise. With a powerful flap, the hawk sprang into the air and took off.

But a minute later, as Ami and I were turning to leave, Brightest landed back on a low bough of the chain tree, their mouth open with exhaustion. "How did you find the way here without me?" they asked.

That question was more confusing than the hypothetical about a jewel thief. "Uh. We didn't," I said. "You led us here."

Both Ami and Brightest gasped at the same time.

"That wasn't me," they said. "I . . . got snared in a spider-silk trap on the way to the tree. It dropped out of the sky."

I remembered briefly losing sight of Brightest and wondering where they'd gone. Then, they'd appeared beside me, seemingly from nowhere. Was Brightest claiming that wasn't actually them?

"Oh, no," they groaned. "No, no, no! Not *again*! What did the mockingbird say? What did she tell you?"

"Mockingbird? She looked like a hawk. Like you."

"That's because she's a mimic whose false form can be anything." Their wings spread, they slow-dropped to the ground and kicked a dry leaf. "Over the past three years, she's tricked my family, my friends, and even me. We've tried to be kind. I even invited her to my birthday party. But she prefers to play mind games. It got so bad, a mob of robins, sparrows, blackbirds, and even other mockingbirds grouped together and chased her away. Guess she's back. I'm worried she'll get in real trouble someday. She's just a kid, really."

Ami wrapped his arms around Brightest's left leg, squeezing it in a fretful hug.

"Are you implying she has the power to imitate both bodies and voices?" Usually, mimic-type animal people could imitate just one component of another person. The physical form, the voice, or the scent. The mockingbird girl must have been unusually skilled.

"Not just implying. It's a fact. She's great at nailing mannerisms, too. I don't get it, though. What was her goal today? What did she tell you?"

I racked my brain. "Nothing much. She showed me the chain and then asked a bunch of philosophical questions about the meaning of self. That's it. Oh. One more thing. Before leaving, she complimented my cooking . . ."

The answer occurred to all three of us simultaneously. Ami threw his arms up, and Brightest shot into the air, shouting, "Your dinner!"

The jog home, with Ami cupped gently in my hands, took only five minutes. Apparently, that was all the time the mimic needed. One of my tilapia fillets, which had been meticulously seasoned with sage from my garden, was missing.

"Augh! Jerk!" I cried. "She stole half my dinner!"

Ami patted my shoulder in commiseration, while Brightest shook their head. "Sorry. I can't help but feel partially responsible."

"Why? You didn't eat my fish."

Inquisitively, I flicked my tongue a couple times, tasting the air. It carried traces of toad, hawk, cottonmouth, tilapia, lake, bacteria . . . and something nearly undetectable. Something I would have missed completely if I hadn't been searching for it. Mockingbird.

"She won't trick me again," I promised. Then, I raised my voice and reiterated, "I'm onto you!"

In the distance, shrill and sweet, the mockingbird giggled.

NINA, AGE 15

*T*he St0ryte11er app had a suite of free tools, including sound effects, atmospheric music, narration overlays, screen splitters, and even voice modifiers. They were all intended to enhance the narrative aspect of uploaded videos. However, Nina rarely used the tools. At most, she'd deploy the "background noise scrubber" to eliminate sirens. Once, when her father was watching basketball in the living room, he cheered so exuberantly at a three-pointer that his voice infiltrated Nina's story about the alley raccoons. The interruption cracked her up, so she used the "isolate and enhance" tool to amplify her father's shout of "That's a bull's-eye!" But otherwise, Nina preferred simplicity. All she needed was a camera, her voice, and a story.

Because of her newfound St0ryte11er diary passion, Nina's room had a two-faced quality; she'd shoved her shelves, laundry basket, trash can, school supplies, and assorted stuff around her computer table out of the camera's line of sight. Thus, one side of the room was a mess, while the other was clean and clutter-free, with a self-curated selection of posters taped to the wall. Nina followed several pixel artists online, mostly young creators who sold their work in small digital shops. Over the years, she'd purchased art of futuristic cityscapes, expansive deserts with yellow sand and pink skies, and fantasy cities teeming with strange little residents. Nina's favorite poster was a five-inch-by-five-inch square depicting a family of bunnies shopping for carrots in a marketplace. Each bunny wore a different hat; their white, black, and brown ears poked through holes in the bright fabric. As Nina slowly spun in her computer chair, gathering her thoughts, the bunnies caught her attention. She used the ball of one foot to stop her dizzying motion.

For a long minute, Nina stared at the animals in human clothing. Then, she turned to her camera, which was secured in its desktop stand.

"Nifty, turn on," Nina said, connecting to her digital personal assistant.

Good afternoon, Nina, chirped every speaker in her room. *How can I help you?*

"Start protocol three."

The St0ryte11er recorder popped up on her computer screen, with her custom settings loaded. Nina stared, unblinking, at herself in the monitor. She scooted a half inch to the right, centering her round face. Her hair was growing long, but Nina couldn't get it retouched for cheap until school started again. Her classmate Jess gave free haircuts to anyone who agreed to appear on their public St0ryte11er channel. That was their gimmick: they told tales as they cut hair. Jess claimed that anyone who wanted a chance at fame on the app had to have an appealing gimmick.

Maybe so. But in Nina's opinion, if gimmicks and skill were all it took, Jess would be a universe-tier St0rye11er already, 'cause both their stories and their haircuts were great. She idly wondered if they'd agree to visit the bookstore sometime. Jess was witty, friendly, and read the same series as Nina; plus, they were the only other ace sophomore she knew.

"Record," she said. A tiny red light on her camera blinked to life.

"Hey, friends." Nina said. Lately, her St0rye11er diary entries addressed a nonexistent crowd—friends, folks, everybody, y'all—as if Nina were uncomfortable telling stories to nobody. That hadn't always been the case. She used to address her video diary to "Future Me." In moments of introspection, Nina assumed she was being influenced by popular St0rye11er videos; universe-tier St0rye11ers assumed that a million strangers would listen in, and they chose their words accordingly. Nina might not want that level of fame, but it was becoming increasingly difficult to believe she didn't want her voice to be known by anyone. Perhaps she was practicing for the day when she switched her recordings off of from private.

"I have a question for y'all," she continued. "Have you ever seen something or someone who made you wonder whether animal people still walked the Earth? By 'animal people,' I don't mean humans in fuzzy costumes. I'm referring to spirits. Or maybe you know them as guardians. Whatever the name, they aren't supposed to be here anymore."

She glanced at her bedroom door, confirming that it was closed and locked. Sure, her father always knocked before entering a shut room, but he'd be mighty disappointed if he heard

Nina blabbing about his favorite bookstore clients. She'd have to explain what she did with all the stories she recorded. Things like that were best kept quiet. It wasn't that she distrusted her parents. They'd never rifled through her stuff before. But what would they do if they learned about her video diary? To Nina, secrets were mosquito bites; they itched the worst when she tried to ignore them. Assuming that her mom and dad felt the same way, she wanted to spare them the inner conflict.

"Don't get me wrong," Nina continued. "I'm not one of those conspiracy theorists who believes the two worlds are still actively connected. The joined era is over." A solemn shrug. "That said, I suspect that some spirits and monsters still conduct business on Earth. Specifically, they buy books. Let me get to the point. I have physical evidence that animal people walk among us . . ."

She conspicuously placed a shoebox on the desk, in view of the camera.

"Dad has two really unusual clients. They're father and son, I think, 'cause they look similar and walk with the same long gait. For years, they've visited the bookshop twice a month after sundown. That's why Dad works late every other Wednesday. And the thing is, the two guys, um, look shady. They wear long trench coats and extra-dark sunglasses like stereotypical Hollywood bad guys. Or . . . people with lots to hide.

"That's where the story gets interesting. Last Wednesday, I decided to observe their visit closely. Unlike regular customers, the trench-coat guys enter the bookshop through the back entrance, which is located in an alley. I have a perfect view of that door through my bedroom window.

"At sundown, I turned off all the lights in my room and

cracked the window open. Then, I waited. It was a stakeout. They usually arrive sometime between nine and eleven-thirty. That night, I got lucky and only had to wait forty minutes.

"They loped down the alley. That's the best way to describe how they walk. The trench-coat guys move with long strides. Like this." To demonstrate, Nina stood, pushed her chair aside, and bounded back and forth, pretending to be speed-walking on the moon.

"They're tall, too, with long legs." She settled in front of the camera again. "Without even knocking, the trench-coat guys entered the bookstore. They never knock. I guess they've been customers so long, they're always welcome. Dad keeps their books in the stock room, far away from the main shelves. Every visit, they leave with two medium-sized cardboard boxes filled with books. Interestingly, unlike most regulars, the trench-coat guys don't care about the condition of their purchases. The books can be 'like new' or 'lightly worn' or even 'well read.' Also, they don't have a preferred type of book. Sometimes, Dad sells them paperback mystery novels. Other times, they buy anatomy text-books. It's really random.

"Anyway, after fifteen minutes in the shop, they exited back through the alley. As expected, each trench-coat guy carried a cardboard box. And here's where things get, um, unusual. The young one staggered 'cause his box was heavy—or maybe he tripped over the uneven pavement; I don't really know—and slammed straight into a metal recycling bin. There was a big clang, and he toppled on his butt. The older guy laughed in a shrill, kinda grating way, and the younger one cried out, 'Can't see with these.' Then, he flung his sunglasses across the alley.

They ricocheted off a brick wall and landed behind a garbage bin. Then, he ducked his head, as if embarrassed, and grabbed his book box. After that, the trench-coat guys left. As they walked out of sight, I heard them speaking in harsh tones—probably arguing—but the words weren't clear.

"Now, the trench-coat guys both have really thick, long hair. Plus, it was night, with just a couple streetlamps illuminating the alley. So this next part I'm iffy about. But during the collision with the recycling bin, I think I saw a pointed ear sticking out of the young one's loose mane of hair. And the ear looked . . . furry.

"That's not the proof I mentioned, though."

She paused, mentally revisiting a conversation she'd had that morning. Nina and her father had been standing in the cubby-small kitchen, eating microwave-heated strawberry Pop-Tarts and listening to the Weather Channel.

During a commercial break, Nina had asked, "Dad, you know the trench-coat-wearing men?"

He'd grinned. "My clients? The ones you shouldn't be pestering because they're the only reason the store hasn't closed?"

"Yes, those guys."

"Rings a bell. What about them?" At that point, her father bit off the bready corner of his Pop-Tart; he always ate the dry, flavorless edges first. In contrast, Nina liked to snap her Pop-Tarts in half and begin with the frosted, fruit-filled center.

"One of them dropped this in the alley." She'd placed a pair of aviator-style sunglasses on the kitchen counter. The ear loops were long and hook-shaped, as if designed for a head with unusually shaped, back-set ears.

"Oh, thanks! I'll be sure to return them."

"Look at the ear hooks, Dad. They're designed for animal people." Tightrope had been looping calmly around Nina's legs; she reached down, cradled him in the crook of one arm, and pointed at his velvety, triangular ears. "If I had a pair of these on my head, the glasses would fit perfectly."

"That's very possible, yeah."

"We're now confident that animal people are your clients. Why are you so unenthused?"

"I'm not. You're probably onto something. But just . . . it doesn't really change anything."

"Seriously? Yeah it does! What do spirits do with all those books?"

"Read them, I suppose."

"Okay, but why guess when you can ask? After all these years, they should trust you enough to drop the act a little."

"It's not like we go for drinks and watch games together. We're still just acquaintances." Nina's father had waved his tart back and forth, trying to fan away the excess heat. "If I asked questions, there's a good chance the animal people—if that's what they are—would turn tail and never come back."

"Yeah. That's what Grandma said."

"Your mom feels the same way." He'd reached out to give Tightrope an affectionate pat on the head. "It's not that we don't care. Actually, I probably care too much. I'm petrified of hurting them. I even had a nightmare about it last year."

"You did?"

"Vivid one. In my dream, I was waiting for their visit, but they never came. So I went outside—the bookstore was in the middle of a cornfield for some reason—and wandered around until I found a pair of bloody, torn coats on the ground. Somehow, I knew they were dead 'cause of me."

"That's terrible."

"Yeah, it is, but nightmares don't have to be prophetic. Over time, my clients may decide that we can be trusted. Could take decades or generations, considering the life span of spirits. Which is why I hope you'll be the one to forge a friendship someday. Wouldn't that be amazing?"

He had a point. It would.

"Why are they so afraid of us?" Nina had wondered.

"That's my biggest question," her father confessed. "Sincerely, it is. Knowing humans, they probably have a very good reason."

"Do you think there are really people who hunt them? I've seen that claim online."

"No doubt. People will hunt anything, Nina."

Now, in her locked bedroom, Nina opened the shoebox, looking down at the scarf-wrapped glasses. A sudden, overwhelming pang of protectiveness urged her to snap the shoebox lid shut.

"Nifty," she said, "delete recording and close program."

Are you certain, Nina? her phone chirped in a smooth voice with a slight Texan accent. *Do you really want to delete?*

She didn't want to risk hurting the wolfmen, however unlikely; even with passwords and locks, no St0ryte11er diary was one-hundred-percent safe from prying eyes. "Yes."

The monitor went black.

Then, there was a gentle knock on the door.

"Nina?" her father called.

"Come in!"

He cracked the door open, leaning inside. "Good news and bad news."

"Bad first," Nina said. She always chose that option.

"I'm taking a train to Grandma's place. Might spend the night."

"What for?" They usually planned visits days in advance! "Oh. Oh, no. Is she sick?"

Nina always took Grandma's good health for granted. To be fair, she was unusually hearty, breezing through cold season without a sneeze. Case in point: during the most infamous family gathering, she was the only person to escape a terrible case of food poisoning. Which really wasn't fair, considering that Grandma ate two heaping bowls of Uncle Carl's mystery casserole.

Still, hadn't Grandma said she'd been feeling off lately?

"No," Nina's father said. "Nothing to worry about. The city gave her a warning."

"Um. What? Why?"

"One of her oaks is dropping leaves outside her property line. If we don't trim it, we'll be fined."

"Who cares? It's not like anybody lives there!" Unless . . . "Wait. Did Paul report her?"

"How'd you know?"

"Because he called her place a mess. I don't get it! His camper is a quarter mile away! Plus, he lets his place grow wild, too, except for that little square tucked inside barbed wire . . ."

Her father shrugged. "It's no big deal. I only need to cut a few branches."

"I just don't understand why Paul reported her. It can't really be about leaves."

"It's not."

"So what's going on?"

"Petty bee-ess. Not long ago, he made a couple offers to buy Grandma's property—the first was an offensive lowball, but the second was decent. Of course, she turned both down. I don't know his goal—don't know why he's buying up so much land. First Paradise, and now the old orchard. But I know his kind. Some folks won't lose gracefully."

"Wow. I knew there was something off about him," Nina said. "Stalking around Grandma's land with a compass . . ."

"At least he hasn't returned." Her father stepped back, as if fixing to leave.

"Wait! What about the good news?"

"Aw, right!" He grinned. "You got mail."

"Is it the dictionary?"

"I didn't open the box, but it weighs more than a block of bricks."

"That's gotta be the dictionary!" Nina jumped upright, accidentally sweeping the shoebox off her desk. Its lid popped open, spilling her blue scarf onto the floor.

The sunglasses were gone, as if they'd vanished into thin air.

COTTONMOUTH MEETS A BOUNTY HUNTER

In my defense, when I agreed to be Reign's "living manne-quin," I didn't fully comprehend what the term *mannequin* meant. Thanks to the influence of the daredevil world-journeyers in their pack, she and Risk dropped the most obscure Earth terms in their parlance. "Basically," she explained, "you'll help me design clothes. I need somebody to wear my dresses when I make finishing touches."

"But I'm this much taller than you," I said, spreading my hands till they were four inches apart.

"You don't have to be a perfect fit," she assured me. "Any-way, my current line of clothing is supposed to be loose. It's com-fier that way."

We were drinking morning tea on my raft, drifting in the calm shallows within sight of the basking rock.

"Still," I said, "isn't Risk a better mannequin? She's your iden-tical twin."

"Pfft." Reign blew a raspberry at me and waved her hand

dismissively, as if my idea had transformed into a pesky fly. "She's too preoccupied with her new friends. It's like she joined their pack. I blame Zale. Risk thinks he's so impressive."

"Who?"

"Zale. He's a wolf hybrid from a pack of book-smuggling scribes."

"That's actually impressive."

"Not you, too!" Reign cried, throwing up her hands. "This is all your fault. You and your insatiable hunger for books. You're the only reason me and Risk got tight with the scribes and the importers. We used to be happy with the occasional Earth scrap from Great-Uncle's random adventures. Phones, bottles, garbage. But you! You read a book a week! And now my sister is always gone! In fact, I think she wants to marry him someday!"

"So?" From what I gathered, it was common for coyotes to marry a partner for life. They'd find a special somebody, fall in love, and make vows of eternal loyalty. In contrast, with cottonmouths, that kind of relationship was the exception, not the rule. Personally, I didn't have strong feelings either way. I guess marriage could be okay, if the right person came along. They'd have to enjoy living near the water, though. "If Risk loves Zale, isn't that a good thing?"

"I guess." Reign sighed. "Yeah. It is."

I finished my tea, which had cooled to an unpleasantly lukewarm temperature. "OK. I'll be your living mannequin. Feel better?"

Reign snorted. "Yeah. It's a start. Also, I brought the book you wanted." She passed me a paper-wrapped parcel. "It has a day left before vanishing, so read fast."

"Not a problem. Momma always joked the eyewear gave me my impressive reading speed." I tapped my spectacles. "But Sona needed spectacles, too, and she'd have to stare at a page of words for half an hour before the language made any sense."

"What's your time?" Reign wondered.

"Now? Almost instantaneous. It used to take a few minutes, but I practiced."

After a beat of thoughtful silence, Reign asked, "Do you ever miss your family? Your siblings?"

"Yeah," I confessed. "I worry about them, too. It's been a long time since the water monster answered my question, said they were all alive. Even if I trust her, a lot of bad can happen in a year. You're lucky to live with a community of family. Aunties, uncles, cousins. Even when your sister is distracted by wolves, at the end of the day, you know she's safe."

"We can adopt you!" Reign offered. "The species difference doesn't matter. There's a coyote pack 'round the lake with a possum member."

I laughed. "Thanks, but I'm doing all right."

"Just keep it in mind. What should the next book be? You want a romance? Or a mystery?"

"Something exciting," I said, "so I can pretend to go on adventures without actually risking my life."

"Got it." A moment of silence. Then: "Thank you for agreeing to be my mannequin."

So that's how I found myself decked out neck to knees in a white linen dress the next morning. Reign and I were situated on a flat patch of land between my tent and the basking rock. She flitted around me with a hedgehog-spiky pincushion in one hand, pinning a web of bright ribbons to the outfit. Every time she pinched the fabric and jabbed it with a pin, I flinched, but she never actually broke skin. Ami sat on a plump white mushroom in the shaded tree line and watched us, fascinated.

"My first show will be in the valley," Reign said. "You're both invited." That day, she was dressed less elaborately than usual. She wore a sleeveless dress with blue fringe around the hips. "Hey, Ami, what kind of clothes do you like?"

My neighbor lifted his tiny hands, as if shrugging, and silently puffed out his blue throat.

"He doesn't wear any," I said.

"My auntie's like that; she despises the way they rub against her skin. It's distracting, or something."

"This is different. Ami doesn't use his false form."

"Never?" Reign circled me twice, then started pinning a blue ribbon down the side of the dress. "Why? Do you hate your false form?"

In response, Ami dropped off the mushroom and scurried away.

"Um. He doesn't like to talk about it," I answered.

"You think his species is going—"

"Can we change the subject?"

She looked at the abandoned mushroom, blushing slightly. "Yeah. Sure. What's up with the weirdo with the binoculars? Friend of yours?"

"Excuse me, what?"

Reign pointed down the bank with her nose. I slowly turned my head, careful not to jostle the pins poised to sting the inexplicably tender skin of my false form. A grizzly bear person was lying on her belly in the high grasses bordering the forest. She stared at us through a pair of binoculars that seemed absurdly small compared to her round face. They were the kind of binoculars children used for field lessons, and although the weirdo wasn't a full-grown adult grizzly, she'd clearly outgrown her equipment years ago.

"That's a complete stranger," I said.

Reign snuffed in frustration. Then, she shouted, "Hey! You! Quit peeping! You're making it difficult to concentrate!"

I flinched at the volume of her voice. "Don't be too confrontational, okay? If we need to escape, all your work will get ruined."

"You'd run away?" she yelped.

"Swim away," I corrected, nodding at the lake. "There. Where you mammals can't get me."

"Oli! Scaredy butt!" She tensed. "The bear's approaching."

"Yeah, I noticed."

Sure enough, the weirdo had lowered her binoculars and was speed-walking straight at us. Her thick arms, which were dusted by bristly fur even in her false form, swung back and forth in sync with her long steps. In one fist, she carried a clipboard. The binoculars dangled from a yellow cord around her neck.

"I think we're about be courted by a camp-to-camp salesperson," I guessed. "Could be worse. They're irritating but mostly harmless."

"Incorrect," the grizzly said, her voice deep and smooth. She must have had excellent ears; I'd nearly been whispering. She stopped in front of me. Because I was standing on an overturned wooden water bucket, we were eye to eye.

"What are you, then?" I asked.

In response, the grizzly rustled through the papers pinched against her clipboard and plucked one sheet free. After glancing between the paper and me a couple times, she flipped it around to reveal an ink caricature of a bespectacled, leering cottonmouth. "Is this you?" she demanded.

"Where'd you get a portrait done, Oli?" Reign asked.

"I didn't!" I jabbed a finger at the caricature. "Seriously? That looks nothing like me, except for the spectacles!"

"Oh really?" the grizzly wondered. "Note the unique scaling pattern." Like me, the sketched face had scales instead of eyebrows.

"That doesn't mean anything," I protested. "Lots of cottonmouths have scaly foreheads in their false form. Like my momma!"

"Runs in the family, eh?" the grizzly asked. "Is mother dearest a foot biter, too?"

My mouth dropped open. It had been over two years since my ordeal in the forest. I hadn't thought about Bruhn the alligator in ages. But apparently, she'd been dwelling on me.

"You're a bounty hunter," I guessed.

"That's right."

"Oh, Creator!" I clasped my face in my hands, horrified. "Did she lose a toe? Or . . . or . . . the whole foot? I'm sorry! It was an accident, and I thought she'd be fine. A person that size—"

"Relax." The hunter smiled in a tight, perfunctory manner. "It's nothing like that."

"What?"

"My client is in good health."

"So why are you here?" Reign demanded. Her head of hair bristled with annoyance.

"The woman you injured requests an in-person apology and compensation for two days of bedrest. Let's go. It's a long walk." She held out her clawed hand, as if expecting to whisk me away, designer outfit and all.

"Come on!" I cried. "Bruhn crushed my tail, tried to lop off my head with a tentpole, and then stole my blanket."

"Not my problem." She flexed her fingers impatiently. "I said let's go."

I was a second away from jumping into the lake when Reign asked, "How much is the bounty?"

The hunter snorted and flipped my Wanted portrait around, pointing at a line of text that read: REWARD IS BREAKFAST.

"That's all?" I gaped.

Reign yapped with laughter. "What kind of bounty hunter are you? Breakfast?"

"Trainees don't get the consequential jobs. That doesn't mean this work is easy. You know how tricky it was to find you, snake? Half my leads swore you got abducted by a monster two years ago."

"Nearly did," I said, thinking. "So you're hunting me for the experience?"

"Yep," she confirmed. "We all start somewhere."

"In that case, I'd like to request a job. Two fish breakfasts for my blanket."

The trainee hunter blinked slowly. Her large amber eyes seemed to glitter, as if dusted by mica. "I dunno," she said. "That's an ethical gray area."

"Didn't realize bounty hunters cared about ethics," Reign snipped.

"And," I hastily added, "I'll write a formal apology for the bite incident. It's all you'll get without a chase."

The hunter looked me up and down, her attention lingering on the intricate web of ribbons that ran down the sleeves and skirt of the dress. Reign had also embroidered a coyote heart under the collar. The vibrant ribbons were supposed to resemble blood vessels. It was all very high concept. Personally, I just thought the design looked pretty. It wasn't my personal style, but that didn't mean I couldn't appreciate the look on other people. The hunter seemed tempted to cooperate, her eyes softening subtly.

Then, Reign chimed in. "Scratch that. There will be no chase. Accept his terms or prepare to fight!"

I hissed, "Don't," but it was too late.

"Heheh," the hunter chuckled. "Riiiight." Knowing Reign, laughter was probably the most insulting response possible to her threat.

"I'm not joking," she said. "You can't threaten my friend and expect to—"

"Think you can take me? Really?"

Reign's mouth snapped shut, and she ground her teeth. Then, the response I dreaded: "I know I can."

"Don't forget your auntie's wisdom, Reign!" I begged. "Remember? Deescalate! Weigh the risk against the reward!"

"This is different than the catfish, Oli," she said. "There is no risk. She's a poser. All talk."

"You're the one talking," the hunter retorted, still smirking.

"We can settle this right now," Reign said. "Unarmed, one-on-one tussle. First one to tap out loses."

"Just a second," the hunter said, delicately removing her binoculars. She placed them and her clipboard on the ground. "I don't want to break these when I kick you into the lake."

"Does this fight have to happen?" I asked. "Can it . . . not?"

"It's just a friendly match, Oli," Reign said. "I win them all the time in the valley."

"Fine." I gingerly sat down, spreading the ribbon-tacked fabric around me. Then, to emphasize that I wanted no part of their nonsense, I crossed my arms.

For a couple minutes, the hunter and Reign circled each other, neither eager to make the first move. Then, Reign feinted to the right and threw a punch. The hunter blocked her strike with one muscular arm and tried to retaliate with a knee to the gut, but Reign nimbly skipped aside. I winced and hid my face behind my hands, peeking at the fight through the gaps between my fingers. Although Reign had agility and speed on her side, it was clear that the hunter was a trained fighter. And—based on her patronizing grin and the lack of force behind her kicks and punches—I got the sense that she was playing, much like an adult bear play-fights with a cub. If that changed, my friend was in trouble.

There wasn't any blood yet, though. No bruises, either. I lowered my hands, relaxing slightly, suddenly hopeful that it really would be a friendly match, painless and fun.

Then, with a quick foot sweep, Reign tripped the hunter.

"Got you!" she barked, lunging down and trying to wrestle the hunter into a headlock. "Give up?"

The grizzly bear's smile snapped into a vicious grin. "You don't got anything yet." She laughed. Then, without a trace of exertion, she stood. Reign clung to her neck, as harmless as a coyote-shaped cape.

"Let go!" I cried.

The hunter jumped and dropped, trying to body-slam Reign into the dirt. If Reign hadn't rolled away in time, she would have been crushed.

"It's a tie!" I announced. "Hooray!"

Instead of listening to me, they collided in an earnest exchange of blows, deflections, and dodges. Before long, blood trickled down Reign's upper lip; she licked it up, glancing to her left, as if searching for something. She'd been doing that a lot throughout the fight.

It finally occurred to me that she must have been instinctually looking for her sister.

I had to stop them. They weren't listening, though. Not to me. Not to the wisdom of aunties. What did my momma do when my siblings and I fought? How had she regained order?

She'd dip a bucket in the lake and dump cold water on our heads. But I had no bucket, and the hunter was rearing back, her fist raised, her mouth a snarl of bone-cracking, meat-tearing teeth.

With a cry of horror, I tightened willpower into a basket, focused on the lake, and scooped several gallons of algae-clouded, cold water into the air. Then, I flung every drop at Reign and the hunter.

Splash.

I'd never attempted world-shaping at that scale before, and the aftermath left me feeling shaky. An ache pulsed behind my temples, as if I'd held my breath too long. But it worked.

"That's enough!" I shouted. "Reign, stop fighting, or I'll never be your mannequin again. Hunter, stop fighting, or I won't cooperate at all. Do you understand?"

Sopping wet, the pair blinked at me. Then, after ten seconds of baited-breath silence, Reign and the bounty hunter simultaneously stepped away from each other, as if repelled by an invisible force. My friend stalked around the basking rock, detangling her hair with her clawed fingers, while the hunter plucked two blank pieces of paper from her clipboard and handed them to me. "Affirmative. I'll need a picture of your . . . alleged blanket," she said. "Think you can manage something more informative than a rectangle?"

"Yeah. Like I said, Momma wove it. The pattern's our family fingerprint. I'll never forget those details."

Reign passed me a charcoal stick, one of many implements she used for sewing. Then, she moved in front of me, offering her back as a solid surface. Without stepping off my water-bucket pedestal, I started drawing.

"You can have my clipboard instead," the hunter begrudgingly offered.

"No," Reign said. "He's been my living mannequin all morning. I'm returning the favor."

"Living desk," I said, "why is your spine so bumpy?"

"It's my sharp bones. Draw around them."

I did my best, and before long, the hunter's clipboard carried a bounty for my blanket and one handwritten apology: *Sorry about your toe. It won't happen again.*

"Guess that's contrite enough," the hunter said. "Client won't be satisfied, but one breakfast isn't sufficient to make me worry 'bout that."

"What if your client offers a bigger reward?" Reign wondered, still positioned between me and the hunter. "How far would you go?"

The hunter shrugged. "Until later, snake," she promised.

I didn't correct her with my real name.

The good thing about living in a tent is you can pack up and move on a whim. Later that day, Reign helped me relocate a quarter mile away, setting up my new camp in a region of the lake where the forest practically spilled into the water. I didn't appreciate the extra distance between my bed and the basking rock, but it was in my best interest to hide after dark. After we finished, Reign and I sat on a fallen tree half-submerged in the lake, making ripples with our toes.

"Bounty hunters are creepy," Reign said. "You can change your mind about joining the pack. There's safety in numbers."

"I'm not afraid of a grizzly bear with baby-sized binoculars," I said. "Anyway, don't bounty hunters have rules? Like they can't use force unless a serious crime's been committed?"

Reign laughed. "Yeah, but since when do rules matter?"

"If the alligator wanted me dead," I reasoned, "she wouldn't have enlisted the help of a trainee."

"I guess." Reign back-rolled from a sitting to a standing position and then spun across the fallen tree, as if performing a dance. With a final jump, her arms spread, she returned to land. There, she grabbed the basket filled with her sewing supplies. "Good night, Oli. Be safe."

"You too," I said.

Anxiously, I watched her leave. I wondered if Risk really would get bored with her poetry-spouting fella. For the past week, she'd spent all her free time with him in the valley. And during that period, every time Reign visited me, she had to travel alone.

It was almost sunset. Coyotes and cottonmouths aren't usually afraid to be awake at night—many actually prefer a nocturnal lifestyle—but I was haunted by one particular fear. Although two years and an unknown distance separated me from the clicking monster, I vividly remembered the ember brightness of its eyes and dreaded glimpsing their steady glow in the shadows of the forest.

"We should walk with her next time," I said, patting the empty patch of bark beside me. Ami climbed out of my chest pocket, down my arm, and onto the tree.

"Thanks for coming," I added. "Life wouldn't be the same without my favorite neighbor."

Ami opened his mouth in a smile. Then, he clambered away to find a bed for the night. He enjoyed sleeping on tufts of moss within the cozy nooks of exposed tree roots. There'd be plenty of options in the area.

I didn't plan to live there forever. If the alligator decided to retaliate, she'd act within the season. Hopefully, that wouldn't happen. I wanted to move on. To forget about both her and my embarrassing, terrifying stumble into adulthood.

Weeks later, on the cusp of autumn, the hunter returned. I was making the quarter-mile hike to my basking rock, carrying Ami in a basket of dew-slick leaves, when she called to me from the forest, "Hey! Snake! I have something for you!" It took a moment for me to recognize the smooth, deep voice.

"Is that the bounty hunter girl?" I wondered aloud. Ami propped his head on the edge of the basket, his round eyes trained at the tree line. I tasted the air, but she was still too far to sense chemically. And she must have been walking carefully, because I didn't hear the crunch of ground beneath heavy feet.

"I have your blanket!" she shouted, and that's when I finally saw her. The hunter was draped in bark-colored strips of fabric, well camouflaged among the trees. With a thumbs-up, she jogged the last few paces between us and thrust a tightly bound cube of wool at me, a folded blanket in brilliant shades of sunset red and orange. I gently placed Ami's basket on the ground. "No," I said. "My blanket was green and brown." Still, I took the bundle from her and cradled it in my arms. The wool smelled faintly of silk and smoke. Of home.

"That's impossible." She waved her clipboard. A single sheet of paper—my bounty request, complete with a detailed charcoal sketch of the blanket pattern—flapped in front of my face. "The design matches one hundred percent. You think I'd just pluck a random blanket off a clothesline? Huh?"

"Where'd you find this?" I asked. The cords fastened around the blanket were tied in an elegant bow. I loosened the knot, my fingers unsteady.

"At the cliffside city of Redstone," she said.

I unfolded the blanket from eighths into fourths into halves, revealing my mother's meticulously even stitches and the tightly woven geometry—zigzags and diamonds—of our family pattern. "Did you see another cottonmouth there?" I asked. "Somebody my age? Momma wove this for my sibling."

"Oh," she said. "Ohhh. Oh, dang. Really?"

"Yes! It's orange and red. Mine's green and brown. Didn't I specify that on the bounty slip?"

"You know the ways colors go," she explained. "You can't rely on them. Every animal sees the world a different way. Most bears are red-green color-blind. Didn't you know that? It's biological."

"That's fine. Really. Just tell me—was my sibling at the city? His name is Wist, and he looks like a taller, paler version of me. No spectacles, but our brow scales are the same shade."

"It's not okay. I made a mistake, and that's on me. But you have to admit that the description was misleading. I was acting under the misimpression that your blanket would be the only one with that pattern."

"Right! Whatever! Who did you take this from?"

"Excuse me?" She drew up to her full height: at least six feet. I wondered if she was even taller in her bear form. Didn't want to find out, quite honestly. "Watch your tone, snake."

Ami hopped out of the basket and clung to my big toe. I couldn't decide whether he was trying to comfort me, or hold me back from a tragically lopsided fight.

"Sorry," I said, lowering my volume. "It's just that I haven't seen my siblings in years. Don't even know if they're all alive. This is the first sign . . ." I looked down at the blanket. "It's the first physical sign that my family's out there, you know?"

The hunter crossed her muscular arms, a stance that seemed more defensive than threatening. "Unfortunately," she said, "it was being sold by a merchant. He deals mixed goods. I didn't notice any vipers. Maybe your sibling traded the blanket for something else."

"Wist wouldn't do that. He'd sell an organ first. The blanket was a gift from our mother. Her greatest gift, aside from life.

Who was the merchant? I need to know when he got the blanket and who he got it from."

"Uhm." She consulted her clipboard. "He's a porcupine named Furious. But trust me. You don't want to mention this to him."

"Why not?"

"One. He's named for his general temperament. Two. I stole the blanket. Well. Technically, since I'm your agent, *you* stole the blanket."

"Whaaaaaiii?"

She raised her free hand in a placating manner. "Relax. Nobody knows, and I'm a professional."

"A professional? What does that even mean?"

"Confidentiality. I'll never turn you in."

"But I never agreed to be a thief by association!"

"You want me to return the dang blanket?" she asked, hands now on her hips, with the clipboard pinched between two of her clawed fingers. "That's always an option."

My grip tightened on the blanket, as if I was afraid she'd pluck it from my grasp. The wool felt rough and heavy, but it didn't itch. Good blankets never did. I thought of Wist, second to last child to leave. The way he'd glanced over his shoulder as he marched away from home, looking at me. Not Momma. Not the house. Me. And I wondered if he'd delayed his departure on my behalf. He must have known I'd be lonely.

Why didn't I follow Wist? We could have teamed up and survived the first few days or months together. It wasn't common for cottonmouth siblings to cooperate as adults, but that didn't mean it was wrong. Looking down at Wist's blanket, I thought of all the pain and loss that could have been avoided if I—if he—hadn't been so alone. Was he even still alive? With a snap of my arms, I completely unfolded the blanket and spread it across the forest floor. Then, after dropping to my knees, I hunched forward and delicately ran my hands across the wool.

"What are you doing?" the hunter asked.

"Looking for blood." My spectacles slipped down my nose; I pushed them into place again, sniffling. "I'm looking for Wist's blood. In case . . . in case . . ."

She bent at the waist, looming over me, no doubt trying to seem helpful. "Tricky. Half the yarn's red."

I gaped a silent scream of despair before collapsing facefirst on the blanket. With my face smooshed into the wool, the world was darkness and sage and smoke. I inhaled deeply and held my breath. Tried to hold home inside me. Cottonmouths can hold our breath a long time, even in our false form, but one breath can't last forever. Ultimately, nothing can.

My exhale came out with a pathetic sigh. Ami hopped onto my head and gave it a sympathetic pat.

"Uh, hey." I heard the crackle of heavy footsteps. I turned my head—slowly, so Ami didn't tumble off—to squint at the hunter through knocked-asunder spectacles.

"Relax. If your sibling had been violently murdered on top of that blanket, there'd be a massive puddle of blood. Impossible to miss. Right?"

"Maybe," I conceded.

"When did you lose your blanket?"

"Over two years ago."

"Right. Immediately after your mom gave it to you. And how'd that happen again?"

"You know how it happened."

"A lady ran you off her fishing spot with a tentpole. Isn't it possible something like that happened to your sibling?"

I sat up. "Yeah." Ami dropped onto my shoulder, shuffled down my arm, and sat beside me.

"Or somebody could have stolen it when his back was turned? Same way I stole it from the merchant?"

Both Ami and I nodded. Yes, that scenario was very possible.

"So what do you want to do, Oli? Or, more accurately, what do you want me to do?"

I stood and lifted the blanket by a corner, brushing off the dry leaves that clung to its surface. Then, with precise folds, I recubed it. "Thank you for finding Wist's gift, Hunter. I'll keep it safe for him."

"Right." She held out the clipboard with my bounty request pinned at the top of the job pages. "All I need from you is a written confirmation of my success."

"Got a writing implement?" I asked, placing the blanket on a relatively clear patch of forest floor. Ami climbed the folds, as if scaling a soft mountain, and huddled on top. He blinked up at me. It was nearly his midmorning nap time. Mine, too, to be honest.

"Of course." The hunter dug through a pouch clipped to her utility belt and handed me a sharpened stick of graphite wrapped in string. I took both the clipboard and the stick and moved a couple steps away from her, to stand in a pool of sunlight that had wriggled through the dense canopy. As I wrote *JOB COM-PLETED THANKS* in the first language, I intentionally rubbed my clammy palm over the sketch of my blanket, smudging away the details of my family pattern. Some knowledge—like the story of the path to anywhere-you-please—is most powerful when it's known by everybody. But other knowledge is best protected, held close.

Plus, I wanted to destroy any link between me and the theft. The last thing I needed was an adversarial relationship with a porcupine. He might put quills in my bedroll. Or worse!

If the hunter noticed that I'd erased the sketch, she didn't care enough to comment. "Good luck," she said, tucking the clipboard back in her pouch. "I hope you find your family."

"You don't want the breakfasts I promised?"

"Nah," she said. "I messed up, so let's call it even." She smoothed back her dark hair, which was oil-sleek. "If you want help, go to the caves at the base of the third mountain in the seven-peak range. That's where my family works."

"They're all bounty hunters, too?" I asked.

"Many, yeah. Others are investigators 'cause they don't deal with criminals; that's what you need. I recommend my aunt. She specializes in finding lost children, but I figure a lost sibling is in her wheelhouse. Sometimes, she even travels to Earth."

"Seriously?"

"Sure. We have lots of connections there. Human allies, all very trustworthy. They even help us avoid the King's knights."

"Whoa," I said. "You mean the Nightmare?"

"Yeah. That jerk."

"How far are the mountains? I've never been there."

"You know how to use a compass?"

I nodded.

"Slither northwest. Two-eighty degrees. Forty miles. One word of caution: her schedule's packed, and my aunt hasn't been a trainee in decades. Be convincing, or she'll kick you outta her cave."

"What does that mean?" I asked. "Convincing?"

She chuckled. "It means you can't expect to compensate her with breakfast. Good luck, Oli."

I watched the hunter trundle away, her body quickly merging with the texture of the forest. It wasn't until later—as I gently transferred Ami from the blanket to his leaf basket—that it occurred to me: I never told her my name. So how did she . . . ?

"Reign was right," I muttered. "Bounty hunters are dangerous."

I didn't want the help of an investigator. I'd find my siblings—all eight of them—myself.

COTTONMOUTH REACHES A FORK IN THE ROAD

I wonder if I missed any signs. Throughout summer and fall, I became so wrapped up in my plans—such uncertain, hopeful things—that I had little time for anything else. There were no naps on the basking rock. Poor Reign had to find a different living mannequin for her design projects. Meals were consumed unseasoned and barely cooked. The road to anywhere-you-please had transported me across two forests. But the bottomless lake fed many rivers, and according to a map I'd acquired, that included the river flowing past Momma's cottage. I could follow it to the dammed city and start my investigation by questioning the city innkeepers.

After leaving home, my siblings had probably spent days or weeks in the city, adjusting to independence in a familiar setting. That's what I would have done, if I hadn't followed the wrong branch in the river. I'd often yearned to visit, but the path to anywhere-you-please had taken me far away, too far for a journey by foot or belly. Some nights, I dreamed that my whole family, even adventurous Sona, was waiting for me at our favorite food cart in the city. Waiting and waiting until we were all large enough to swallow mountains.

After I awoke from these dreams, the homesickness drove me to work on my raft. It had to be transformed from a lake drifter to a boat that could travel down rivers, surviving rapids without breaking apart or overturning. That process strained my foraging and carpentry skills to their limit, and I hammered bruises into both of my thumbs. Twice.

Fortunately, the payoff was a not-bad-at-all boat, one I trusted to keep me dry across a hundred miles of river. "I think it's time," I told Ami, surveying my new rivercraft, a wide skiff with two benches. "Once Risk and Reign find a more detailed waterway map, I can leave . . ."

Ami was huddled in his basket of leaves and moss. He'd been sleepy lately—I assumed his species of toad was extrasensitive to the cold. Although the growing chill hadn't frosted the morning grass yet, the leaves were browning and dropping, making the forest crunchy and rich-smelling.

"After the winter," I amended.

When I was a child, I'd pass the winters in front of the fire ring in Momma's stone cottage. At night, my siblings and I all snuggled together, comforted by the collective warmth. I could remember how unpleasant the winters became as more and more siblings left home, until, at last, I was alone and cold. At first, I slept close to the firepit embers, basking in their dying heat. But one night, during a dream, my arm slipped into the pile of charred wood, and a red-glowing chip of oak burned me. There's still a scar on my forearm, a rectangle of shiny dark skin.

Unlike certain alligators, I didn't blame the embers for hurting me. Instead, I lived in my snake form until the burn stopped stinging, then gave the firepit a wide berth, shivering myself to sleep instead.

As an independent snake, my tent was too small and flammable to contain a fire. Instead, during cold seasons, I wrapped myself in blankets and insulated the dome-shaped exterior of my home with brush and mud. In my false form, I wasn't completely cold-blooded, but it was still difficult to control my temperature. There was no chance I'd survive a journey down the river in subfreezing conditions. If I came into contact with more than a couple drops of frigid water, I'd probably curl up and freeze into a spring-shaped snakecicle.

"I'll bring just my important supplies," I continued. "That way everything should fit in the back. See?" I climbed into my skiff and sat, knees tucked, behind the bench. Ami peeked over the edge of his woven basket.

"The unimportant stuff, I'll bury or give to the twins for safekeeping. You don't have to worry about anything when I'm gone. Reign and Risk promised to visit once a month to make sure nobody steals my basking rock. They'll also check in with you."

I paused, waiting for Ami's response, but he made no sign to indicate his feelings on the matter. He just propped his head on the edge of the basket and blinked.

"Is that okay?" I prompted.

Nothing.

"I know you can take care of yourself. We all do. Just. Friends check on each other. It's what they do."

He closed his eyes. His lids were the same blue-gray tint as his throat.

"What's wrong? Are you sad I'm leaving? It won't be soon." I climbed out of the boat and crouched beside my friend, lowering my face to his level. "Hey. Do you want to come with me?"

Ami opened his eyes. His irises, pretty gold circles, were bisected by long, flat pupils and speckled with constellations of black flecks. It occurred to me that he had the prettiest eyes I'd ever seen. They were small, though. Too small for me to normally appreciate.

Then, he extended his right hand, as if trying to give my nose a comforting pat. But before Ami could reach me, his body went slack, and he collapsed onto the leaves.

NINA, AGE 16

*T*he stone wall around Grandma's land hadn't been built for permanence, and it was neither high nor solid enough to keep people out. Constructed without mortar, the wall could be disassembled piece by piece, and over the decades, both human hands and natural phenomena had began the process. In some regions, the only sign of a barrier were a few calf-high sedimentary rocks lined up in a row. Vegetation pushed through cracks in the wall elsewhere, knocking hearting stones to the ground. With the closing of the gated communities, most of the vandals had gone, and left Rosita and now Grandma with the assumption that there'd be plenty of time for her to tidy things up. She hadn't counted on Paul. When he wasn't making offers on Grandma's land, he was bombarding her mailbox with legalese-sprinkled complaint letters. After the oaks were trimmed, he even threatened to file a noise complaint because the wild chachalaca were too loud. For obvious reasons, that particular threat went nowhere.

"We need professional help," Nina's father said, glaring at an outer region of the wall. Somebody had spray-painted a declaration of love across the stones. Unfortunately, half the message was in a pile on the ground, leaving only LIN LOVES and OREVER standing. To Nina, the absence was quietly heartbreaking.

"If everyone came home for just one week, we could do the job," Grandma said.

"The family's scattered, Mom. It'd cost ten thousand dollars just to fly everyone in. Plus, it's spring. They're all busy at school or work."

"For extra cash, you could sell the rocks to a seawall builder," Nina suggested, kicking a stray pebble. One side was bright red; once, it might have been part of the word FOREVER.

"We could, sure," her father agreed. "Mom, I know a contractor who's willing to give you a senior discount. He can be here soon as Wednesday."

"How much is a senior discount?" Grandma asked.

"Twenty percent off, and that's a deal. He's also happy to remove just the trashieist sections." He pointed at a rusty old can shoved in a crack between two rocks. It was a brand of soda that'd been out of distribution since the nineties. "That's less than half the wall."

"Guess I can't complain," she sighed. "It'll be an improvement. If I'd had the money, I would've hired your friend sooner."

Technically, Grandma still didn't have the funds for major acts of landscaping. But Paul had complained that her wall was a blight. There were steep fines for blights. Didn't matter that the graffiti had been left by strangers. It was her wall, her responsibility.

"What will he do next?" Nina asked. "What else can be reported?"

"Who do you mean?" her father asked.

"Paul. First the trees, now this."

"He's out of options, thankfully. Once the wall gets tidied, we're good. Hopefully, that'll end his one-sided feud with your grandmother."

"You said folks like him don't lose gracefully, though, remember?" Sure, Paul might run out of legal methods to drive Grandma from her home, but there were still plenty of other options. Mysterious fires. Vandalism. Anonymous threatening letters written in angry all caps. Sure, Nina wasn't giving Paul much credit, but he'd spent the last two years hounding an elderly woman, so he hadn't earned any credit to begin with.

Honestly, Nina still struggled to understand the guy's goal with Grandma's land. Fifteen acres weren't cheap, and this wasn't prime "house-flipping" territory. Paradise had closed for a reason. Plus, if he really wanted to collect plots of South Texas, there were nearby sellers itching for a deal. Yet it was Grandma's he coveted.

Thinking back to her first and only meeting with Paul, Nina remembered the strangest part of their conversation. He'd showed her a compass and asked about iron deposits.

"You sure there aren't metal mines around here?" Nina asked.

"One hundred percent positive," Grandma said. "The best natural resource this land has is mesquite."

"Hm. I wonder if Paul knows that."

"He wouldn't be the first person to mistake pyrite for gold," her father joked.

While the adults discussed contractor specifics, Nina wandered to a shady spot under a mesquite tree. There, she could see her phone screen, as direct sunlight turned it into a blank-looking rectangle, despite purported "outdoor-friendly" technology. "Nifty," she said, "show me geologic maps of my region." Color-coded images with lengthy keys popped onto the screen; she read tongue-twister terms like *siliciclastic sedimentary* and *complex lithology*. The maps eventually just confirmed that Grandma was right about natural resources. The area wasn't even known for iron, and that raised other questions.

"Nifty, what makes a compass stop working?"

Nina skipped the first few results because they linked to iffy forums, places where any anonymous user could comment, whether they should or not. Fortunately, the fourth result sent her to an academic web page with teaching resources, including an explanation of compasses. Nina knew all the basics. They pointed to magnetic north, they shouldn't be used around magnets, and their accuracy was affected by metals, such as iron tools. However, nothing in the Intro to Navigation e-course explained why a compass needle would spin and jump. Magnetic deposits didn't even cause that behavior.

So, she refined the question, asking: "Why would a compass spin like a broken clock?"

Good question, Nifty said, raising a smile on Nina's face. It was a purely random response, but she still enjoyed the praise.

When the results loaded, Nina murmured, "No way." One of the top links was a pop-science essay entitled "Millennia after the Joined Era, the Science of Two Worlds Remains Elusive." High school had refined her speed-reading skills, enabling Nina to skim the article until her eyes reached the word *compass*. From there, she slowed to fully absorb the content.

". . . nor is it clear how many so-called crossing zones exist, although estimates range from 500 to 500,000. Size estimates are similarly variable. Researchers hypothesize that the largest, strongest crossing zones—through which most spirits journey—exert an influence on Earth, resulting in measurable magnetic and temperature anomalies. However, to date, zero peer-reviewed studies support this belief. A recent video by J. C. Jackson, a self-described spirit hunter, purports to show evidence of a crossing zone anomaly. In the 2-minute clip, which was filmed in Northern Canada, a compass needle spins like the hand of a clock. Notably, a source close to the spirit hunter reports that the video is a hoax . . ."

Nina lowered her phone. It was certainly possible that Grandma's land was a "crossing zone," an area where spirits could go back and forth between their world and Earth through the sky, the land, and the water. That would explain the Odd Jobs man and the little fish girl Rosita tried to rescue ages ago . . .

At that thought, Nina's gaze lingered on the well, so deep she'd never been able to measure its bottom. Did Paul suspect how special it was? After all, he'd been holding a compass when they met. Surely, he was a curious enough man to research the various causes of a jumpy needle.

She'd never seen him carrying a gun, but there were other ways to hunt. Traps. Poison. Perhaps he knew exactly what the compass malfunction implied.

As she fretted, Nina found her gaze wandering from the well

to the stream, which ran through Grandma's land, down a slight slope, and into a pipe near the silver camper parked on Paradise.

During her fourteenth birthday, Paul had been so focused on that stream. She'd assumed that his warning not to dump anything in the water had been an attempt to annoy her, to exert his control over some small part of Grandma's property.

"I think I know what he wants!" she exclaimed, standing. "Grandma, you do have a valuable natural resource!"

The two adults, who were still chatting, turned. "What's that?" her father called back.

"Water!" Beverage companies were always vying for new sources of freshwater. In particular, cola-bottling monopolies loved picturesque springs, just like the spring that flowed through Grandma's land. Heck, Nina wouldn't be surprised if Paul had investigated the well, too. It would be super easy for him to sneak across the yard and lower his own distance-marked cord into the water. If so, he'd recognize its monetary value, even if he didn't understand the well's greater importance.

That possibility was better than living next to a spirit hunter. But it still didn't mean good things.

With a fortune at stake, Nina doubted he'd stop pestering them any time soon.

COTTONMOUTH
CHALLENGES DEATH

I'd only traveled to the valley a handful of times. Sure, that's where Risk and Reign lived, but they preferred to visit me. Claimed it was more peaceful at my place. I suspect that "peaceful" was a roundabout way of saying, "There's less nosy family at the lake."

Honestly, I was kinda charmed by their pack of boastful cousins, but I experienced them in moderation. Plus, Risk and Reign were fond of wandering. Even when they stayed in one place, they didn't stay still, always jumping, dancing, standing and then sitting and then standing, balancing on one foot, or circling my basking rock like vultures eyeing prey. It seemed as if the twins were privy to a secret, catchy beat, an internal soundtrack that was so captivating, they couldn't help but move.

In contrast, I didn't care much for travel. Never had. And getting chased up a tree by that monster didn't help. For example, the mere thought of boating down a river coiled me into loops of anxiety, made me want to open my mouth in a silent scream of *do-not-want,* and I'd had months to plan the journey.

That said, when Ami collapsed onto his back and didn't respond to my cries of "Hey, buddy, wake up! What's wrong?"— he didn't even open his little gold eyes—I knew I had to find a healer fast, even if that meant a trip to the valley. There were two ways to get there. I could follow a broad cart path that meandered through the forest, avoiding uneven terrain. I'd taken that route several times and knew it was reliable, well trafficked, and easy to follow. Unfortunately, the path was far from a direct line between me and the valley. All its cautious winding increased the travel time by an hour. That's why Risk and Reign rarely took the cart path when they visited me. Instead, they cut straight through the forest, guided by landmarks and their keen sense of direction.

I'd gone that route only once. One morning, while Ami and I were making pottery—his clay bowls were the size of thimbles, and mine were lopsided but functional—the twins had barged into my camp, yapping about "the cookout, the cookout, you're going to miss the cookout!"

"What cookout?" I'd asked, wiping my clay-crusted hands on a linen rag. Ami had used a leaf to clean his.

"It's the valley wildflower festival," Risk had explained. "Mom and Dad want you to be our special guest this year!"

"Come on, hurry!" Reign had added. "We're going to miss the smell-off! That's at noon!"

"What does that even mean? I . . . I'm so confused."

Reign, while tugging me off my basking rock: "The gardener

with the best-smelling bouquet arrangement gets a cake. You can help judge!"

Risk, while helping Ami climb into the basket: "Really? Him? Judge?"

Reign, while straightening my spectacles: "Why not?"

Risk, while taking me by the hand and leading me to the forest: "Can noncanines appreciate a complex aroma?"

"Just a minute." I dug my heels into the ground. The sisters stopped, staring wide-eyed at me. "First, yeah, I can smell flowers. Second. Isn't the path that way?" I pointed with my nose toward the east.

"There's no time for the cart path!" Reign said. "We're late, remember?"

"Whose fault is that?"

"Ours," Risk said. "Don't worry. We cut through the forest every day. It's safe. Right, Ami?"

My neighbor blinked.

"Fine," I said. "But if a monster appears, I'm going straight up a tree."

"Some monsters can climb—"

"We'll kill any monster who bothers you, Oli," Risk interrupted. "Not that I'm worried. None live in these parts. They got chased off ages ago by the valley defenders."

"Twenty of our sixty-four great-great-great-grandparents were part of the original defenders," Reign added.

"That's a lot of ancestors," I admitted. "Okay. Let's go. The sooner we get there, the sooner I can eat all your food."

As we hiked, the twins called out landmarks—crooked tree, badger cabin, thicket of thorns, toad-shaped rock. Every so often,

Reign would scamper up to a birch tree and slash its pale bark with her claws, saying, "Sorry, sorry."

After the tenth apology, I'd caved in and asked, "What are you doing to those poor trees?"

"They're markers so you don't get lost on the way back."

"Hah. Thanks, but I'm taking the cart path home."

"Why?" she'd asked.

"Risk aversion."

I'd shrugged. She'd shrugged. And fifteen minutes later, the trees cleared, and the wind embraced us with sweet flower scents and cheerful voices from the celebrations in the valley.

Now, while cradling Ami's basket against my chest, I looked between the two paths—one lengthy but safe, the other quick but uncertain—and made a choice.

My friend was unconscious, maybe dying.

I sprinted into the forest. Hopefully, the landmarks hadn't changed. Hopefully, the birches still carried scars from Reign's long claws. Hopefully, Ami would survive the journey.

I passed the crooked tree. The cabin. The thicket of thorns. My strides were long but steady; I didn't want to jostle Ami. He was still breathing—slowly, deeply, his sides going in and out with each breath. "We're halfway there," I promised. "I know the way."

What if the healer was busy? People were always breaking bones and catching colds in the valley.

Another landmark on my right, the ancient tree with a chain embedded in its trunk. I paused and peered upward, searching the branches for red feathers. "Brightest!" I shouted. "Brightest, I need help! Please!"

It was a long shot. I hadn't spoken to Brightest in a couple months, although I occasionally noticed their silhouette in the sky, making easy circles above the lake until the thermals enticed them landward. I sometimes wondered if the sensation hawks experienced, as they surfed the earth-warmed, rising air, resembled the joy I felt when I basked on a toasty rock.

I waited. At that point, I was desperate for any winged helper, even Mockingbird. A moment passed without any encouraging sign that Brightest was listening, so I shouted one last time. "Ami's sick! Please help us!"

A rustle of leaves, and Brightest dropped onto a low bough, cocking their feathered head in curiosity.

"Sick?" they asked. "Huh?"

Brightest glided off the branch and landed on my shoulder. I flinched as their talons gripped me for balance, their sharp tips wedging through the weave of my tunic. "He really does look terrible," Brightest remarked, peeking into the leaf-cushioned basket. "How long has the little guy been ill, huh?"

"Less than an hour. He just passed out."

"Shoot. How can I help? I'll do anything."

"Can you fly to the valley and find the healer? Alert her that we're coming, that it's an emergency."

"Consider it done." They disembarked with a quick flap of their wings. Once above the highest canopy, Brightest shouted, "Run, Oli! Good luck!"

I straightened my spectacles, which had been knocked ajar by their wing tip, then continued speed-walking. In the second half of the route, the landmarks thinned; I suspect that, during my first trip, Risk and Reign had gotten tired of reciting objects. So, I instead eyed the forest's birch trees, searching for brown scratch-made scars in the bark. There was one. And another. Then, nothing. Hopefully, that meant I'd reached the final stretch. Any minute now, the trees should thin . . .

"Oli! There you are!" Brightest dove through an open spot in the canopy and landed on my head, their talons prickling my scalp. I felt like one of the birch trees Reign had scratched. "The healer is waiting for you. Hurry up!"

"Am I going in the right direction?" I asked.

"Yeah. Sure are." They stretched out one wing, pointing. "Follow my primaries. By the way, the coyote sisters you like are wailing with concern. We'll probably hear their howls soon."

"Risk and Reign. They're Ami's friends, too."

Brightest relocated to my shoulder. Strands of my black-brown hair were tangled around their toes. "Hey, Ami, if you can hear me, it'll be all right," they said. "Think positive thoughts, okay? You, too, Oli." They head-butted my ear.

"I'll try," I promised.

We traveled like that—Brightest balanced on my bony shoulder, guiding my steps with a single outstretched wing—until the sun fell, unimpeded, on a meadow of long grasses and yellow wildflowers. The valley was a vast, subtle bowl in the earth. A line of family homes bordered the far edge, resembling a thin line of wood delineating the horizon, while most of the valley's activities and public structures filled the concave part of the earth. I saw Risk and Reign cutting through the meadow at a sprint. Risk wore her typical sweatshirt and shorts, while Reign's outfit resembled a black jumpsuit paired with several filmy, multicolored capes. They flapped behind her, snapping side to side with every whim of the wind.

When we met, the twins' questions tumbled out so rapidly, I could barely keep track of who asked what.

"Was he attacked?"

"What happened?"

"Has he ever fainted before?"

"Does he have any enemies?"

"This looks like poison!"

"No," I responded. "I don't know. No. Definitely not. Where's the healer?"

"Follow us," Risk said.

◊

While the healer treated Ami, we sat on the soft grass outside the hospital. Brightest, still in their bird form, waited on the roof, idly preening their fluffy leg feathers.

"Who is that?" Reign whispered, rolling her eyes upward.

"A neighbor."

"Not a friend?" Risk asked.

"We're friendly. They're closer to Ami, though. I'm surprised you haven't met. Brightest is"—I paused, considering—"nicer than the average person."

"Birds live in a world of their own," Risk explained, fluttering her fingers. "Isn't it difficult to connect with somebody who spends half their life above you? In the air, the trees."

"Eh." I shrugged. "Not always."

Silence. The twins plucked at the ground anxiously and wove

necklaces with long blades of grass. Each time they completed a loop, they tore it apart and started again. The air soon smelled of cut plants.

"I've never seen a toad like Ami before," Reign commented somberly. "He's rare."

Her implication was painfully clear. No, I thought. Not that.

The healer's assistant, a young hare with silky gray fur down her head and neck, wrenched open the hospital window and leaned outside. "You can visit your friend now," she said.

"Will he get better soon?" I asked immediately. The last word—*soon*—felt awkward as it left my mouth. I knew it was naïve to frame recovery as the inevitable outcome, but could not bring myself to ask the real question. Will he recover at all?

"Hm," the assistant murmured. "My boss will discuss all that inside."

The hospital was shaped like a clover, with three round rooms branching from a narrow front lobby. Risk, Reign, and I filed into the center room. There, a mature coyote woman sat beside an examination mat. Ami's empty travel basket was on the ground. I noticed that its leaves had been replaced with damp, sweet-smelling purple moss. Ami, however, was nowhere to be seen.

"Your friend is unconscious," the healer said, standing, "and I've done all I can to improve his condition."

"What is his condition?" I asked.

She shook her head. "It rarely happens so suddenly, but I've witnessed this type of decline in health before. I'm sorry."

Not that. Not that. Not—

"It's extinction."

NINA, AGE 16

*A*fter a moment's consideration, Nina slipped a black hoodie over her neon green T-shirt. A patch of color peeked above the hoodie's V-shaped collar, giving her outfit a color-block quality that looked good on video. Her hair, gathered in a high bun, was streaked with pink and orange wash-out color. She'd also applied bright coral lipstick, a color that complemented her skin tone better than the rose-toned pinks in her mother's makeup cabinet. Nina had purchased that tube of coral lipstick herself, but—like the temporary hair dye—she never wore it outside of the house.

Well, that wasn't completely true. Once, she tried to bring colors to school. She streaked her hair in different blues, applied the lipstick on the bus, and tucked the tube in her jean pocket for touch-ups. The early classes seemed to go well; Nina's teachers smiled warmly, and she thought Jess sounded impressed when they said, "Hi. Morning."

Then, at lunch, a senior with exquisitely plucked eyebrows slid into a seat across from Nina. She smelled like the expensive section of a perfume aisle: ginger, almond, vanilla. And for a moment, Nina believed that this beautiful, cookie-scented stranger was going to pay her a compliment.

"Honey," the senior said, "clean your teeth."

Without a fifth word, she walked away.

Baffled, Nina swept her tongue over the front of her teeth, feeling nothing. It wasn't food, then. Because smartphone use was banned on school grounds, she couldn't use the selfie camera to check her face, so Nina left her untouched lunch box in the cafeteria and speed-walked to the nearest restroom. In the streaky oversink mirror, Nina saw bright orange smudges on her white incisors. The lipstick had left residue. What's more, her neck and collar were covered with blue splotches, transfer from the temporary hair dye.

That was the last time Nina tried to be colorful in public.

But here, in front of a camera, she could always film a redo. And the only audience for Nina's stories was herself.

"Start protocol three."

She waited a few seconds, holding eye contact with her mirror image projected on the computer screen.

"This is my favorite story," Nina said. "My grandmother shared it with me, and her grandmother shared it with her. That's the way it goes, all the way back to the original storyteller. The person who witnessed—or experienced—the event.

"Now, let me tell you how a coyote girl trapped the world's most beautiful ballad in a locket.

"In the Reflecting World, where spirits and monsters are born, lived a coyote family: uncles, aunts, grandparents, children. Coyotes survive in packs of relatives, not unlike many humans.

"Now, I don't know if you've heard a coyote howl. Take it from me: they got a powerful voice. So do coyote people. Some claim that they're prone to singing in haunting, high-pitched vocables. I wish I could confirm or deny that, but the joined era happened long before record players. There was no good way to record stuff, which means I'll personally never hear an animal person's voice unless I meet one on Earth. That goal is . . . a work in progress. I digress!

"A coyote woman named Musical served as the unofficial leader of the pack. She earned her name by singing. Allegedly, Musical's voice was so piercing, so moving, even monsters loved to listen. She had a talent for composing, too, and invented new tunes on the daily. With time, Musical had many children, and naturally, she always sang them to bed with a special lullaby.

"Well, one day, Musical's eldest daughter, a huntress named Fearless, came of age and fell in love. Supposedly, when two coyotes marry, it's common for one spouse to join the other spouse's family. True to her name, Fearless joined her bride's pack in a distant forest.

"Before I go on, it's important to mention one thing. When it comes to magic, coyote people have a special knack for tricks of sound. Perhaps that's 'cause of their fondness for howling.

"Anyway, Fearless was generally very happy in her new home, with her new family. But she often longed for her first pack, too. Over time, Fearless developed terrible insomnia. Day or night, she barely slept. 'What's wrong?' asked her wife. 'Is the ground too hard? Is the air too cold?'

"'It's nothing,' Fearless lied. 'A passing illness.'

"However, when exhaustion began to affect her concentration, her waking joy, she had to admit, 'Actually, I might miss my mother's songs.'

"The next day, her wife traveled by wagon to the nearest artisan market and returned with a gift for Fearless. A silver locket on a chain. 'The next time you visit your parents,' she said, 'put her song in here. That way, you can carry it with you.'

"See, using world-shaping, it's possible to trap sound—vibrations in air—in pots, boxes, and even lockets. That was really handy before the first gramophone. Unfortunately, once the sound is released into the world, it's gone forever. So you can't replay a conversation in a barrel, or a song in a locket. Also? It takes practice. Fearless normally spent her free time whittling cedar, and she had no use for magic during the daily hunt.

"Nonetheless, with the guidance of a wise old fox (they're also skilled at tricks of sound; could be a canid thing), Fearless learned to trap laughter under overturned bowls, screams in sealed conch shells, and stories in glass jars. Her house became the noisiest place in the village. One time, Fearless's wife, a chef, invited the pack for a catered meal. When she opened her dish trunk, a howl tumbled out. When she removed the lid from a clay pot, whispers rose into the air like steam. And when she popped the lid off a salt shaker to season her masa, both grains of sea salt and mutters shook out. 'I think you're ready to trap a song in your locket, dearest,' she said.

"With that, Fearless journeyed across the forest, and into the desert where her old pack lived. There, she was welcomed by a celebration. Feast, games, and song. Her relatives offered Fearless many gifts, but she politely turned them down, explaining the need to travel light. 'All I want is a song,' she said.

"Her mother happily obliged, singing the lullaby. Then, she sealed a promise into the locket. 'Be strong, my daughter,' she said. 'We'll always be here for you.'

"Gathering her mother into a hug, Fearless said, 'Next year, I'll bring more lockets.'

"After the visit, Fearless carried her song home. She wore the locket on every hunt, to every meeting. And although she did not listen to the song, reluctant to lose it, its nearness was a comfort. Peacefully, she slept.

"Until, the following winter, a messenger owl flew circles in the moonlit sky above the village. Some claim that owls delight in delivering terrible news, but that's an unfair characterization. The thing is, they are often asked to carry urgent messages at night. And, as you know, night is a common time for monster attacks.

"'Fearless One,' said the owl, his voice more piercing than the winter chill. 'Your mother has been slain by an automaton monster with bear-trap teeth. It happened as she slept. Quickly. Instantly. I'm so sorry.'

"'Tell me you are mistaken!' Fearless had been on night watch with two other pack warriors. Now, she chased the retreating owl. 'Why would it do such a senseless, terrible thing?'

"'I'm so sorry,' the owl repeated, its voice murmur-soft with distance.

"Despairing, Fearless sprinted back to the night watch bonfire and flung her shortbow into the sparking flames. That weapon was built for sustenance hunting. It could not kill beastly monsters with metal bodies and glowing eyes. It would not intimidate the ten-armed, giggling fiends who attacked travelers along cart paths. And a bow and arrow would just annoy the mountain giants whose appetites grew with every bite of flesh. Fearless needed stronger weapons, because from that moment on, she'd only hunt monsters.

"Of course, Fearless had no vendetta against the vast majority of monsters. Contrary to popular belief, they aren't all cruel. She targeted those who killed purely for the joy of it. Fearless, the first coyote person in a long line of monster hunters, tracked down the living automaton who'd murdered her mother, and then she turned her blades on its homicidal . . . er . . . coyotecidal . . . kin."

A breath. A sad smile.

"You know the way these old stories go. Usually, there is no single, all-encompassing end. There are little resolutions and enduring questions. One story bleeds into the next. You may wonder: what happened to the locket? Did Fearless symbolically release her mother's lullaby after slaying the automaton? Oh! Maybe Fearless actually used the lullaby in the battle! As I mentioned earlier, Musical's voice captivated everyone who heard it. A distraction like that could tip the scales in a closely matched fight.

"But no. Fearless didn't want to lose the precious song. She carried the locket through every adventure and heartache in life. And over time . . .

"Over time . . .

"She learned how to survive without her mother's voice in the world."

During the story, Nina had started crying. Now, she swiped a hand across her cheek. "The end."

COTTONMOUTH MEETS
THE SCRIBES

*I*t had been generations since my many-great ancestors more or less gave up living on Earth. It was beautiful, but too dangerous, too heartbreaking. So—like most animal people—they slithered through the burrow between worlds, taking refuge in the world of monsters and spirits. Sometimes, I almost forgot that Earth existed. Other times, it was just a source of vanishing novelties. But, like all people, I was inextricably linked to life up there.

That rarely worried me. Cottonmouths were doing great on Earth. They'd probably flourish long after I died. Coyotes? Same thing. And I knew Ami was probably among the last of his kind, but that didn't mean he had to die.

"How's that possible?" I asked the healer. "Ami hasn't been sick until this morning."

"You had to suspect," Reign said. "I mean, he's not even powerful 'nuff to transform."

"So what?" I asked. "He's rare. That's different than going

extinct. I know him better than anyone, okay? He's been happy and active. Something must have happened on Earth. Something sudden and terrible. A disaster!"

"You may be correct," the healer agreed. "But the cause is beside the point. In my experience, your friend's illness indicates that his animal species has been irreversibly damaged."

"But it hasn't gone extinct yet, right?" I asked. "He's still alive."

"For now. Yes." She handed Ami's basket to me.

"Can I talk to him?"

"He's unconscious, but you may visit." She pointed at the door with her nose. "This way."

She led us out of the hospital, through a lush herb garden, and into a small wickiup cooled by the shade of a red-leaved oak tree. Inside, against the far wall, Ami slept on a square silken pillow that smelled of the purple moss in his basket. It must have been filled with the stuff. Although my friend's pallor had improved slightly, his eyes were tightly shut, with moisture welling along his eyelids, as if Ami was dreaming of a sandstorm, of being pelted by grains of dust.

"Ami," I whispered. Then, louder, "I'm here."

"We're all here for you," Risk said. The three of us knelt around his pillow.

"Can you hear me?" I asked. When he didn't answer, I looked toward the healer. She stood in the entryway, a broad-shouldered silhouette against the brightness outdoors. "Can he hear me?" I asked her.

"Possibly. In his dreams."

"I hope they're good ones." I leaned closer to my friend's

spotted head. "I promise you, I'm gonna do everything in my power to make you feel better. On my family line, I swear."

Risk and Reign exchanged one of their inscrutable, meaningful looks, but they didn't speak until we left the healing cottage.

"A promise like that can't be broken," Reign warned as we walked into the valley.

"I know."

"You understand what 'extinction' is, right?" Risk asked.

"Yep."

The twins and I walked circles through the bustling valley hub. There, true-form coyote children (and a couple young raccoons) wrestled for cornhusk dolls and scampered around the legs of their elders. To the right, a row of weavers worked behind enormous looms, their nimble fingers callused by the repetition of creation. To the left, traders swapped pottery for meals, toys for tools. I was driven by a sense of dissatisfied restlessness, as if going nowhere-in-particular was preferable to going nowhere-at-all. Was that how Risk and Reign always felt? Did I finally understand their wanderlust? Above us, Brightest glided in tight circles. I wondered if they could read our lips from that height. Hawks were supposed to have amazing eyesight. I couldn't relate.

We passed a food cart loaded with roasted corn, each cob brightly spiced and steaming. Reign normally couldn't resist warm snacks, but that afternoon, she didn't even dawdle upwind of the cart, although her nose twitched at the scent.

"I didn't promise anything impossible," I said. "I said I'd try my best to help, and that's what I'll do."

"So what are your plans?" Risk asked. "I mean, our plans? What can we do to cure extinction?"

"Our plans," I repeated, questioning, and she nodded.

"That depends, doesn't it?"

"Depends on what?"

"The root cause of Ami's illness. It happened within a day. I really suspect that something massively bad impacted his species. A catastrophe on Earth." Nearly in unison, we all stopped walking and looked up. Past Brightest's silhouette. Past the clouds, which were feeble and wispy, like the smoke of a sputtering campfire. Our gazes settled on the bloated yellow sun, which—unlike the real thing—was not quite intense enough to sear the eye, but still left spots in my vision when I looked at it too long.

It was a mere reflection.

And a passageway to Earth, one accessible by winged people or anyone in possession of a reliable hot-air balloon. Apparently, all you had to do was fly straight toward the pseudosun. It'd get bigger and brighter and unbearably hotter. And when you thought your feathers were gonna sizzle right off or that your balloon couldn't rise a centimeter higher, an irresistible gravity would seize you, pull you straight through the light, and spit you out on Earth. Or—more specifically—into the air of Earth, ten thousand feet above ground level with no way to turn around and go home.

The exact nature of the pseudosun passage was difficult to verify. Very few travelers could go that high without fainting from exhaustion or choking on the thin air. Fortunately, there were easier ways to reach Earth. And by *easier,* I definitely mean "somewhat less treacherous," not actually easy.

"We have to visit Earth," I reiterated. "It's the only way to understand why Ami got sick and how to help."

"What if it was a vast wildfire?" Reign wondered. "Those keep happening, and it's not like three people can stop the whole world from burning."

"Or a meteor. Lots of extinctions have been caused by impacts from space," Risk added.

"Wouldn't that hurt many species, though?" her sister asked.

"Yeah, I guess. Could be a disease, then. Fast-spreading virus? They're generally selective. Or a bomb. If something exploded in a swamp full of rare toads—"

"The point is," I interrupted, since the last thing I needed were more reasons to feel like curling up and screaming, "that the cause of Ami's decline is a mystery we gotta solve. And maybe . . . maybe we can reverse it."

"Reverse the irreversible," Risk restated, her bushy eyebrows squishing with incredulity.

"Listen, I respect the healer, and I'm grateful for her help, but that whole irreversible comment was a guess based on statistics. Just 'cause something usually happens doesn't mean it always happens, or has to happen. We can't afford to be defeatist, got it? This is personal. Ami is our friend. So, um, from now on . . ."

Overhead, Brightest screeched. I took it as encouragement.

". . . positive thinking!" I concluded.

Risk and Reign looked at each other, no doubt communicating through lip quirks and eye glints. "Agreed," Risk said.

"I'll still have negative thoughts," Reign admitted, "but will keep them inside my head."

"Thank you." I exhaled a hiss of frustration. "So how do we do this? What will it take to reach Earth?"

Risk grinned at me. "I know a guy," she said.

The scribes worked beyond the valley, among fields of blueberries tended by student scribes for nourishment and ink. As Risk, Reign, and I walked between two rows of waist-high bushes, their branches sprouting gray-blue, juicy spheres, I noticed the bushy head of a possum person three rows down. She seemed oblivious to our presence.

"She's picking berries," Risk explained, as if I couldn't guess that somebody crawling around berry bushes would be picking berries. "Hey! Daysona!"

The possum stood and regarded us with splendidly large brown eyes. Her thin lips were flecked with blue-black berry juice.

"I thought the berries were supposed to go in your basket, not your mouth!"

"I'm multitasking," Daysona shouted back, holding up a nearly full woven blueberry basket.

"Where's Zale?" Risk asked.

"In the peace dome, with the other scribes. We just received a box of textbooks that need transcribing."

"Yeah? What kind of textbooks?"

"No idea. I'm busy finishing morning chores. Need to get back to them now, if you don't mind." Daysona crouched, all but the crown of her head hidden by the dense bushes. Risk nodded at me and then inclined her head toward an earthen dome beyond the agricultural field. It was smaller and more geometrically precise than a hill, but, unlike most built structures, was covered by a layer of living earth. Grasses, dandelions, and clover sprouted from the roof. To reach the dome, we continued walking down the alley between the berry bushes.

"Daysona is nocturnal," Risk explained. "That's why she does morning chores in the midafternoon."

"Must be lonely," I said, my voice a nearly whispered hiss. I didn't know how keen Daysona's senses were.

"Some people like solitude," Reign said. She looked at me questioningly, no doubt wondering: *Don't you, Oli?*

At that point, we reached the clearing around the peace dome. A pair of coyote pups, both in their animal form, tussled on the ground. Their minder, a harried young coyote man who wore an ink-stained apron, seemed torn between greeting us and supervising the rowdy babies. After a moment of dizzying indecision, his head whipping between us and the babies and then us again, he scooped up his charges, a child tucked under each arm, and walked up to Risk.

"Childcare duty, Rue?" Risk asked.

The right-side puppy gnawed contentedly on Rue's sleeve, while the left-side puppy wiggled in a spirited attempt to break free.

"Yup," he said. "It's nap time for the other young 'uns, but these two been teething and wouldn't give it a rest."

"It's your lucky day. We need to speak with Zale. I bet he'd take your place outside the dome for a couple hours."

"Ah, it's a rotten day for visitors, Risk. The new chemistry books are in, and Zale's one of our fastest transcribers. He's racing to copy a textbook before it vanishes."

"Excuse me," I said, stepping beside Reign. "I wouldn't interrupt critical scribing work for anything less serious than life or death."

"Wait, really?" Rue asked. "Life or death?"

"Yes. My friend is sick, and Zale may be able to help."

"You shoulda led with that! Obviously, I'll fetch him." Rue tucked the puppies into Reign's open arms. "Watch the two scoundrels like a hawk."

"Babies!" Reign kissed the puppies on their foreheads and cackled with delight when they tried to climb onto her shoulders. Their sharp nails tore holes in the gauzy fabric of her capes, but she didn't seem to mind. Instead, she sat and arranged the puppies on her lap, and sang, "Go to sleep. Close your eyes. No more trouble." Each puppy curled into a tight ball; one yawned, flashing an assortment of new teeth. Then, the other yawned.

"Should I go with him?" I asked Risk, stifling my own sympathetic yawn. Rue had already darted into the peace dome through a curtained entry. The curtain was a tightly woven tapestry depicting a gray wolf scribe. The tapestry wolf stood on his hind legs, with an open book in his upper paws and a long, fluffy quill clenched between his canid teeth. That had to be artistic license. Aside from primates, animal scribes worked in their false forms. Books were the creations of five-fingered humans; it was difficult to replicate their crafts without thumbs.

"Don't," Risk said. "It's a maze in there. The dome's just the entry. There's several chambers underground. Cool, dim places to work in silence. That's why kids"—she pointedly looked down at the puppies—"aren't allowed. Every day, one adult is chosen to watch the rascals while their parents are working."

"The kids are quiet now," Reign said.

"Did you know that my sister is freakishly good with tiny beasties?" Risk asked me.

"I do now."

With a slight smile, I returned my attention to the dome. The tapestry flapped outward, and a wolf-coyote hybrid scrambled into the sun. In his fake form, he wore shorts and a loose black shirt cinched at the waist by a belt with a heavy silver buckle. His long-fingered hands were stained by blue ink and had patches of thick fur across the knuckles. Notably, he wore a pair of reading glasses with wide rectangles of glass within thin copper frames.

"That has to be Zale," I said.

"It's him," Reign confirmed.

Zale noticed us and hustled over. "Sorry . . . Rue . . . Rue said . . ." He bent slightly at the waist, panting. "Sorry. Need to catch . . . my breath."

"Did you run up three flights of stairs?" Risk asked.

"Yes. Sorry. Rue said . . . emergency?"

"Thank you. It's an emergency, all right! My name is Oli—"

"I know who you are, Oli." Zale wiped his sweaty forehead, accidentally transferring smudges of blue ink from his hand to his brow. "Risk tells me all about you."

"Really?" Not gonna lie: I was pleasantly surprised to learn that.

"She says you can read like that." He snapped. "Instantaneous textual understanding. If this weren't an emergency situation, I'd try to recruit you as a new scribe."

"Um, wow," I said. "I'm flattered. Speaking of your work—"

I glanced at Risk, as if searching for her approval. That was silly of me. She'd been the one to recommend Zale. Still, it strengthened my resolve when she nodded.

"Yes?" Zale asked, crossing his arms.

"How do you get the books from Earth?"

"Twice a month," he said, "my dad and older brother travel through the sun. They have a reliable supplier who sells them books. No questions asked."

"Have you ever visited Earth?" I asked.

He shrugged. "Once. It didn't go well. My dad's a wolf, but I'm wolf-coyote."

"What difference does that make?"

A quirk of his lips, not quite a smile. He removed his glasses and rubbed them clean using part of his shirt. "There aren't many wolves left on Earth, so Dad's weak up there, and he can only stay a dozen hours before he's transported back home. However, it turns out that I take after my mother. There's a bazillion coyotes on Earth, so I was stuck there for days. Spent most of the time in my true form, surviving off garbage and hiding under an abandoned factory. When I finally returned, my dad was so stressed, he swore I'd never step foot on Earth again. 'I looked all over for you,' he said. 'I went through the sun ten times. I thought you were killed by the King's knights.'"

"That must have been terrible for you both."

"Less so for me; the garbage I ate was from a really nice restaurant. I had fried chicken every night." He pointed at my chest with his index finger. "Why are you curious about books? Do you need something special from Earth? If it's a medical emergency, we've transcribed lots of anatomical and medical texts already. They're stored in the cliffside caverns. That's what the library of lifesaving knowledge is for."

"It's not the books he wants," Risk interrupted. She shooed his index finger away from me. "Cut that out. You're gonna get ink on Oli's nice shirt."

"Oh, sorry."

"We need to go to Earth," I explained, "because my best friend Ami is fading fast. His species is going extinct, and I'd like to know why."

Reign hunched over the sleeping puppies, as if subconsciously trying to shield them from the horrors of two worlds: here and there, inextricably tethered together.

"Extinction," Zale said. "I'm so sorry." That time, his apology sounded genuinely sympathetic.

"It hasn't happened yet. If I'm successful, it won't happen anytime soon."

"What do you expect to do up there?"

"Whatever I gotta do. Our question is: how does your father make the journey so often?"

"Tell him about the secret route," Risk encouraged.

"I'm not supposed to share that with anybody—"

"Please," I begged, clasping my hands together. "Will you make an exception to help Ami?"

Zale shook his head with amusement. "Of course," he said. "Just promise to keep it quiet."

NINA, AGE 16

Thursday 9:35 P.M. (NINA)

Our plan is working. Rosita's story already
makes more sense. I already ran through the
whole Lipan dictionary and am working on
Jicarilla.

Thursday 9:38 P.M. (NINA)

What time zone are you in? If it's morning, good
morning. If it's night, good night.

Thursday 9:45 P.M. (NINA)

Message me when you're free.

Friday 1:00 A.M. (MOM)

I'm six hours behind you (it's 7 P.M. in my slice of
Earth). Guess what. I just devoured the most
delicious bowl of vegetable stew. Truly, the galley
on this research vessel deserves to be recognized
as a 3-star Michelin restaurant. Wish you could join
me for dinner.

FRIDAY 1:11 A.M. (NINA)

>We ate soup from a can yesterday. I give it two stars.

FRIDAY 1:15 A.M. (MOM)

>Nina, go to sleep! Tomorrow is a school day! It's not quite summer yet.

FRIDAY 1:16 A.M. (NINA)

>I'm in bed, but I couldn't fall asleep.

FRIDAY 1:18 A.M. (MOM)

>Is everything ok?

FRIDAY 1:19 A.M. (NINA)

>Yeah. Just busy. Homework took all night, and then I had other projects.

FRIDAY 1:21 A.M. (MOM)

>You mean Rosita's story? Pace yourself. Creating a key might take years. It's hard work.

FRIDAY 1:22 A.M. (NINA)

>I do! And yeah. It took forever to learn pronunciation. I'm getting close, though. The story almost makes sense.

FRIDAY 1:25 A.M. (MOM)

>That's wonderful, but what's the rush? Why can't you do this on the weekend?

FRIDAY 1:26 A.M. (MOM)

>Grandma doesn't have years. Lately, she can't leave town without getting sick.

FRIDAY 1:26 A.M. (MOM)

>I don't understand the connection between your grandmother and this story.

FRIDAY 1:27 A.M. (NINA)

OK, so here's my current theory.

FRIDAY 1:29 A.M. (NINA)

There's something about Grandma's home that heals people. That's why Rosita lived so long. That's why Tightrope got better ridiculously fast. That's why the story includes the words "healer" and "homeland." That's why animal people (probablyyyy) hang out around Grandma's house.

FRIDAY 1:32 A.M. (NINA)

It makes sense, right? Grandma is skeptical because she gets scrapes and bruises that don't heal instantly but maybe the power is selective?

FRIDAY 1:33 A.M. (NINA)

I'm REALLY afraid that if we lose the story, we'll also lose info that can save her life.

FRIDAY 1:35 A.M. (MOM)

Is your grandmother doing poorly?

FRIDAY 1:37 A.M. (NINA)

Not right now. She's at home, though. What'll happen when she *has* to leave? You're always gone during hurricane season, so you don't see how worried Dad gets. He tries to hide it, but I notice.

FRIDAY 1:39 A.M. (MOM)

I'll talk to him later.

FRIDAY 1:40 A.M. (MOM)

Nina, have you ever witnessed one of Grandma's
sick spells?

FRIDAY 1:41 A.M. (NINA)

No. She told me about them.

FRIDAY 1:42 A.M. (MOM)

What did she tell you?

Nina typed: **Don't you believe her?**

Deleted.

Retyped: **Don't you believe me?**

Deleted.

Typed: **Do you remember the school play, the one
you couldn't see because you spend half the year in a
different time zone?**

Simply typing the words was enough to stifle the intense
surge of hurt, of resentment Nina felt. Calmer, she reworded the
message before sending it.

FRIDAY 1:46 A.M. (NINA)

Do you remember the last school play? Weeks ago.
Grandma couldn't be there. Only Dad saw me act.

FRIDAY 1:47 A.M. (MOM)

You were wonderful!! I watched your performance
livestream.

FRIDAY 1:48 A.M. (NINA)

OK, but that's not the point. I got sad, and the next
time we were together, I asked Grandma why she
couldn't be at the play.

Nina thought back on that day. They'd been in a car together, driving to the diner near Grandma's house. "You've never missed a play before," Nina had commented, trying to keep her tone light, unaccusatory. "Were you busy?"

Grandma responded so quickly, Nina wondered if the subject had already been on her mind.

"See, Nina, I've always felt strong at home," she said. "On the homeland, I sleep deeper. My mind is clear. I don't ache in the morning, and my steps are quick. You know, I was born where I now live. Things sometimes go full circle that way."

"Yes." They did.

"When I was young, that sense of wellness seemed like a side effect of familiarity. Why wouldn't I feel safer and more comfortable at home? So, I chalked it up to psychology and traveled freely. I even lived in Arkansas for twelve years. That's where I met your grandfather. He was a cook. Did you know that?"

"No," Nina said. "But I should have guessed. That's why his barbecues were the best."

"He loved to feed people," Grandma continued. "When your grandpa was hired as head chef at the Tex-Mex place downtown, we moved from Arkansas to Texas, and it was like taking a pill, a big painkiller. Again, I thanked psychology. New child. Steady job. We were living our dream. Of course I'd feel good. Even with the stress of debt and running a business, our life together was idyllic."

"It wasn't psychological, though."

"Yes. Now I know that." They were driving between two bare fields, abandoned farmland being reclaimed by wildflowers and spiny-leaved succulents. The sky, though sulking gray, didn't rain. "But it wasn't until recently that I realized I can't leave even if I need to. That if I try, I'll die."

"Grandma?"

"During your cousin's wedding in Iowa, I wanted—really wanted—to be there. That trip should have been simple. It's a direct route by train to Des Moines. I bought a ticket on the fast rail, but the farther it traveled, the faster my heart sped. Didn't even make it twenty minutes before I collapsed in the dining car. The pain in my chest was an explosion. Next thing I remember, I'm in an ambulance. Needle in my arm. Oxygen tubes in my nose—"

"*What?* That's horrible! Does Dad know it got so bad?"

"Nobody does. When they stuck me in the ambulance, they thought I was a goner. I felt peachy by the time we reached the hospital. Tests identified zero issues, so the doctors sent me home with the same old diagnosis: it's all in my mind."

"You should have said something!"

"And ruin the wedding? Nina, you oughtta know me better than that."

There were buzzards standing alongside the empty road, picking at something flat and furred. Nina lifted a hand to block the sight and didn't peek between her fingers. Some people rubbernecked when they passed fresh roadkill. Nina wasn't some people.

"So what now?" she asked.

"I recently did my own tests. Forty miles, and my heart skips beats. Fifty miles, and it races so fast, I can't stand. But if I stay near home, everything's fine. So . . . life will remain business as usual, I guess. With less traveling."

"Do you ever wonder," Nina mused, "if the doctors can't help 'cause they don't understand who you really are?"

"Hm. They're only human."

"Are we?"

"Of course," Grandma answered, "but that doesn't mean we can't be mysterious, too."

In the present day, Nina's thumbs remained poised over her smartphone screen; how could she convey the importance of that conversation through texts?

FRIDAY 1:48 A.M. (NINA)

Trust me. She genuinely gets sick.

FRIDAY 1:49 A.M. (MOM)

There must be health specialists she can visit. Like I told your father, if money is the issue, I can extend my contract another year.

FRIDAY 1:51 A.M. (NINA)

NO DONT. There are no specialists near her home and she can't travel!

FRIDAY 1:52 A.M. (NINA)

Like I said I have a plan!! Rosita's story may have clues to help us understand the power of this land. That's why its urgent! Someday, a hurricane is gonna hit her place full force. What are we supposed to do if Grandma cant evacuate?

FRIDAY 1:54 A.M. (MOM)

That's a question you should not contemplate in the middle of the night. Please go to sleep, Nina.

FRIDAY 1:55 A.M. (NINA)

OK. Love you.
FRIDAY 1:55 A.M. (MOM)
    Love you too!!!

Nina lowered her phone, stared at the ceiling for a minute, and then rolled out of bed. In her fleece onesie, she shuffled to her desk, where a Jicarilla-to-English dictionary lay open on pages 22–23. She'd work on the key for fifteen more minutes. Then, she'd go to sleep.

She was too close to stop now.

COTTONMOUTH HATCHES
A PLAN

We met again at sundown. The wait hadn't been easy. Since learning Ami's diagnosis, my sensitivity to the passage of time had increased. I was aware of every creeping minute and yet powerless to slow the march toward the demise of my friend. But Zale could not take us to the secret path through the sun until later.

"We can't travel to the mountain till nightfall," he'd explained. "That's when the foot traffic on the road clears up."

"Which mountain?" I'd wondered.

"One near the pseudosun."

That meant height. The greater the altitude, the easier the journey to Earth. "The fourth peak," I said.

"You guessed it!"

On clear days, from the right vantage point in the valley, you could see the mountain range: seven peaks, all tinged pale blue with distance, jutting skyward like fish teeth. The mountain range had a lovely, steplike symmetry. From east to west, the mountains' heights increased until the towering fourth peak, and then they decreased progressively.

"How will we reach it in one night?" I asked. All rivers, the quickest routes of travel, flowed away from the mountains.

"Easily! Ever ridden a motorized vehicle before?"

I groaned. "Briefly. It made me ill."

"This one won't," Zale promised. "Make sure to bring everything you need."

Four hours and twenty-six minutes: that's the amount of time I had to prepare to leave home for the unknown.

"The last time I left home," I confessed to Risk and Reign, "I almost died. Creator, give me strength." We'd returned to the valley. The sisters each snacked from little bags of blueberries, their lips stained purple.

"You mean two years ago?" Risk asked.

"When your momma chased you away?" Reign added.

"Yes."

"No offense to your momma," Risk said, "but she didn't give you any time to prepare. That's not happening here. You have hours to strategize with your clever brain."

"And you aren't alone," Reign added. "You think that alligator woman would have given you guff if me and Risk had been there as backup?"

"Yeah, yeah!" Risk chimed in. "And you know the clicking monster who chased you?"

"What about it?" I prompted.

"He would've been the one hiding in a tree if I'd been there."

"Earth has worse monsters," I worried. "That's where the Nightmare lives. If he or his followers learn about us, we're in trouble."

"The wolves have avoided those losers for generations," Risk assured me. "Zale's people have a group of human friends who monitor them. It's easy with technology like security cameras, keyword trackers, face recognition, chat monitoring, that kind of stuff. Right now, they say the King is in France, and his followers aren't planning a hunt or attack."

"France?"

"Across the ocean from our entry point. Honestly, the Nightmare King doesn't care about occasional world-jumpers either. He'll only kill us if we're conspicuous. He's got no problem with world-shapers who lie low. Secretly I bet he likes it. When we hide, it means he's winning, right? It means we're so scared, we play by his rules."

"Still . . . it's a risk. His followers aren't the only dangerous humans. Are you certain you want to come with me?" I asked. "You've already done so much to help."

Risk and Reign simultaneously burst into fits of high-pitched laughter. "Says the guy who is scared to wander off the cart path," Reign barked.

"Hey! I cut through the forest this morning."

"We know," Risk said. "But sometimes, it's like you don't know *us*."

"My sister didn't get her name 'cause she won't take risks."

"And if my sister cuts through the forest on an average day, think of what she'd do to save her friends."

"I know you're brave," I explained, "but our situations are

completely different. I'm just an isolated snake. Nobody depends on me to survive." *Not technically true anymore,* my inner realist interjected, but I pushed that realization aside. "Won't your pack object?"

"Nah. Reign and I always go our own way."

"Everyone knows we'll be back eventually."

"We should give Mom and Dad a heads-up, though. Warn them to distribute our chores."

Reign worried one corner of her pink cape between her fingers, squishing wrinkles into the gauzy fabric. "Oh, great. You know what the cousins will say. 'Why do your adventures always happen during laundry day?'"

I smiled at that. "All right. Do what you need to do. We can regroup here before sundown."

"In the meantime," Risk asked, "what are you doing, Oli?"

"Quick trip home for my travel clothes." I looked past the ring of food carts that circled the village center, where a group of children played in the shade of a five-hundred-year-old oak. Its lower branches had grown so long, they no longer grew upward. Instead, slumping under their own weight, they made a circle of wooden arches radiating from the great trunk. A square of bright red fabric emblazoned with a white patch, shaped like a starling in flight, hung from one branch. "First, I have a message to send."

The children, who'd been kicking around a large wicker ball, stopped playing as I approached the message tree. They parted around me, their curiosity mostly expressed as quick glances in my direction or side-eyed stares. I say "mostly" because the youngest coyote girl, who was smaller than the wicker ball, toddled beside me, staring up at my face, as if she'd never seen anybody like me before. "Hi," she said.

"Hel—Watch out!"

One of her bare feet wedged between an exposed root and the ground. As the child stumbled, I reached for her hand in a frantic attempt to prevent injury. But gravity acted with swiftness, and although I could move fast in my snake form, my fake form was comparably gangly and slow.

However, instead of landing on her face, the child dropped into a graceful somersault. Then, she hopped back upright, wobbling only slightly. "Oops."

"Are you okay?" I asked; now, I was the one staring with disbelief.

"Yah."

"By any chance, are you related to sisters named Risk and Reign?"

She snickered behind her hands, shook her head, and then scampered back to her group of friends. Not for the first time, I wondered how much of the twins' acrobatics was instinctual and how much was learned. Could be a mixture of both, I supposed. Like how I read well when I was a child, but learned to read extremely well with practice.

I'd known them for two years and never thought to ask whether they took tumbling lessons with a balance master in the valley. Sure, I'd sometimes remark, "How in the worlds did you do that?" after they pulled off an impressive move. But Risk would just shrug and respond with "I'm a coyote." And Reign would just laugh and dance for me, as if proving that her grace wasn't a one-time fluke.

Next time, I'd insist, "No, seriously. I'm curious."

Under the oak's boughs, the air was perceptively cooler. I looked up, searching for feathers among the leaves. "Excuse me! Is anybody available to deliver a message?"

A swallow dropped from the upper canopy, swooped over my toes, and circled my body in corkscrew loops. Then, she perched on a twig above my head. "How far?" she asked.

"The third mountain in the seven-peak range," I said. "There's a family of bounty hunters and investigators who work out of the caves."

"Too far," she twittered. "Sorry."

"Too far for a sparrow," said a familiar bird, "but not for me."

I turned and looked down at Brightest. As always, they were in their true form. "Hey there," I said.

"Hey to you. What's happening?"

"Ami's suffering 'cause of extinction—" I began, but Brightest ruffled their feathers.

"Yes. The healer and I talked. She says you've got impossible plans, and I disagree. As long as Ami is breathing, there's hope. So what can I do to help?"

I held out my arm. With a hop and two flaps of their wings, Brightest jumped on my offered perch, and I lifted them up to face level. "Tonight, we're taking a motorized vehicle to the fourth peak. The highest mountain. You know the one?"

"I do indeed."

"We're going to Earth. Um. On the other side, we'll need support—"

"Say no more." They patted my nose with their wing. "I'll come with you."

"That's great, but it's not exactly . . ." They tilted their head at me. "I need you to deliver a message to a bounty hunter trainee. Her family is based at the third mountain."

"I see. Is that third from the east or third from the west?"

"East," I said. "It's always from east to west. That's how people do things."

"Most people," they agreed.

"This is a long shot, but the bounty hunters are supposed to know humans on Earth, and according to Zale, we won't get far without human allies. Any chance you can beg the bounty hunters for help? We'll be at the fourth mountain by dawn, so there's not much time."

"I'll do my best. Oh! Question."

"Yes?" I encouraged.

"Will I need to be in my false form for the journey to Earth?"

"I . . . really don't know."

"Just in case, bring me something to wear?"

I couldn't stop myself from gaping, though my mouth only dropped open a couple centimeters. Trouble is, when the inside of your mouth is the color of fresh milk, it's hard to miss an incredulous jaw drop. Even a tiny one.

"What? What's wrong? I'll return your pants. I'm not a thief like the mockingbird."

"Sorry. It's not that. Of course I'll lend you an outfit. It's just . . . I've never seen your fake form. I was starting to wonder if you even had one."

They hopped from foot to foot, dancing in a jovial rhythm that reminded me of laughter. "Oh, yeah. I have one, but I don't like it. See my wings?" Their speckled wings, when stretched, exceeded the length of my arm.

"Uh-huh. They're difficult to miss."

"In my fake form, they grow out of my head. I have a pair of wings where my squishy round ear skin should be and, uh, ear holes behind them. Which is fine. Except . . . when I get, like, startled? Or when I forget I can't fly? My wings do this—" They flapped twice, powerfully; their grip on my arm tightened to prevent them from sailing into the air and colliding with an oak branch. "And that sends gusts of wind straight into my ear holes. Which hurts a lot, even when I got scraps of cotton shoved in them like dampeners. The movement also gives me a wicked headache."

"I'm sorry about that," I said.

"It is what it is." Brightest head-butted my cheek affectionately. "By the way, yellow is my favorite color, but I'll wear anything that doesn't itch too bad."

They winked at me. Then, Brightest glided to the ground, hop-ran out of the shadow of the tree, and shot into the air.

"Show-off," twittered the sparrow.

After leaving the message tree, I jogged straight to the forest. Once again, there'd be no time for the winding cart path. I sensed the minutes flowing forward, drawing me closer to something big. It pained me that I couldn't escape the current. Couldn't delay my inevitable arrival at the result of a million actions, whatever it would be.

All I could do was make the most of the time I had and hope that my actions mattered.

NINA, 3 DAYS
BEFORE LANDFALL

W ith some creative interpretation," Nina told the camera, "and a year of work, I've found meaning in the story." She held up the Jicarilla-to-English dictionary, her arms trembling with the strain. Nina's father had been able to purchase a "large-print" edition, which weighed twice as much as the "small-type" edition. In other words, Nina possessed a whopper of a book. She flopped it on her desk—*whump*—and flourished her notebook, showing the camera its label: *Rosita's story*. The notebook was now filled cover to cover with color-coded notes. Since beginning the translation project, she'd rediscovered her love of gel pens.

"I wish I could take all the credit for this progress, but my mom helped. First, she told me that Lipan Apache and Jicarilla Apache are similar languages. By that, I mean there are words that sound practically identical and other words that sound similar.

"See, when Rosita spoke, my translation app had no clue. It might contain a thousand different dialects, but not a one is Lipan. Not a one is Jicarilla. In fact, the app doesn't even understand Navajo, which is spoken by lots of people. That's why—instead of giving me an English script—my phone spat out nonsense. Strings of confusing vowels and consonants. It was the big barrier to understanding.

"So my mom—one time she was home, I think when I was fifteen—me and my mom started talking about the story. She's a translator, so all this"—Nina flapped the pages of her notebook for emphasis—"is professionally interesting, I bet. Mom said, 'It's like a puzzle. All we need is a key. Our own Rosetta stone.' Every Lipan word is linked to a specific series of app-generated letters. Well, that got me thinking: why can't I make my own key?

"Of course, I asked Mom, 'Is there a dictionary of Lipan words?' She thought a bit and then went, 'Yes, but it's very incomplete.' I asked for a copy, and she came through. It wasn't easy. You can't find our language in bookstores or libraries. Mom had to reach out to a tribal linguist, and he collected materials for her. She isn't part of the tribe like me or Dad, but Mom has a good way with people; she makes friends so easy. I wish I inherited that trait instead of her ingrown toenails.

"After working on my pronunciation, I recited the whole dictionary into the app and saved the output as an initial key. That part went fast. As I said, there weren't many words to run through. It helped interpret a few new phrases, though. *They—singular—hunted. They—plural—died. Their—plural—son.* I need to explain it that way because the Lipan language doesn't use gendered pronouns. There is no *he hunted* or *she hunted*. There's only, like, *they—singular—hunted*. We do have pronouns that indicate whether the plural version of *they* means two people or more than two people, though. I won't get into that now.

"Afterwards, I repeated the process using the Jicarilla dictionary, and . . . uh . . . that's been tedious." Nina patted her five-pound tome. "At least it's easy to read. Plus, once you make a key for core sounds, it's possible to narrow things down. By now, I think I've done enough work to understand Rosita's story. More or less.

"She told the story of a family. It begins with a man from afar—using context, I assume that's the Reflecting World—and a woman from Earth. They meet in the place of water, in the homeland, and have one son. The father has to go back and forth between worlds. The mother has to stay near the water. They make it work, and the son grows into an adult. In the story, he travels and does amazing things. He is a friend to animal people. Essentially, the son behaves like the spirit humans of the joined era. Like a legend.

"That's probably what makes him the target of hunters. I'm not clear what happens, but he—with his father—is killed on Earth. The woman remains on her homeland and raises an infant child—a daughter—alone.

"It's the last line that chills me. To paraphrase, Rosita said: 'Remain hidden here, or you
and your children
and their children
and their children
will also be prey of the nightmare.'"

Nina looked down at her hands, at her chewed-ragged fingernails and the mole on her wrist.

"Rosita heard that story from her mother," she said. "And I think the warning was personal. What else could it be?"

Exhaling slowly, as if meditating, Nina clenched her hands and focused on the tension in her muscles, trying to mentally push that strength outward, to exude magic—shouldn't it come naturally to the child of a child of a child of a child of a child of a spirit? If the story was her family's history, as she now believed, why couldn't Nina perform a miracle in front of her camera?

Truthfully, very little was known about human spirits. In the old stories, they sometimes participated in the adventures of animal people, but they were uncommon, and they all but vanished before the end of the joined era.

Nina didn't even know whether the magic trait could be inherited. Or if, like many elements from the Reflecting World, the trait was governed by dreamlike laws.

Move something, she thought. Or . . . *heal something*. She tensed her fists until her fingers ached. In the end, that's all that happened.

"Nifty," she said, "end video."

As if on cue, there was a knock on the door.

"Nina?" her father called. "Are you awake?"

That was a decent question. It was half past noon, but during the summer, Nina sometimes slept until 3:00 p.m. "I am! Come in!"

He cracked the door open, stepping inside. "Bad news," he said. "The latest predictions show Hurricane Jeremy-2 heading toward Grandma's house."

She rubbed her forehead, trying to will the dizziness away. "Huh? Didn't a hurricane just hit Louisiana?"

"Yep," he confirmed. "But this is a different one, and it's wild strong."

"How wild?"

He spread his arms as wide as they'd go. "They predict a category 5. But it's still early. At least three days till landfall. The weather people aren't even confident where it'll strike. To be safe, I'm gonna drive to Refuge County and board up Grandma's windows. Get her place ready."

"What if she has to evacuate?" Nina asked. "Grandma finally told you about the wedding incident, right?"

"Heck," he sighed. "She did. Let's cross that bridge if we must."

"And what if we must?"

"Nobody actually knows why she's ill. You got your ideas. Doctors have theirs. If the situation becomes dire, we'll try a calm evacuation. It might work."

"I hope so."

"Will you be okay while I'm gone? I'm closing shop, but somebody needs to be in the stockroom for a delivery at 4:00 p.m. I made chili and sourdough bread for supper."

"I'm almost seventeen. Don't worry."

He laughed. "Nina, we were literally just worrying about a seventy-something-year-old woman. With family, you always worry."

That was all too true. As they hugged goodbye, Nina said, "Drive safe." And her father promised to do his damnedest.

Returning to the computer desk, Nina settled into her

ergodynamic chair and said, "Nifty, show me the forecast for Hurricane Jeremy-2."

A weather map of the southern United States popped onto the screen. It displayed a bright swirl of red spinning across the Gulf, looping toward Texas.

The great eye pierced Refuge County.

COTTONMOUTH JOURNEYS TO THE FOURTH PEAK

*T*he last time I rode in a motorized vehicle, my siblings and I were visiting a traveling park. The park people set up wondrous mechanical contraptions in a clearing near the river. There were spinning chairs on seesaw levers, a tower of metal bars they painstakingly pieced together rung by rung, gigantic wheels you could run inside without actually moving an inch, and the big attraction: single-person railcars on a train track that circled the whole clearing.

There were only five cars, so my siblings rode the little train in groups. Straightaway, I volunteered to ride last, uninterested in bickering and shoving my way into the first group.

Turns out, I shouldn't have volunteered to ride at all. The bumps and rattling of the car, the disorienting blur of the scenery zipping past me, the sensation of moving so quickly without feeling the land beneath my feet or belly: all these factors, when combined, made my stomach clench and complain. I squeezed my eyes shut, but that just made the dizziness worse, especially since I tasted a cacophony of chemicals in the air hammering against my face. I couldn't switch to my true form without potentially losing my spectacles and clothes. So, before the train completed half a lap, I flung myself out of the car.

In briefer words, the last time I attempted to ride anything motorized, I tolerated a grand total of five minutes of travel. The drive to the mountain would take hours.

And despite Zale's reassurances that I'd be fine, the truck didn't seem capable of a smooth ride. After we met up at sunset—Risk, Reign, and I carrying knapsacks—Zale led us on a half-hour stroll to a wooden shed near the cart path. His father's truck, which was a beetle green shell of metal balanced on chunky black wheels, was parked inside. An array of tools and mechanical parts hung from hooks on the walls. The wrenches and gears cast bizarre geometric shadows as Zale swept his electric torch side to side, checking the shed for any unexpected people. It wasn't quite dark outside, but very little red-violet light filtered through the cracks in the wall's wooden slabs.

"My dearest one, how well can you operate this thing?" Risk asked Zale. I laughed; it was a purely startled response. I couldn't think of another time she'd uttered an affectionate term in my presence.

"What, Oli?" Risk demanded, squaring up. "Did you remember a funny joke? Want to share it?"

"No. I, uh, swallowed a fly."

She stared at me a second too long for comfort, a silent confirmation that my lie wasn't tricking anyone in that shed, and then turned back to Zale. "Sorry. What did you say?"

"I was going to say . . ." He considered the truck, shining the torch through the window hole. Briefly, the pale interior of the truck lit up, and it resembled a giant's lantern. "Pretty good? I've never driven all the way to the mountain. But I once handled the return trip when my father and brother were, uh, unwell. They ate bad fish on Earth and . . . let's just say they had to ride with their heads out the windows."

"In that case, we oughtta split the work," Risk said. "I'll drive everybody to the fourth mountain, and you can drive back home alone."

"You're practiced enough to do that?" he asked.

"Sure. Reign and I have traversed this land on everything from go-karts to motorcycles."

"Really?" I asked. "When we met, you had to borrow my shitty raft. When'd you get go-karts and motorcycles?"

"Borrowed them, too," Reign said, snickering.

"We even once drove a monster truck."

"A mechanical monster?" I asked, cringing. "That's horrific."

Risk smirked at me. Then, she wrestled open the squeaky door and sat in the driver's position. The cabin of the truck had a single long bench that had to be shared by the driver and all passengers. Risk rested her hands on a metal steering wheel. It was shaped like a ring with several evenly spaced, squat spokes. Like the sun, I thought. The wheel resembled a pictograph of the sun.

"Oh, no, Oli. It's not a real monster," Reign explained. Instead of going around the vehicle, she climbed over her sister and plopped on the far end of the cushioned bench.

"It's a giant truck humans build for the sole purpose of crushing littler trucks," Risk continued. "As sport."

"When we were still pups, my great-uncle rode one straight into camp. He said, 'I stole this from Earth, so everybody take a spin while it lasts.' Me and Risk fought cousins twice our size to drive it first.'"

"I almost lost a tooth."

"She did! Worth it, though. The aunties were shouting, 'Stop wrestling. Settle down. You'll all have a chance.' But that wasn't true. The monster truck ran out of gas. Half our cousins missed out."

"Including the guy who elbowed my mouth."

"Serves him right," Zale said, loading our bags in the back of the truck. Then, he passed Risk an hexagonal medallion dangling from a beaded lanyard. "Fit that in the starter, and turn one-eighty degrees," he instructed. "That'll unlock the spinner. And promise me that you won't crash. Dad built this truck by hand. Designed every piece using blueprints from Earth and one-of-a-kind Reflecting World tech."

"I'll be careful," Risk promised.

"Appreciate it." Zale sat in the middle spot, awkwardly folding his long legs in the woefully small gap between the dash and his seat. "Don't forget your seat belts, okay?"

That's when I noticed a big problem. "Where should I sit?" There wasn't an additional bench, and Zale was squished hip to hip between the sisters.

"Around my arm?" Reign offered. "There's plenty of room for a snake!"

I cringed, shaking my head. "I'll take the back."

"Wouldn't recommend sitting in the cargo bed if you get sick on kiddie trains," Risk warned.

"Sorry," Zale said. "I can't trade because I need to sit up front to supervise."

"Oh, fine." Reign didn't bother to open the door; she climbed headfirst out the window, dropped into a hand-stand, hand-walked forward, and then flipped upright. "I like to feel the wind on my face, anyway."

"Thank you," I said, genuinely relieved I wouldn't need to switch forms in front of so many people. Too often, limbed creatures treated my change like a spectacle, oohing and aaahing as my false limbs sucked into my elongating body. Reign didn't have that problem. As I took my seat, strapping the leather belt across my waist, I noticed a flash of gray-brown fur through the open window behind my head. Then, Reign stuck her long canid snout through the gap. One cape, a bright sky blue, was still draped across her true form.

"Let's ride."

I watched as Risk inserted the medallion into the hexagonal indentation. A thunk rang out from deep within the truck. Then, she put her hand on a crank protruding from the dash. "How many revolutions will it take to start the motor?" she asked.

"About ten," Zale said. Then he ducked his head, hiding a smile behind his hand. "But that varies depending on speed. For example, my great-grandmother drove once. She turned the crank so gently, it took at least one hundred revolutions to start. Maybe more. I stopped counting after minutes of this." With precise, excruciatingly slow movements, he mimed turning a hand crank.

"I can do it in eight," Risk promised. Then, she proved

herself. The crank whirred vehemently with each revolution. I counted seven distinct whirs before the truck began to vibrate, its belly emitting a low hum that resembled a gnat's busy wings. We rolled forward; at the first shudder of movement, I grasped the belt across my lap so tightly, the leather bit into my fingers. At a walking pace, the truck crept from the shed and turned onto the cart path. I squinted in an attempt to see. The path was so narrow, any deviation to the left or to the right would send us into the shrubs. And although the truck was open to the sky, leafy trees blocked most of the moonlight. I struggled to make out a single detail of my surroundings.

"How can you drive with no light?" I asked. "Are your eyes really that good?"

"There's plenty of light." Risk kicked at a pedal; I heard a thunk under her booted foot. Then, the truck lurched forward and began to accelerate.

"Wish you could see the world like we do," Reign commented from behind my ear.

"Don't pity the snake. He has sensory advantages." Risk flicked her tongue, demonstrating.

"My senses don't make this any less terrifying," I muttered. I tasted the air, my tongue capturing a medley of earthy, floral, and metallic scents. In a disorienting sequence, they swirled and clashed; only the mechanical aura of the truck remained constant. "Oh, it's worse. It's so much worse." I snapped my mouth shut and pursed my lips to seal out the air.

"It's a straight path," Zale reassured me. "Very easy to travel."

"How long is the trip again?" I wondered.

"Depends on speed. We can go fast and get there in a couple hours. Slow will take four. Either way, nobody can climb the mountain until morning since the guides will be sleeping."

"What do you think, Oli?" Reign asked. "You're the only truck-shy person here."

The truck lurched over a bump in the road. As it bucked upward, my body squished against the bench, but on the way down, I felt weightless. Only the seat belt prevented me from sailing up into the air.

"I've made my choice," I said. "Slow down."

"Bad news," Risk said. "This is the slow speed."

I clutched the edge of the window and steeled myself for a bumpy four hours.

"Let's talk logistics," I said after a while. "How long were you stuck on Earth, Zale?"

"Hmmm. Six days and a little extra."

"We can plan to be up there a minimum of six days, then. My ally, Brightest, wants to journey through the sun, too. They're a hawk. Are they doing well on Earth?"

"It depends on the species, Oli," Reign said. Her voice was muffled; I turned in my seat, squinting, and made out her silhouette near the back of the truck bed. "Some hawks are going extinct also, you know," she continued. "But probably not your friend. They're too chipper. Plus, they can transform, right?"

"Evidently."

"In that case, I wager they'll last six days, too."

"Right. Okay." We had six days. But what about Ami? Did

he have the luxury of six days? "On Earth, we need to find two things as soon as possible: shelter and a human to assist in our investigation."

"Why do we need the second one?" Risk mused, half-smiling.

"Earth is their home. It's where they're influential, powerful."

Reign raised her pointy index finger. "You know what else is powerful? Money! Great-Uncle says money is the best way to get stuff on Earth. You could buy almost anything."

"Yeah, but who would we pay to stop extinction? Is that even possible? Even if we had a whole bucket of coins, we need human guidance."

"Fair enough," she agreed. "So if your bounty hunter plan falls through, how do we find a friendly one?"

"I . . . don't know." Another bump in the road shook the truck; this time, I was ready for it, so I did not flinch. "We have four hours to make a backup plan."

NINA, 3 DAYS
BEFORE LANDFALL

*N*ight had fallen and taken root by the time Nina got an update from her father. "I'm definitely staying overnight," he said. "It'll take a lot of work to make your grandmother's house safe this time. She's got so much stuff. Be ready to go when I return. We oughtta drive north, just in case. Please take out the garbage before locking up."

Although it was farther inland than Grandma's house, the bookshop—and their apartment above it—was still in the predicted path of Hurricane Jeremy-2. Nina and her family typically waited out bad storms in a roadside inn near Austin. It had among the best continental breakfasts in Texas: grits, home fries, fresh fruit, and buttermilk pancakes with genuine, tapped-from-the-tree maple syrup.

Warding away bad thoughts with memories of pancakes, Nina heaved a black bag of garbage through the house and into the alley. There, she chucked it into a half-full metal bin, the lid closing with a thunderous *CLNG*. Light raindrops dusted her bare arms and brow; to escape a soaking, she reentered the building through the alley door, which led to an inventory room. Cardboard boxes of used books were stacked along the walls, and a wooden table was piled with graphing notebooks containing handwritten lists of the title, condition, ISBN number, and price of each book her father decided to sell. Only a small fraction of the inventory ended up on the store shelves. Nina didn't know what happened to the rejects. She imagined some were donated, while others were recycled.

After removing her tennis shoes and shaking excess raindrops onto the welcome mat in the doorway, Nina turned on the yellow overhead light, locked up, and took a deep, stress-fighting breath. She loved the smell of the room: old paper and suggestions of the books' former homes. Candles, perfume, spices, smoke, air freshener, coffee. As if each used book carried the ghost of whatever library or drawing room it had come from.

Overhead, trapped in the second-floor apartment, Tightrope meowed plaintively. It was his "You're home. Why aren't you feeding me?" cry for attention.

"Hang in there, Tightrope!" Nina shouted. After throwing her jean jacket on a coat-and-hat rack, she hustled to the stairwell. The stairs ended at a white door; during work hours, it remained locked to prevent lost shoppers from wandering into the living room. As Nina stepped onto the upper landing, she heard gentle scratch-scratch-scratching—her cat pawing for attention on the other side of the door.

Nina wasn't sure about nine lives, but Tightrope had at least two.

The kitten head-butted Nina's legs until she acknowledged him with a scratch on the head. At that, he purred so adamantly, his whole body vibrated. That was the way he was: aggressively cuddly. Lanky and black, with eyes like rings of yellow glass, Tightrope enjoyed sprawling over shoulders—especially when it was way too hot for a purring scarf—or curling into a ball on her lap.

Now, he made figure eights around Nina's legs as she entered the apartment. "Hey, sweetie," she greeted. "You need to eat fast tonight. Will that be a problem? No?"

In response, after Nina spooned half a can of wet cat food into his bowl, Tightrope shoved his face into the brown glop and devoured it in quick bites. He always ate like somebody would steal his meal if he took a break to breathe. Nina pulled his carrier out of the storage closet and folded clean baby blankets inside the mesh-lined pod. "Cozy," she said. "You'll sleep well in—"

Suddenly, his whiskers still messy with dinner, Tightrope scrambled out of the kitchen, across the living room, and behind the couch. "Aw, no!" Nina cooed. "Did you bite your tongue? What's wrong, little guy?"

That's when she heard the knocks. *THUD. THUD. THUD.* Somebody was pounding on the door downstairs. Was it her father? He wasn't supposed to be back tonight . . .

Nina's phone was so low on power, it wouldn't turn on; she plugged it into the charger near the television. Then, she crouched between the sofa and TV stand, waiting for the low-battery icon on her screen to stop blinking, and listening to bursts of *THUD THUD THUD*. There was a doorbell near the side door, but the noisemaker didn't seem to notice it. That meant they probably weren't her father. Could be a neighbor in need of help.

The window in Nina's bedroom overlooked the alley. She could peek outside and check.

"Stay," Nina hissed at Tightrope. Sometimes, the optimist in her half-believed that he obeyed her commands. To his credit, Tightrope did not budge from the narrow passage between the sofa and the wall.

Nina relocated to her bedroom and pushed one edge of the rainbow curtains aside, half-dreading the person she'd see below her window. Thing was, there wasn't a *single* person in the alley: there were two. Or three? Hard to tell from her vantage point. Nina ducked down before anyone could notice her. What were they doing outside the shop? It was a miserable, rainy night before the year's worst hurricane. She ought to ignore them.

THUD, THUD, THUD!

They were knocking; then, a high-pitched voice yelped, "Bookseller? Hello, bookseller?" The knocking started back up again, convincing Nina that she should go downstairs and tell them to scram. It'd be fine; Nina didn't even have to open the door, which was heavy and well reinforced in order to discourage break-ins.

Taking the stairs two at a time, she was nearly at ground level when the *THUD, THUD, THUD* culminated in a *thunk!* of the door swinging open and hitting the wall. They'd unlocked it! Nina couldn't slow her downward momentum; she stumbled into the inventory room. There, in the open doorway, stood three strangers: twin siblings with heart-shaped faces, sharp overbites, and manes of wavy hair; and a young man with a hawk on his shoulder. They were all younger-looking than Nina had expected; she wouldn't have been surprised to find them at her high school. Except she hadn't seen them at school. She hadn't seen them anywhere before.

The guy with the hawk gingerly stepped around his friends. He exchanged his sunglasses for a pair of wire-framed round spectacles. His eyes were deep brown with diamond-shaped pupils; he had shiny brown scales instead of eyebrows. "Please don't be too angry," he said. "We desperately need your help."

COTTONMOUTH MEETS
AN ORIGINATOR

*D*uring the last section of the drive, we turned off the cart path and onto a well-worn dirt road. "My family made this road," Zale explained. "Generations ago. Back when we used a wagon to tote the books home. It was tricky. Ten wolves had to pull the wagon, and one trip could take a day or more. That's one reason why Dad built the truck."

"What are the other reasons?" I asked.

Zale pointed with his nose at Reign, who was panting happily into the wind. "Going fast is fun."

"You've never hit anybody? Or crashed?"

"Never," he said. "People expect us, sense the truck coming. Plus, the path is ours at night." He paused, making a thoughtful hum. "I do worry, though. There's a first time for everything."

"You ought to return to the old ways," Reign said, "and only use this beast for emergencies."

"Problem is, there aren't ten young wolves left in the pack," he explained. "The survivors on the last team of pullers . . . well, they're elders."

"I'd help," Reign promised.

"Coyotes pulling book wagons," Risk added, laughing. "How many of us would that take? Fifty?"

"Oli would also help."

"Careful who you volunteer. I doubt I could drag half a book down the cart path." I tried to imagine a snake-drawn wagon. The attempt didn't pan out.

"It's fine," Zale said. "Our truck does the job."

We slipped into silence. On the horizon, the mountain range resembled a jagged black wall with no end. As we drove closer to the fourth mountain, the indistinct blackness seemed to eat the sky.

"We can wait here till sunrise," Zale said, pointing to a camp-site off the road. Risk rolled into the clearing, parking near a stone firepit. When she removed the hexagonal medallion, the truck fell silent. We'd stopped in a patch of footstep-hardened dirt, wiry grasses, and any weed that could survive the site's frequent use. I tasted fresh water in the air, dew and a nearby spring. The mountain was far enough that I could see its white-speckled peak, but near enough to protect us from the wind.

"It's warm back here," Reign offered. She was curled between two knapsacks, her nose resting on her tail. Risk and Zale joined her in the cargo bed by climbing straight through the back window.

"I'll sleep on the bench," I said.

But that was untrue; I didn't sleep at all. I had a persistent, terrible feeling that Ami would die in the night. He'd die among strangers. Alone. Or maybe he'd die tomorrow, when all his friends were in a different world.

I wondered if we were in denial. Was I abandoning Ami when he needed me most? Harming instead of helping?

The pseudosun rose in front of the fourth mountain a little while later, bathing its craggy face in a golden brightness. After drinking our fill in a nearby stream and snacking on dried fruit and fish, we climbed back into the truck. Everyone was quiet, as if subdued by the earliness or by the journey ahead. As Risk drove, I looked up through the sunroof.

"What are you doing?" Reign wondered. She'd transformed back into her false form and was sitting with her back propped against a mound of supplies.

"Looking for Brightest," I said. "They promised to meet us at the mountain. My eyes aren't the sharpest . . ."

"There's a bird." She pointed at a low-flying black silhouette. "But I think they're a starling. Hello!"

The silhouette dropped into fleeting vertical dive and then zipped upward again, as if pulled by an invisible elastic string. They were either hunting bugs for breakfast or greeting us with acrobatics.

"Our big plan hinges on human assistance. Ideally the bounty hunter's contacts," Risk griped. "If Brightest doesn't materialize soon, do we wait for them?"

"There isn't time—" I paused, allowing my surge of anxiety to settle. "They'll find us. Brightest cares about Ami, too. But . . . if we need to go ahead without the contacts, we'll improvise. There's always the bookshop humans, right, Zale? Can we trust them?"

"Yes, but there's one problem," Zale fretted. "We have a very nice arrangement. They pretend to think we're human, and we pretend that we don't know that they do know that we aren't . . . wait. I'm confusing myself."

"Can we trust them or not?" Risk asked, snickering.

"Uh huh." He sniffed. "The bookstore family's safe. Around others, though? You must pretend to be humans. Convincingly. Can you do that?"

"Sure can," Reign promised. "As you know, Oli reads books about humans every week. And my sister and I know a lot about Earth 'cause of our great-uncle. He's a daredevil, always finding ways to visit the place. I even invited him help save Ami, since he has experience going on adventures, but his hind leg is bothering him—"

"Honestly," Risk interrupted, "that's for the best. He tells a good story, but do you seriously believe that he's Earth's greatest magician, beloved by millions?" She deepened her voice and freed her hair from the thin leather rope binding it into a ponytail. "Fellow humans, behold!" Risk snapped the rope in half with a quick pull and held the two segments over her head. "Has this ever happened to you? I have the perfect solution. Magic!" With a clap, she snapped her hands together, crushing the leather between them. When she opened her hands, the rope was whole again.

Zale and I applauded.

"Yep," Reign answered, nonplussed. "Why not believe him?"

"Because if our great-uncle habitually transformed trailer homes into skyscrapers, or lassoed tornadoes, his grandstanding would attract the King so fast. When it comes to that guy's cult of murderers, no disappearing act could save Great-Uncle's hide."

"Risk has a point," Zale interjected. "If you have to use a major act of world-shaping, keep in mind that it'll make you a target for the Nightmare King. Fortunately, he never leaves Earth, and his response time is slow. These days, his human followers do most of his dirty work. They can be dangerous, too, but you'll survive, as long as you're secretive."

"Has your pack ever met them?" I asked.

"Thank Creator, no." He hummed softly; the sound resembled an anxious whine. Outside, a dozen long, black-tipped ears popped out of the grass, alerted by the rumble of our truck. Six young hares gathered alongside the road to watch us pass. In their true forms, they had to stand on their hind legs to get a clear view; Zale waited until their inquisitive faces were behind us to continue his story. "But we know—knew—people who drew the Nightmare's attention. They were knowledge seekers. A multispecies clan with a shared goal to understand Earth. Observers, really. For a long time, they were able to visit without trouble.

"Then . . . one member, a fox, made a mistake. She was observing life in a city when an earthquake struck. Right in front of her, a building crumbled with half its residents inside. She said she could hear cries within the earth. People pleading. They were too desperate to ignore.

"When the fox did not return to the clan's rendezvous point that evening, her friends journeyed to the city. They found her there, with her furred ears uncovered and tipped toward the ground. She'd been helping a rescue effort all day. News crews filmed her; reporters exclaimed, 'A spirit has returned to Earth to save our families.' Her clan was heartbroken because they knew that the Nightmare King—or his so-called human knights—would see the reports. They also knew that their friend would rather die than abandon the voices calling her from below.

"So the clan's moose and elk people used their great strength to lift slabs of rubble. The clan's fish people sent sips of fresh water to thirsty people who were trapped underground. The bird people cleared dust from the air. The coyote people helped the fox woman listen for signs of life. They worked all night; some members of the clan did so much world-shaping, they burned through their time on Earth and were safely transported home. But the others? The ones who remained until sunrise? They became sick. Deathly. Most, including the fox woman, died on an alien world."

The cry tore from my mouth. "Why? How?" The Nightmare was a human spirit, possibly the last living originator, but he couldn't cause people to spontaneously die. He was simply immortal, and seemingly unkillable. That said, Earth's weapons could be deadlier than offensive feats of world shaping, and he had thousands of human supporters to back his cause.

"It's believed that the King's followers poisoned them." Zale looked at Risk. "Be careful. Promise me."

"We will," she said.

For another ten minutes, we drove down the winding path. I felt a familiar dizziness pulse behind my eyes; apparently, my vehicle sickness only flared when the vehicle was chugging around extreme loops and turns.

"Almost there," Zale reassured me, perhaps noticing my ill-looking complexion. I could see the top half of my face in the rearview mirror, a rectangular strip of high-polished silver attached to the truck's frame. The color of my scales popped as the blood seeped out of my surrounding face.

Mercifully, it wasn't long before we reached the literal end of the road. It simply stopped at the mountainside. Before us, the land—formerly bumpy but now relatively flat—shot upward in bursts of brush-scruffy, rocky inclines. The distant peak was white with snow. Reign helped me out of the truck, since my legs were wobbly with vehicle sickness, and walked me toward an outcropping of stone. There, we sat together, enjoying the building warmth of morning, while Zale and Risk unloaded the knapsacks.

"You look nice today," I said. "But different. I've never seen those clothes before."

"That's because they aren't mine." Reign stood, her arms spread, and did a slow turn. She wore a knee-long woven tunic with leather leggings and boots. The deep red and soft yellow of the tunic reminded me of the sun over the desert. "Mom lent me her second favorite set of adventuring clothes. Risk got her first favorite, but that's because she likes blues more than I do."

Sure enough, Risk's outfit was similar to Reign's. Except instead of red and yellow, her tunic was black-blue and bright sky blue.

"I hope humans still wear stuff like this," Reign said, returning to her seat beside me. "Mom swears they do, but she got all her info from Great-Grandpa, and he hasn't been to Earth since, uh, a hundred years ago?"

"In the state of Texas," Zale said, joining us with a bag on each shoulder, "which is where you'll land, if all goes according to plan, humans wear lots of different styles. What you're all wearing will be fine. But if you want to really blend in, find a pair of jeans and a T-shirt. Also, don't go barefoot in your false form. They pave every walking inch of their cities, and that material—especially the black kind—gets griddle hot."

"I hope Brightest can fit into the sandals I brought them," I said.

"They can always fly and ride on our shoulders," Risk said. "Seems to be their preferred way to get around. Speaking of, have you noticed a hawk in the sky? Because we need to leave."

We all looked up. The sky was empty, with no cloud or Brightest in sight.

"Let's give them five more minutes," I suggested.

Time passed, pulling us closer to the result of all our choices, including the one to wait or leave. Should we give them five more minutes? Ten more? Or should we leave?

"What do you think?" I asked.

The sisters looked at each other, and judging by their uncertain expressions, they were unanimously undecided. "Let's go," Risk said. She spoke quickly, firmly, as if ripping off a bandage.

"Yeah," Reign agreed, glancing at the sky. "Yeah."

"Okay," I said. "What's next, Zale?"

He jogged back to the truck and removed a wooden box from the cargo bed. Zale wiggled the tight lid off the box; inside was a handheld drum, rawhide stretched over a round frame. It came with a single drumstick, a sturdy wooden stick with an egg-shaped leather head.

"This is what my father told me before we journeyed through the sun," he said. "It's important, so pay attention." He seemed to direct that statement at Reign. She smiled sweetly at him, flourishing her right hand in a motion that seemed to say: proceed.

"First things first: that big round circle in the sky isn't really the sun. We just wish it could be the sun, I guess. But no. It's a passageway. Only bright because the Earth is bright. Dark because the Earth is dark. And vast because . . ."

He pointed at me.

"Because the Earth is vast?"

"That's right. Guess what else the Earth is."

"A spheroid with a core of iron."

"Uh. Correct. But I was hoping for the word *moving*. The sunny passage rises in the morning and sets in the evening because, like the Earth, our world is always moving. And that makes things tricky. During our journey, everything has to be choreographed perfectly. Timing. Direction. Otherwise, we could land in the middle of a highway in Houston. And if you think Dad's truck goes fast, wait until you see the vehicles on a highway."

"Has that mistake ever happened before?" Risk asked.

"Not for a long time. We tend to land on the same patch of isolated land; it must have an anomalously strong pull. But, especially when the ancestral packs were perfecting this technique, there were slipups. People would get lost and reappear with bullet wounds or snares around their hands. Once, a scribe died on Earth because she dropped into a flooded river."

"It's dangerous," Risk summarized. "We're prepared."

"When we reach the peak, do exactly what the guides say, and it'll be all right."

"Okay," I said. "Where are the guides?"

Zale stared hard at the mountainside. "Never can see them," he said. "But they'll come. They always do." Then, he cradled the drum in the crook of one arm and readied the drumstick. In rapid succession, he beat the drum five times. Waited a second. Beat it twice, more slowly. Waited. Then five more quick beats.

THNK-THNK-THNK-THNK-THNK

THNK, THNK

THNK-THNK-THNK-THNK-THNK

The resonant sound dispersed around us, echoing off the mountainside and then swallowed by the sky. "Look at the mountain," Zale said. He lowered the drum, moved to stand beside Risk, and pointed at the craggy incline.

It was the movement that drew my attention. High above us, bodies emerged from the landscape of weathered shrubs and uneven gray stone. A herd of bighorn sheep, all in their true forms, had been within sight the whole time. Except for a pair of tiny yearlings, the sheep were imposing. Their paired horns ranged from narrow, slightly bent points, to weighty curls spiraling out from either side of the head. So why hadn't I noticed them?

"Where'd they come from?" I asked. "Were they in a secret cave?"

Reign snickered. "Sheep in a cave, Oli? Really?"

"Hey, anyone could be in a cave." Distracted by her teasing, I looked away from the bighorns for a second. That's all it took to lose sight of them. For a moment, I skimmed the mountainside in confusion. Then, the quick movement of a hoofed foot attracted my attention. They were exceptionally well camouflaged.

"Oh," I said, feeling extremely naïve. "That explains it."

Near the base of the mountain, the herd stopped. The adults surrounded the babies in a protective ring and then bowed their horned heads together, conferring in private. Snippets of a hushed conversation drifted toward us, though I couldn't make out full words. Reign tilted her head; her right ear twitched. "What are they saying?" Risk whispered. Although the twins had similar-looking fake forms, when they stood side by side, it was obvious that Reign's ears were larger and more canid. In fact, every lingering coyote trait—from their claws to the fur down the backs of their hands—was amplified in Reign. That puzzled me. Nobody could consciously control the details of their fake forms. For example, I couldn't will my white tongue to turn red. Couldn't reduce the number of scales on my face. Why, then, did Reign look more coyote-like than Risk? Could it be a function of their personalities? Or was the whole thing random?

"I think they're annoyed," Reign said. "They weren't expecting anyone to ascend the mountain today."

The largest bighorn, who could probably pull an entire book cart by himself, raised his head. His horns were two tight coils of spirals, as if they'd been growing for many lifetimes. None of the other bighorns could compare. With a loud snort, he loped over to us. His back hooves knocked loose a tiny avalanche of pebbles with every powerful kick. Still gaining momentum, he crossed the strip of grass between the truck and the mountain and barreled toward us. I stepped back, reaching for the sisters, as if I could save them from a collision with four hundred pounds of muscle and wiry gray fur. But, as my fingertips brushed Reign's sleeve, the bighorn skidded to a stop.

"Kuh-chu!" Reign sneezed, squinting against the cloud of fine dust his stop had launched into the air. Risk took three big steps, moving out of the sneeze zone. Her face went blank, as if she were so unimpressed by the bighorn's show of speed and agility, she couldn't even muster the energy for a visible emotional response.

"A viper?" the bighorn rumbled. He had golden eyes with horizontal pupils; at the moment, they were focused on me.

"Yes. My name is Oli."

"Why are you here?"

"To journey through the sun," I said. "Sorry for the short notice, but—"

"Excuse me," Zale interrupted, shuffling between me and the bighorn. "He's my friend. The sisters are, too."

"Where's your father?"

"Not involved." He tucked his chin, a sign of respect. "This isn't a typical book run. My friends need to visit Earth, and your route is the safest."

The bighorn snorted. "We only help wolves. No coyotes. Never again. In fact, those two"——he bowed his head to point at the sisters with his horns—"bear a striking resemblance to the rabid coyote man who exploited our hospitality to steal a monster truck. Frivolous creatures."

"I'm a wolf," Zale said.

"You're a hybrid, and your father forbade you from traveling through the sun, if I recall."

"How could anybody forget that?" shouted a bighorn woman. During the course of our conversation, the huddle had crept ever closer, and now stood on flat land, well within eavesdropping distance. "We spent a week sending your papa back to Earth. Each trip, he looked a little sadder. We all thought you'd died."

"I promised my father I would not set foot on Earth again," Zale said, "and intend to honor my word. Only my companions will make the journey today."

"Why?" Again, the extra big bighorn looked at me. "What motivates you?"

"My friend is very sick," I said. "This is the only possible way to save his life."

"Is that so? What do you expect to find, viper, that cannot be obtained from our own healers? What possible medicine or treatment?"

"I expect to find the disease that is killing him."

The bighorn nodded his heavy head and then returned to his group at an unhurried trot. "Come," he called back. "Bring your supplies."

I shouldered my bag, and the sisters each grabbed a knapsack. Then, single file, we followed the sheep around the mountain. The terrain was fairly level. However, we barely kept pace with our guides. Even the yearlings were more agile than I was. I wasn't surprised; a single misstep could lead to death on the steep inclines of the fourth peak. Their home was also their greatest challenge.

After traveling for half an hour, we came upon a statue: a gigantic bighorn sheep emerging from the mountain itself. Its body was furred with desert brush, its face etched from gray stone. Each horn was the bright yellow-gold of jasper, and white moss grew down its nose. Dewdrops moistened the crease of its mouth. If I hadn't known better, I might have mistaken the statue for an animal. Just like I'd mistaken the herd for the land. It still amazed me how effortlessly the sheep had blended into the mountainside.

Then, the statue—thirty feet tall, heavier than a boulder—turned and opened its eyes.

I don't remember whether I screamed out loud, but I guarantee my mouth dropped open, because Reign poked my cheek until I closed it.

"Grandpa, Grandpa!" The yearlings danced around the stone sheep's legs. With a crack that sounded like the splitting of a tectonic plate, their "grandpa" lowered his head until his brow nearly scraped the ground, and allowed the babies to playfully head-butt his horns. They tired out after a half dozen charges, and returned to the safety of the herd.

"Is he an originator?" I whispered to Zale.

"Yes."

We were meeting one of the first bighorn people. Born the day his species came into existence. More ancient and powerful than I could conceive. Capable of living in both worlds, a bridge of creation. The originator raised his head and took a step forward. More of his body appeared, as if emerging from a fluid surface that just resembled stone. Soon, only his hind legs and tail were still within the mountain. I wondered if he were tethered to it somehow. Bound to the body of the highest peak in the land. Or maybe he chose to be materially connected to his home.

"Our friends want to ascend, Grandfather," the leader of the herd explained. He spoke deferentially, but warmly, as if addressing an elder member of his family. "Will you help them?"

The originator bighorn snorted; a puff of fine gray dust blew from his nostrils. Then, he lowered his head toward us.

"Does he want us to do this?" Reign gently head-butted her sister, forehead to forehead.

"No," Risk said. "Don't even play. His horns would crack our heads open."

"He's agreed to help you," Zale explained. "Climb on his back. Just watch your step."

To demonstrate, Zale approached the originator bighorn, whispered a thank-you into his ear, and crawled up the stony slope of his neck.

"Oh, thank you, Grandfather!" Reign exclaimed.

"Thank you," Risk agreed.

The sisters delicately followed Zale. The originator was so large, they could sit side by side between his shoulder bones. Identical sagebrush bushes grew from either side of his front legs and his back haunches. Upon noticing them, I wondered: were the roots of the plants skin deep, or did they grow throughout his body like veins? Either way, they were part of him. The sisters held the sagebrush trunks for balance and beckoned to me with their free hands. "Come on, Oli," Reign urged. "We'll help you up."

I can't say the originator frightened me. No. His eyes were too gentle for that. He looked at me the same way he looked at the yearlings. I suppose, we were all infants compared to him. Fragile and new. But I did hesitate. He was probably the wisest, most powerful person I'd ever meet.

In front of the originator, I knelt and said, "Thank you." Part of me wanted to ask, "Are you sure we're worth your time? Why are you helping us? We're strangers. We're nobodies. You have the strength and memory of the mountain. You've probably seen a million cottonmouths and coyotes live and die. Witnessed extinctions, the birth of species. But you're willing to carry us up a mountain?"

As if privy to my thoughts, the originator nudged my hand with his left horn. Then, with a voice deeper and more resonant than the quaking earth, he said, "Anytime."

Risk and Reign took my hands and pulled me between them. We linked arms so they could steady me as the originator stood. His movement was fluid, but quick; he might resemble a statue, but he had the grace of his kind. I also noticed that the originator's warmth, which radiated through his stone-tough skin and coat of desert grasses, was more intense than the heat of my basking rock. Perhaps, like the Earth, his heart was a pool of molten iron.

"Hold on!" Zale called. The sisters tightened their grip on the sagebrush bushes.

Suddenly, I lurched forward as something crashed into my shoulder. It took me a moment to recognize the familiar grip of hawk talons.

"You made it!" I cried out. "Hey, everyone! It's Brightest!"

"Sorry about the lateness," they said. "Long story. I have good news and ba—aaaAAAAK!"

The originator shot up the mountain. Brightest flapped their wings, trying to remain on my shoulder.

"What's happening?" they screeched.

"We're going to the top." I had to shout to be heard over the wind in our ears.

With long, smooth strides, the originator rapidly gained elevation. I turned to nod goodbye to the herd, but they'd either left, or blended into the landscape. "Brightest," I said, "you had us worried!"

They huddled against my neck, finally balanced enough to stop battering the air. "You won't believe this. Guess who I encountered on the way here."

"Your cousin?"

"No."

"A monster?"

"Closer, but no."

Suddenly, I remembered the day Brightest and I met and the person who'd delayed their flight to the chain tree. "The mockingbird? No way! What did she do?"

"Followed me, mostly. From the valley to the third mountain to here. She took different forms—I wasn't sure it was her, at first. But then, she slipped up and imitated . . ." Brightest shuddered. When they continued speaking, their voice was soft, almost too soft to hear over the thrum of wind in my ears. "She imitated the form of a dead eagle," they said. "He passed not long ago. I shouted, 'Leave me alone! This isn't a game! Ami is dying!' After that, I didn't notice her again, but that doesn't mean she left."

"What did she want?"

"Probably mistook this pouch for a mouse. See?" Brightest lifted their right foot. A small leather pouch was tied around their leg. "She's a breakfast thief, as you know."

"That's a lot of effort to steal a pinch of food," I said.

"Maybe she was just bored."

I grunted in a somewhat affirmative response. It was possible she'd followed Brightest because of boredom, but the mockingbird's inner thoughts and motivations eluded me.

"How did the meeting with the bounty hunters go?" I asked.

"The trainee was at the mountain. She remembered you. Apologized for 'the blanket'—what does that mean?"

"Just a mix-up," I explained. "Nothing worth retreading."

"She couldn't disclose the names of their Earth allies. Apparently, that's confidential. But she's going to discuss our predicament with her family of investigators and hunters. If they approve an away mission, she'll meet us at the bookstore on Earth."

"They know the location?"

Brightest ruffled their feathers; I could feel them against my cheek. "I'm sure they know a lot."

I watched the mountain pass around us. The originator's legs, which were a blur of motion, seemed to flow through the rock. He left no hoofprints or destruction behind him. No sign that he'd passed. I wanted to ask, "Have you become the mountain?" But, more importantly, I didn't want to insult the originator by interrogating his own state of being. So the question remained unspoken.

Well, until Reign noticed my fascination with the originator's feet. Curious, she peered at the ground a moment, then barked out, "Grandfather, are you swimming through the rock?"

He snorted. "I am not."

"It looks like it to me!"

"Me, too," I admitted. "It's almost like you're fused with the ground, and it's carrying you up the side of the mountain the same way a river carries a leaf."

"Interesting," he said. "What do you see, hawk?"

Brightest tilted their little head and glared at the ground with the intensity of a bird of prey during a hunt. "Oh, hey!" they said, ruffling their feathers. "It's an optical illusion. His lower legs just blend in with the ground when they go fast. You're very graceful for a giant, Grandfather. I'm impressed!"

Try though I might, I couldn't see what Brightest saw. I guess they had the benefit of eyeballs that could pinpoint a solitary vole in a field from a hundred feet above the ground. Plus, everyone but they and the originator were in our fake forms. The transition affected most senses. It's like trying to function in a bulky costume.

Somehow, the elder accelerated over time. As our height increased, as the incline steepened, and as the air chilled and thinned, his leaps sped up. Halfway up the mountain, we were going faster than the truck. Two thirds up the mountain, we could probably race a speeding arrow. My arms still interlocked with Risk's and Reign's elbows, I hunched forward, and ducked my head to stop the wind from beating against my face. Brightest had moved behind me, but every so often, he called out, "I'm still here!" to stop me from worrying. Zale and the sisters clung to the originator's back like squirrels on a tree. Tendrils of fine green vines, once part of the originator's floral coat, curled around their hands and wrists, as if trying to steady them.

We needed all the help we could get. We started to travel up a slope so steep, it resembled a vast gray wall. Around us, caps of snow glinted atop jutting rocks. I was afraid to look behind us, to see the world so far below us we might as well be flying. The temperature had dropped gradually, so I could not pinpoint the exact moment when unpleasantly cool became painfully cold, but my exposed ears and nose stung, and a deep ache pulsed in my head.

Then, with a final kick, the originator leapt over the edge of a sharp outcropping and landed on a crescent-shaped, natural platform hugging the mountain. We were not yet at the peak, which still loomed before us like a mini, cone-shaped mountain.

The green tendrils that had bound the sisters' hands now turned a sickly yellow and snapped like brittle, sun-dried hay. I noticed that a few delicate coils remained looped around Risk's fingers. Reign, on the other hand, quickly brushed the stragglers off.

"Is this as far as we need to go?" she asked, jumping from the originator's back. Her landing was unusually awkward; she stumbled a couple steps, her arms pinwheeling for balance. "Can't breathe properly," she muttered. "My lungs feel like I've been running, too."

"It's the cold that gets me," I said. Risk, Zale, and I did not attempt to somersault off the elder. Instead, we climbed down the gentle slope of his neck. My limbs were leaden, sluggish. As if they were trying to move through thick honey instead of elevation-thinned air. And once I wasn't perched on the originator's back, the cold intensified; I was no longer warmed by his body heat, which had seeped through his skin of stone and plants.

"We can't take you all the way," Zale said apologetically. "It's too risky. At noon, the pseudosun will pull anything on the peak to Earth."

"That's okay," I said. "Can you go over the procedure again?"

"It's very easy. Here's what you need to do. Hike up the trail slow and steady. Once at the peak, hold tight to the cord—you'll see it—otherwise, the pseudosun may pull you too soon. On the peak, there's a glass ball that concentrates a ray of sunlight on a pictograph. When the light shines in the center of the turtle's shell, let go of the cord and fall to Earth. Timing is crucial. Don't hesitate. The moment that light hits the center of the tortoise, you need to let go. It's better to try again tomorrow than to mess up today. We'll be waiting right here."

"This location is still very high," I said. "Why won't you be pulled with us?"

"There's a threshold," he says. "Below it, the gravity of Earth can't touch you. That's why we don't attempt the journey on any other mountain in this range. They're all just a little too small."

"I hope you succeed in reviving your friend," the originator rumbled, "if only for a moment longer."

"Me too," I said.

"D-d-drive safely," Risk chattered. "We'll be b-back soon." Risk and Reign, whose arms were bare from the elbows down, shivered in the cold. They bared their chattering teeth, as if snarling at the temperature. I couldn't help but pity them.

"Don't worry about me," Zale said. "I'm not the one visiting Earth. Oh! And don't forget: once you land, go west. You'll reach a gray road. Follow it north till you see a sign commanding you to STOP. There's a trailer nearby. The human women who live inside will give you a ride to the bookstore, no farther. Tell them you're with the scribes. Then, you can thank them, but don't talk about anything else during the drive."

"Awfully kind," I commented.

"They aren't all scary," he said, smiling. "Good luck. I'll be waiting."

In response, Risk reached out to affectionately ruffle Zale's tuft of thick gray hair. Then, the sisters turned in unison and started hiking up the narrow mountain path. Wordlessly, sluggishly, I followed. It was a quick but painful journey. By the time we reached the highest point of the fourth mountain, my fingers, toes, nose, and ears were numb; my eyes stung behind the ice-cold glass shields of my spectacles; my lungs ached. Even my joints burned with pain, as if the cold had aged me by centuries within a matter of minutes.

The peak, a flat oval of land swept snow-bare by gusts of wind and the daily pull of the pseudosun, was large enough to comfortably hold thirty people in their false forms. Risk, Reign, Brightest—who was still perched on my shoulder—and I moved to the center of the peak. Above the clouds, within the grasp of Earth's gravity, I felt unusually light. My steps were too long, too high. As if I was on the verge of floating away. But that was the point, wasn't it? We'd float, and then we'd fall.

Several metal stakes, which were hooked at the top like needle heads, had been hammered into the stone around us, creating a ring; they were connected by a thick woven cord. Within the ring was a disk of stone under a heavy orb of glass; the glass, which concentrated the pseudosunlight into a point of intense brightness, was secured in a metal frame. Risk swept the dusting of snow from the stone disk's surface, revealing a turtle etched into its surface. Although the light was near the center of the turtle's back, it hadn't quite reached the middle octagonal plate.

"W-w-won't be long," she said. "Hold on to the rope."

We sat side by side, close enough to share our body warmth. Brightest perched on the cord and clutched it within their strong taloned feet. In contrast, the sisters and I hooked our elbows around the cord; in their half-frozen state, our fingers were useless appendages.

"G-gotta be precise," I said. "W-w-watch the turtle."

"On it," Brightest volunteered.

Before long, I felt the curls on my head stand on end. Beside me, Risk and Reign looked like they were moments away from being struck by lightning. Their loose hair rose, as if charged by static electricity. "We must be c-close," I reassured them.

"Almost," Brightest agreed, staring intently at the turtle disk. I felt weightless, the same feeling I'd experienced every time the speeding truck dropped over a bump in the road. But this time, the sensation did not go away. It expanded, urging me off the ground. Trying to flip me around and upside down. I squeezed my elbows, pinching the cord more tightly, forcing my legs to stay against the frozen ground. The sisters took a different approach, dangling straight into the air, as if performing awkward handstands. They cackled shrilly in either anxious delight or delighted anxiety; I couldn't tell. With a flutter of wings, Brightest flew onto Reign's foot, perching upside down.

"Aaaalmost," they promised, their gaze locked on the turtle.

"Next time, I'm b-bringing gloves," Risk said. Clouds of her chilled breath slipped from her mouth and rose toward the pseudosun, which was now so near to us, it seemed to encompass the whole sky, except for a ring of blue at the edge of sight. My spectacles began to slip off my nose; in order to grab them, I switched to a precarious one-arm hang. My bicep strained to hold the combined weight of my false body and my overpacked knapsack.

"A few more seconds!" Brightest cheered.

"Do you hear that?" Reign wondered. "Listen! Voices! And . . . machines? What's that? Oh, wow! It's Earth!"

Unfortunately, my ears weren't keen enough to register the murmurs of a different world. But Risk, after tilting her head, barked in laughter, "You're right!"

"Now!" Brightest shouted. "Fall!"

In my peripheral vision, I saw their streamlined body dive toward the pseudosun. Beside me, the sisters loosened their grasp on the cord and dropped straight up.

I did not hesitate. Not because I was confident. Not because I was unafraid. On the contrary: hesitation would mean I'd land far away from my friends. And that terrified me.

So, I released the mountain and fell into the sky.

COTTONMOUTH FALLS TO EARTH

*T*he heat was an enveloping warmth. Gentle as a hug. Not fire. Not agony. In fact, the only pain I felt radiated from a single point, where Reign's fingers squeezed my hand, her grasp boa-constrictor-tight. She'd reached out during the fall, first grasping for her sister and then—when that failed—for me. Now, Reign giggled hysterically. Risk's laughter answered somewhere above us. Below us? Beside us? In the gap between worlds, direction ceases to exist.

I closed my eyes against the brightness, but it seeped through my eyelids, tinted by the color of my false blood and skin. Little different than light passing through stained glass or a fine chip of rose quartz.

The light's intensity increased, then I tasted mesquite and felt ground beneath my feet.

"Open your eyes," Reign said.

I did, hissing with pain as I looked straight at an intensely radiant circle in a vividly blue sky. My face had been tilted toward the sun.

The sun.

For a minute, a black dot—the emptiness left in its wake—hovered in my vision. "Is everyone here?" I asked.

"We all made it," Risk confirmed. Brightest landed on my shoulder and made a pleased click with their beak. "What do you think?"

"Earth is . . ." I hesitated. What was it? We'd landed in a clearing among honey mesquite; hearty shrubs and yellow grasses grew between the trees. A stump—so similar to Ami's favorite perch, I half-expected him to be sitting there, waving—was squeezed between two gray rocks. Somewhere, a bird chirped.

If not for the sky, I might have mistaken the Earth for home.

NINA, 3 DAYS BEFORE LANDFALL

*A*t one point during Oli's long explanation, Nina visited the minifridge in her father's office and poured each of her visitors—except for the hawk, who was perched on the edge of a wire bookshelf—a cup of generic sugary cola. Reign shrieked with glee when she tasted the bubbles in her drink. However, the others seemed unimpressed by their first experience with soda, wrinkling their noses at every sip. In fact, Nina suspected that Oli wasn't really drinking his; he'd bring the glass cup to his mouth, tip it back, and let the amber liquid sit against his shut lips a moment without actually swallowing.

"I can bring you water, too," she offered.

"Water! Yes, thank you! I was going to ask, but . . ." Oli looked at his hands, which were clasped on top of the storeroom table. "We know about the droughts."

"The droughts? Oh, you mean in Texas?"

"Lots of places," he explained.

Nina side-eyed the rain-streaked window. "Don't worry

about it. As you can tell, we're having a moment of relief. During hurricane season, flash floods are the new threat." She stood. "I'll be right back."

Setting off for the apartment kitchen, she ascended the stairs two at a time.

After Nina filled three cups with water from the kitchen tap, which had a bulky white fixture for filtering impurities, she paused to check the messages on her phone. There was one from her mother, a generic good night, and five old ones from her father: one announcing that he'd arrived safely, one warning that the latest projections were dire, one confirming that he was staying a couple days in case Grandma needed to evacuate, one reminding her to turn on the security systems and call Aunt Leslie if she needed urgent help, and one that said: "Sleep well, love you."

He probably assumed she'd gone to bed long ago. Nina considered firing off a text to explain the whole animal people situation, but she knew what would happen then. The moment her father heard the shrill, factory-setting message alert on his phone and glanced at its screen, he'd interpret her message to roughly mean, "Dear Dad: three strange teenagers and a hawk are in the house, and I'm giving them all your emergency work cola. Come home immediately, or we'll burn down the bookstore." Then, he'd jump in the car and rush home, leaving Grandma to fend for herself.

Nina had a better idea. She'd bring the animal people to him. She didn't have her own car, but there was a bus stop down the street and a train station in the heart of town.

Satisfied with her plan, Nina balanced all three glasses on a wooden cutting board and carried them downstairs waiter-style. On the staircase, the water sloshed dangerously close to spilling, but she managed to save every drop. Although there was enough water to drink, Nina didn't want to waste any.

When Nina reentered the stockroom, she noticed that all three glasses of soda were now sitting in front of Reign. "Don't drink those too fast," Nina warned. "They're full of sugar and caffeine."

A sly smile from Risk. "Sugar and caffeine? You'll make her want to chug 'em faster."

"Do you have soda in the Reflecting World?"

"Nah," Reign said. "Not really. Carbonation never caught on."

"The exchange of customs between our world and yours really slowed a few hundred years ago," Oli explained. "When were bubble drinks invented?"

"Nifty," Nina said, "I have a question!"

Her pocketed phone asked, *How can I help you?*

"What year was soda invented?"

Eighteen-seventy-four by Dr. Anachronismus. Should I elaborate?

"No," Nina said. "Over and out." She distributed the water around the table and took her seat. "Did you hear that? It's been way over a hundred years."

"Technology," Oli said, his eyes wide with amazement. "What a marvel. Can you ask it anything? Nifty, how much do you know about saving frogs?"

Silence. Nina placed her phone on the tabletop. "It only responds to my voice," she explained. "But you're right. This"— she tapped the phone's rectangular screen—"is the right place to find information. We'll need to ask more specific questions, though. Hey, where's your friend? Um . . ." She closed her eyes, trying to remember the hawk's name. It was something unique. A descriptive word, like Risk and Reign.

"Brightest?" Oli supplied.

"Yes!"

"Getting dressed in the washroom. On Earth, it's impossible for us to speak with humans in our true forms, so they transformed."

"Won't that decrease their time here?" Nina asked, recalling an earlier part of Oli's story. How he'd explained that he and his friends would remain on Earth a week, give or take, and then vanish like evaporating mist, returning to the Reflecting World. "So we can do, er, magic," he'd explained, "but at a cost. Every transformation or act of world-shaping decreases our hold on this world. The greater the act, the greater its cost. If I stepped outside right now and pushed away all the rain clouds, I'd probably transport home in the morning."

"Transformations aren't that big a deal," Risk answered Nina. "They'd have to go back and forth a bunch to seriously reduce their time here."

"I bet Brightest just wants to eat and drink like a human," Reign said, flicking a half-drained cup of cola. "When you were upstairs, they flew onto the table and shoved their beak in my cup of soda. That's when they decided to transform."

There was a loud *thunk* from the washroom, followed by a cry of frustration. In unison, everybody around the table stood and looked toward the closed wooden door.

"Are you okay in there?" Oli called.

An energetic voice with the slightest unplaceable accent hollered back, "I'm good! Don't fret! Tripped on the pants. Legs are too long in this body, is all!"

"You need help dressing?" Risk asked, exchanging an amused look with her sister.

"I do not! Is the human back?"

"Yes, I'm back," Nina said.

"May I remain barefoot in your home?"

"Sure. Actually, it's polite to remove your shoes in many human houses . . ." Nina noticed the other three animal people begin to bend over to whip off their footwear. She hastily added, "But since this is a bookstore stockroom, anything's fine."

A couple minutes later, the doorknob rattled, as if Brightest was batting at it helplessly. "How do you open this type of door?" they asked.

"Turn the knob," Nina said. "While you're turning it, push outward."

"Turn the . . ." A click, and the door swung open. Immediately, she understood why the poor hawk had had such a difficult time getting dressed. Their pants were at least one size too tight, and a quarter foot too short. At least the loose yellow tunic fit. Strikingly, Brightest hadn't lost their pair of wings; they'd just migrated to the sides of their head and nicely framed their messy cascade of black hair.

"So, that's what you look like," Reign commented. "I like it. Very tall. Nice face."

"Thanks, I know," Brightest said, laughing. "Of all my siblings, I have the shiniest eyes and the sharpest cheekbones. My parents almost named me Beautiful One. Can you imagine? A name like that would go straight to my head." Then, they moved to sit on the edge of the table, propping their bare feet on the armrest of Oli's chair. "What did I miss? Do we have a plan to save Ami?"

"We're working on it," Oli said.

Nina tried not to stare at the wings, just like she'd avoided gaping at Risk and Reign's soft, pointed ears. She had the urge to take a picture. But that might not be safe.

There was no doubt in her heart that, if hunters still existed in the shadows of society, they'd be tapped into social media. Maybe even private phones. They'd develop sophisticated algorithms designed to identify animal features on humanlike bodies. To look for incontrovertible proof. One photo in the cloud could endanger everyone.

"First," she said, glancing at Oli, who averted his eyes out of either politeness or nervousness, "when did your friend get sick? What day?"

"Two days ago," he said. "Almost three."

"Can you tell me anything else about his species? What they look like, where they live?"

Oli tapped his chin, his scaled brows scrunching in concentration. "Our home is linked to this place. Here."

"Texas," Risk elaborated.

"Yes. I don't know whether Ami's species lives anywhere else. I guess it's possible that he's from a faraway island or forest. There are certain roads that span continents."

"Pal, I dunno about that," Brightest said. "When I first met Ami, he was half a tadpole. The little guy was born in the lake."

"For now, let's assume he's a toad from the southern United States," Nina said. "Northern Mexico too, maybe."

"His throat is blue," Oli said, "his eyes are gold, and his back is a green brown spotted with black. He's this long"—Oli held his hands a couple inches apart—"and this tall"—he decreased the distance between his hands—"and can listen to you talk for hours."

"Shoot," Nina said. "I think I know what happened. Maybe."

Her audience gaped in astonishment. "Already?" Reign wondered. "Is it because you read so much?"

Nina had to smile at that. She did read a lot, but her space operas and epic fantasies weren't exactly relevant to wildlife. "There was a major disaster last Wednesday," she explained. "A hurricane, the first in a pair. It raged up the Gulf of Mexico and tore through Louisiana. That ain't far away."

"There have always been storms," Oli said. "Why did this one have such a devastating impact on Ami?" He lisped when he spoke, with soft whooshes of air past his fangs that endeared him to Nina. Made him seem more human, as funny as that seemed.

"Let's find out," she said.

It took one minute and fifteen seconds to rattle off a list of Ami's physical features and search for a matching species. *Anaxyrus dallasensis*, Nifty informed her. *Colloquially known as the Dallas toad.*

"Search keywords: hurricane, *Anaxyrus dallasensis*," Nina urged. "Filter results: no later than Wednesday." The phone was still lying faceup on the table; its screen flashed bright white, and the search results loaded. All four animal people leaned forward, crowding the phone, forcing Nina to halfway sit up in her seat and push shoulder to shoulder into the huddle. She noticed that Risk, Reign, and Brightest wore expressions of concentration, but Oli's eyes widened, as if he was reading something shocking.

"What does that mean?" he asked, pointing at the third search result, the title of a news article.

"Let me see," Nina said. She picked up her phone, expanding the article with a click. The title, "Floodwater Destroys University Facilities," was above a photo of a blue-throated toad sitting serenely in a woman's open hand. She skimmed through the first couple paragraphs, and then read, "A one-thousand-acre *A. dallensis* breeding center was submerged after Hurricane Illeana-2 damaged Bigswamp Dam. According to Dr. Louisa Fennel, senior herpetologist, the flood is a 'critical setback in the struggle to revive wild populations of the Dallas toad.' It is unclear when or if facility reconstruction will convene, given recent cutbacks to funding."

She lowered her phone. The stockroom was silent, except for the low hum of the minifridge. It occurred to Nina that her guests were a bedraggled bunch. Hair frizzy or tangled after air-drying without a good brush. Pants and shoes muddy, eyes hollow or red-rimmed with exhaustion. They looked like she suddenly felt. For a couple hours, she'd managed to forget the four-day countdown looming over her own family.

"What does that mean, exactly?" Reign asked. "All the frogs were living in one place?"

"Toads," Oli corrected, his voice soft, his thoughts clearly elsewhere.

"Pretty much," Nina said. "They were trying to rally together a population of toads to release into the wild, but a dam broke and ruined everything. That's kind of ironic, considering that they're in trouble 'cause drought has reduced their natural habitat. Now, there isn't enough money to rebuild. If that'd even help . . ."

"There you go," Risk said. "Night one, and we know what happened."

"But now what?" Brightest asked.

"We give them money," Oli said, smiling, as if that was the simplest task in the world. "Nina will help." If the situation hadn't been so tragic, Nina would have laughed.

"I'll do my best," she said. "But . . ."

When she hesitated, all four animal people leaned forward in anticipation. Their eyes, slightly inhuman variations of brown or yellow, focused directly on Nina's face. "So, here's the thing," she continued. "Another hurricane might hit my grandma's house in three . . . no . . . two days. She's stuck at home, and—"

"Say no more," Reign interrupted. "For you, we'll fight this storm."

"Um . . . what? How?" Nina filed through her mental playlist of old stories. Although animal people did incredible feats, she wasn't aware that they dueled storms.

"We'll help protect her," Oli clarified, while Reign muttered something about her great-uncle and a lasso. "It's the least we can do."

It was past midnight, and although Nina didn't feel sleepy yet, the evening's events felt distinctly dreamlike. There were four animal people sitting in the bookstore stockroom, offering to help her family. This must be how lottery winners felt right after learning the good news, she decided. She didn't trust her happiness, her good fortune, but couldn't find a reason to doubt herself. This is real, she kept thinking. Tonight is happening, and it's happening to you in real time, real life. Earlier, gradually, during Oli's explanation of events, Nina's trust in her inner optimist had increased. Now, her initial shock and disbelief were almost completely overwhelmed by awe.

The legends weren't all gone. They were here, in her family's bookshop.

NINA, 2 DAYS BEFORE LANDFALL

*N*ina occasionally dreamed of raking in enough money to buy anything she wanted. Those types of daydreams were most common when two expensive games were released during the same year, forcing her to choose just one, if any. But overall, she was too comfortable in life to dwell on money. Therefore, Nina didn't have a get-rich-quick-scheme list lying around her bedroom. And there were some questions Nifty couldn't answer. She was 99.9 percent confident that a search of "how to make lots of cash fast" would result in nothing but scammy websites and possibly a computer virus.

Exhausted from their journey across two worlds, the animal people were resting; she'd carried spare blankets, sleeping bags, and pillows—even a couple of old cat beds—to the living room, and they'd improvised sleeping arrangements for everyone, with Brightest sprawled across the sofa, Risk and Reign on the floor, and Oli sleeping with his head in one cat bed and his feet in another.

"Are you sure that's comfortable?" she'd asked, and Oli looked at her like she'd asked him whether water was wet.

"They're so soft," he'd said. "Of course!"

She almost left them in the living room unguarded, but as Nina brushed her teeth in front of a streaky bathroom mirror, the absurdity of her trust in four unsupervised strangers became an issue. Sure, they were animal people, not humans, but weren't coyotes supposed to be tricksters? Weren't birds supposed to be thieves of sparkly, expensive objects? Weren't cottonmouths . . . well, she couldn't recall a traditional story about a malevolent cottonmouth person, but that didn't mean such stories didn't exist.

To be safe, Nina turned on the motion-sensitive alarms in the kitchen and hallways. Then, she locked her bedroom door. From a pile of dirty clothes in the open closet, Tightrope mewed.

"There you are," she cooed, picking up her cat by the waist. He flopped over her hands, momentarily a fluid creature of fur, and then wiggled into the cradle of her arms. Nina pressed her cheek against Tightrope's soft forehead. He purred and leaned into her hug. "Were you hiding?" she murmured. "I'm sorry."

She slowly lowered Tightrope to the floor. Then, Nina paced around her room, observed by her cat, who'd jumped onto his favorite spot on her pillow.

She had an idea. A far-fetched, optimistic idea that would probably end in disappointment. Hey, they had to start somewhere. Might as well go big. And if the long shot failed? Well, as her father said, they'd cross that bridge when—and if—they needed to.

Nina crawled under her bright yellow bedsheets, but instead of sleeping, opened the St0ryte11er app.

◆

A shrill beep woke her. Nina must have dozed off while researching, because she was still clutching her phone in one hand. Its screen was broadcasting a motion-triggered security stream of the hallway. The gray video feed showed Oli walking toward her door, hesitating, and then tapping the wood with his fingertips.

Tp tp tp.

She could hear him knocking in real time. Then, came his hissed question: "Nina, are you awake?"

She rubbed her eyes and called, "Yes."

A pause. Then, through the door, his answer. "It's morning."

A bleary glance at her phone clock confirmed that he was technically correct: 5:45 a.m.

"I'll be out in a couple minutes," she said. "Get everyone ready to go. I have a plan to get rich fast."

◆

At 6:30 a.m., the city bus was mostly empty. Nina paid the fee for three student riders and urged Risk and Reign to the back bench, which was wide enough to seat them all. She'd dressed the sisters in floral maxiskirts, oversized T-shirts tucked into the elastic waistbands, and her father's shoes. Although the shoes were loose, even with two layers of socks, they did a manageable job concealing the twins' long, clawed feet. Their ears were hidden under flowery silk scarves, and they wore simple white driving gloves to conceal their heart-shaped patches of fur.

It was certainly a look.

As they walked single file down the narrow bus aisle, Reign greeted every passenger she passed with a "Hello!" The first grunted a sleepy greeting, the second smiled, but the third pinned her with an annoyed glare.

"It's too early to be friendly," Nina whispered.

"Oh! Sorry." Reign slid into the left window seat of the rear bench, delicately holding a backpack on her lap. As soon as she settled down, a feathered head popped out of the partially unzipped bag.

"What is the correct time for friendliness?" Risk asked, taking the other window seat. Her backpack was filled with snacks and Oli, but he'd been warned that a cottonmouth snake could cause panic, so he didn't peek out of his carrier.

"It depends," Nina said, sandwiched in the middle. "You really need to judge social stuff case by case. When in doubt, stay quiet." She wrapped her arms around her backpack of filming supplies, hugging it tightly as the bus lurched away from the curb, afraid the rough drive would jostle her equipment. Sometimes, Nina wondered if she deserved to have such a high-tech camera, one with all the bells and whistles, the kind of camera pros used. It would be one thing if her story channel was profitable. Or, barring that, public.

How much did the camera cost, anyway? How much had her parents sacrificed to indulge Nina's hobby, a souped-up diary? Her mother at sea, her father running a business alone. But they'd both looked so pleased when Nina, fifteen years and two weeks old, had unwrapped the tech-loaded camera and, after a shriek of surprise, cried out, "Is this for real?"

Her mother, dressed in denim coveralls and sunburned from her recent time at sea, had nodded, beaming. "Happy belated birthday, Pumpkin. I found it in New Zealand."

"She didn't really," Nina's father had stage-whispered. "We visited an electronics place in Houston."

For the most part, the twenty-minute bus ride was quiet, which surprised Nina. She'd expected the coyote sisters to bombard her with questions about Earth. Instead, they stared intently out the windows, as if watching a fascinating movie. As the bus neared their destination, Nina unfolded a handkerchief from her pant pocket, leaned over Reign, and used the handkerchief to press a red stop request button under the window. That's when Reign asked her first question of the ride.

"Why did you do that?"

"Now, the driver knows we need to disembark."

"He won't stop unless you press a red button?"

"Not unless he sees people waiting to get on."

"Why did you use a cloth?"

"So I don't spread germs."

"Can you catch rabies by touching a button?"

Before Nina could answer, Risk barked with laughter and shrieked, "Are you kidding? Rabies comes from bites!"

"According to our auntie," Reign explained, "rabies is the second scariest thing on Earth."

"What's the first?" Nina wondered.

"That's easy. The King's knights."

"Who?"

"They're a cult of humans who kill animal people. It's . . . their thing?" She glanced at Risk, her eyes questioning.

"Zale and I suspect that they're excessively territorial," Risk took over. "That the knights all got an overactive, violent territorial drive. In their heads, the whole Earth is theirs, and we don't belong."

"Huhm. I always assumed they just hate us and enjoy killing things," Reign replied.

"You could both be right," Nina said, leaning into her role as expert on humans. "Why do you call them the King's knights, though? Who is the King?"

"Their leader," Risk explained. "The cult organizes under his ideas."

"Why haven't I heard of these creeps?"

The sisters simultaneously shrugged.

"Maybe 'cause our bodies don't stay behind for long," Reign guessed, looking down at the bag in her lap. "They go back home."

Well. That explained the level of secrecy and fear. The trench coats, sunglasses, and nighttime visits. The rumors she'd heard about hunters who killed spirits for sport—she'd assumed they were isolated monsters who worked alone, serial killers, not a club of wannabe murderers.

"Should you be here?" Nina asked, her hands suddenly clammy, her cheeks flushing with anxiety. "With me, on this bus? I thought you said this was a great plan! Can they track you? Is it safe?"

"Yeah, yeah." Risk leaned over, nudging Nina with her shoulder. "Don't worry—we told you it was cool! It's not like we give out a signal. We're humans—or animals—until proven otherwise. Just don't take pictures of our transformations."

"O . . . oh. Oh, good!" Nina extracted several cotton face

masks from an outer pocket of her camera bag. Although she usually wore them in crowded places during virus season, they also came in handy when the wind kicked up dust, a common occurrence in the warm months of Texas. "Still . . . we should do whatever we can to protect our identity. Not only 'cause of hunters. It's just good practice. Do you know what deepfakes are? Face miners?"

She found herself sandwiched between blank stares.

"Um, basically, it's very easy to alter videos," Nina explained. "Go online, and there are millions of convincing ghost sightings, UFOs, and animal people encounters. Although . . . now I'm wondering how much of that is actually real."

"Our Great-Uncle once made the local news in Kentucky," Reign said. "He was standing in a crowd and acting like a typical human grocery store customer. Nobody noticed."

Poised just inches from Risk and Reign, Nina tried to search for clues that they were spirits. The scarves and gloves covered their most obvious tells, and their teeth, although prominent and relatively sharp, weren't canine-shaped. It's the eyes, she decided. That shade of yellow couldn't belong to a human without a pair of cosmetic contact lenses. Thankfully, those were more common than rainbow-colored hair. In fact, after years of pushback, the school no longer banned "extreme or extraordinary" contact lens colors, but students did have to sit through a 30-minute lecture on eye safety every year. The primary takeaway? Get all contact lenses through your optometrist, kids!

At that thought, the bus began to slow.

"We're here," Nina said, "so act like typical humans. In all seriousness, if my camera captures any sign that you're animal people, I'll need to delete the whole video. I'm even iffy on the eyes. We should be fine without any close-ups."

"But—"

"No buts!" Their ride lurched to a stop, and the side door opened with a mechanical squeal. Nina led her friends outside in silence, only continuing when they were alone. "I know. Really, I know. You'd risk your life for Ami. You already have, just coming here."

The twins nodded without hesitation. From within a bag, Brightest screeched in muffled agreement.

"Names aside," she shot an amused look at Risk, "we shouldn't increase that risk unless it's totally necessary."

"Fair enough," Risk agreed.

Their stop was at the outskirts of the city, near the railroad tracks. Across the street was a run-down strip mall. It had once contained a grocery store, a few take-out places, a laundromat, and a liquor depot, but now, only the laundromat and liquor store remained. The rest of the storefronts were dark, their doors chained shut. Because of the early hour, there were no cars in the parking lot, which made Nina feel uneasy as she crossed the cracked asphalt field. Her internal warning bells rang: you're in an isolated, unknown environment; people go missing in places like this. Her only weapon was a can of Mace in her utility belt. Nina had to reassure herself that she wasn't alone. She had backup, and her backup knew magic. Risk and Reign followed at a casual trot, their masks now hanging under their chins. Both Oli and Brightest peeked out of their backpacks, as if enjoying the fresh air.

"The next bus arrives in an hour," Nina said, "so we need to get everything in a few takes, if possible. Can't miss the bus, either. My dad's gonna check in before lunch."

They rounded the strip mall, passing a row of green garbage bins. A flock of grackles that had been pecking at discarded fast-food wrappers screeched and took to the air. They flew in frenzied loops overhead, eventually landing on a patch of oil-stained asphalt between two bins.

"Whatever they were eating smells delicious," Reign said. "Can we get some later?"

"Uh-huh," Nina promised, though her attention was elsewhere. They'd arrived at a wire fence between the back of the strip mall and a newly wooded area. According to the video of a local urban explorer, a section of the fence was bent toward the ground, allowing easy passage into the woods. As expected, nobody had bothered to repair the fence yet; in fact, its condition had degraded further, as if multiple people had stomped over the metal links.

"There's a tunnel in the woods," she said, "that's supposed to be haunted. People go there a lot to film videos. According to legend, its echoes carry terrible secrets. Obviously, that's all fake."

"We have a real cave like that in the Reflecting World," Risk said, smiling coyly. "It's on our list of destinations to visit."

Nina did an actual double-take, unsure whether the comment was a joke. For all she knew, conscious, communicative caves were commonplace in the Reflecting World. It still seemed bizarre that Risk was blasé about the subject, though. "Why would anybody intentionally go to a place like that?"

"The cave shares warnings, not terrible secrets, so it'll be very practical, as far as our adventures go."

"That makes sense."

"I'm not convinced," Reign said. "For all we know, the warnings could come from a pithy bat hiding behind a stalagmite. 'Don't stay awake too late! Be kind to the people you love!' See? It's easy."

"Only one way to know," her sister said. "The wolves and I are visiting the cave this winter. You don't have to join us."

"Of course I'm gonna!"

From their backpack, Brightest screeched conversationally, as if trying to speak, and then clicked their beak in frustration. Nina couldn't help but giggle.

The group followed a footpath down a hill and around a copse of juniper trees. Finally, Nina stepped onto the remnants of a street leading to a yawning concrete tunnel. Thin, young oaks grew on either side of the tunnel mouth, framing it between their bar-like trunks. "We're here! It's setup time!" she cheered. "Everybody out!"

The moment their backpacks were unzipped, Brightest and Oli burst and slithered out, respectively, into the sunlight. They stretched—wings spreading, body uncoiling—and blinked up at Nina, who was busy unfolding her camera stand.

"The goal is authenticity," she reiterated. "If the video seems obviously staged, it's useless. So, show me your startled faces."

Risk and Reign took turns miming shock and pointing at Oli.

Nina, thoroughly impressed, had to stop herself from cooing "Good job!" in the same high-pitched tone she used to praise Tightrope when he fetched a toy mouse. She hadn't quite decided yet how to view the animal people. On the one hand, there was an exceptional beauty about them, an otherworldliness. Their "human" bodies moved across the world with an unusual ease, as if Earth's gravity did not pull them too tightly. And their voices had a keenly musical quality. It wasn't that the animal people barked out literal instrumental notes or sang when they spoke. Rather, their words ignited emotional responses Nina had previously only experienced through music. When they were worried, she experienced the squeal of violins, the quick-heartbeat thrum of a thriller soundtrack. Risk and Reign's bickering had the impact of a rattling gourd and snare drum. Oli's hopeful questions were reminiscent of the lo-fi hip-hop Nina played when she studied.

On the other hand, in many ways, their facial expressions and behavior reminded her of their animals. That, more than anything, made Nina's heart sting with affection for her new friends. She'd known them less than twenty-four hours, and was already willing to drop everything in the middle of hurricane season just to help them save a toad.

For a moment, she watched them practice their roles. Risk and Reign were still gasping and feigning surprise. On the ground, Oli—who was a much smaller snake than Nina had expected—was trying to seem threatening by throwing back his head and flashing his white inner mouth. Brightest flapped their wings aggressively and bird-jogged in circles around Oli.

"I think we're ready," Nina said, checking her camera settings. Through its viewfinder, she could see the tunnel entrance and part of the disintegrating path through the woods. "Brightest, see that high branch? It's a good place to wait until your cue. Oli, I want you mostly hidden behind that bush. Risk and Reign, you're with me. Masks on."

Everyone scrambled, flew, or slithered into their places. Nina surveyed the area one last time; aside from a few birds in the trees, they were alone. That was one reason she'd chosen the tunnel. It was an interesting spot for dares and ghost-hunter videos, which gave her an excuse to be taping, but it wasn't overly popular. Nina didn't need any interruptions.

Once the sisters were in their spot behind her, Nina took a deep breath. These days, that was all she needed to steady her nerves before filming. The rest came easy, if she didn't think too hard.

She stepped into the camera's line of sight and looked at the round glass lens, ensuring that it had a clear shot of her mask-shielded face. "Nifty, turn on Nina tracking mode in Visualizer."

Tracking mode activated, her phone promised. A green light blinked in the camera; it had successfully locked onto her body, and would follow her movements using AI-assisted technology and a robotic swivel attachment on the stand. That meant she didn't have to worry about stepping beyond view.

"We almost died trying to climb down here," Nina conversationally began, approaching the tunnel. "You think it's actually cursed?"

"Yeah," Risk said. "That's why we decided you should go first."

"I'm scaaared," Reign whined. Her tone was slightly over the top, but that was okay. Visiting a "haunted" tunnel was supposed to be cheesy. The sisters had learned how to enunciate their lines in English, instead of relying on their special spirit language, since Nina wasn't sure how that would translate to video.

"The tunnel knows when we'll die, so if you hear today's date in an echo, we're done for." Nina kept her voice light, playing into the too-cheery persona of an entertainer who didn't actually believe the stories they were spewing.

Then, they approached Oli's bush. With impeccable timing, he shot onto the path, his tail shaking, his mouth flung open in warning. Risk and Reign shrieked with fear.

"Oh, shit! That's a cottonmouth!" Nina cried.

Then, Brightest dropped out of the sky in a classic bird-of-prey hunting dive. They landed a couple feet behind Oli and flapped their wings. In response, openmouthed Oli lunged, but Brightest hopped beyond striking range. The pair engaged in a faux deadly dance, swaying and striking, until Brightest pinned Oli under one talon, and Oli, in response, wrapped his tail around Brightest's neck. That's when the girls fled; the camera followed Nina, cutting away from the action.

"Done!" she shouted.

Perfect. Everything had gone seamlessly. The performances were genuine, the fight exciting. But Nina was not satisfied. Leaning against a juniper trunk, she held up her phone and said: "Nifty, replay the last two minutes of Visualizer footage."

"Ooooh!" Reign cooed.

"We look great," Risk said.

They stood on either side of Nina, trying to see the little screen by shouldering close. She spread her elbows, gently pushing them away from her personal space, and once again thought of Tightrope, how he always head-butted her leg insistently when he wanted something.

"You do," she agreed. "Completely human. But . . . ugh. This isn't going to work."

"What?" Reign cried.

"Why not?" Risk asked.

"It's interesting," Nina replied. "People will enjoy watching it. But . . . to make big bucks, we need spectacular." Nina looked down at Oli. He was curled in a polite little spiral, his eyes glittering innocently. "He's just . . . not threatening enough."

Oli tilted his head, as if asking, "What?"

"You're too cute for this video."

He threw back his head in an openmouthed gasp of despair.

"What about a coyote attack?" Risk suggested.

"Two little puppy-looking critters? No. Sadly, you'd be extremely cute. Plus, a hawk is no match for coyotes."

"Oli can summon other cottonmouths. Would that be scary?" Reign asked.

"What do you mean?"

"We have a bond with our species. For example, if there are coyotes in this forest, me and my sister could think, 'Hey, friends, come here!' and they'd surround us."

"Could Oli also stop the cottonmouths from biting me?"

"Er . . ." Reign shook her head. "No. It's not mind control. Just a summons."

"Then we better not take the risk." Nina paced, thinking. There was enough time left for one more video, but if a hawk and a snake weren't compelling enough, what next? The animal people knew magic—world-shaping, they called it—but if she understood correctly, they couldn't use it without seriously reducing their time on Earth. Plus, what type of world-shaping could help create a viral video without potentially attracting the King? She had to be clever. The movies were for special effects. The stage was for levitation and rabbits hiding in big black hats. On St0ryte11er, people wanted to witness an authentically surprising or remarkable moment.

Sometime during her brainstorming session, Oli and Brightest had disappeared behind a juniper tree to transform and get dressed. In contrast, Risk and Reign now stood near the mouth of the tunnel. "Hello!" Risk barked. "Hello, hello!" Then, they fell silent, ears twitching under their silk scarves.

"I hear something," Reign said. "Ahhh. It really is haunted!"

"Wait, what?" Nina jogged up to the sisters and peered into the tunnel, which was so long, the exit resembled a quarter-sized circle of light, and the interior was concealed in shadow. "Do it again!" she encouraged. "I want to hear."

"What's up, ghosts?!" Risk shouted. Her voice had a hollow quality, as if it had been sucked through the tunnel like water through a straw. There was no echo. But then . . .

Nina did hear something.

It was a low whuffing sound. A rumble. At the end of the tunnel, a black silhouette lurched in front of the circle of light. What was that? It was too far away for her to be certain, but if Nina had to guess, she'd say the figure resembled a Sasquatch. She held out her phone.

"Nifty, turn on the light."

The flashbulb emitted an intense beam of white light. At the end of the tunnel, two eyes flashed yellow. Then, the grizzly bear charged.

COTTONMOUTH STARS IN AN ACTION MOVIE

*A*lthough Brightest no longer struggled with the mechanics of pants, T-shirts still gave them trouble. I finished dressing to find them rolling on the ground with one arm sticking out of the head hole, one arm sticking out of an armhole, and their face pressed against the cotton fabric, gasping for breath. "Oli, a little help?"

"Stay still." I helped them into a sitting position, pushed their wayward arm into the right place, and carefully lowered the collar over their feathered head. Brightest was red-cheeked with exhaustion. "Wooh!" they said. "Thanks. I felt like a bug in a web."

"You'll get a hang of clothes soon."

"Do I really have to—"

"Yes. On Earth, always." I helped them to their feet and tied a violet scarf around their head.

"How does it look?" Brightest asked.

"Pretty, but also like we draped a blanket over two hawk wings. Maybe Reign can design a hat for—"

That's when the three others shrieked. Their voices tangled into a single knot of high-pitched shock. I turned, half-expecting them to be standing in a circle, playacting for a second take. Instead, they were all pointing at the tunnel. "What do we do?" Nina asked frantically.

"You run!" Risk said. "We'll . . . stop it."

"Stop a grizzly bear?"

I could hear it now: the low thrum of feet and claws. The whush of a one-ton muscle-and-fur cannonball charging down a concrete tube. Despite opposition from every instinct in my body, I ran toward the tunnel, standing beside the sisters. The grizzly bear was cloaked in shadows, but I could tell two things: she was massive, and she was seconds away. "Do as they say!" I shouted at Nina. "Go!" She was frantically patting her belt, as if distracted. That seemed impossible; what could be more distracting than an aggressive bear?

"My Mace . . ."

I grabbed Nina by the elbow and pulled her away from the tunnel entrance. All the while, she continued to fuss with a strap fastening a bright red can to her belt. Simultaneously, Risk and Reign exchanged a glance, and then leapt at one of the young birches growing near the tunnel entrance. By jumping off Risk's shoulders, Reign grabbed onto the top of the birch, and used her weight to bend it in front of the tunnel a second before the grizzly burst into the light. The bear collided with the tree, her momentum ripping it from the ground. The birch's shallow root system sent a spray of dirt into the air.

There was something very familiar about the stature of the bear. Hope surged through me. Grizzlies were rare on Earth, right? So what was more likely: that we had a chance encounter with an extremely pissed-off grizzly bear, or that the bounty hunter had found us, and was playing into our act?

Well, Nina had asked for a more spectacular encounter . . .

"Brightest!" I shouted. "Throw me your shirt!"

Together, Risk and Reign picked up the fallen tree by its trunk and held it like a lance, trying to keep the grizzly away by using its brush-like crown of branches. This, I suspected, was only a temporary distraction, considering the size, weight, and agility of their opponent. Already, the grizzly was trying to lope around to attack them from the side.

A bunched-up, yellow cotton T-shirt flew through the air. Thank the sun that Brightest had an easier time taking off their clothes than putting them on. As I grabbed the shirt one-handed, Nina finally held up the red can. "This will burn its eyes!" she declared.

"We don't need that! Risk, Reign! Drape this over the bear's head!"

As I flung the shirt at the sisters, the grizzly rounded on me, distracted by my burst of movement. She fell to all fours and knocked me to the ground with a single swipe of her crushing forepaw. Her mouth opened wide, her bone-splintering bite falling toward my shoulder. In the approach, I caught a glimpse of walnut-brown eyes.

The bounty hunter's eyes had been amber.

As I gaped in silent horror, Nina sprayed a stream of burning liquid at the grizzly's face, and then Reign ran up its back, flipped over its broad shoulders, and managed to bag its tooth-filled face with Brightest's shirt. Risk dragged me away and helped guide me down the tunnel; my spectacles were flecked with either drool or fine droplets of Mace. Sightless and bruised, I tried to taste the air, but there must have been Mace on my lips, because my mouth burned, as if I'd bitten into Earth's spiciest pepper.

"I can't see! I can't taste! What's happening?"

"Just hold my hand and run, Oli!" Risk said. Around us, the sound of several footsteps ricocheted off curved walls. I listened carefully, afraid to hear a date of my death in the echoes.

Then, a deep, gravelly voice shouted after us. "Hey! Heeey! Come back! What did you do to my eyes? They're burning like a forest fire!"

"It's the bounty hunter!" I exclaimed. "Stop!"

We slowed to a walk. After pulling out of Risk's grasp, I whipped off my spectacles and squinted down the tunnel. A blurry, humanoid shape stood in the sunlit entrance.

"Another animal person?" Nina asked. "Oh my god! I'm sorry! I thought you were going to kill everyone!"

"Trust me, if I'd wanted to kill you, even a scorpion to the eyes couldn't stop me." The bounty hunter laughed. "This stuff hurts pretty bad, though. What is it? I want some."

We gathered near the entrance; the yellow shirt was tight around the bounty hunter's torso and barely covered everything it needed to conceal. Reign, laughing riotously at the sight, ripped half the fabric off her maxiskirt. "I'm gonna make you a wrap so the humans don't lock up your bare butt."

"Ah, thanks," the bounty hunter said. "Wouldn't want that."

"How did you follow us without your own clothes?" I wondered. "It's not safe for carnivores to walk through human cities. And you can't be naked in your false form."

"I have my ways."

"Hmm . . ."

"So you're a bear person?" Nina asked, fetching her camera from its stand. She and the sisters all tore off their masks, while I wished that I'd been wearing something to protect my mouth.

"That's correct. Born and raised."

Reign tied a makeshift skirt around the bounty hunter's hips. "By the way," she said. "Now, we're even."

"Huh? How so?"

"Fights. This counts as a win for me."

A pause. Then, "If you say so."

That's when my suspicions went into overdrive.

While the twins fussed with the bounty hunter's outfit and Nina reviewed her camera, I pulled Brightest aside. "Pretend you're helping me wipe the Mace off my face," I said.

"Uuuuh. What if I didn't just pretend? No offense, but you look like a swarm of red ants had a go at your mouth and eyes." They poured a bit of canteen water on the edge of their scarf and started dabbing my cheek.

"Remember when you visited the third mountain?" I asked.

"Sure I do."

"The mockingbird followed you, right?"

Brightest stood so close to me, I could see their expression clearly, even without my spectacles. It became tense, worried. "Yes."

"Did she witness your conversation with the bounty hunter?"

They shrugged, dabbing at my other cheek with a different scarf corner. "Not that I'm aware of, but . . . it's hard to know for sure. She can pretend to be anyone."

I pointedly turned toward the bounty hunter.

"Her? Really?" Brightest asked, clacking their teeth with disappointment. "Can you sense it?"

"At the moment, the only thing I taste is pain. But I didn't catch a hint of grizzly bear on the walk from the bus. You know what I did detect?"

They pointed at their bare chest, which was coated by downy feathers from their collarbone to their stomach, almost like an undershirt. "Birds?"

"Birds."

"What's the next step, pal?"

"In private, I'll share our suspicions with the twins. Can you keep one eye on the bounty hunter?"

"Absolutely. Both my eyes." They handed me my freshly wiped pair of spectacles. "I'm not a fighter, Oli. You know that. I'd rather make friends than enemies. But if she interferes with our rescue mission. If she even tries . . ." They crossed their arms, made a soft *hmm* sound. "Actually, I don't know what I'll do. There's no context for this feeling. I've never had so much at stake."

"It'll be—"

"We did it!" Nina interrupted, her voice an excited shout. "It's perfect! My camera filmed all the action!"

At that, the tension seeped out of Brightest's stance. "Huh. She was helpful."

"This time," I conceded.

"But we should still do one more take!" Nina called out. "Risk and Reign, be less awesome. You're imitating humans, not superhumans."

I don't know who groaned louder: me or the twins. "For Ami," I said.

The bounty hunter shrugged.

Two takes later, I sat beside Nina on the bus ride to the bookshop. Behind us, the other four shared the back bench. For the third time, Nina played the video of our tussle and escape. "Seamless," she said. "If this doesn't get Thou Own Dave's attention, nothing will."

"I don't completely grasp . . ." I gestured to her phone screen. "Technology?"

"No. Well, yes. But that's not what confuses me the most about your plan. Why does Thou Own Dave matter so much? Who is he?"

"A top creator on St0ryte11er. He's universe tier. Look." She navigated to Thou Own Dave's landing page and pulled up an announcement: SHARE YOUR CONTENT AND GET 50% OF THE PROFIT. "I'm not a big fan of his stuff," she said. "But every day, he uploads a submission from somebody else, provides commentary, and splits the profits."

"Why share any of the money? Aren't you a storyteller, too?"

"Yeah, but . . . it's complicated." She eyed me, as if trying to decide whether I was worth the effort of an explanation. "So . . . there's only one way to make money on St0ryte11er. Basically, a committee has to unanimously decide that your stories are good enough to represent the application. At that point, they make you a star-tier storyteller. Every minute somebody spends listening to your content, you get paid a fraction of a fraction of a cent. If you're popular and consistent enough, the committee will promote you to a galaxy-tier storyteller. Those folks make more money per minute. It's still not much. But every year, ten galaxy-tier creators are promoted to universe-tier storytellers. They're given big money. I'm talking millions. Nobody else has that privilege. Nobody. There can only be ten. Which is why I need Thou Own Dave to host my story."

"Because there's no way for you to make money without his help."

She nodded, beaming. "Yes! You're clever!" I had the alarming sense that Nina wanted to reach out and pinch my cheek. Fortunately, she refrained from touching my still-stinging face.

"Thanks," I said. "My momma would agree." I thought of Ami, of minutes passing and the dreadful toll of time. "Will you be paid quickly?"

"I don't see why not." She was sitting near the window; until that point, Nina had been looking at her phone or at me, but now, she looked outside. We were going so quickly, the buildings resembled a blur. They made me dizzy. "I'll edit the footage today," Nina said. "Won't take more than a couple hours. Then . . . fingers crossed. Do you know what that phrase means?"

"Hope for the best," I guessed. To be fair, it was an educated guess, because my internal translator had provided a rough interpretation of the phrase.

"How did you know? Snakes don't have fingers!"

I wiggled my false hands in front of her face. "Sometimes, we do."

The *look* returned. The fiercely affectionate gleam in her eye that made me want to guard my cheeks from pinches. "You're wonderful," she said. "All of you." And then, with sudden meekness: "I wish you could stay longer. If you lived here, Grandma would give you presents every day."

"This isn't our home," I explained simply.

"It used to be, once."

"No," I said. "My home is a warm rock near the bottomless lake."

"Oh."

"But I'd happily visit, if the Earth became a safer place."

"Let's hope that happens," Nina said. Then, more softly: "I'll make it safer. Somehow."

NINA, 2 DAYS
BEFORE LANDFALL

*N*ina's finger hovered over the send icon. One click, and the edited bear attack video would zip into Thou Own Dave's submission inbox. After that, she'd have to wait.

Wait and imagine: a tech room deep within a Los Angeles mansion, where Thou Own Dave's staff works and lives, an intern sitting cross-legged on a plush gaming chair, surrounded by monitors, reviewing hours of videos, drinking ink-dark coffee straight from the carafe. Nothing new on the monitor screens. Dancers and daredevils. Interesting but not the next big thing. Occasionally, a lewd or violent video slips through the AI filter and causes the intern to flinch, turn away, curse the troll who had no better goal in life than the ambition to annoy a nineteen-year-old media science student. And then, Nina's video plays. Teenagers standing outside a "haunted" tunnel; if it weren't for the all-caps submission title—BEAR ATTACK—the intern would delete the submission without watching a single minute. But they're intrigued. And then thrilled. They call a supervisor. The supervisor calls Thou Own Dave. "Did the bear escape from a circus?" he asks. "I can work with this. Send them a contract."

Wait and dread: the video is published on a St0rytel1er account with 30 million subscribers. Nina makes lots of money, but at what cost? In response to public outcry, animal control scours the backwoods of South Texas, searching for an aggressive bear. There haven't been wild grizzlies in the region for generations, but this one must have escaped notice. Now, it's attacking children. Parents are terrified. First a hurricane, and now this? Animal control promises to relocate the animal, but a day passes. Then two. No grizzly. In the shadow of roiling thunderclouds, hunters load their guns and aim into the woods.

Or—just as bad—copycats decide that antagonizing dangerous wildlife is a surefire route to fame. They wouldn't do that, would they? Random St0ryte11ers wouldn't start poking beehives and screaming at mountain lions, right?

Of course they would.

Nina hadn't even pressed send, and she was already on the verge of a panic attack. She'd spent so much time ensuring that the submission was King-and-Knight safe, she'd barely considered other issues. Her chest jumped in shallow hiccups of breath. Sweat slickened her hands, leaving greasy-looking prints on supposedly streak-proof screens. She grabbed Tightrope from his perch on the windowsill and dragged him into her lap. He reclined across her knees, purring. A reminder that it was possible to chill. Why dwell on the worst-case scenario? St0ryte11ers posted wild videos every day without causing chaos and doom. Her friends were safe; she'd left them in the living room with a stack of books about toads, three bowls of popcorn, a carton of lunch meat, pizza bagels, and a playlist of St0rytel1er content from Thou Own Dave's page. Soon, she would take them to the train station, and they'd whisk off to Grandma's place. If their video miraculously got viewed by millions, she'd anonymously confess that the bear was just a flair of special effects. A digital magic trick, nothing more. And Thou Own Dave was a universe-tier St0rytel1er, which meant he could not promote dangerous behavior. He'd sprinkle plenty of warnings into his commentary on Nina's video. She could imagine his boisterous voice-over now: *I don't care if those girls are the luckiest kids in the world. They shouldn't be alive. Daviesapiens, this is another reason why I don't condone leaving your bedroom.*

Calmer, she released Tightrope, and he slid fluid-like to the floor. A successful video would have more pros than cons. Nina would be rich. She could use half the money to save a species of toad that had been living along the Rio Grande longer than her own people. And the other half? She could rebuild Grandma's house and fill it to the brim with shiny new stuff. No threats of fines from scheming neighbors would ever frighten the family again.

Nina clicked send.

"I hope that was the right choice."

With the perfect, devastating aim of his kind, Tightrope jumped off the windowsill and landed directly on Nina's chest. She wheezed, slightly winded. "You little . . ."

Shamelessly, Tightrope curled up and tucked his head under Nina's chin.

"Little goofball." She kissed his head in forgiveness.

A shout from the living room. Then, shattering glass. Nina leapt to her feet and ran to throw open her bedroom door, her panic now replaced by an electric surge of fear.

COTTONMOUTH CONFRONTS AN IMPOSTOR

*O*nce Nina was safely ensconced in her room and occupied with video editing work, I pretended to choke on a popcorn kernel, the sign that it was time to confront the mockingbird. After pausing the St0rye11er videos of Thou Own Dave, which had been blasting through the television for the past half hour, Reign subtly moved to lean against the window. Brightest sat cross-legged in front of the stairs. Risk took two steps across the room and planted herself in front of the hallway, scowling.

"Okay, what's up?" the fake bounty hunter asked. "I was watching that." She lounged lengthwise on a sofa. A half-finished bowl of popcorn was balanced on her tummy.

"Um. First, you aren't in trouble," I said. "We just want to understand your goals."

She sat up, relocating her snack to the coffee table. "It's no mystery, Oli. I want to prove that I'm an asset to you and your friends. A successful mission on Earth will further my long-term goal to become a bounty hunter like—"

"Mockingbird," I scolded, "stop. I warned you that shape-shifting can't deceive me anymore. So enough with the act. Why are you here?"

She grunted unhappily. "That was fast."

"Yeah, well. Earth's dangerous."

"You carnivores know all about danger, huh?" She plucked a kernel of popcorn from her bowl and threw it in the air. Her head tilted back, her mouth wide open, the fake bounty hunter caught the corn kernel. Then, she crushed it between her sharp teeth in a single, bone-snapping crunch. "Sorry. I meant us carnivores."

"You aren't really a bear," I said, "and technically, grizzlies aren't actually carnivores. They're omnivorous."

"Huh. Thanks for the clarification. I'm still working on this character."

"Is . . . is the real bounty hunter still coming?" Brightest asked.

"I wouldn't count on it. Good thing the book girl's so help-ful, right?" Mockingbird put one hand on her chest, as if com-ing clean to a terrible secret. "Okay. Truth time. I followed you to the third mountain, Brightest. Watched you beg the grizzly bear for help. 'I'll do my best,' she promised. Just like that. But guess what happened after you flew away? Seriously, guess."

"She . . . spoke to her clan as promised?"

"Nooope. She shook her head. Like this." Somberly, the mockingbird demonstrated. It was a slow, sad shake. "Then, the grizzly bear said, 'Not a chance.' Just like that. You never had a chance."

"Answer my question," I insisted. "Why are you here?"

"Does there have to be an answer?"

"Yes!"

"Well, okay. Fine. Confession time. I love all of you. You, you, you, you." Jabbing the air with her heavy, clawed hand. Pointing at Risk, Reign, Brightest, and finally, me. "That's why I'm going to help you. Or maybe . . . that's why I'm going to ruin everything. Aren't you supposed to tease and torment the people you love?"

"Not intentionally," Risk said.

"You can't really love us," I added, trying to remain calm. I didn't want to make an enemy of a trickster. Not when Ami's life depended on the success of a mission so difficult, we'd failed to recruit a young woman who once agreed to find my blanket for the price of two fish breakfasts.

"Why not?"

"Uh. Because you don't know us?" Reign ventured. "Maybe you're infatuated, which is just . . . Yeah, no thanks. Not interested. I don't go for tricksters."

"Ouch. I'm heartbroken." The mockingbird hopped upright. Her body shrank until her clothes dangled loosely from narrow shoulders and thin limbs. Her eyes shifted to a familiar shade of brown. Fur sucked into darkening skin, and black scales grew from her pores like widening sores. Now, her hair was curly and short. Now, her tongue was white. If not for our different attire, I could have mistaken her for my reflection.

"She's right, though," the mockingbird said, grasping my hands. "I'm only here for one person. You know that, don't you? Oli?"

"Ami." He must have charmed her, too.

A smile, a flash of fangs in milky gums. "No." Now, a lithe

but muscular arm snapped around my neck, squeezing me in a headlock, and a clawed hand ruffled my hair. Reign's voice boomed, "I'm here to destroy you, snake! Then, I'll be undetectable again! Ahaha!"

The real Reign and Risk leapt to help me, but in the blink of an eye, the constricting arm was gone. Fake Reign dove straight into the glass window, bursting free in a shower of glass, blood, and delighted laughter.

Then, a little gray mockingbird flittered into the air and flew away.

"What was the point of that?" I shouted. "Hey! Heeeey! What is wrong with you?"

"Let her go," Brightest advised, sighing. "I've tried reasoning with her before. It . . . pretty much ends in chaos every time."

"What an enigma," Risk said.

Reign muttered, "Enigma isn't the word I'd use." Most likely, both sisters were correct.

"Is she really here to destroy me?" I rubbed the soreness from my neck and stared at the damage. Glass was such a delicate commodity. Hopefully, Nina's family could afford to replace the window.

"Probably not," Brightest promised.

From the hallway, Nina cried, "What happened?" A moment later, she appeared with a defensively-held broom in one hand and her phone in the other. "The window!"

"The bear decided to leave," I explained.

"Does she know how to use a door?" Now, Nina turned the broom bristles down and started sweeping popcorn and glass off the floor. Fortunately, most of the shards had landed in the empty alley.

"Yeah," Risk said, stooping to pick up a triangular blade of glass. Nina gasped, "Careful!" and shooed the sisters away with a wave of her hand.

"The bear wasn't actually a bear," I tried to explain. "She's a shape-shifter, so . . . be on your guard."

When Nina gave me a look of joy and bafflement, I worried that she'd misunderstood the term *shape-shifter*. Errors in cross-language communication were uncommon, but they did happen, especially with unique or complex concepts. In her mind, every sentence I spoke was squished into the mold of her preferred language. The molds weren't always perfect fits. In fact, sometimes, they were downright terrible fits, but nothing better existed.

"So she can look like anyone?" Nina asked. "Whoa. That's a superhero power."

Not a problem of communication, then. "Yes. Her imitation isn't always perfect, though. Still. She's very good. Better than most mockingbirds, and they have a knack for shape-shifting."

"What powers do you have?" she wondered, scooting a mound of glass into a dust pan. "I remember you mentioned cottonmouth people are usually good at water magic, but what does that mean? Can you create rain? Could you . . . end a drought?"

Risk and Reign were inching close to the metal water canteen on the coffee table, their eyes bright with anticipation. They were either gonna trap a whisper in the canteen or ask me to pull a little droplet of water from the half-full canister. Those might be tiny, barely difficult examples of world-shaping, but I was unwilling to reduce our time on Earth for a bit of fun. I shook my head at them. No.

"I can do this!" Brightest said, swooping to a bowl of popcorn. They grabbed a handful of white kernels, held them to their lips, and blew, as if trying to extinguish a candle. The little white kernels tumbled and fell. "Except instead of using my breath, I manipulate the air around my body. Hawks are the best at flight-related world-shaping."

"Ohoho. The best?" Risk asked. "Careful. Don't say that around eagles."

"Or falcons," added Reign.

"Or owls."

"Or hummingbirds."

"Or—"

"Leave me alone, ladies!" Brightest cried, throwing up their hands in mock surrender. "We can all be the best in our own way."

"And coyotes?" Nina prompted. "What are your powers?"

The twins eyed the canteen again, Reign biting her lower lip, as if struggling with the temptation to throw a show. "All sorts of wonderful, useful tricks," Risk said. "We can trap a scream or song in a bottle. Vanish within shadows. Fuse fragments of ropes or papers together. Walk soundlessly across dry wood chips."

"I know how to make my eyes glow red," Reign bragged. "It's a personal skill."

"That's true. Even I can't manage the eye trick."

"Incredible," Nina praised. "You four would make a great superhero team. I'd be your tech person. Every superhero needs a tech person." She'd finished sweeping the food and glass mess into a glittering mound and was now pushing a bookshelf in front of the shattered window. I scurried to help, squeezing beside her, throwing my weight against the wooden furniture. Together, we managed to scoot the heavy thing a few feet.

"Your nemesis could be the shape-shifter," Nina continued, leaning against the wall, worn out. "I'm going to call my father now. He should know you're here."

She stepped back, hunched over her phone, and whispered to Nifty, "Call Dad."

I picked up a large piece of glass, holding it at just the right angle to catch the glow of the electric light. It was similar to the glass in my spectacles. Thinner, though. Flatter. The edge so sharp, it could slice through skin. Like a clear tooth. A dagger.

Nina's voice hitched in volume, drawing my attention. Into her phone, she cried, "Wait for me, okay?"

A pause. Reign's ears twitched, and she not so subtly shuffled closer to Nina for better eavesdropping access.

"Um, what? No, wait. I want to be there when the test evacuation happens. That's why I'm bringing a compass."

Now, Risk was crowding closer. The sisters both stood on their tip toes—don't ask me why—their ears twitching. Nina, still on the phone, gave them an amused smirk, spun on her heels, and speed-walked to her bedroom. The door snicked shut in front of the sisters' faces.

"She locked us out!" Reign exclaimed.

All four of us gathered on the couch, with Brightest perched along one armrest, their legs crossed elegantly, and the sisters sulking on either side of me. We stared at the TV, where a frozen image of Thou Own Dave grinned back at us. His outfit was brighter than feathers on a parrot. Vivid green shirt over baggy yellow pants with a hundred little pockets, all different shades of orange. He stood on a balcony, his arms spread, throwing squares of paper into the air. Poised in a single slice of time, they resembled flecks of snow. I hadn't been paying attention to the videos, instead opting to skim through facts about endangered toads, each paragraph more discouraging than the last. I had read about their diminishing habitat. Their susceptibility to contaminants. How small they were. How delicate. How overlooked. Once, after a heavy rain in Nina's homeland, you could step outside and hear the ruckus of a thousand toad songs. I hadn't heard a single croak. Even when we traveled to the woods, where a toad might live in the leaf litter or within the haunted tunnel, the only sounds had come from birds and insects. And the whoosh of cars on the paved road, beyond the empty palace of concrete and dark glass.

"Why is he throwing paper into the air?" I asked.

"It's a game," Brightest said. "Thou Own Dave signed his name on one piece of confetti. All the rest are blank. His house, it's on the side of a steep hill."

"Hollywood," Reign supplied. "Far, far away."

"Hollywood," Brightest agreed. "Off his balcony and down the hill is a crowd of people, waiting. The one who finds his signature will win money."

"I wonder what'll happen," Risk said, reaching for the black control to the television.

He was moving again. Laughing, jubilant. Thou Own Dave's voice-over explained his inner thoughts: *I really didn't expect the situation to escalate. Things got scary fast.* The video zoomed in, focusing on the young man. He looked down his nose, down the mountain, down at unseen participants in a game of chance. A murmur of voices rose, distant shouts. Still looking down, his smile sharpened, and then he doubled over, as if cringing so adamantly, the move hurt his guts. "Oooooh, no! Stop, stop!" At first, he was laughing and pointing. Then, he wasn't laughing, but an edge of glee still sharpened his voice. "Ah, no way! Those ladies are really fighting. We need to get down there." The voice-over reiterated: *It was supposed to be fun. Not everyone wins the grand prize, but they all get a six-pack of caffeinated spring water and a gift card to the Dave Depot.*

He ran through a room of white. White furniture, white carpet, white walls. White contraptions that might have been sculptures, machines, or toys, although I couldn't guess their purpose. Down a spiral staircase, each step a different color. Into a room of green with a carpet so thick, it resembled the short, bright grass humans planted around their houses. Then, he descended another multicolored staircase. His house never seemed to end, as if it filled the hill with rooms. *This is the problem with humanity*, his voice-over lectured. *People all want to be the big winner. They aren't content with less. But now, I need to break up a catfight, which means the giveaway may be canceled. Nobody wins anything.*

"I want to see this fight," Reign complained. "When does the house end?"

"I think he has to run through all the colors in the rainbow," Risk said.

Brightest propped their chin on their hands and said, "I wish I lived in a rainbow."

At last, he emerged into a sunlit room on the ground floor, but the journey didn't end there: Thou Own Dave burst outside through a heavy pair of doors, using both of his hands to shove them open simultaneously. Then, he jogged down a winding path, passing a row of minicars—Dave buggies, according to their license plates—and a swimming pool with a diving board. There were inflatable swans floating on the blue water. A young woman dozed on a towel, her yellow hair fanned out across the sun-heated poolside. I felt a surge of longing. It had been days since my last nap. On Earth, the sun was bright and warm, its rays as gentle as a lullaby.

Finally, Thou Own Dave reached a gate with high, spiked bars. He flipped a lever and threw his shoulder against the gate, knocking it open. The sound of chatter swelled as he walked around the base of the hill, approaching a crowd of fifteen young adults. They stood among dirty scraps of paper, forming a ring of spectators around two women. Based on Thou Own Dave's buildup of the fight, I'd expected blood or bruises. Humans were great architects of weapons. They'd invented guns, bombs, and swords. Even Nina carried a weapon with her: the can of Mace, a deterrent no less effective than my bite. But the women weren't even wrestling. They stood face-to-face, holding hands. The camera zoomed in, revealing that they were both grasping the same piece of paper. Part of Thou Own Dave's signature was visible between their thumbs, the ink smudged.

"If you rip it, no prize!" Thou Own Dave cried.

I made that last-minute rule to prevent them from hurting each other. If they wanted to stand in the sun all day and see who could last longer, I couldn't stop them. It's a free country.

Picnic blankets, like islands of food, were spread around the two women. The rest of the spectators dispersed to eat, soak in tiny plastic pools of water, and drink fruit juice from large, clear pitchers. Thou Own Dave gave the two women cups of ice water and stools. One of them asked for a bathroom break. He brought a cup—*The look on her face! I can't believe she actually thought I'd be such an asshole!*—then laughed, and said, "Just kidding. You both have ten minutes. Go!"

The moment it became clear that there'd be no real fight, Risk and Reign lost interest in Thou Own Dave and started reading the toad books, their brows scrunched in concentration. Brightest was standing near the broken window, staring out through the centimeter-wide slice of open space between the bookshelf and the window frame.

But I couldn't bear to look away. I had to know what would happen. How long could two people stand in the toasty sun without napping? Why didn't they just share the money prize? Perhaps they were both desperate for it all. I could relate. Frankly, I'd play tug-of-war with a piece of paper till my whole body gave out, if it meant saving Ami.

The standoff was getting ridiculous. The mosquitoes were having Sunday brunch on their legs. I had to broker a peace agreement.

"New rule. The first person to release the ticket cannot be voted out of the house this week," Thou Own Dave announced, clasping each woman on the shoulder. "Who wants the money, and who wants the immunity?"

"The story just lost me," I confessed. "Why are people being voted out of houses?"

"I dunno, Oli," Reign said. "Can you shut it off and help us read?"

That's when the squeak of wheels announced Nina's return. She was pulling a large purple suitcase into the living room. "Okay, everybody!" she announced. "Time to visit Grandma."

NINA, 2 DAYS BEFORE LANDFALL

Recipient username: Nina's Stories

Received: 2:59 P.M.

Read: 3:38 P.M.

Subject: CONGRATULATIONS!

Hey, Nina's Stories! Guess what? Thou Own Dave wants to feature your submission, GRIZZLY BEAR ATTACK IN A HAUNTED TUNNEL, in his stories! You know how it works, right? Did you read the user terms? Of course you did. Simply sign the attached NDA and release form.* That's it. We'll handle the rest. Your video will appear on THURSDAY. Half of the profits GRIZZLY BEAR ATTACK IN A HAUNTED TUNNEL raises in the first 24 hours will be deposited in your St0ryte11er account. You're welcome.

What are you waiting for? Respond!

Thanks for the entertainment.

TEAM DAVE

Sitting in a train car with Risk, Reign, Brightest, Oli, and Tightrope, Nina lowered her phone. "Whoa," she said. "Tomorrow is Thursday."

"Huhm?" Oli asked. He'd been curled with his head nestled against the vibrating train wall, fighting motion sickness in the windowless car. Nina had spent every dollar of her savings on five economy tickets and one pet pass on the fast rail; she couldn't afford to splurge on window seats. Fortunately, the trip was less than two hours long, and her father would be waiting with his truck at the station. But he was only expecting her, and the thought of explaining the animal people situation made Nina's stomach flip almost as enthusiastically as Oli's stomach.

Oddly, the message from Thou Own Dave didn't improve her mood. The hurricane had jumped to the top of Nina's hierarchy of worries.

"The video," she said. "They're uploading it tomorrow. Thursday."

They'd have the profits by Friday, shortly before the hurricane struck.

What would happen on Saturday?

"Hooray!" Reign grabbed Tightrope's front paws and raised them in the air, making the cat cheer. It had taken ten minutes for Tightrope to escape his pod-shaped pet carrier. Ten minutes and a hundred plaintive meows. That's when Brightest cried, "I can't take it anymore! He's so sad! Free him!" Tightrope had spent the rest of the ride alternating among laps.

"That's good, right?" Oli asked, cracking open one eye to look at Nina. "The money will save the Ami toads?"

"Well . . . it might help. I've contacted the reintroduction program, asking what we can do. They haven't responded yet, but I think it'll take a lot of work and time. In any case, I'm sure the money will be huge. And I promise: after you go home, I'll continue helping the toads. My mom is friends with a lot of scientists. They're studying changes in the ocean—it's a big project. International. I'm just saying: she has to know at least one amphibian expert. I can keep you updated by putting notes in the books Dad sells the wolves."

"Thank you. I know this is a lot to ask."

"Nah. It's the right thing to do."

Reign released Tightrope's paws, and he primly jumped onto Risk's lap. "You seem sad," Reign observed. "Is it the storm? Don't worry, Nina. You helped us, so we'll help you."

"Can you stop a hurricane?" she asked. "Magically?"

To her surprise, the animal people seemed to consider her question, as if there might be an answer more encouraging than, "Sorry, no."

"When it comes to shaping the air and wind," Brightest finally said, "all my skills are flight-related. I can manipulate the area around my wingspan. It helps with midair acrobatics, but I can't dampen a storm."

"A group of people might pull it off in the Reflecting World," Risk added, "if they worked together and had the guidance of a skilled elder world-shaper."

"Wait, really?" Nina wondered. "Hey, you're a group. Can't you try that here?"

"Earth physics complicates matters," Oli said. "Plus, we're far from elders."

"Great-Uncle once lassoed a tornado!" Reign said. "On Earth! Alone! Remember?"

"Uh-huh," Risk intoned. "Suuuure he did."

"What's with the sarcasm?"

"No offense to Great-Uncle, but isn't it funny how all his best stories happen when nobody is watching?"

"There weren't witnesses because everybody had to hide in their storm cellars."

Risk smiled sweetly. "Of course. It doesn't matter, anyway. A hurricane is wider than a hundred tornadoes. It can't be lassoed."

"Could you block hurricane winds from damaging one small area?" Nina asked. "Like a house?"

Oli rubbed his face and made a hissing sound, signaling his thoughts. "Maybe for a few minutes? What do you think, Risk? Reign? You're the most experienced world-shapers."

"By combining your control of wind and water with our trick-related skills, we might be able to shield a house, but it'll drain our time on Earth too quickly. We'd vanish before the eye of the storm passes."

"Where do you go when you vanish from Earth?" Nina asked.

"Home. Or if somebody has no fixed home, they'll go

somewhere comforting, like a flower-filled meadow in the Reflecting World. But I don't understand. What sickness does your grandma have? Can you put her in an ambulance? They're like movable hospitals."

"She knows what an ambulance is," Risk said. "She's literally from here."

"It wouldn't help." Nina shook her head, dismayed. "Her heart gives out when she leaves home. She can't evacuate anymore. That's what really worries me. It's not just this hurricane. It's all the others. Because there will be more. Next year and the year after." She considered the predicament. "Hm. Do any of you know healing magic?"

"Sorry," Brightest said, imitating Nina's headshake. "That kind of world-shaping is rare these days."

Rare meant possible. That made her wonder . . .

"Oh." Nina felt silly posing the follow-up question, kind of like a poker player asking for a royal flush. "Even so, could somebody with the skill . . . subconsciously heal themselves?"

"Possibly." Brightest tilted their head, seeming to reconsider. "That's a good question for a healer."

The train began to slow, and from every speaker, the conductor's voice intoned, "We are approaching Cedar Station. Next stop: Cedar Station." Nina picked up Tightrope and gently placed him in the blanket-lined carrier, a violet pod with gridlike airholes. "That's us," she said. "Get ready."

"Ah," Oli sighed. "Finally."

Risk and Reign grabbed the cat carrier and suitcase, while Nina led them down the aisle between compartments. The metal floor vibrated and swayed, and she had to lean against the wall twice to stay upright. Oli and Brightest also seemed precariously unsteady; they clung to each other, their legs shaking.

"Will we need to leap off while the train is moving?" Oli asked, his voice tight with concern.

"No," Nina said. "It'll come to a full stop. Be careful, though. There's a gap between the train and the platform. Drops straight to the tracks."

Only one other person, an elderly woman wrapped in shawls, waited at the exit. She stared at Nina's group with undisguised interest, her eyes glittering under thick gray eyebrows. Cedar Station was between cities and seemed more like an afterthought than an actual station. When the train jerked to a complete stop, a green ceiling light turned on, and the door slid open with a ding. Outside was a narrow platform and a twenty-car parking lot with only one truck in it.

"My dad's already here," Nina said, politely waiting for the elderly woman to step off. Then, Nina took Brightest by the hand and helped them onto the platform. Oli followed, his posture relaxing noticeably once he was on solid ground. Risk and Reign didn't hesitate to cross the threshold, their steps as balanced and swift as always.

A minute later, as they approached the truck, Nina realized she'd been mistaken. Her dad wasn't behind the wheel.

"You brought friends!" her grandmother exclaimed, rolling down the window. She shook her head, turning off the vehicle with a twist of the ignition key and stepping outside to have a better look at Nina's group. "Five teenagers. I didn't expect a full truck, but you're welcome to pile in. It's lucky your father stayed behind to pack my papers."

"I call the open-air part!" Reign cheered, throwing the luggage into the truck bed and climbing in after it.

"Me too," Risk said, passing Tightrope to Nina before joining her sister.

"That won't do!" Grandma scolded. "It's too dangerous; you'll sit in the backseat with your seat belts fastened. My god. Will there be enough room?"

"I can always fly," Brightest volunteered.

Nina's grandmother resumed shaking her head with disbelief. "Fly?"

"They aren't human," Nina said. "They're from the Reflecting World, Grandma. Two coyotes, a cottonmouth, and a hawk. All this time, Dad's been trading with wolves! I knew it. I knew it! Aren't they wonderful?" Nina pointed to Oli with a pleased flourish; she felt a bit like a ringmaster highlighting the star of a grand show. Now bearing the brunt of all human attention in the parking lot, Oli smiled stiffly and bent his fingers in a tiny wave.

"You're serious?" Grandma asked. "That kid is an animal?"

"Yes. I've seen him transform."

"I can also transform," Brightest chimed in. "Check out these head wings." After glancing around, ensuring that the parking lot was empty, they yanked aside the floral scarf Nina had tied around their wings. Grandma's wary smirk vanished when she saw the feathered appendages, which flexed in the sunlight, as if testing the air.

"What in the . . ." Grandma stepped closer, leaning in to inspect the connection between Brightest's temple and the base of their left wing. "Don't they get heavy?" she asked.

"Not really. They sometimes squish my false ears, though."

"Don't forget about our ears!" Reign called, wrestling with the knot of her scarf. At last, she gave up, and just slipped the fabric back until it dangled around her neck. "They hear everything."

"Beautiful," Grandma said. Her eyes, deep-set and cradled by laugh lines, glistened. "You must be proud of them." Then, she looked at Nina. Clasped her hands, kissed her cheek. "I never thought I'd meet anyone from the Reflecting World."

"But you have. The wolves, the Odd Jobs Man."

"Those meetings weren't proper. I have so many questions!"

"That's good, 'cause they know so much!"

Grandma stepped away from Nina and slid into the truck, settling behind the steering wheel. "Load up," she ordered. "Sit wherever you please. Just be careful!"

With the sisters in the bed of the truck, Oli, Tightrope, and Brightest in the backseats, and Nina in shotgun, Grandma turned the key in the ignition. The engine stuttered alive with a couple high-pitched *vrrrooms*, then settled into a low hum. There were no charging ports at the train station, but the old truck had more than enough juice to take them home.

"Before we get small-talking, tell them about your condition," Nina suggested.

"Ah." Grandma clicked her tongue. "I'll give the whole spiel."

"Don't worry. This isn't a doctor visit. They have a different perspective."

"We also know very little about human health," Oli said. "Practically nothing."

That was all the convincing Grandma needed to launch into

her history, beginning in her hearty childhood, and ending with the near-death experience on a train to Des Moines. "I couldn't ask for a lovelier cage," she commented, pointing with her nose at the world beyond the open driver-side window. "But a cage is still a cage, and I want to understand why I'm in one."

"We're baffled," Risk called from the bed of the truck.

"Nobody in our pack has got sick like that," Reign explained.

"Well, Nina has a theory. Don't you, sweetheart?"

"Yes. At first, I thought the land itself had a healing quality. Like the fountain of youth, except the ground of health. If that was true, we could grab shovels and fill the truck with dirt to help Grandma survive an evacuation."

Oli hissed thoughtfully. "Huh. That doesn't line up with experience, though. Locations don't do magic. People do magic at different locations."

"Tell him about your latest theory," Grandma urged. "I'm honestly surprised you didn't lead with it." There was a teasing edge to her voice, but Nina got the impression that she was being teased for her reticence, rather than the idea itself. "Nina has been studying a family story for years," Grandma explained. "It was originally shared by her great-great-grandmother."

Assorted ears swiveled or turned toward Nina. Brightest even extended their head wings to more clearly hear her response.

"Hey," Risk said. "You've been holding out on us?"

"We've told you hundreds of stories," Reign said, only slightly exaggerating.

Laughing, Nina apologized. "Sorry. It's just that I don't have solid evidence. Only the partially translated words of a woman who is gone now. And I only just figured them out."

"Seems like plenty good evidence to me," Oli encouraged.

"Alright. The story . . . it hints that my great-great-grandmother was a child of a woman from Earth, and a spirit from the Reflecting World. I know it's unlikely, since human spirits disappeared 'round the end of the joined era—"

"Not all of them," Oli interjected, his voice apologetically soft. "The Nightmare is still around somewhere."

"France," Risk said.

"That's right. And a small group survived his war on—"

Now, it was Nina's turn to interrupt. "Hold it. The Nightmare?"

"Yes," Reign explained. "He also calls himself a King. Remember that guy we mentioned earlier?"

"No. Way. The Nightmare! El pesadillo? He's a human spirit? Would he kill another human spirit, too?"

"Yeah," Oli said. "Actually, that's his favorite kind of murder."

The truck decelerated, as if Grandma had reallocated more of her concentration from the empty road to the conversation. With the change in speed, Oli cringed, as if pained by the choppy movement.

"What about descendants?" Nina asked. "Like . . . hypothetically . . . the people in my family line?"

"From what I know, he won't hurt mortals, but I guess it also depends on their world-shaping strength? Good news is, as distant relatives, I bet you're safe. Actually, Nina, I doubt you got any skill for shaping. Your grandma might've inherited a small amount."

Nina's relief that the Nightmare wouldn't hunt down her family far exceeded her disappointment that she had little to no magic. But the disappointment was still there, like a gloomy lining of a silver cloud.

"And you four? Are you really safe?" she asked, probably for the hundredth time since they first discussed hunters on the bus.

"Yeeeees!" Reign promised.

"Pinky swear," Brightest agreed, picking impatiently at the faded fabric seat cover. They'd learned about the sacred "pinky swear" during one of Thou Own Dave's videos and—maybe because they had wings—seemed completely charmed by a promise sealed with locked fingers. "I need to hear your story now, Nina. We've spent way too long telling our own!"

"Share it." Grandma's voice lacked its previous levity. "Go ahead."

Before Nina could begin, she heard a hiss of surprise.

"This place," Oli said, his eyes round and big behind his spectacles. "It's so familiar."

He pointed at the old gas station, its tanks empty, the weed-cracked ground still spotted with oil stains. At the former farmhouse with newspaper-covered windows. And finally, at the row of windmills with blades shaped like seagull wings.

"We landed here!" Risk shouted in response. "I can smell it! Hey, you live in a part of the Earth that pulls on the tethered world."

"That's good news for you!" Reign added. "World shaping is easier in places like these."

"We've gone in a circle," Brightest said, awestruck, as if that meant something deeply significant.

"The homeland," Nina agreed. "It makes sense. Compasses don't work here. Here, where the story begins . . ."

Here, where the two worlds embraced, and magic rose to the Earth like the enduring water in Rosita's well.

COTTONMOUTH
REMEMBERS FLOWERS

I'd spent hours in one room—the "guest room," although there wasn't much space for guests. Sunlight no longer fell through the slender gaps between the planks across the window. Around me were waterproof containers full of things. More things than I could properly describe in one story. I'd never seen so many Earth objects. Papers and tools, machines crafted by machines. For a moment, I was delighted by the unnecessary, overwhelming abundance. As I packed, I turned each object in my hand, pressing buttons. If there was text, I read it. Instructions on how to use a footbath. Menus describing feasts of meat, fried potatoes, and cakes. Then, I saw a wooden doll with a smiling face and a seam along her belly. With a twist, she popped in half, revealing that a second, smaller doll was hidden inside her hollow body. Instinctually, I turned to my right, looking for Ami, eager to share the discovery of dolls inside dolls. That's where he'd sit at the lakeside: on a flat stone—barely larger than a pebble—to the right of my basking rock, in the shade of the grasses.

His absence was a stark reminder of the world beyond the cluttered boundaries of Grandma's guest room. I stopped lingering over every fascinating object and packed in earnest. Risk and Reign were helping Nina flood-proof the living room and closets by stowing important belongings in waterproof containers. Brightest was chattering Grandma's ear off and assisting with miscellaneous prehurricane chores. Nina's father, alone, worked outside; every so often, he'd peek into the house and shake his head, repeating, "I'll be damned." The first time he said that, I had to reassure my friends that the expression conveyed a sense of disbelief and wonder, despite its literal meaning. My time on Earth, with its many written directions and unusual English phrases, was really highlighting the value of my communications skills.

Even after hours, my work in the guest room was just partially finished, but I'd managed to uncover a mattress previously hidden under piles of books. The scribes ought to visit Grandma's house sometime; it was closer than the bookshop and had enough material for months of transcription work. Satisfied with my accomplishments, I curled up on the dusty mattress, wrapped myself in a polka-dot blanket, and fell asleep. Dreamlessly, the night passed.

There was a tickle on my cheek, an insect's gentle feet. I brushed it away.

"Oliiiii!"

"Oli, hey! You overslept!"

"Whua?" All this time, the insect had been Risk and Reign leaning over me, the tips of their loose manes tickling my face.

"Sun's been up for three hours," Risk teased. "Have you decided to embrace the nocturnal lifestyle?"

I rubbed my eyes and then patted the mattress, finding my spectacles by touch. Reign helpfully flipped a switch embedded in the wall, lighting the room with yellow electric lights. Such lights were in the ceiling of every room, some protected behind a glass bowl, others bare coils of incandescence. "I stayed awake too late," I guessed, "and the boarded windows sabotaged my internal clock."

"Excuses," Risk snickered. "Guess what happened while you were sleeping."

I shook my head and wriggled off the mattress, standing. My clothes were wrinkled, and my fake hair stuck up in wavy clumps.

"We're famous," Reign said.

"You mean . . . ?"

From the belly of the house, four voices lifted in unison, cheering, "One million!"

Risk and Reign grabbed me by the hands and guided me down the hall in a scamper. Around the kitchen table, their faces glowing in the light of a laptop screen, sat Nina, her father, and her grandmother. Brightest was bouncing on the balls of their feet, making an excited "Waaaaaaah!" I could hear Thou Own Dave's energetic voice coming from the computer speakers; from the context alone, I knew he was narrating our video.

"You know how I suspect the bear escaped from a traveling circus?" he asked. "Now I'm confident that the girls did, too. They have to be Cirque acrobats. Patrick, are you sure this video is real?"

A softer voice chimed in, "It's been reviewed, Dave. No sign of manipulation."

"In that case, check the news feed for an article on four missing kids. If the bear didn't get them, the tunnel did. It's full of cannibal ghosts, right? I may be thinking of another, similar nope-tunnel."

"Does he actually think we died, or is that just his sense of humor?" Risk asked.

"It's humor," Nina said, winking. "He'd never post a snuff film."

"Not even for the views?" her father asked. Judging by his scowl, which hadn't faltered since the video started playing, he wasn't the biggest fan of Thou Own Dave.

"Dad, of course not. That would violate the St0rytel1er code of conduct. He'd never risk a demotion to gold tier."

"I don't know anything about this man."

"Know this: he's going to make us rich." Nina pointed at me with her index finger. "And half of that goes to the toads."

"We did it, then?" I sat heavily on the only empty chair, wooden with a high back and a creaky leg. A mound of fine-smelling eggs and potatoes steamed on the counter, and Nina's grandmother stood to get plates from the cabinet. We weren't packing anything in the kitchen; the bowls, plates, and pans could survive a flood. But the refrigerator, which had been decorated with a collage of art—hand-drawn pictures of houses and animals, "love you grandma" written in unsteady characters—was bare now, the papers stuffed into plastic bags.

"Yeah," Nina said. "It's a good first step."

I allowed myself to smile.

Like that moment in the guest room, briefly, everything was fine.

But time continued flowing.

As I drew farther away from breakfast—as clouds multiplied in the sky, as boxes filled with oddities, as the weatherwoman on TV was replaced by a weatherman, as we completed chore after chore until there was nothing left to keep Risk, Reign, and Brightest busy, nothing more Nina and her father could do to protect Grandma—I realized that my optimism was like a tree growing along a river.

Specifically, the flowering desert willow.

She grew alongside the river between my mother's cottage and the dammed city. The desert willow's branches were always bright with pastel pink flowers. No matter the season, she bloomed. When my siblings and I passed her on the riverboat, we'd press our bodies against the railing, leaning as far as we dared, and shout, "Hello!" The desert willow would respond with a rustle of leaves, shaking loose petals that drifted, spinning, into the water. I always wanted to introduce myself properly, but the current was too quick. We had just a moment to appreciate her beauty. Then, she was a vague smudge of color on the horizon. Then, she was gone.

With a snap of clasps, I sealed the final box in the guest room. The window board gaps were bright with a murky light, the sunset filtered through dark clouds. I stood, my movement stirring up dust motes, and gave the room a final once-over. All the delightful clutter of the previous evening was hidden within walls of opaque plastic. Boxes were neatly stacked against the walls and around the entirely cleared mattress. Good enough. The wooden floor creaked under my bare feet as I walked to the living room, where Risk and Reign were playing a board game with

Grandma and Nina. Brightest stood against the window, peeking between two boards. I wondered what they saw out there. What they were looking for.

"All done," I said, kneeling near the table.

"Thank you, sweetheart," Grandma said. "You've been very helpful."

On the low table, a wooden bowl was filled with chocolates wrapped in silvery foil. I took one, carefully unfolded its glittering wrapping, and popped the whole candy in my mouth. As it melted, the deep, complex flavor of cacao spread across my tongue. In the dammed city, they serve chocolate thick and spiced, not delicately sweet. I liked both versions.

As I reached for a second candy, Grandma pushed a polka-dotted paper bag across the table. A clump of festively springy blue strips was taped to one face of the bag.

"It's a gift," Nina explained. "You all get something." That's when I noticed the plush puppy dog toys sitting between the twins. And around their neck, Brightest wore a new white scarf with a bluebird print. An obvious theme emerged when I found a rubber snake coiled on the bottom of my gift bag. The color of pine needles, it wiggled when I freed it by the tail. "So lifelike! Thank you!"

"I wanted to give you a cottonmouth toy," Grandma explained, "but couldn't find one in my gift reserves."

"That's okay. This little guy is the spitting image of a tree snake who once waved at me." I draped it around my neck, imitating Brightest with their scarf. Conveniently, the fake snake curled into a loose ring.

Grandma leaned back from the game board, a square of cardboard covered with bright rectangles, glass pebbles, and numbers. "Now that you're all here, I need to say this: if the evacuation doesn't go well tomorrow morning, I want you to continue without me."

Three voices responded simultaneously.

Nina: "No!"

Risk: "Huh? Why?"

Reign: "Seriously?"

Grandma responded to the loudest of the three. "Yes, seriously. The winds could blow my house over. The tornado shelter could flood. It's too dangerous."

"Not with us around," I said. "If I get pinned under a slab of roof, I'll resist the rain using all my world-shaping power. Within minutes—I promise—that'll send me safely home. You are at the greatest risk."

"I'm also an adult who can choose to put herself in danger."

"So are we," Risk argued.

"It's true, Grandmother. My sister and I are grown! You think our pack would let a couple babies journey to Earth?"

"Maybe it will be dangerous," Nina cried out, standing. "So what? You're family, Grandma. Dad, why've you been so quiet? Tell her. We don't abandon family."

Nina's father, who'd been listening from the kitchen entryway, joined us in the room with two long strides. He plunged his hand into the bowl of candy, emptying it with one grab. However, after a moment's hesitation, he thoughtfully returned a couple pieces. The rest went directly into his windbreaker pocket.

"Wait, what happened to your good jacket?" Nina asked. "That one looks like it's from the early 2000s."

"I found it in the back of a closet," he said, smiling. "So maybe it is from then. Amazing what she's saved. Mom. Listen . . ."

"Yes?" Nina asked.

He bit a chocolate in half and swallowed the piece whole. "We've just forgotten the reality of our worlds."

He knelt beside me, resting a hand on my shoulder and squeezing. "When it comes to survival, Oli here could live to see the mountains crumble and re-form as the continents collide. He could live until the last cottonmouth on Earth either dies or transforms into something new. I reckon snakes will reign supreme far longer than humans, don't you?"

"No idea," I said, "but it would be neat to watch a mountain form."

"Sure would." He stood, crossing over to Brightest. "What about birds? Descendants of dinosaurs, lords of the sky? Do you know the most dangerous element of a hurricane, Mom? It's the wind. Do winds scare you, Brightest?"

"Never have," they said, still fixated on the view out the window. "Nina's . . . father?"

"That's 'Nina's dad' to you," he corrected.

"What about us?" Reign asked. "Can you convince her that we're heroes?"

"Well—"

In the moment of thoughtful hesitation, Nina spoke up. "Half of the greatest legendary stories begin with the daring spirit of coyote folk," she said. "Monster hunters. Adventurers. If I had to choose two people to defy a force of nature, I'd chose you every time."

"So you should! We'll do our best"—Risk turned from Nina to Grandma—"to protect your family."

The vertical wrinkle up Grandma's forehead deepened with thought. "Right," she finally said. Then, with an almost painful severity in her tone: "I need to fetch more candies. Somebody took them all."

Nina's father grinned, shrugging. "Mechanical work burns calories. Speaking of, I better get back to the shed. Almost finished repairing the old boat. You know how to use boats, right, Oli?"

"Yes."

"Fantastic." With a nod, he strode out the front door, his bright yellow jacket flapping like a cape. Grandma shook her head and puttered to the kitchen, closely followed by Nina. Soon, I heard them rummaging in a cabinet.

"What have you been gaping at this whole time, Brightest?" Risk asked.

"See for yourself," they offered, stepping aside. With that invitation, the twins and I joined them at the window. Across the lawn, the open garage was aglow, a rectangle of yellow light. Tools hung on the walls, and a single car was parked alongside a gas-powered generator. Nina's father—dressed in his standard jean jacket—was filling the generator with the contents of a red canister.

"Has he been there the whole time?" I whispered.

"Yup. Wasn't completely sure who was whom."

I tasted the air. Faintly, there it was: the hint of a mocking-bird. "Well, that explains the jacket."

"Do we tell the humans?" Reign asked.

"Nah," Risk whispered. "That would complicate everything. Plus, she convinced Grandma to let us stay."

"I wonder," Reign said, "whether she's trying to help us, or get us killed."

That—in my opinion—was a very good question.

NINA, SHORTLY BEFORE LANDFALL

Friday 6:01 A.M. (MOM)

Update?

Friday 6:02 A.M. (NINA)

Dad's loading the truck. Almost ready to leave.

Friday 6:03 A.M. (MOM)

Drive carefully. You know how people get when it rains.

Friday 6:04 A.M. (NINA)

We're going to go really slow. 30–40 mph

Friday 6:05 A.M. (MOM)

Driving under the speed limit can be dangerous, too.

Friday 6:06 A.M. (NINA)

Got no choice. Grandma needs time to adjust. Dad says he'll turn on the emergency blinky lights.

Friday 6:07 A.M. (MOM)

What's her heart rate now?

Friday 6:08 A.M. (NINA)

74 bpm

Friday 6:09 A.M. (MOM)

> Pull over if it spikes & double-check via the pulse on her wrist or neck. Finger monitors aren't 100% reliable. Don't show her the compass. It may cause anxiety.

Friday 6:10 A.M. (NINA)

> OK.

Friday 6:11 A.M. (MOM)

> This week has been TOO MUCH. Animal spirits and hurricanes!!!

Friday 6:12 A.M. (NINA)

> Yeah. You're missing out.

Friday 6:13 A.M. (MOM)

> I really am.

Friday 6:14 A.M. (NINA)

> It's time to go!! Text you soon!

Friday 6:14 A.M. (MOM)

> Love you.

Friday 6:15 A.M. (NINA)

> Love you too.

Friday 6:16 A.M. (NINA)

> PS why are you awake so late? Go to bed, Mom!!

Friday 6:17 A.M. (MOM)

> Very funny. :) And no.

The outer bands of Jeremy-2 hadn't reached Texas, but overhead, the clouds moved quickly, spilling bursts of fine drizzle, hinting at the storm to come. Nina slipped her phone in her hoodie pocket and jogged across the crunchy gravel driveway. With an exhausted yawn—it had been difficult to sleep a wink that night—she slid into the back of the truck cab. Risk and Reign were seated beside her; in their true forms, they resembled small dogs. A ruffled Brightest sat on Risk's head, and Oli slithered around Nina's feet, half-concealed by shadows.

In the front passenger seat, Grandma glanced at her pulse oximeter and reported, "Seventy-eight. Average." Shaped like a squat clothespin, the device pinched the tip of her pointer finger and measured her heartbeat (among other things). She'd purchased it from a medical supply depot after the Des Moines incident.

"It'll stay low," Nina's father commented, as if he could predict the future, as if death could be charted on a map like the red swirl of a hurricane. But they all had to hope—on some level—that Grandma's illness was not actually so bad. Otherwise, what was the point of escaping? Even Nina, who'd championed Rosita's story as the key to all their family secrets, was not 100 percent confident that Grandma's health depended on the power of the Reflecting World. That's why she'd come prepared with tools to test her hypothesis.

"It didn't stay low last time," Grandma sighed. "But we'll see."

Nina placed a dollar store compass in her lap. Its red needle jumped back and forth between west and east, dancing to the rhythm of an alien magnetic field. If Grandma was using world-shaping to stay alive, there should be a correlation between the strength of the magnetic interference and her declining health.

As the truck turned onto the paved road, Nina pulled Tightrope out of his carrier and onto her lap. Clearly born with a faulty sense of self-preservation, he batted at Risk's leg, trying to play. "Don't do that to any other coyote," Nina warned the cat, sticking him back into the carrier. "Remember how we found you?"

Bleeding, his stomach punctured by teeth.

"You know, Grandma . . . lately, I've been wondering if you healed him. Magically."

Her grandma chuckled. "I wish. If I had the ability to heal, I'd use it to help more than one cat. Remember when you broke your wrist, son?"

"Unfortunately, yes." He said. "Twelve years old. First time using a skateboard. Just my luck, right?"

"Nina, there were a thousand times I wished I could've fixed his fractured bone, but it still took weeks to heal."

"It could have been unintentional, subconscious." Nina leaned forward, sticking her free hand through the gap between front seats. As always, her nails were chewed to the skin, with plenty of ragged hangnails. "Before we leave the neighborhood, try to fix one of my fingers."

"The state of those nails, Nina!"

"I know, I know. It's a bad habit."

"I'll do my best." Nina felt the warmth of her grandmother's hands as they clasped hers. In the following minute, they passed Paul's camper. His windows hadn't been secured, as if he didn't get how to respond to bad hurricanes; perhaps he'd moved there from a landlocked state. Hopefully, he knew enough to evacuate. He might be a pest, but Nina didn't want him to suffer.

"Nothing," Grandma said, releasing Nina's hand.

"Nothing?" She inspected her fingers in the bleak gray-sky

light. Sure enough, none of the little cuts had healed. "Yeah. Nothing."

They drove in silence for a while, passing a hill beyond a wire fence.

"There was the cricket . . ."

Nina, who'd been inspecting her hangnails, looked up. "Cricket, Grandma?" She couldn't see her grandmother's face, its expressive web of folds around her mouth and eyes which conveyed every emotion.

"I was a girl. Barefoot, playing outside, running through the grass. Something small crumpled under my toes. I'd stepped on a cricket, this plump, fragile bug with long, bent legs. They were twitching in desperate spasms. I was so young. I'd never seen anything die. But I knew. I just knew.

"The ants were already gathering, so I scooped up that cricket and cradled its body in the palm of my hand. And I remember this part so clearly: it twitched once more, a full-body snap of motion, and then it simply hopped away."

Brightest ruffled their feathers and chirped softly, inquisitively.

"Maybe you do have powers," her father said. "But . . ."

The pause dragged on.

"But what?" Nina urged.

"But they only work when somebody is dying."

In the troubled silence that followed, the compass needle continued jumping. However, with every mile, the speed and amplitude of its movement lessened.

Twenty-five miles later, Grandma said, "Eighty-one beats per minute."

Then, ten miles later, "Eighty-five."

At eighty-nine beats per minute, Nina glanced at her phone to check the time and noticed the notification symbol—a red exclamation point—above her St0ryte11er app. She had a message.

It was from Thou Own Dave.

"Whoa. Twenty-four hours have passed since the video uploaded."

With a flick of his eyes, her father's attention darted from the road to Nina, then back to the road. "That's good?"

"It means I'll get paid soon. Last I checked, the video had over seventy million views."

"You can't be serious. How did almost a quarter of the country's population watch that in a day?"

"It's an international audience, I guess. Universe-tier St0rytellers are big." She opened her account and scrolled to the full message.

🝡

Recipient username: Nina's Stories

Received: 8:00 A.M.

Read: 9:08 A.M.

Subject: PROFITS OF GRIZZLY BEAR ATTACK IN A HAUNTED TUNNEL

Hey, Nina's Stories! Guess what? Your video, GRIZZLY BEAR ATTACK IN A HAUNTED TUNNEL made bank! Thou Own Dave has deposited $58.31 USD into your St0ryte11er account.

Buy something nice.

TEAM DAVE

"What." Nina reread the message, convinced she'd misunder-stood something. Fifty-eight dollars? She couldn't rebuild a toad sanctuary with fifty-eight dollars! She could barely buy a new pair of shoes with fifty-eight dollars! "This can't be right."

"Huhm?"

"No. It's impossible." She rechecked the view count of GRIZZLY BEAR ATTACK IN A HAUNTED TUNNEL. It had spiked since early morning and now exceeded 80 million views. That was immensely successful, even for Thou Own Dave, who averaged 19 million views per story. She might have pro-vided his most-watched commentary video ever, and at the rate universe-tier people were paid, it should have fetched at least half a million dollars.

"They made a mistake," she said. "Fifty-eight dollars and thirty-one cents? I should have a quarter million!"

The coyotes tilted their heads, listening. Brightest stopped preening their wing and straightened, peeking at the phone screen.

"Money doesn't come easy . . ." Nina's father said.

"No. It does. For him, it does. This has to be a mistake. I signed a contract."

Nina jabbed the reply button and sent off a quick, collected message:

Recipient username: TEAM DAVE

Subject: Question about the profits of GRIZZLY BEAR
ATTACK IN A HAUNTED TUNNEL

Dear Team Dave,

Thank you for featuring my video! I can't believe how
popular it was. 80 mil already!!! I have a quick question
about the profits. I thought the video would make
more than $58? Is the rest coming later?

Thanks for helping me understand!

Nina

"Ninety," Grandma said. "I'm starting to feel . . . off."

Outside, the silvery clouds seemed to dip in upside-down
waves, their bellies rippling over fields of grazing land. Nina
dropped her phone, apologetically touching her grandmother's
shoulder. "I'm sorry, Grandma, I shouldn't raise my voice. It's
too stressful."

"No. It isn't you. This always happens after thirty miles."

The compass needle was barely twitching; in fact, Nina
couldn't tell whether it was from the truck's motion, or because
the joined world still exerted a slight influence on the land.

"I'm pulling over at the next rest stop," Nina's father said.
"Should be coming up. We can take a break. Maybe it'll help."

Sure enough, a sign reading SAFETY REST AREA directed them to a turnoff. Nestled against the highway was a long parking lot, a strip of grass and trees, and a brick building containing bathrooms, vending machines, and a rack of tourism pamphlets. The parking lot was empty, except for a pair of motorcycles. As the minutes stretched past, Grandma's heart rate didn't increase, but it didn't decrease, either. "Let's give it another ten minutes," she suggested. "I'll focus on living. Is that the right approach to magic?"

Brightest raised a taloned foot, flashing an imitation thumbs-up.

Feeling helpless—there was nothing she could do to quicken the passage of time, or affect the outcome of their wait—Nina refreshed her messages. The payment had to be a mistake.

That's when the bold, unread "New Message" appeared in her inbox. It was a reply to her question.

◆

Recipient username: Nina's Stories

Subject: REPLY to Question about the profits of GRIZZLY BEAR ATTACK IN A HAUNTED TUNNEL

Please refer to section 3b-9 of the terms you signed during the submission of materials to Team Dave. As stated in 3b-9, for the purposes of our transaction, the profit you are entitled to receive is NOT defined as half of the TOTAL profit. It is defined as half of the "profit generated by new subscribers," i.e., "accounts that subscribed to Thou Own Dave within 24 hours after your content was posted." To put it simply, although GRIZZLY BEAR ATTACK IN A HAUNTED TUNNEL was viewed 79,400,312 times within its first 24 hours, >99% of the views were from unsubscribed accounts or accounts that have ALREADY subscribed to Thou Own Dave's stories. Thus, Team Dave is entitled to the entire financial benefit of these views.

Further questions can be directed to our legal representatives.

P.S. A word of advice: always read the fine print, and don't forget your NDA.

Team Dave

That settled it. Nina's get-rich-quick plan had failed. Although she'd tried to keep her expectations low, hope had an insidious tendency to grow.

She lowered her phone.

It didn't seem fair that a guy could promise to share "half of the profits" and then redefine the meaning of the word *profit* on page twenty-four of a thirty-page legal document. Fifty-eight dollars? Really? She could have sold the video to a clickbait media outlet for a thousand bucks. That still wouldn't be enough money to rebuild the toad sanctuary, but at least she'd feel well compensated for a whole morning of acting, and a whole afternoon of editing and stressful indecision.

Her finger hovered over the reply button. Maybe, if she

explained the situation, Thou Own Dave would reconsider the terms of her agreement. Just this once, to save a species, he could share the total profits of his story. A story she helped make successful. After all, behind his always-entertaining public personality, was a human. A man. If only she could reach him at a sincere level . . .

That's when the reply button changed from yellow to gray, indicating that Team Dave had blocked her account. She wouldn't have a chance to plead the case for Ami.

How could she possibly break that news to Ami's friends, who were all staring at her with confused, concerned little eyes?

"I . . . need to use the restroom," Nina said.

"Already? Well, it's as good a place as any." Her father held out a creased five-dollar bill. "If you see anything appealing in the vending machine, feel free. Get some beef jerky for the coyotes, will you? I'll honk if we gotta leave in a hurry."

She smiled, but as soon as Nina pushed through the swinging door of the restroom, she turned on the tap water, moistened one corner of her sweater sleeve, and rubbed the fresh tears off her cheeks. They'd started falling the moment she turned her back to the truck. She blew her nose on a square of toilet paper, crumpled it up, and stared at her reflection. Why did her eyes become so puffy when she cried? She could blame the streaks running down her face on the quickening rain, but red-rimmed eyes were trickier to explain away.

The door squeaked, and an elderly woman stepped deftly into the bleach-scented restroom. "Oh," she remarked, gawking at Nina. "Sorry. Are you upset?"

"It's allergies," she replied softly. There was something so familiar about that woman. "Hey, weren't you on the train earlier? We shared a stop."

"I was on a train this week, yes." Her eyes softened. "I thought you looked familiar. But . . . you also resemble my daughter. When she was young." She lifted an arthritis-curled hand and gently touched Nina's arm. "Please tell me why you're crying."

"Just . . ." Nina shook her head. "It's hard to explain. Lots of things. I made a mistake."

"What do you mean?" The woman's face pinched with concern. "What happened?"

"Nothing important. Sorry, excuse me." Nina stepped toward one of the stalls. She respected her elders, but there was a time and a place for heart-to-hearts, and a rest stop bathroom during a storm constituted neither.

"Wait." The elderly woman sighed, releasing her breath in a frustrated whoosh. "It's me."

Nina paused, staring. "Huh?"

"Remember when I pretended to be a bear and then broke your window?"

"Do I remember? Seriously? Mockingbird, you *followed* us?" She shuffled through memories of the prior two days, searching for hints that the shapeshifter had been lurking in the periphery. Aside from the train, Nina drew a blank, which made her wonder if Mockingbird had spent time as an actual bird, too. They were so easy to overlook; just part of the living background in Texas.

"What else am I going to do?" She flicked her hand in an impatient manner. "The tears. Is it your grandmother?"

"Yes and no. She's . . . struggling, which is not ideal. But it's expected. We'll probably need to turn around."

"What, then?" A bony finger jabbed toward Nina. "Has somebody threatened you?"

"No." She crossed her arms. "Why do you care?"

"I've told y'all, in many ways, that I want to help." Mockingbird gazed forlornly at her wizened face in the streaky bathroom mirror. "That's the problem with being a shape-shifter. People always assume you're in disguise. My best friends don't trust me at all, do they?"

"Um, no. But I suspect it's less that you're a shape-shifter, and more that you're always pranking them."

Mockingbird snickered. "Yeah."

"Um. Just a suggestion, but . . . if you want to be nice, you could stop with the mind games."

"What if I don't want to be nice, Nina?" Mockingbird poked her cheeks and winked at the reflection. "By helping them, I could be doing a very good thing for a very selfish reason. Ever consider that?"

"Are you?"

"Eh." She dropped her hands, turning. "What do you think?"

"For what it's worth, I believe you may actually care. There are less dangerous ways to pull pranks than journeying across worlds. Doesn't matter. You couldn't help on this one, anyway. Thou Own Dave made me sign a bad contract. Long story short, he got all the money for our video. It's . . . no big deal. I'm just a loser. Should've read the fine print."

Unexpectedly, the mockingbird grinned. Her teeth were small and white, like a child's teeth. They seemed misplaced in the head of a ninety-year-old woman. Her body changed, then. Stretching and expanding, features shifting like pieces of clay under an invisible sculptor's hand. Nina watched the little old woman transform into a sandy-haired, six-foot-tall man with dimples and a strong chin. Dave. He stood there in too-tight pants, the blouse buttons straining over his muscular chest.

"Whoa," Nina said. It was the first and only word that came to mind.

"Turn that frown upside down," Impostor Dave encouraged, winking. "The story isn't over yet."

"You aren't going to hurt him, right? Please don't!"

"Violence? Never. It's against the St0rye11er code of conduct."

"Whatever you're planning, chill! I know you're creepily good at"—Nina gestured to the mockingbird's current configuration—"but really, where will you begin without an address?"

"That's the great thing about thirteen-story houses, kid. They're hard to miss."

"This is disturbing, Mockingbird."

Impostor Dave spun around, kicked open the door, and stepped into the gray daylight. "Who's Mockingbird? I'm Thou Own Dave. 'Scuse me. I got turned around at the vending machines. Where's the minigolf course? Those are toilets. I can't hit a golf ball into a toilet. Too easy."

The door snicked shut.

"Well, okay then," Nina said.

She'd have to explain this to everyone, which might raise more questions than answers, given Mockingbird's seemingly uncontrollable chaotic energy. But at least Nina didn't feel terrible about the Dave situation anymore. Worried? Yes. Confused? Slightly. Both were preferable to the helplessness of earlier.

Which was super, since she had more pressing dangers to angst over.

Back at the truck, Grandma's heart had started beating irregularly, fast, and then slower. "This is what happens before I get real sick," she explained. "I don't know how much more I can survive." Nina, while slipping into her seat, looked at the compass. Its needle was steady. "This confirms it," she said. "The joined world has no pull anymore."

"Hold on, Mom," Nina's father said, squealing out of the parking lot. "We're going back home."

He drove quickly, the scenery passing in a blur. Before long, Grandma's heartrate settled into a healthy pace, and her breathing calmed. "I really can sense it," she said. "Yes, I really can."

Nina looked up from the jumping compass needle. "What, Grandma?"

The answer, spoken quietly, reverently, barely lifted over the ambient rush of wind against the car. "The rightness of home."

COTTONMOUTH, HAWK, AND THE COYOTE SISTERS FIGHT THE WIND

*L*ater that day, after the electricity went out, we sat around drinking strawberry-flavored bean milk and listening to a chattering radio. Nina and her father were doing a video call with Nina's mother, in the weak light streaming through the front screen door. All other sources of natural light were impeded by the plywood over the windows, so a wide, three-wick candle lit our faces. I'd seen candles before—I've even made them from beeswax—but the Earth candle was special. It smelled of pine, but I tasted no trees, no fallen needles or prickly cones. It was like the ghost of a forest grew in the dim house.

"According to the radio, the first hurricane bands are coming soon," Grandma said. "They'll rattle the house like a healthy thunderstorm. Nothing I haven't survived before. It's earlier than expected, but that's fine. I'd rather survive a storm in the daylight than at night."

"Are there hurricanes every year?" I asked.

"Oh, yes." She nodded. "But they don't always hit me. And

those that do usually pass quickly. Thing is . . ." Grandma sat back on the sofa, nearly vanishing within her cocoon of blankets. She chilled quickly. That endeared me to the woman. I understood what it felt like to shiver at the slightest breeze. "Thing is," she continued, "they're getting stronger. It's the heat. Hurricanes are juiced up by the heat of the ocean, which has increased in my lifetime, and it makes me feel unbearably old. I mean. Okay. If you put more than seventy candles on a birthday cake, it would be an inferno. I'm well aged. But that kind of temperature change usually happens over generations. A human body shouldn't live through it."

I thought of an ancient elm tree, confused and crying for home, and the memory sent a shiver through my body that was completely unrelated to the temperature.

"I once met a crow who was a thousand years old," Brightest commented. "If we celebrated our birthdays with candles on a cake, we'd need massive cakes."

"That's not a bad thing," Risk admitted.

"What's the climate like in the Reflecting World?" Grandma asked. "Does it imitate ours?"

I understood the point of her question. Earth's recent transformation was common knowledge. Sea level fluctuations. Increases in the average temperature. Ecological devastation. Explosions in some species (like mosquitoes, which I personally enjoy eating; that said, I respect that they have a scary side as disease spreaders and itchy-lump makers). The decimation of other species. But until Ami got sick, it was never personal. It didn't affect me.

So, to answer Grandma's question . . .

"No," I said. "Not directly. I guess that's 'cause we don't share the same atmosphere."

"Thing is," Brightest added. "Our worlds are connected by the living." They looked down at the flames, and I was struck by Brightest's beauty in the golden light. Fire has a way of making everything it illuminates seem to dance. My friend, observant as always, noticed my attention and asked, "What?"

"I was just thinking: that's why we're here in the first place," I said. "Ami's connection."

"Ami is the friend you came here to save?" Grandma asked. She leaned forward to pull the illustrated book into her lap, tapping the picture of the "Dallas toad," with its spots and intense gold eyes. "I swear . . . I've seen one before. When Rosita was still here. We must have been near the well."

"Not surprising, since our home is like the Reflected World version of Texas," I agreed. Intensely hopeful. "Have you seen an Ami toad recently? Or more than one?"

She shook her head. "No, but this land's home to plenty little creatures, many hidden. They keep me company. Make it less lonely after . . ." Her voice cracked, lost its strength. In the pause, she glanced at a stack of boxes filled with toys. Teddy bears. Dolls. Plastic cars and neon bouncy balls. ". . . others leave." In terms of items, I had so little to tie me to the family I'd lost, but she was surrounded by reminders. How must it feel?

Suddenly, Reign jolted upright, knocking her glass of pink drink off the coffee table. Her ears twitched, swiveling, listening.

"What is it?" I hissed. "What do you hear?"

"A howl," she murmured. "But it doesn't come from the living."

That's when the radio spat out three loud screeches followed by a high-pitched shriek. The sisters flinched, their ears lowering. The screech stretched out for several seconds, much longer and more insistent than the blips and dings of Nina's phone. Still, I recognized it as an alert. A warning. It was confrontational, with the feel of a prairie dog yapping at a predator or a crow screeching at a stranger. I hear that type of warning way too often.

The National Weather Service has issued a tornado warning for Hidalgo County. At 11:34 a.m. central daylight time, a tornado was located nine miles north of . . .

"That's not us," Grandma said, lowering the volume a click.

"I thought this was a hurricane!" Reign cried.

"Sometimes, hurricanes pair with tornadoes. Don't fret. If the radio tells us that one is coming, we can go underground until it's safe. But Hidalgo County is far enough that I'm not worried . . ."

Three loud screeches. A high-pitched shriek of sound. *The National Weather Service has issued a tornado warning for Nueces County . . .* In unison, we all looked at Grandma, wondering.

"That's not us. We're in Refuge."

"It's louder," Reign whispered to her sister. "The howl outside."

Risk shook her head. "I can't hear anything."

I couldn't hear anything, either, beyond the ebb and swell of the wind and the radio's constant chatter. Heavy footsteps announced that Nina and her father were running through the hall. A moment later, their faces flicker-lit by palm-sized candles, they appeared in the doorway. "Guess it's gonna be one of those storms," her father sighed.

A few minutes later: three loud screeches. A high-pitched shriek of sound. *The National Weather Service has issued a tornado warning for Dew County . . .*

Then:

The National Weather Service has issued a tornado warning for Harrod County . . .

"To state the obvious," Nina's father said, scooping the mewing cat off the ground, "that's a lot of tornadoes. Basement time."

Grandma stood, her blankets like a cape. One—a pink knitted shawl—slipped to the ground; I plucked it up, draping it across my shoulders for safekeeping.

Single file, with Brightest carrying the portable radio, we followed the humans down the hall. Beside the guest room was a skinny white door with a dull brass knob, which led to a steep gray staircase plunging into the shadows. Nina held out the candle; however, its light wasn't strong enough to reveal the end of the stairs, so she blew out its flame and switched to a flashlight. The rising air was cool and musty. I sensed the promise of water, saturated earth on the cusp of flooding.

"Richie, I'm going to need your help," Grandma said. "These stairs are too steep."

Dutifully, Nina's father—Richie! So he did have a name!—took Grandma by the elbow. She grasped at the thin metal railing for additional support as they started descending. At step two, Richie hollered out, "Kids, quickly, grab blankets. Bring a litter box, too."

"Right, Dad!" As she passed me, Nina touched my arm and waved her flashlight toward the guest room I'd packed. "I think there's quilts in there. We should get food, too. No telling how long we'll be downstairs."

"If a tornado comes," Reign said, as Nina went to the room, "I know exactly what to do." She threw her heavy flashlight from hand to hand, as if planning to beat up the weather.

"Oh no," her sister muttered. She matched my sentiments exactly. I'd been dreading this moment since Reign mentioned her Great-Uncle on the train.

It's not that I believed she'd somehow manifested the tornadoes outta sheer willpower. No coyote could do that, thank the sun. However, Reign had clearly recognized all the signs of an impending twister, and now that the big, threatening windstorm was indeed acting like a big, threatening windstorm, she'd jump headfirst into a self-fulfilling story. Assuming she'd play the role of a hero, instead of a tragic victim of impulsive decisions. So, yeah. I'd been dreading this outcome.

But I also knew my friend well enough to believe she *could* be the hero.

"We need a long rope," I conceded.

"Quick question about the . . . concept of lassoing a tornado," Brightest said. "Assuming you can loop a rope around it—"

"Oh, that's not necessary. You just need to snag a little bit of the wind," Reign interrupted. "Then give a good pull. I guess it's a fusion of fishing and lassoing."

"Okay. Right. But won't that drag the tornado straight at the house?"

"Not if I go like this"—Reign threw her arm outward—"and fling it aside. Kind of like kicking a spinning top."

Risk clicked her tongue. "You can't wrangle a tornado. It's

too powerful. Remember what happened to Great-Uncle? He played tug-of-war for a couple seconds and then got chucked into the stratosphere. Assuming you believe his tall tales, the lasso trick nearly killed him."

"I wouldn't do it alone, though, would I?" Reign asked. "Would you rather it takes our shelter before a hurricane?"

"There hasn't been a warning for us on the radio yet," Nina said, returning, her arms piled with blankets.

"But I can hear it getting closer." Reign's voice dropped in volume, her smile tight. "We don't have much time."

Risk sniffed. "Where's our ridiculously long rope?"

"Would cords work?" I asked.

◆

Racing, we overturned boxes onto the guest room mattress, building a mound of electrical cords. Most were black lengths of copper coated by a flexible skin of insulation. Some were thick, with three-pronged metal plugs. Others were thin and seemed to fit into rectangular or circular ports. A few orange, green, and blue cords were tangled among the pile, which went up to my chest after the last box was emptied. "It'll take hours to make a rope outta these," I realized, hissing. "And they have to be untangled first!"

"How can I help?" Nina asked, grasping at the wires. "Tell me what to do."

I passed her a folded quilt. "Be with your family. Where it's safe."

"But—"

"The howl is near," Reign warned. "It's becoming a roar."

"Hurry, Nina! Please. It's okay. You don't have world-shaping powers, so there's nothing you can do up here. Go!" At my urging, she made a conflicted sound, something between a sign and a groan, and then darted from the guest room. I'd been gritting my teeth with worry; now that she was gone, the tension in my jaw decreased. Slightly.

"Ropes, ropes." Risk closed her eyes. "It seems possible. What do you think?"

"What?" I asked.

"Can you? With so many?" her sister wondered.

"What?" I repeated. "Can you what?"

"A magic trick!" Risk cried. She grabbed the polka-dotted bedsheet off the floor and snapped it over the pile. As the blanket's corners settled, she paced almost restlessly. Then, with a grin bright with confidence and teeth, she boomed, "Attention, carnivores and omnivores. Reptiles and birds. You witnessed me cut the rope into a thousand different pieces. It'll never be whole again . . ."

"Never!" Reign agreed.

"Or will it? All that was done can be undone!" With a bark of joy, Risk grabbed the blanket and whipped it into the air. Brightest and I had to dodge polka dots. On the mattress, which had once bent under a chaotic mess of a thousand different cords, was a long, continuous coil. The wires had fused together; we had our tornado lasso. "Thank you, thank you!" When Risk bowed, her hair flipped over her head. "Now, we need to hurry."

At this point, I could feel it, too. The approach. The howl of wind sweeping everything into its frenzied dance. My first instinct urged me to slither down the basement stairs and seek refuge with

Grandma. But there were other threats in the near future. The eye of the hurricane, cradled by a wall of violence, would pass directly over us, and if that didn't flood the basement, what would?

Grandma needed a roof over her head for as long as we could provide one.

I knelt, wiggling my fingers under the heavy coil of insulated wire. "Somebody help!" I grunted, trying to wedge it upward. "This is heavy as a boulder!"

We managed to flip the entire thing over the mattress and onto the polka dot blanket. Then, Risk, Reign, Brightest, and I dragged it down the hall, through the living room, and toward the exit. At first, the door resisted us, as if the wind was a heavy body leaning against it. Then, we had to turn the coil on its side and shove it wheel-like down the porch stairs; it partially unwrapped during the roll. Winded by the effort, I sucked in heavy breaths of rain-dense air, and futilely swiped at the water droplets now on my spectacles. My sleeve left streaks across the glass, and the storm wasted no time in replacing the droplets. That's probably why I was the last to see it.

Of course, Brightest spotted the tornado first.

"Whoaaaa!" They patted my shoulder and urgently pointed at the horizon. "Over there!"

From afar, the tornado seemed almost graceful; it was a narrow-stemmed cone of dark gray against the silver sky. At its base, an upside-down skirt of disturbed dust billowed upward. The dust resembled something Reign would sew from filmy gray tulle.

"It's not coming at us," Risk said.

"No." Brightest squinted. "Actually, I think it's headed for the neighbor's house!"

According to Nina, the man who lived there was land hungry and untrustworthy. "He gives me a really bad feeling," she'd explained. "I wouldn't put anything past Paul. If you see him, hide. Avoid at all costs!" She didn't have to warn me twice. After my run-ins with Bruhn the Hotheaded and the catfish cultist, I never wanted to deal with a massive jerk again.

"He's gone, right?" I asked. On a clearer day, from the porch, I had been able to see the vaguest suggestion of a tiny silver house across the street. With raindrops streaking my spectacles, that was no longer the case.

"Hopefully." Reign pretended to wipe sweat off her brow, instead flicking rainwater aside.

"Um. He's . . . outside, actually. Running our way . . ."

"He won't make it," I hissed. With only two legs, humans were nimble, but not especially quick. That said, even a horse would struggle to outmaneuver a tornado. I squinted, still unable to see well. So in my mind's eye, I pictured Bruhn fleeing a tornado, urged on by her flock of robins and other birds. *Run,* they'd chatter. *Run!* Strangely, the thought wasn't funny at all.

It did make me wonder: what would have happened if I'd saved Bruhn's life the day we met instead of biting her toe?

"He won't escape," I repeated, grim. "Can we . . ."

Reign seemed to understand. "Give him a fighting chance?" she said, holding up a three-foot-long loop. "Yeah! Risk? *Risk?*"

Just a couple seconds ago, Risk had been standing on the lowest porch stair, hands on hips, staring down the storm. But she wasn't there anymore. She wasn't anywhere.

"Risk!" Reign shouted. "Oli, where'd she go?"

I shook my head, baffled. "Nowhere. Unless . . ."

Of course. Risk's world-shaping trick had drained her time on Earth. She'd also been the one to shape open the bookstore door.

"I think she transported home."

"*What?* No! I can't do this alone!"

"Please try!"

With a quick shake of her head, Reign kicked the mile-long length of wire; it flopped right side up, like a coiled snake. Then, she picked up the loop and ran several paces in front of the house, watching the tornado pass in front of Grandma's yard. There was no spark of lightning, no shriek of wind, but the air seemed to rumble, as if we stood in the middle of a ghost stampede. "How does somebody chuck a lasso that far?" she cried. "There's no way!"

Without hesitation, Brightest grabbed the loop in their hand and started running across the field. "Don't worry," they shouted. "The wind can't hurt me. I won't let it." Then, in a burst of transformation, Brightest shifted the loop to their talons and spread their wings. The wind swept them up, quick as a kite, with a mammoth black string for a tail. They were a flash of gold against the tornado's pillar of debris. No ordinary bird could have flown against the wind like that, but Brightest was not—had never been—ordinary. They were a sculptor of the air itself.

That said, I still gaped with silent-scream horror as I watched my friend approach the tornado, aware that one mistake could lead to death.

"Almost there," Reign shouted, but I doubted that Brightest could hear her. With the roar of the tornado, the patter of a million raindrops, the distance between them? I wiped the raindrops off my spectacles and squinted at the sky, failing to see my hawk friend anymore.

There! That telltale, beautiful fleck of feathers. Brightest swooped, releasing the loop at their peak height.

Then, in the blink of an eye, they vanished.

And in that blink, Reign pulled on the rope, her stance wide and braced for a struggle. The cord snapped taut, as if it had snagged a hook within the rapidly moving column of spinning dust. The tornado seemed to slow; perhaps it had stopped, but its momentum resisted her attempt to snap it off course. Reign's feet began to drag across the soggy earth. With a cry of alarm, I grabbed her by the waist. "The guy isn't clear yet!" she cried. "Augh! He fell! Get up! Get up and run! Run, human! Oli, I'm losing control of this twister!"

A voice rose over the storm. Nina, bursting onto the porch behind us.

"Can you capture it instead?" she shouted.

NINA, COTTONMOUTH, AND COYOTE FIGHT A TORNADO

*T*his was how old stories went: first came a problem, then a plan. A tornado was approaching. The plan? Lasso the wind. How would the story end? Nina had no point of reference, but she'd heard a hundred other stories, the histories of a more magical era.

Risk and Reign, newcomers to the storm rodeo, might fail. In fact, that outcome seemed likely, unless they were incredible world-shapers, able to master random skills in a snap. They'd try their hardest, sure. But confidence and good intentions were no substitutes for practice, and there was a hurricane on their heels, too.

Then again, she could be wrong about that assumption. Nina didn't know much about Risk and Reign. She knew even less about magic. Its governing laws might reward determination. And assuming the plan worked, the tornado would go careening off somewhere else. It might tear through the only remaining livestock in town—the milk cows on the Ritter family farm or the longhorns on the ranch belonging to wealthy retirees. The poor animals wouldn't stand a chance. The tornado might also destroy the nearest grocery store, the hospital, or the pharmacy. Grandma needed access to food and medicine. And she couldn't travel far; they'd proved that much.

Thinking, Nina paused at the head of the basement stairs. Down the hall, the screen door slammed in its frame. Her friends started shouting.

Over there!

The neighbor's house!

Did they mean Paul? Frankly, life would be easier if the tornado carried his camper away.

But Nina couldn't live with herself if she blithely let that happen.

And amid the chaos, she wondered: if a song could be trapped in a locket, could a tornado be trapped in a box?

No damn way.

And yet, in the logic of old stories, it made a peculiar kind of sense. Both songs and tornadoes were movements of air.

She dropped the quilt and sprinted to the guest room, her heavy footsteps prompting her father to holler, "Nina, are y'all up there?"

"Yes! Just a minute!" She grabbed the overturned plastic storage box. Its waterproof lid should be tight enough, but just in case, Nina also threw the nesting doll and an empty popcorn tin into the box.

The outdoor shouts, now fearful, had risen in pitch.

Run, human!

So Nina sprinted, bursting shoulder-first into the door,

muscling through a gust of wind. In the yard, Oli and Reign were struggling to hold the tornado in place. Oddly, Nina's first thought was: *They should have worn gardening gloves to prevent blisters.*

"Can you capture it instead?" she shouted, holding up her box of boxes and running toward the pair. "Like a song in a locket?"

"Or a question in a bottle," Oli called back, digging in his heels as the tornado dragged him and Reign forward a foot, then two.

Reign laughed shrilly. "I'll try! Nina, toss me the bottle!" She partially released the lasso, now only clutching it with her left hand, her claws stripping the cords' protective wire coating. Complying, Nina handed Reign the most bottle-like object, the outer nesting doll.

The moment the painted wooden doll hit her palm, Reign released the rope and sprang forward. For a few seconds, Oli held his own against the wind, but then the cord slipped out of his grasp and whipped into the tornado, slurped up like a piece of spaghetti.

It didn't seem to matter. Now kneeling, Reign cracked open the doll. From the porch, Nina's father called, "Get back!" But Nina couldn't pull her gaze away from the sight. Oli held his arms skyward and parted the raindrops between Reign and the tornado, giving Reign a clear look at it. A tendril of darkness— dust and debris caught in a horizontal spin of air—split from the tornado's body, extending toward them. Although the tendril did not stretch across the grasslands, the doll trembled in Reign's grasp.

As Nina watched in astonishment, the tornado transformed.

It was like somebody had pulled a plug on the wind. As the tornado's spin decreased, the doll shook violently.

"Almost got it!" Reign yelled. As if responding to her announcement, the tornado stopped moving altogether, leaving a vast column of suspended particles in the air. In the distance, heavy chunks of debris dropped like hail, while the fine dust settled sluggishly. Reign snarled at the doll, trying to snap its two halves shut. Her arms swung around in circles, barely able to contain the object's thrashing.

"I'll help you!" Nina promised. After two long leaps, she knelt and placed her hands over Reign's hands. "Okay, now!"

In a unified push, they sealed the doll with a click. It fell still, its red lips smiling up at them, secretive and smug.

"Whuoa," Nina said, holding up the toy. "We just trapped a whole tornado."

COTTONMOUTH RETURNS

"We did! We really did! Oli! Did you see that? Sun above!" Reign cackled. "I lassoed a tornado and then put it in a doll!"

"Y . . . yes! That was legendary!" I knew my friend could do great things, but it was still an incredible feat to witness! Rising, Reign threw her arms around my neck, the beginning of a hug.

And then, I was alone.

"Did she go back to the Reflecting World?" Nina asked, the awestruck grin dropping from her face.

"Don't worry," I assured her. "She's at home, safe."

"Are we?" Richie asked. "She just shoved a whole tornado into something smaller than a bread box. All that wind and rain, compacted. Is it going to explode?"

"Not if you keep it closed." Richie seemed skeptical, so I tried to explain. "She adapted a simple world-shaping trick. Take active motion—like the vibrations of sound—and convert it to potential motion. It's the potential for a tornado that's in the doll, not the tornado itself."

"Okay. In that case, I'm going to wrap dollie in duct tape, because it still sounds dangerous."

"How much time do you have, Oli?" Nina asked.

"Um. Probably not much. I deflected a lot of rain." All of my friends had vanished shortly after their act of world-shaping. Parting the rain wasn't on par with tornado wrangling, but it had been my biggest act of shaping ever.

"Goodbye," she said, and although all our faces were wet with rain, with my sense for water, I could feel her tears. "When you see the others, tell them I'm so happy we met, and we'll do our best to help Ami."

"Nina—"

There was a jarring sensation, as if the ground had dropped, and my knees buckled. However, instead of landing on the hard floor, I fell into ankle-deep lake water. My flashlight, which had traveled with me to the Reflecting World, fell out of my pocket and sputtered in the mud. That was fine. I didn't need it anymore.

It was a clear day alongside the bottomless lake.

"Oli, pal, are you okay?"

Brightest. They'd been perched in a tree, waiting. Now, they flew onto my basking rock, and watched me clamber from the muck.

"Reign stopped the tornado, Brightest. It was amazing."

"I knew she could!"

I sat beside them, inhaling deeply, nearly tearful with gratitude for the scent of home.

But when I thought about the humans, abandoned to the wrath of the incoming hurricane, I felt wretched.

"What's wrong?" Brightest asked, bopping my arm with a single extended wing. "Nobody's hurt, right?"

"I'm worried about them. The danger isn't gone."

They sighed, pushing a whush of air through their nares. "It never is. We could return to the fourth mountain peak."

"It'll take too long." I looked at my tent, which was lopsided after half a week of neglect. At my raft, still ready for a journey down the river. Back then, I'd been frightened by the prospect of traveling a couple dozen miles away from home. Or cutting through the forest. Or meeting old enemies.

I was still afraid. Just not of the same things.

"Can you fly to the valley," I asked, "and check on the twins?"

"Sure, sure!"

"And when you're there, please tell Ami that I won't leave Earth until I'm certain that we succeeded. One way or another."

Brightest tilted their head, confused. "You can tell him that . . . ?"

"No." I untied my boots and slipped them off my feet. Next came the socks. Then my shirt. I didn't waste time folding my clothes; they were dropped in a pile on the basking rock. "You know what they call this lake?"

"Bottomless."

"That's technically true. At least . . . I think so. Because some waters connect us to Earth. Endless rivers and streams, bottomless wells and lakes. I hear stories from the depths. If you swim past the light, where the water carries the chill of winter and is heavy enough to crush a horse's back . . . you'll feel the pull of an ocean."

"The Gulf?"

"Probably."

"Oli," Brightest said, "there's monsters in the darkness. It's safer to take the long route, you know?"

"Says the bird who flew at a tornado."

"I never claimed to be cautious!"

"You inspired me." With a chirp, Brightest bowed their head, and I scratched the soft feathers on the back of their neck. Then, before I could change my mind, I dove into the lake.

My siblings and I used to play "stay below" in the river near Momma's cottage. We'd slither down the bank, slip underwater, and wrap around submerged blades of grass or waterlogged branches. Anything to keep us secure. Elvin was always the first sibling to give up. Boredom was his failing; he couldn't last more than twenty minutes. Next, Bleak or Al would be enticed to land by Elvin's jeers. The rest of my siblings usually survived another hour. At that point, the game became challenging. Your lungs started tingling. Nothing painful. Nothing urgent. But Fourier couldn't tolerate discomfort, and was therefore likely to give up. At that point, the real game began. Although I never won a round of "stay below," always falling short of Pilot, with his prodigious lungs, or Sona, who'd sooner suffer than lose, I came close a few times. And the experience taught me my limitations. I could hold my breath for two hours.

I'd dive for an hour, and if I wasn't near the boundary between worlds, I'd turn around.

That was assuming the lake didn't kill me first.

The initial descent was easy. After swimming to the edge of the deep section, where the lake floor dropped suddenly, I took one last look at the sky, inhaled, and dove. The transition from sunny water to blackness wasn't sudden, but it did happen quickly. There was a minute in the depth of eternal twilight, where fish were indistinguishable smudges of darkness and silt fell like snow, when I was intensely frightened of the unseen. But the moment true darkness enveloped me, the water's unknowns seemed to disappear. Instead, I was alone with one goal: swim, swim, swim.

Minutes passed. Minutes more. There was a thrum in my ears, a rhythmic, gentle beat, the music of my heart radiating through my body and into the lake. The water over my tail accumulated so gradually, I wasn't aware of its vast weight until my head began to ache.

At this point, Fourier would have given up. But not me.

So I swam.

It was later, though not much later, that I heard the second heartbeat. It hid within my own, a deeper thrum. One that sped slowly. Gurgling. Becoming laughter.

In the darkness, the monster said, "You're in my home now, viper."

"I have a story for you," I explained, swimming onward. "One that's too big for a bottle."

NINA, SHORTLY
BEFORE LANDFALL

*T*hat night, before they weathered the hurricane storm, Nina descended to the basement with her phone. There, patches of the cement floor were dark with moisture; puddles of water welled from the seam along the wall. There was a large metal cylinder—a boiler—in the middle of the boxy room, but the basement was much emptier than the rest of the house. Only a stack of paint cans and a metal chair, the clever type that could fold into a flat frame, were visible. Grandma had to keep most of her clutter aboveground to prevent water damage.

In her private St0rytel1er video diary over the years, Nina had recorded about twenty-eight different stories, her favorites. The act of recording was a comfort. If—fate forbid—she vanished from the face of the Earth, the stories—in her voice—would persist. In some way.

Now, she had a new one to preserve. She'd record it the old-school style and save it on a thumb drive, far from the reaches of anyone but family.

Her camera propped on the stack of paint cans, Nina sat in the metal chair.

"Nifty, connect to Visualizer. Start recording. All filters off. All extras off."

In the light of a single electric bulb, Nina's face was chiseled with shadows.

"This is a story of change," she said. "I learned it from a cottonmouth person named Oli, who learned it from his mother, who learned it from her mother, who learned it from an ancient snake who was born in an age when peoples moved freely between the Reflecting World and Earth.

"That age is over, and for the first time, I understand the forces that brought our coexistence to an end.

"Billions of years ago, the Earth formed, but the early planet was no place for life. It took a long, long time for the violence of planetary birth to subside. Even longer for microbes to evolve into bigger, more complex creatures. Eventually, the first organism to dream was born. Oli says that's possibly when the Reflecting World came into being. He's not sure. There are several theories. You'll meet lots of people who insist their theory is the cold, hard truth. Maybe the Reflecting World is timeless and has reflected many universes, many planets before ours. Or it could be the Earth's dream. It could even be something stranger.

"Personally, I'm curious, but the answer to that question doesn't matter much in the grand scheme of this story. What matters comes later.

"With the creation of a species, originators are born. They appear in the Reflecting World, the first of their kind. When the originators are on Earth, it can be the home of their children.

So there was a time when all animal and plant peoples mingled with each other. It was an era of adventures spanning worlds. Of legends without language barriers. It was the joined era.

"I don't know exactly how the joined era collapsed—Oli says the motivation is a mystery—but a handful of human spirits, claiming to be royalty and gods, declared war on each other. Their peaceful fellows were killed or chased into hiding. That includes animal people, who don't war. Ultimately, all the pain and bloodshed culminated in this: one originator human emerging victorious.

"The King.

"The most skilled killer in existence, or so he bragged. And the spoils of his war were simple. He wanted to be the only immortal on Earth. It was the only way to prevent another war. The two worlds should be separate for the sake of peace. That's what he claimed, anyway. And many humans believed him. Many still do.

"I asked Oli why the King remains unchallenged, and he guessed, 'Because he's dangerous.' See, if you try to slap the King, he'll put an arrow through your heart. If you try to imprison the King, he'll murder your family and friends. Want to kill the King? Well, you better succeed on the first attempt, or he'll return the attack, guaranteed. And he isn't alone. His supporters remain numerous and dedicated. They have day jobs, sure. But in their free time, they train to hunt spirits.

"So all originators—even the few surviving humans—retreated with their children to the Reflecting World, the dream of a living planet. And the hunter was given a new, more appropriate name: the Nightmare."

COTTONMOUTH'S HEART BREAKS

*A*fter the water monster carried me to Earth, I slithered down a rain-slick path between the well and Grandma's home, transforming only long enough to knock on the front door and shout, "I'm back! I'm back!" There'd be no long good-bye from Earth until Ami was well enough to open his eyes.

At first, when my human friends opened the door, they didn't seem to notice me—I guess I'm fairly small. So I flashed my white mouth and waved 'hello' with my tail.

"It's Oli!" Nina exclaimed, gathering me into her arms and out of the cold. I waited out the storm with them indoors. At times, the wind shrieked so loudly, battering the house with debris, I feared that the roof would blow away. But eventually, miraculously, the hurricane swept north, leaving the house behind. I didn't need to do a single act of world-shaping.

In the day that followed, the sun bathed the land in warm, golden light. Every lingering droplet of rain on the leaves, stones, and branches—alive or dead, upright or bent sideways—glittered.

Together, the humans and I stepped into the light and strolled around the house to survey the damage. The garage seemed fine, and the house was scraped up, but otherwise was standing strong.

"Seems like I lived through another storm of the century," Grandma said, and although her lips quirked into a smile, the deepening furrow down her brow hinted at fear. Who could blame her? I lived in a tent, always poised to flee at the slightest hint of danger. A trainee bounty hunter once scared me up the bank. But Grandma was linked to her homeland. She couldn't even travel for fun.

"What comes next?" I asked.

"Usually, we pick up debris, unpack, and get the solar panels running until the main power's back."

Beside me, Nina stooped to pick up a paper-sized sheet of corrugated metal. It must have been carried by the wind, finally dropping in the branches of a sage bush. "I wonder what happened to Paul," she said. "He just ran off."

"The guy probably took a vacation after he saw a tornado vanish," Richie said. "I know I would."

"Me too. Maybe he'll rethink his plans to snatch up your land, Grandma. Whatever Paul wants, it can't be worth the hassle, right?"

The others treated her statement as rhetorical, but I sensed a genuine question there.

"What would be worth the hassle?" I pressed.

She shook her head, shrugging. "It depends on him. You know, there are people who get into fistfights over parking spaces. I kinda get that vibe off Paul. But you know what else? Sometimes, I remember the day we met, and it scares me. His eyes were so mean. Like there's a real depth to his danger. Deeper than the well."

I instinctively gasped, showing the white of my mouth.

"Soon as possible, I'll talk to him," Richie decided. "Until now, I've been wary of antagonizing the hornet's nest, but it's gone too far. You shouldn't have to live in fear, Mom, always wondering what the neighbor's plotting."

"And you," Grandma said, poking my shoulder, "shouldn't leave our sight until you jump back home."

That's how we spent the day: chatting, cleaning, and brainstorming plans to help Ami. There was even time for a nap with Tightope before supper. I tried to absorb every ray of sunlight, aware that this would be my last week to enjoy it. At night, I slept in the guest bedroom, clutching the rubber snake, the present I couldn't take home. As I explained to Grandma, nothing created or born on Earth could stay in the Reflecting World. If I took the toy home, it would vanish after a few days.

"Would it return here?" she asked.

"Honestly, I don't know."

I'd wondered about that often. What happened to all the books the wolves smuggled between worlds? Did they reappear on the bookshop shelves? Or did they choose different homes in random houses? Maybe Zale or Richie had an answer. Later, I'd ask.

For the next couple days, while waiting for the power to return, we shared meals on the porch. That's why Grandma, Nina, and I were outside in the afternoon when a shiny, rat-snake-black car grumbled onto the driveway. Nina slammed down her plate of eggs so quickly, it must've been a small miracle the porcelain didn't crack. I understood her excitement a second later. "Mom!" she shouted.

The driver-side door popped open, and a statuesque woman with a short tuft of gray-streaked hair stepped outside. Because she wore a loose rain poncho, clearly planning for a stormier day, her spread arms resembled a pair of wings. There was certainly a parent-child resemblance. Like I share my momma's scale pattern, the humans both had bushy black eyebrows and wide noses. Pleased as a possum in a blueberry patch, Nina dashed toward her mother. The camera dangling around her neck jostled with every step, but she didn't seem to care. "How long do you have?" she asked, enveloped in a hug.

"They gave me two weeks emergency time off. And it's paid. Now and then, the job has its benefits." The woman glanced up, clearly noticing me. "Oli?" she asked. "You must be!"

Nodding in agreement, I descended the porch stairs, closely followed by Grandma. "It's good to meet you—"

I never had the chance to finish my introduction.

Never saw it coming.

There was a crack of sound, the taste of metal. Instead of pain, I felt numbness spreading through my false body. Blood welling from the hole in my chest.

Nina, screaming, tore away from her mother and ran toward me. Grandma, gasping, caught me as I fell. The sun was not yet at its apex, but I saw a halo of light.

Too quickly, darkness overcame my vision of the sky.

NINA DEFIES
THE NIGHTMARE

*B*lood welled from Oli's body and spread across the rain-saturated ground, staining Nina's jeans red. There was so much blood, so quickly. Had the bullet passed through his heart? Injuries like that couldn't be healed, could they? Not without magic.

"Grandma, help him!" she begged. In response, her grandmother put her hand against the hole in his chest, applying pressure. The blood squished between her fingers and trickled down in rivulets along her wrinkled hands.

Somebody—who? Who would do such a terrible thing?—had shot her friend, and they could snipe more people. Nina shouldn't be outside, in the open. None of them should. But she couldn't let Oli die. This cottonmouth spirit, who'd fallen through the sun and swum through the waters of two worlds; who'd survived attacks by monsters; who'd trusted her with the life of his best friend.

"What happened?" her mother asked. She kept looking at the

sky, at the blue spaces between the clouds, as if convinced that a meteorite had hit him. Something purposeless and utterly random. Nina had been through enough active shooter drills to recognize reality.

"He was shot!"

With a hiss of breath, Nina's mother knelt in front of her daughter, perhaps hoping that her poncho-armored body could absorb a bullet. "Run inside," she ordered. Half-obeying, Nina tried to lift Oli by the shoulders to drag him behind the porch.

"Leave it!" a man shouted. The women, now all huddled around Oli, scanned the area, searching for the shooter. Nina's gaze paused at the line of oaks along a nearby ditch. "There," she said, lifting one of her blood-drenched hands to point. "Is that . . . ?"

It was.

Paul, dressed in his same camo from years before, and carrying a scope-equipped hunting rifle, approached them from the tree line. Nina remembered the moment they met. How he'd stared at her with a compass in his hand and eyes sharp with suspicion.

"He's one of the Nightmare's knights," Nina whispered. "A spirit killer. We can't let him get Oli." Bitterly, she understood now: that day, Paul really had been tracking a coyote. He hadn't wanted the land for its water, and he'd never needed a compass to find north. No. Compasses led knights to fertile hunting grounds.

"Stop!" her mother shouted. "My husband is calling for help!"

Was that true? Nina wondered. Had her father heard the gunshot from within the house? Would he save them? Could he? Grandma owned a lot of stuff, but there wasn't an armory hidden in the house. Nina shifted, ensuring that the camera around her neck had an unimpeded view of Paul, and thumbed the record button. The machine could be their witness, for whatever that was worth.

"I can't get imprisoned for shooting a snake," Paul replied simply, enunciating every word loud and obnoxiously clear, as if speaking down to an audience of children. "That's what he'll become when he dies. It's what he always was."

"You think Oli is a spirit?" Nina's mother bluffed. "Why? Because of his makeup? The joined era's over."

"This isn't my first rodeo," Paul snorted. "He did magic. Made a whole tornado vanish into thin air. There are places where the wall protecting our world is easy to jump. Now, I finally know I've found one here."

"What?" Grandma wiped tears from her face, accidentally marking her cheek with a streak of Oli's blood. "You just shot a boy. If it's my land you want—"

"Enough with the crocodile tears. Where is the fox girl?"

He knew about Reign. Knew that she and Oli had saved his life. That favor didn't seem to matter to Paul.

"Let my daughter leave, please," Nina's mother begged.

"Don't pretend to be momma of the year," he taunted. "You let your daughter play with snakes."

"This is a nightmare," Grandma wept.

"Nightmare?" Paul's face hardened, and he raised his rifle, swinging its muzzle toward the women. "That's what the beasts call him. Do you believe their stories?"

"No!" Nina's mother said. "We're just scared."

Then, the crunch of footsteps. Nina's father rounded the

house at a stroll, one hand hidden behind his back, the other waving. "Hey, neighbor," he said, his tone warm and personable; it was the same voice he used to placate difficult clients at the bookshop. "None of us want trouble today. Do me a favor, will you? Back up. Way up. Give my family room. That's all I ask. If you want to revisit a land deal, fine."

The knight's demeanor shifted, from disgusted to wary. As if doing them all a favor, he took a few steps backwards and addressed Nina's father. "I need to see this through, sir."

That's when Nina realized that the puddle of blood around Oli hadn't spread recently. She gently shifted Grandma's hand to the side.

The hole in his chest was gone; not even a scar remained. Grandma *had* saved him. But could she do it twice? Could she heal everyone if the knight started shooting?

"Hey, what are you hiding?" Paul demanded. Nina jolted, certain that he was speaking to her. But no. He was glaring at her father. "Before I back up any farther, show me your hands, man. I'm not playing."

"Just a toy." Nina's father slowly revealed that he'd been hiding the tornado doll behind his back. For better or worse, Paul didn't recognize its power; rather, he seemed puzzled. "Put that thing down," he said, "and join the others."

As if lowering a newborn infant, Richie gingerly placed the doll on a tuft of grass. Its serene round face smiled at the sky. Hands raised, Richie walked over to Alicia and knelt beside his family. They no longer had anything to use to defend themselves.

"The snake should be gone by now," Paul said, his voice

cracking. "Is it dead yet?" With that question, Paul's shoulders squared up, as if he'd been backed into a corner and now had to decide whether to slink away, tail tucked, or lash out in a flurry of teeth. He muttered something, looking directly at Grandma's hand over Oli's chest.

Then, Paul lifted his rifle again.

A flash of white beside the man's boots was the only warning Paul had before the wild cottonmouth struck. The snake's teeth sank harmlessly into thick leather, but Paul still yelped and kicked, sending the poor hero who'd answered Oli's call flipping head-over-tail into a sagebrush plant. In the second of that distraction, a column of water shot out of the old well, rising thirty, forty, fifty meters, quickly resembling a waterfall from the sky. Nina saw Oli sit up, shaking with the strain, but by the time Paul realized his target was alert, Oli's strength gave out completely, sending tons of water plummeting earthward. He hadn't been able to bend the column; not a drop touched them or Paul.

But maybe, it didn't have to.

"Oh," Nina whispered, understanding.

With the deluge roaring downwards in the background, Oli twisted, wrapping his arms around the people who'd protected him, showing his back to the knight who was raising his gun once more. And in that moment, Nina knew there were one of two ways their story could end, so she squeezed her eyes shut, and hugged her family too.

Nina smelled the ocean in her mother's hair, mud, and dead leaves in the breeze. The sun's warmth, though present, was gentler now, and when Nina opened her eyes, she saw the banks of a bottomless lake.

"It worked!" Oli cried, pulling away from the others. After quickly counting their heads—one, two, three humans, all accounted for—he stood, hands on hips, and surveyed the area.

"Did you take us to the Reflected World?" Nina asked. "Or is this some kind of afterlife?"

"You're alive," Oli promised. "This is my home. And while you're here, it can be yours, too."

He grasped Nina by the hand, helping her stand. Richie and Alicia tried to lift Grandma upright, but the older woman brushed aside their help and jumped to her feet. "I feel wonderful," she said. "Even my knees don't ache."

"World shaping is easiest here," Oli explained. He glanced at the forest, thoughtfully straightening his spectacles. "Do you want to visit Ami? He's with the healer, and she may be able to help you, too, Grandmother."

Nina's parents, seemingly at a loss for words, simply nodded in response and then continued staring wide-eyed at the trees, the basking rock, the water, the sky.

"Yes," Nina translated.

"That's good! I know a shortcut," Oli waved them toward the treeline. "We should hurry. I don't know when you'll fall back to Earth."

And with that, together, they journeyed into the forest.

THE KNIGHT FLIES AWAY

*T*hey'd vanished!

The whole lot of 'em, gone, or so it seemed. A prime demonstration of why knights couldn't afford to miss any bullseye. The snake should have been shot and gone, no time for magic. But clearly, when it came to marksmanship, Paul had become rusty over the last few years, preoccupied with observing this clump of Nothing, Texas. At least now he knew he'd been right. The old woman's property was a crossing zone, and the whole brainless family had been aiding and sheltering beasts. They'd regret it. With this encounter, he'd finally gathered enough evidence to contact the King.

Experimentally, Paul shot at the empty space where the family had been sitting before they'd disappeared. The bullet thudded into the dirt, kicking up dust. They weren't invisible, then.

He stalked around the outside house, pausing at the object Richie had dropped. A doll? Why had a grown man been carrying a toy? Paul picked it up, turning it over, noticing the seam around its belly. It was one of those hollow dolls; maybe there was a weapon hidden inside. A knife or a handgun.

Once he'd returned back home, Paul cracked open the doll to check.

TWO WEEKS LATER

*A*t the edge of Grandma's land, part of the wall was transforming into an anthill. Grain by grain, the worker ants used fragments of the crumbling sedimentary rocks to build their colony's home. Nina observed the ants from afar—although she wore closed-toed shoes, with her pants tucked into her socks, she knew full well that a determined insect could find a way to bite her. She switched her camera to video mode and directed its lens toward the busiest segment of the anthill, where a stream of red bodies poured into a hole near the top "crater" of the conical structure.

"Nifty, zoom and focus on moving targets: ants."

The video magnification increased until a single ant spanned the width of the digital screen, but Nina's hands were too unsteady for her to identify the species. Their subtle tremors caused the image to jump around, as if she was filming in an earthquake. She needed a good shot for her latest series of stories about the hurricane's aftermath. It was hosted on her new account, a public one under the name Child of Refuge.

In one week, the ants had rebuilt their city of mounds, but the nearest grocery store still had a gaping hole in its roof, the houses along the river were flooded, and half the trees in their area had been either stripped of their leaves or torn from the ground. She was collaborating with other Gulf storytellers to share their experiences: Jellybean Kel from Fort Worth was living in her car because a tornado tore up her family's house; Listen to Jerome was documenting the efforts of a Houston-area shelter to find homes for all the cats and dogs who'd been displaced during the storm; the Sebastian Sisters were interviewing their neighbors, including the residents of a retirement home (elders who'd experienced a lifetime of hurricanes); Jess, taking a break from their haircutting series, was focusing on the inequal distribution of government relief funds. For her contribution to the St0ryte11er anthology, Nina planned to introduce the residents of Grandma's land and tell their stories in the weeks following the storm. "Nifty," she said, still holding her camera toward the diligent red ants, "apply automatic image stabiliza—"

Her phone chimed insistently. Once, twice. That was the sound of a "time-sensitive" alert, as flagged by the sender. "Nifty, who is bothering me?"

You've received an alert from Thou Own Dave.

Well, that was unexpected. Guess Team Dave had unblocked her account. She lowered her camera, letting it dangle from a strap around her neck, and opened the message.

Recipient username: Nina's Stories

Received: 11:28 A.M.

Read: 11:29 A.M.

Subject: YOU INSPIRED ME

Hey, Nina's Stories! Since featuring your video GRIZZLY BEAR ATTACK IN A HAUNTED TUNNEL, I've been following your work. Check out my livestream RIGHT NOW. You INSPIRED me.

Do it. I'm making a speech. Here's the link.

All my best,

THOU OWN DAVE

Well, that was suspicious. Nina thought of the mockingbird, wondering . . .

But how? The email read like a missive from Team Dave, complete with CAPS LOCKS for emphasis and vintage slang. Was the mockingbird really that skilled at imitation? Perhaps. Somebody could watch a lot of Thou Own Dave videos in one week. Read his announcements, study his act for their own.

She clicked on the link and was directed to an ongoing livestream on Thou Own Dave's St0rytel1er page. He stood on his favorite balcony, the one that overlooked the hillside. Behind him stood four serious-looking adults, all dressed in gray or black suits. In contrast, Thou Own Dave wore a shimmery gold jumpsuit and bright red boots. His smile was brighter than his outfit.

"Let's get started!" Dave shouted, clapping, his exuberance stirring up a low hum of applause and cheers. There must have been an in-person audience at the base of the hill, out of sight. "This announcement will change lives, so pay attention."

He looked at the camera; Nina had the uncanny sense that Thou Own Dave could see her, as if she was peering through a window instead of looking at a smartphone screen. That was another trick of Dave's art, a tried-and-true way to make his stories feel personal; he'd stare directly into the camera, as if holding eye contact with his audience of millions.

"Thanks to St0ryte11er, I've witnessed the devastation of the hurricanes in the Gulf region. It's like being there and suffering with you." He patted his chest. "Families left homeless. Buildings in ruins. Floods and power outages. There's even a species of toad in dire straits because of this storm. Poor little guys. Toads never hurt anybody. And. And then it came to me. The most incredible realization. An epiphany. You know what that word means? Don't give me the dictionary definition. I'm referring to the actual experience of a life-shaping revelation. 'Cause that's what I experienced."

Dave thudded a fist against the balcony railing, and continued.

"I have the power to decrease *your* pain with *my* money. That's an incredible trade, don't you think? There's half a billion dollars in my bank account. I couldn't spend that if I tried. And trust me, I've tried. I live in a color-coded mansion like a fresh new

Prospero, for freaksake. Come here, lawyers! Let's make this official. Right now, in front of the world, I'm donating my savings
to help rebuild the Gulf Coast. I hope my friends on St0ryte11er
will join me in the pledge to DECREASE PAIN by being
SOMEWHAT LESS WEALTHY. We may not be able to fix
everything, but we can make things easier!"

Again, the murmur of applause. The lawyers surrounded Thou
Own Dave, shoving papers and pens into his arms. He signed
each contract on the back of a dour-faced, gray-haired man.

"This isn't a publicity stunt," Thou Own Dave said, his attention returning to the camera. "I need you to hold me account-
able. Yes, you. I may get cold feet. If that happens, tell me to
stop whining, and buy thicker socks."

After the livestream went black, Nina stared at the ants,
as if looking to them for answers. Then, she fired off a single
question.

💧

Recipient username: TEAM DAVE

Subject: Re: YOU INSPIRED ME

Dear Thou Own Dave,

Is this really you?

💧

The response came a minute later.

💧

Recipient username: Nina's Stories

Received: 11:48 A.M.

Read: 11:48 A.M.

Subject: Re: Re: YOU INSPIRED ME

That's a good question. Who is Thou Own Dave, really? A man, or an act?

The world may never know.

◆

Before Nina could press the issue, Team Dave blocked her again. That was probably for the best. It was almost noon; the visitors would arrive soon. She hiked to the eastern edge of the land, where Grandma and her mother were already waiting at an old picnic table near the creek. For the moment, they were safe; Paul had been missing since their encounter. It seemed a freak tornado—Nina had her suspicions about its origin—blew him and his house away. Silver pieces of his camper were scattered down the countryside, but a body hadn't been found yet. Coyotes might have gotten it; that's what locals speculated. If other knights came someday, Nina's family would be prepared to protect their homeland. She was confident of that.

"Have you seen any toads yet?" Nina asked them.

"No, but this is where I saw one ten years ago." Grandma pointed at a stout oak growing on the other side of the creek. It had been rattled by the wind, shedding twigs and leaves, but was otherwise growing strong. "They're teeny tiny. Could be hiding anywhere."

Suddenly, Nina noticed movement in her peripheral vision. She turned just in time to witness the spirits arrive on Earth. They didn't plummet down like falling stars. Instead, although the air was clear and bright, the animal people seemed to emerge from a fog. One moment, they were vague blurs across the field. The next, they were as solid as the oak tree. Oli, who carried a bundle in his arms, stood between two wolfmen; the moment he noticed the humans, he called, "I brought him!"

Oli cut through wild grasses and brush, his long pants gathering brambles. As the distance between them closed, Nina observed that his bundle was a wicker basket wrapped in a wool blanket; clumps of snow melted on the green fibers.

"This is Ami," he said, gently lowering the basket onto the tabletop. Oli flipped the lid open, revealing a little toad sleeping on a bed of soft moss.

"Hello there," she said. "I've heard so much about you."

Ami didn't open his eyes; in fact, if Nina hadn't noticed the rhythmic rise and fall of his back, she might have mistaken him for a plastic toy.

"He's been sleeping," Oli explained. "It's the illness."

"He might still hear us," Grandma said, her eyes crinkling with melancholy affection. "I'm glad to meet you, Ami."

"Very pleased to meet you, too," Nina's mother agreed.

The wolves stood a respectful distance away, their hands clasped behind their backs. Nina nodded at the young one, grinning when he adjusted his new pair of sunglasses. Then, she watched as Oli lifted Ami from the basket and placed him atop the folded wool blanket.

"He's always wanted to feel the warmth of the sun," Oli said.

They sat around the table, waiting. Since his species was nearly extinct, they figured Ami only had an hour before he'd transport back home. Risk and Reign were waiting for his return alongside the bottomless lake. "Call to them," Oli said. "Please call to them."

The shadows of the oak tree lengthened; fifteen minutes passed in silence. Nina was afraid to make any sudden movements; she didn't even attempt to brush a red ant off her hand. If Ami toads did live here, that was a big win. Much of their habitat had dried up, but Grandma's land benefited from a steady supply of water from the bottomless lake. It could be a good location for a thriving new population. That's what her mother's friend—a biologist from the research vessel—believed.

Fifteen minutes became thirty minutes. No toads yet.

That didn't mean none were left in the wild.

That didn't mean it was too late.

At thirty-seven minutes, there was a suggestion of movement in Nina's peripheral vision. She turned, looking down the creekside. A yellow leaf wobbled. A blade of grass shook. Insect-sized shapes moved among the plants, approaching the bench.

"Look!" she said, standing. "Whoa. They're so tiny! What are they?"

Gently, Oli picked up Ami and lowered him to a clear patch of ground. The baby toads—none larger than a dime—surrounded him. They waddled closer, snuggling against Ami's side. Their eyes were specks of gold; their backs were flecked by pinpoint spots. Nina counted them—one, two, three, four, five, six. Six baby toads.

It seemed impossible that six baby toads were all that kept Ami alive. There had to be others out there—survivors from Bigswamp Dam, or toads living in pockets of land throughout Texas. Groups stranded on shrinking islands of habitat. There had to be! And if that was true, there was hope.

A baby hopped onto Ami's nose and sat on the crown of his spotted head.

As if emerging from a deep sleep, Ami opened his eyes.

ONE YEAR LATER

*A*t sunrise, I dismantled my tent, prying its stakes from the rich earth, gathering its aluminum poles into a twine-secured bundle, and neatly folding its waterproof exterior. The tent might prove useful someday, but I didn't plan to pitch it near the bottomless lake anymore.

A lot had changed since I returned from Earth.

The valley coyotes were building a cottage behind my basking rock, a two-room stone house. They told me it would have a domed roof, a fireplace, and round windows with real glass. It would be finished before I returned at the end of the summer; there'd be a great party to celebrate my homecoming. According to Risk and Reign, the valley community always built houses for new packmates, and though I wasn't technically part of any pack—I didn't even live in the valley—I was, and I quote, "Close enough, okay? Just accept the gift, Oli. It's really no big deal."

I smiled at the stacks of hand-chiseled stone, the building blocks of my cottage. They'd been carted down the wagon trail ton by ton. I wondered where the stone came from. Was it cut from the valley beyond the seven mountains? Later, I'd ask. There'd be time.

For now, I carried my tent down the bank. Past the reeds in the shallows. Past my boat, which was moored with a single length of rope. I walked until the rising pseudosun warmed the dewdrops off the ground. At a fallen tree hairy with yellow mushrooms, I turned onto a footpath through the forest. The poles on my back knocked together with every step I took.

Clack, clack, clack.

"Good morning!" Brightest said, dropping from the sky onto my shoulder. "My bag is on the boat." Reign had sewn shoulder pads into half my shirts—including the brown tunic I currently wore—so I didn't feel the pinch of their talons.

"You're only bringing one?"

"It's all I need; you know my lifestyle. Possessions just weigh a bird down."

Brightest and I came upon the tributary a few minutes later. A river-ready houseboat—borrowed from a lapsed catfish guardian—waited at the dock; we'd been loading it all night, and now that I had my tent, there was nothing left to do but leave.

"All aboard," Reign shouted, leaning out of a port-side window. "Next stop: the dammed city."

"I'm trying to sleep," Risk barked. Her muffled voice came from the lower story; in there, hammocks dangled from the reed ceiling. I planned to sleep in my true form, leaving the rocking beds to the sisters.

Our home for the next three months resembled a little wooden house, stacked on top of a bigger wooden house, stacked on top of a long, narrow boat. I was still skeptical about its stability, but we'd taken it on a few test runs, easily bobbing across rough patches of water. As long as we avoided waterfalls, my friends and I would stay dry.

"You're going to love the city," I said, climbing onto the deck. "The food. The entertainment—"

"Entertainment?" Reign asked. "Like what?"

"Twice a week, there are shows in the amphitheater. Comedies, mostly, but I once saw an epic romance; I was a toddler, so all the dramatic moments were confusing. Oh! Also, beyond the logging trails, there's a natural cavern with great acoustics. Musicians perform there every night. Gets a bit loud, I hear. Maybe we should stick to the comedies."

Reign snorted. "Can't be louder than the howls of a hundred coyotes during the blueberry wine festival."

"We should experience everything," Brightest said.

I crossed the deck and crouched beside the navigation table. There, nestled atop a folded wool blanket—Wist's blanket—Ami pored over my map of the tributaries. "What do you think?" I asked him. "Are we ready to leave?"

He tilted his head thoughtfully and then hopped across the map, following the main river—a diagonal vein of blue branching off into a hundred different paths. Countless routes we could follow, futures we could live.

With an openmouthed smile, Ami patted my hand. Then, he pointed with his nose to the path ahead.

"Great!" I agreed. "Let's go!"

The path to anywhere-you-please cannot be found, and I never expect it to find me again. That's okay. I'll always be grateful for our single encounter, and for its grace to guide me home. A place where the water binds two worlds; where coyotes confide in monsters; where hawks and mockingbirds discern revelations from ancient trees; where my best friend basks in the sun beside me; and where I can spend long days in the company of new family, as I search for the family I left behind.

I don't need the path anymore.

THE END

ACKNOWLEDGMENTS

When I started writing *A Snake Falls to Earth* in late 2019, my father—a witty, intelligent, and genuinely good man—was still with us.

Dad did not live to read the first draft.

And yet, I feel his presence in these stories, in every word on every page. Dad was my greatest champion; I would not be here without him. It is a blessing to be his daughter.

Xastéyó, Dad. I love you. I will always love you.

I am grateful for the support of my editor, Nick Thomas, and the hard-working team at Levine Querido (Arthur A. Levine, Alexandra Hernandez, Antonio Gonzalez Cerna, and Meghan McCullough, as well as intern Sanjana Thakur). My stories are in good hands. Thank you also to my agent, Michael Curry, and my writing community at the "cafe."

And finally, to all my readers: you're the reason I publish. I hope you enjoy the book.

ABOUT THE AUTHOR

Darcie Little Badger is an Earth scientist, writer, and fan of the weird, beautiful, and haunting. She is an enrolled member of the Lipan Apache Tribe of Texas. Her first novel, *Elatsoe*, was a National Indie Bestseller, named to over a dozen best-of-year lists, and called one of the Best 100 Fantasy Novels of All Time by TIME.

SOME NOTES ON THIS BOOK'S PRODUCTION

The art for the jacket and case was created by Mia Ohki, who drew first by hand with a Micron pen, then scanned into Adobe Illustrator for refinement and the addition of color. The type for the jacket, case, and display within the interiors was hand-lettered by Jade Broomfield. The text was set by Westchester Publishing Services in Adobe Caslon Regular, a revival of Dutch designer William Caslon's type done by American designer Carol Twombly, and based on Caslon's own specimen pages from the 18th century. The book was printed on FSC™-certified 98 gsm UPM woodfree paper and bound in China.

Production was supervised by Leslie Cohen and Freesia Blizard
Book jacket, case, and interiors designed by Jade Broomfield
Edited by Nick Thomas

LQ
LEVINE QUERIDO